The Madhouse

Cover designer: Ana Chabrand, Chabrand Design House
www.anachabrand.com

Interior Formatting: Iryna Spica, Spica Book Design
www.spicabookdesign.com

ISBNs:
978-1-77374-045-4 (Paperback)
978-1-77374-046-1 (E-book)

Bellevue Publishing
Vancouver, BC, Canada
Printed in USA

Dedication

*To my wife, Jean,
and also to our children: Marilyn, Diana, Michael,
and their families for their love, encouragement and support
while writing this book and for travelling
with me on this journey.*

Also By Dr. Lawrence Matrick

The Quisling
Road to Recovery: Following Your Motor Vehicle Accident

The Madhouse

Dr. Lawrence Matrick

Acknowledgements

With gratitude and appreciation to my editor,
Michelle Balfour.

Table of Contents

"We make a living by what we get,
but we make a life by what we give."
Winston Churchill.

✳

CHAPTER 1

A Clubfoot for Baby Alex

"It was the best of times, it was the worst of times, it was the age of wisdom, it was the age of foolishness, it was the epoch of belief, it was the epoch of incredulity, it was the season of light, it was the season of darkness, it was the spring of hope, it was the winter of despair"

INDEED, it was such a time in history, as Charles Dickens wrote in *A Tale of Two Cities*, when Alexander's mother lovingly accepted her newborn baby in the summer of 1933.

It was in the hospital in New Orleans, and it was from the same nurse who pulled the drapes around her bed for privacy that she accepted the child. With that, his mother dropped her hospital gown to let Alex suckle at her right breast.

The blissful scene was interrupted minutes later when the baby's father rudely opened the curtains and stomped in.

Surprised, Alex's mother looked up. "I'm so happy you stayed in the city until Alexander was born," she said, trying to smile with a giggle.

He said nothing and wanted to chide her again for giving a stupid laugh whenever she spoke. He contained himself this time. He stood aloof and dispassionate, and watched from the foot of the hospital bed.

He ignored little Alex and his deformed foot; he was more interested in listening to the two women in the other beds close by.

They were talking about some man called Adolf, who had just become the chancellor of Germany. He rudely shushed Alex's mother as he cocked his ears to listen.

It was Gretchen, trying to impress the adolescent Afro-American mother in the next bed who had just given birth to twins. "Yes, Beula. I read his book, *Mein Kampf,* last year," she said proudly, and quickly added, "And now, in this year he is the leader of my Fatherland."

After several minutes, Alex finished feeding, and his mother beckoned to his father with a suppressed laugh. "Come, would you like to hold your son?" she asked hopefully.

Her hands trembled as she held him to her chest to let him burp. Little Alex gave out a large, slobbering belch, and she turned him to face his father.

He shook his head and continued to finger the good-luck amulet hanging down his burly chest.

She again lifted her baby proudly and offered him to his father to hold as she tried to suppress a nervous twitter.

The father put up both hands in rejection and peered for some time at the baby's deformed left foot.

His mother, dismayed, took Alex back. She again chortled, embarrassed as Gretchen sat up and gazed at them from across her bed. She heard her say something to Beula about the strange-looking man wearing a rabbit foot draped around his neck.

As Alex's mother dutifully waited, the father pointed to the tiny left foot. It was severely turned inward and greatly deformed. He scowled, turned away, and left the bedside.

It was just then that the obstetrician, Dr. Sondheim, came in to examine Alexander's mother. The nurse followed and smiled at the father as the doctor offered his hand in congratulations.

The father, dark and swarthy, twice the doctor's size, scoffed and pushed the man aside. He said nothing and walked out the door and into the hallway. He was never to be seen again by Alexander's mother.

The doctor was surprised and seemed confused by such strange behavior. Bewildered by the rejection, he shrugged his shoulders and came to the mother, attempting a smile.

She cradled the baby in her arms, but quickly covered the little feet in a towel and wiped her tear away.

Sondheim pulled the drape around the bed and tossed the blanket off his patient. "Now my dear, how are we managing? Let's just spread our legs apart, shall we?"

Alex's mother gave a mortified laugh and did so as she pulled her gown up. The nurse shone a flashlight on her pelvis and the doctor looked into her birth canal.

"Yes, still some bleeding for us, my dear. In our opening there. We have a nervous laugh, my dear, don't we? But our small tear from our birth will heal nicely."

The nurse brought the pan of hot water for him to wash his hands, and after the brief pelvic examination, he reassured the mother. "Everything is as it should be for us, my dear. The nurse will give you more pads for the bleeding. I will explain to you about the tiny foot."

"Yes, please doctor. My husband could not stand to see it. The crooked foot, I mean," she pleaded with another uneasy titter. She was embarrassed to see the other three mothers gossiping amongst themselves as to what they had all witnessed.

"It can be corrected with some surgery, orthopedic boots, and insoles, to have the foot turn back in." He then patted little Alex on the head and added, "Maybe. Yes, perhaps, perhaps."

"What is it, Doctor? Is it something I did? Something I lifted, smoked, or ate?" She didn't ask if it was something she drank.

The doctor shook his head and opened the drape fully around his patient's bed to let in the morning sun. The other two women and the black girl stopped gossiping and turned their attention to their own healthy babies.

"An Equinovarus is what we have, my dear. We call it that, don't we? It is called a Talipes Equinovarus of the left foot. 'Equino,' that is like a horse's hoof. 'Varus,' turned inward, my dear. A clubfoot, my dear, is what we have here. A clubfoot for little wee Alex."

She listened, red in the face, but didn't understand all that mumbo-jumbo, especially when he added, "Yes, we have a clubfoot, my dear. But this year, 1933, has a nice ring to it. Those are all lucky numbers, as my horoscope book reads."

With that, Sondheim left with the nurse, who followed with a full bedpan. Alex's mother only wished he'd stop calling her 'my dear,' as her name, on her wrist band, was Francine.

She also just wanted to call the nurse back to get her the overnight bag. It held her bottle of Jim Beam bourbon.

The nurse did just that when Alex's mother signed herself out the next day against doctor's orders. She took a swig of 'good ol' Jim,' packed up her son, jammed the pad up her crotch, caught the local bus, and went back to her dismal, single room.

It was above the pub where she worked on Bourbon Street, aptly named after her favorite drink.

✳

CHAPTER 2

Aunt Ethel: The Wicked Witch of the West

SEVERAL years later, dragging his left clubfoot, Alex followed his two older, male cousins and his cruel aunt Ethel. It was along the Miami boardwalk, in Florida that summer.

He heard the chatter on the street, in the open cafes, about a war brewing somewhere in Europe. It was that name again, Hitler, causing all the fuss by invading his neighbors.

As he listened to the commotion, he tried to hurry up. He couldn't keep up with Auntie Ethel or his cousins, but he heard her screeching.

"When your father saw your ugly, crooked foot the day after you were born, he left New Orleans. He was never to be seen again." Alex's aunt, the Wicked Witch of the West, reminded Alex again.

The ugly, crooked foot was only partly corrected with minor surgery and after many casts in childhood. Then it required a special boot once Alex turned seven.

"That boot will help keep your ankle partially in line, but it will give you a bad limp," the surgeon added.

As a young teenager, Alex simply accepted his disability. He desperately tried to turn his foot out straight, so that it could be more in-line as he walked. This was a conscious, obsessive attempt, learned from an early age because children at school made fun of his defect.

However, it gave him that obvious, chronic shuffle.

"You're lucky. With that foot, you won't be drafted," his uncle assured him when Alex was twelve. But Alex wasn't worried about that, since the war in the European theatre was quickly coming to an end.

The ache in his left foot always reminded him of the reason his father had left him so soon after he was born. His aunt told Alex that the man didn't tolerate abnormalities. Nor did he recognize the boy as his own, since his mother was often in bed with other men.

Alex knew nothing of his father when he was growing up. He only received snippets of information from his sadistic Aunt Ethel. His mother sent him away to be with her on summer holidays, while she drank and partied with various men.

Alex never liked Aunt Ethel, and Aunt Ethel never liked Alex. When the boy asked his aunt about his father, she sneered. "He went by many names. A half-breed, maybe; from up north, somewhere up there, in the wilds of Canada."

"I don't remember him, Auntie. What was he like?" Alex as a young boy implored. He slowly pulled his clubfoot along.

There was still more hurtful information from Aunt Ethel. "My sister, your mother, drank that awful bourbon hooch and bathtub gin with those wayward drunks while she was pregnant with you."

"Bathtub gin, Auntie—what is that?"

Aunt Ethel ignored that, and she drove the knife in still deeper. "She had two kitchen-table abortions before she met your father and was told she'd never have children again. I blame the Jack Daniels corn whisky for causing that lame foot of yours," she ranted, poking him hard on the head.

"I never met Mr. Jack Daniels, Auntie."

"And you won't. Your dada, he left you as a young baby once he saw that ugly mess of a foot. You're starting to look just like him: large for your age, and your skin is slightly darker, like the perpetual Florida tan," his aunt said with her nose in the air.

Then she put the knife in again and twisted it further. "And you're just like him: you won't amount to a hill of beans."

As a young boy, he was dependent on his auntie, and Alex simply swallowed the abuse. He didn't know how high a hill of beans was, or who Mr. Daniels was, or how you could drink gin out of the bathtub. Maybe with a plastic straw, he surmised.

But it wasn't much later that he became determined to prove her wrong. Such abuse only made him tougher, more obsessive: detailed, resolute, and strong minded; and, indeed, he was lucky.

"What was he like?" Alex continued to ask with childlike curiosity as they walked the Miami Beach boardwalk.

"He was an orangutan; walked something like you do. He wore those stupid lucky charms around his neck," she said as she hunched over. She scratched her sides as monkeys do in the movies. She imitated his father, laughed, and berated the young boy for his awkward limp.

But she did have one kindly memory of him. "He was a powerful man, a swimmer. Every day he swam in your Lake Pontchartrain in New Orleans for the exercise."

Afraid to get angry at Aunt Ethel, since he had nowhere else to go, he bottled up his hostility and instead became compulsive, perfection- istic, and meticulous. This, in turn, strengthened his personality, and did him well in his future scholastics.

He also set up a dart board in Aunt Ethel's basement, where he was given a small, dark room to sleep. Drawing a picture of the Wicked Witch of the West from the movie, *The Wizard of Oz*, he enjoyed throwing darts at 'Ethel.'

So much so that he entered, and became a proficient dart contestant at, his college.

Whenever he received his trophies and scholarships, he hung them up on the wall in the basement. He always told his uncle and snooty cousins, "It's thanks to my Aunt Ethel."

This always pleased Aunt Ethel to no end.

Young Alex worked hard to stand straight, walk erect, and have a smile for everyone. He was kind, patient, and tried to be helpful to his friends, who depended on him for sound, good advice.

Thus, he became quite popular despite his minor shuffle. Later, he used the gym at school thrice weekly to build upper body strength; he was determined to continue receiving scholarships for college.

"What else, Auntie," he often asked.

"A burly monster, no schooling, and he never worked. Your mother was a bar maid, and she was her own best customer. He sowed his wild oats, in these southern parts, if you know what I mean. My sister was no better."

No, Alex didn't know what she meant, but he always stored information like that away. He hoped 'wild oats' would be in the Encyclopedia Britannica. He voraciously read those volumes every night in his auntie's extensive library, since his uncle was a school principal in the city, and she was his assistant.

He also looked up words like 'kitchen-table abortions,' 'bathtub gin,' 'orangutan,' 'a hill of beans,' and some guy called Jack Daniels. He was determined to prove to his aunt that he would be successful.

Years later, Alex discovered that it was his mother who helped men 'sow their wild oats' wherever she lived. Jack Daniels was a bourbon whiskey, sold in bottles, and her favorite.

He forgave his aunt, pushed all that vitriol aside, and excelled in playing chess and arm wrestling. He wrote scholarly dissertations for the high school papers, excelled in debates, became president of his class, and finally graduated with honors.

After graduating from medical school in South Carolina, he entered the post-graduate program in psychiatry in Boston. After his fourth and final year in psychiatry, he returned to New Orleans.

He felt obligated to see how his mother was recovering from her ovarian cancer surgery.

⁕

CHAPTER 3

A Rape on the Mississippi Levee

"SHE'S a-goin' down to the levee with her new friggin' roommate. Shagging away, I's suspect. Need to see your mamma this mornin' does you?" Winnifred, his mother's neighbor, asked as she took a swig from her gin bottle.

Alex had come back to visit his mother in New Orleans to tell her that he had his medical degree from Boston and completed his years in psychiatry, but still required a year in a psych institute. He was worried about her gall bladder surgery three weeks ago, and the recovery from her cancer.

"Yeah, Winnie. She just got out of hospital. I wanted to tell her that I only need one more year to become a psychiatrist after my three years post-grad."

Winnifred smacked her chunky thigh in laughter. Her belly jiggled in unison. "A real shrink? That a feeble specialty, sweetie. Be a brain surgeon, kid. You'se a real-to-goodness doctor?"

"Yeah, Winnie. A real doctor. Three years ago. I'll drive down to her favorite spot on the riverbank. Take care of your diabetes now, Winnie," he warned, pointing to the gin bottle that early in the morning.

Concerned about his mother's health, he found her at her favorite drinking spot on the river's edge. She was drinking with Gottlieb, her most recent live-in boyfriend: an obese, burly Austrian.

They were both camped on a blanket on the embankment, drinking and cavorting loudly as the Mississippi raged by. His mother, inebriated, introduced Alex to her new paramour when he came over to see how her health was.

Gottlieb was disinterested in Alex and continued to massage his mother's breasts under her sweater. The surly, obnoxious oaf took a swig from the bottle of bourbon on the blanket, ignored the introduction, and then contemptuously waved Alex away.

Alex decided to linger, hoping to take his mother out to lunch once she finished with Gottlieb. Or once he was finished with her.

He walked away and joined a drifter, Jimmy, whom he knew from childhood; he had been a long-time letter carrier in his old neighborhood. Jimmy was sitting further back, up on a fallen log at the side of the riverbank.

They both watched the big man groping the inebriated woman and pulling her skirts up over her knees.

"Come sit and rest your bones," Jimmy the drifter shouted out.

"Thanks. Glad to do so, Jimmy," Alex said as he sat down on the fallen log next to Jimmy in the shade. Jimmy cut up a large apple with his red, Swiss Army knife and then sucked on a beer bottle.

Alex accepted a slice of apple.

"Those two are going at it again," Jimmy said as he pointed to Gottlieb with the blade of his knife. Gottlieb was almost on top of Alex's mother, with his pants down to his knees.

Alex stood up. He put his hand over his eyes to shade the glare from the sun. "She's just recovering from pelvic surgery. He shouldn't be forcing himself on my mother, Jimmy," Alex shouted.

He watched in horror as Gottlieb threw his pants aside and pushed himself further into his mother's pelvis.

"I know that motherfucker. Fucking pervert," Jimmy said, offering Alex another piece of the apple. He put his empty bottle of beer down into the case of twelve and got up to look for himself.

It was just then that Alex's mother began to scream. Alex couldn't quite make out what she was saying, since Gottlieb was on top of her. He was a large man, grossly overweight, and he had his hands around her throat.

Jimmy pushed Alex out front. "That motherfucker is raping her. Bastard will kill her. Go help her, son," he yelled. At the same time, he gave Alex the small, red, Swiss Army knife with the blade open.

Alex, in a fury, ran down to the river's edge.

Gottlieb had pushed Alex's mother's thighs apart with both hands and was pumping himself into her. His mother had freed one hand and had Gottlieb by the throat, but she was too weak to hold on.

Alex jumped on the rapist but was no match for Gottlieb's girth and weight. In a panic, he jabbed the man in the back with the small knife several times.

Gottlieb turned over, gasped, and turned blue as his eyes rolled back into his head. He collapsed on top of Alex's mother.

"Fucker died, Alex. Fucker is dead," his mother said as she rolled away from the inert body.

"My God, mother. I didn't kill him. He had a coronary," Alex said as he felt the man's carotid arteries. There was no pulse.

"No ambulance will get here, Alex. Not out here on the river," she said. She watched as Alex pumped the man's chest. There was no sign of recovery after several minutes of attempting to revive him.

"Roll him into the river, Alex. Roll him down the levee. You mustn't be here: trouble for you. You didn't kill him with that knife. Prick had a heart attack," Alex's mother said, suddenly very alert and rational.

"I must have with that knife, mother. Must have," Alex said, terrified at what he had done. He watched his mother roll the body down the embankment.

Alex looked about. There was no one else around. He looked up to see Jimmy.

Jimmy waved and shouted, "Push the body into the fast-flowing river, son. Into the river, buddy. Into the river. Now."

Alex moved down to the river's edge, where his mother had dragged the body by its legs to the water. Alex helped her roll him into the wide expanse of the Mississippi.

They both stood there and watched the river quickly take the corpse downstream. It sank and quickly disappeared.

"Get out of here, Alex. Get back to Boston. Maybe up north, to Canada later on, before Russia nukes us," his mother said, and added, "My operation went well. No spread, the doc told me. I'll be all right. You go. Don't worry; and hurry, for Christ's sake. Get the fuck outta here."

Alex nodded, cleaning the sand off his pants and Gottlieb's blood off the knife with the blanket his mother offered. He talked only briefly with his mother as she walked away to her car up the hill. She didn't look back.

Alex picked up Gottlieb's trousers from the riverbank. There was also a large bottle of Wild Turkey bourbon next to the pants.

He walked back to Jimmy.

"Well done and good riddance. That friggin' motherfucker was always up to no good," Jimmy said. He was happy to have a new pair of trousers: a bit too big, but manageable with some tailoring, he added.

"He had a coronary, Jimmy. Heart attack," Alex said, fearful. He gave Jimmy back his knife and the near-full bottle of bourbon. He prayed that would keep Jimmy quiet.

He watched Jimmy empty Gottlieb's pockets of money, tuck the trousers and whiskey under his arm, and take off on his own.

CHAPTER 4

✳

The MadHouse

"WE must try more hard, Justine. To speak only the true Queen's English. We must always practice it as we leave work every night," Celeste reminded her older cousin.

Both girls had agreed to speak only the 'Queen's English' earlier that evening in the autumn of 1961. Celeste, the younger, was a preemie: a first-year nurse at the Institute for the Mentally Insane just outside of Montréal.

They left the chronic women's ward where they were on duty late that evening. The young girls held hands: to keep warm, and for safety on the dark trail.

They were on their way back to the nurses' residence, which was on the massive, sprawling grounds of the asylum. The maple trees scattered about were turning red that autumn.

"*Oui,* oh, pardon, Celeste. Yes, yes, only real Canadian English. But for you, little one, since you are of such Italian parentage, it will be more difficult," Justine replied to the younger nurse as the freezing air sent a shiver down her spine.

She emphasized the word 'Canadian' again. Justine refastened her nurse's cap with the black band on her head. It signified that she was in her third and final year as a student at the mental hospital.

Shivering in the cold spell, Justine buttoned her blue nurse's cape around her white uniform. It offered some protection from the cold gusts of late October in the eastern Canadian province of Québec.

Celeste was grateful that her cousin was her tutor in nursing on A3, the top floor of the chronic women's building. It housed the most depraved, psychotic women in the psychiatric hospital.

She again expressed her gratitude for her mentorship, gripping Justine's hand as they walked up the hill. It was the howl of coyotes far away that caused Celeste to shiver. "Yes, Justine, but only my father, Vittorio, is Italian; he works here too. A nun, she gave to me my correct, proper French name when my mother died."

"*Oui*, I know Vittorio."

"As a student in my first year I am still, how do I say it?" She paused to find the right words. "Ah, yes: terrified, is the word I mean, of those screaming women. One even struck out at me, Justine."

"We call her paranoid. Sister Denise called her schizophrenic, Celeste. That handsome American psychiatrist told just to me that she was a paranoid schizophrenic. Do not be afraid. No harm will come to you, little one," Justine said, reassuring her and clutching her hand.

"He is the one with the lame foot. He came, I heard, to Canada to stay away from that war in the Pacific, somewhere. But a kindly American doctor, Justine?"

"*Oui*, he is. Oh, sorry. Yes. Doctor Alexander Gage. That war is in Vietnam: far away, Celeste. Many of his kind came to our north. And he can help you with your fear, being terrified."

"How, Justine? How?" she asked, hopefully.

"With a small blotter of paper on your tongue. It will expand your mind as it does mine, my little one. He called it 'LSD', and he can sell some to you."

Celeste didn't like being referred to as slight or little in stature, even though she was only ninety pounds soaking wet. "*Merci*, Justine.

Oh, sorry again; thank you, I mean. You know, for helping me with the charting on that graph of temperatures of those little ill patients. Them very young ones."

Then she recalled further, "And how to write of their strange actions. You are in your last year and very wise." Celeste hesitated. "What is that blotter on the tongue?"

"He calls it 'acid' and gets it from a proper pharmaceutical company. It is inexpensive, my sweet. One of my orderlies, he told me of it."

Celeste brightened, and with a hopeful smile she turned to her mentor. "I know of him: the doctor, the kindly American."

Those were her last words as they both rounded the corner beside a thicket of brush.

Celeste stopped when she heard a rustle next to her in the overgrown branches hanging over the pathway.

"It is nothing, little one. Just some raccoons playing. I saw them this morning as I walked to the wards," Justine said, gently pulling her 'little one' along by the arm.

They never heard, nor saw, the black figure of a man. Hulking behind that very thicket, he bolted out and bowled the youngest one over.

Justine, the larger girl, survived the initial brutal attack. To Dr. Gage, the American who examined her when she awoke from her coma, she said, "It was a large, muscular man, and not a male patient. The male wards were locked up at night, Doctor."

"Are you certain, Justine?"

"It was another man," she reiterated. "But I couldn't recognize him. I could only detect the strong, nicotine smell on his fingers as he muffled my screams with his hand."

"You could smell him?" Dr. Gage asked, perplexed.

"I could. A mask, he wore. He told me to be still, or he would kill me. He called me a *fica;* I know not what that word is."

"*Fica?* What is that?"

She thought for a moment and had another memory. "And he talked with a strange accent. From Europe, maybe."

Just as the brutish assailant had said this to her, she had been struck on the head with the jagged rock the man held.

Justine had faltered and staggered to her knees from the blow but was still conscious. She saw her friend thrown to the ground.

The young one struggled; the man had one hand on her throat and was pulling up her skirts with the other.

Justine was just able to raise her head. Blood streamed into her eyes from the blow, and she reverted back to her own French, yelling, "*Téléphonez la police, les gendarmes.*"

Justine, still confused, yelled out again; but they were alone, and a phone was nowhere to be had. She valiantly tried to rise but fell again onto the gravel pathway.

Celeste gurgled, spittle filling her nostrils. Her eyes bulged out from their sockets, and her lungs gasped for air.

At those garbled sounds, the man simply tightened his grip on her throat and slowly squeezed the last breath out of poor little Celeste.

Justine had awoken again briefly, and desperately tried to lift herself up by her arms to help her cousin. She wiped the blood from her eyes and could just make out in the darkness that Celeste was straddled by this man on top of her.

It was also then that she heard in the distance the sound of women's shouts, somewhere far away from behind.

There was also the sound of a wolf, who howled far away in the woods. Was it Celeste's final plea for help with her last breath, or the beast on top of her cousin grunting like an animal?

It was those eerie sounds that had roused her. Justine gave out a muffled scream where she lay on the gravel pathway: with her face down in a puddle of mud, but with one eye open as she watched her cousin succumb.

The man pushed himself off his victim and searched again for the rock nearby.

"*Aidez-moi, s'il vous plaît,*" Justine screamed again in French. "Someone, help us. Please God, help us," she prayed out loud. She was up on her knees and reached out for her little Celeste.

It was at that very moment that Sister Denise and Mother Superior, known to all nuns as *Mère Supérieure,* came up that path. They always made rounds late at night, and they had both heard the screams. They shouted that they were coming.

However, that was also when Justine received the second blow to her head—with the same jagged rock. She again fell and sank into total darkness.

Oblivion.

✳

CHAPTER 5

A Little Jewish Girl Saved from Auschwitz

THE hospital was abuzz with the brutal rape and death of poor nurse Celeste. Her friends and many sister nurses were beside themselves with grief, and the small chapel on the grounds filled with staff, hospital nuns, and family.

They all talked in hushed whispers. After the service, the funeral parlor from the village nearby took the body away.

Once outside, they did talk about the assault and how the *Sûreté du Québec*, Québec's provincial police, had searched the area for clues. It had been confirmed that no male patients were out that late at night or missing.

"We have such a man in our village, and it must be him who prowled at night," said *SQ* inspector Treudeau. Everyone nodded and, in hushed tones, agreed. Treudeau said that he would have to speak with the suspect.

Justine's scalp was stitched by Dr. Gage when she was taken to the hospital ward. "Your scar will not show once your hair grows back," he reassured her in the sick ward.

Justine put her hand to her head to feel the bandage. Her eyes watered. "Thank you, Doctor. I'm sorry that her father could not be here to be at Celeste's funeral."

Alex was surprised to hear such sorrow from Justine. "And her mother, Justine? Her mother?"

"No, her mother died of pneumonia soon after Celeste was born. In France. Her father, Vittorio, brought her here to work. Here to Canada, and then as a nurse at your hospital, Doctor."

"Vittorio, Justine? You mean Doctor Levy's friend?"

"Yes, but they are not such good friends. Celeste said to me that they knew each other during the war in Italy," she explained, and then turned aside to rest after talking for so long; she was still in shock.

Alex pulled the blankets up over her shoulders. "And you will remain on leave until recovered from the attack, nurse," he whispered to her kindly as she fell asleep.

Alex heard someone in the village say that the suspect, Monsieur Lafarge, had been out of the province at the time, as was confirmed in the local papers the next day. He was away for the month, visiting his family in Labrador. Everyone concluded that the assault must have been the work of a madman.

Mère Supérieure, the head of all nuns at the hospital, also ordered Sister Antoinette Denise to rest for a few days from her post-traumatic stress after finding the dead girl. She had confided in *Mère Supérieure* that it reminded her of the physical and sexual assaults by foreign troops that she had witnessed as a young, Jewish girl during the war in France, in 1942.

But here in the province of Québec, it was the Canadian autumn air that stirred a bronchial coughing fit for Sister Denise when she returned to duty once again.

She felt it her duty to see the new American psychiatrist, called Dr. Gage, and resolve the issues of the young children working at the hospital.

Sister Denise struggled to walk the slight incline; she faltered from time to time with head down, unsteady as she spat specks of blood into a white, lace kerchief. This beautiful, ornate, lace kerchief was presented to her in 1948: just fifteen years ago, when she was baptized as a child of Jesus Christ in the convent in France.

As she walked up the hill, she held her wasted arms folded across her chest to keep her upper body warm under her blue nurse's cape. A simple, heavy, black woolen shawl protected her head and neck from the biting wind.

She needed to rest every few feet to catch her breath, cough, and gasp for air. Taking slow, deliberate steps, she avoided the filthy, gritty slush on the pathway.

It was a freezing day again, with a light snow on the grounds of the mental institution just south of Montréal. *Mère Supérieure* referred to it as the "Hospital of the Incurables" in her lectures to the nuns and student nurses.

As Sister Denise looked around the grounds, her heart was sad to see such miserable patients: young and old, feeble, cold, and hungry, even after their paltry breakfast of dry toast and weak tea.

They worked as exploited gardeners, sweeping and trimming hedges and bushes on command of the director.

As she shivered in the cool air, she was reminded of the grotesque painting by the artist Francisco Goya in a Madrid gallery. The church had sent her and twenty other nuns to Madrid after the war to learn Spanish. She was appalled to see what a mental asylum looked like in 1812, when Goya had painted *The Madhouse.*

Goya depicted the inner cells of that institution to be enclosed, airless, dark, tight, and claustrophobic. The painting's only source of light came from a barred window high up, filthy from grime and unreachable. The patients portrayed in the painting were isolated, distraught, dirty, and bizarre.

When Sister Denise had looked at the painting, she cringed to see that they moved about with deplorable behavior: fighting naked, squabbling, and praying to their god. Praying, perhaps, for freedom from insanity and the confines of that mental hospital near Madrid.

The gallery director, a grizzled old artist from bygone years, was soon to be retired due to his senility. He pointed to the painting with his severely arthritic hands, which had turned into claws. They all dutifully stood there, waiting for his lecture.

"This painter, Goya, was infected with bacteria and suffered from encephalitis; an infection of the brain, we believe. This caused his madness, for he also heard voices, felt dizzy, and was plagued by recurrent headaches. He was sure that he was going insane during a feverish crisis, possibly from syphilis or from the lead in the paint when he painted this."

Sister Denise stared at the painting, and had asked, "Did he enter such an institution himself as he here depicts, *monsieur?*"

The curator wasn't certain; he shrugged his feeble shoulders and walked away. Was the painting a figment of the painter's imagination? Perhaps, they all concluded.

Now, in Québec, Sister Denise struggled through the freshly-fallen snow, made more slippery by maple leaves beneath her feet. She would meet Dr. Gage outside the medical ward where he had examined Justine, the cousin of poor little Celeste.

The ward was just down the hill and past the prison ward. She was successful to come to the crest of the hill but feared the slippery downward slope. The steep decline that she was now on faced the mighty St. Lawrence River.

The small hospital clinic, used by the director, Dr. Cartier, to save money, was housed on the fourth floor. It was basically an attic in the chronic woman's building. It loomed in the distance before her.

Dr. Gage had agreed to meet her after her incessant pleadings to him that he must help her free those waifs: the young, orphaned children who were kept in the bowels of the hospital buildings.

It was *Mère Supérieure* who would soon meet the hospital director in the sick ward about the children. It would be her, she said, as it was her duty to do so as the head of all the nuns. She would confront him with the letter that Sister Denise had written to the college of physicians in Montréal about such deplorable conditions for the young orphan children working there.

Sister Denise had been appalled to learn that the director was accepting government funds for housing hundreds of orphaned children in his institution.

The blood on her kerchief reminded her that she was dying, but she felt fulfilled, having been a good and pious nun.

She shuddered as the heavy, frigid air reminded her of the cold winter of 1942 in France. She thought back to when she was as a young, Jewish girl in Toulouse: when she went through the baptismal ceremony and was told that she had become the bride of Christ in the Catholic convent.

At that time, she had vowed to consecrate herself to God 'until death,' since she was saved from being sent to the camps in Belsen by the Catholic convent; Belsen was where the Nazis had sent her family and all the Jews in her village.

She recalled, with a coughing spasm in her throat, how the German soldiers had battered on the doors of all her kind in the village, and that her father had pushed her out the kitchen window. He did this to save her just as the soldiers stormed through their front door and rushed up the stairs.

She had watched in horror from behind the bushes where she had fallen as her parents and older sister were dragged away. She saw the last of them as they were forced into lorries, and then onto cattle rail cars crowded with other Jews.

Never to be seen again.

Her neighbor had found her where she cowered in the thicket. The kind neighbor secreted her away in a haystack near his farm hut for weeks, feeding her rarely and offering her goat's milk and stale bread to survive.

After that, he hid her in his milk wagon and took her to the convent in the nearby town. There, together with other Jewish girls, she was accepted by the nuns, grateful to be alive.

They all became good Catholic girls, and then later, nuns.

✳

CHAPTER 6

The Ultimate Sacrifice

SISTER Denise was willing to throw herself out of the fourth-story window as a sacrifice if the director and Dr. Gage didn't listen to her pleas. But it would be *Mère Supérieure* who was prepared to do so, she told Sister Denise, since she was already dying of fulminating breast cancer.

Mère Supérieure's martyrdom was sure to be publicized in the local papers and would thus save the little children at this mental hospital. However, *Mère Supérieure* was hopeful that this young Dr. Gage, with Sister Denise's pleadings, would help her return the children back into their communities before such a sacrifice could occur.

Mère Supérieure explained one day, "This doctor is forward thinking, assertive, and wants to create change at this medieval asylum."

Sister Denise had other information. "He is also kindly and sympathetic to drug addicts, Mother Superior. He treated alcoholics, and some addicts, with LSD 'acid,' as he called it—at his clinic outside of this hospital. He called it Casa Loma."

"Yes, Doctor Gage also wants to eradicate that dreaded therapy, prefrontal lobotomies. He called them 'horrendous surgical procedures.' He prefers the newer medications instead of brain surgery, which is irreversible," *Mère Supérieure* was happy to tell Sister Denise.

However, Sister Denise didn't have much time, which she explained to *Mère Supérieure*. "It is the galloping consumption that is slowly eating up my poor lungs. The surgery doesn't seem to be helping, I fear."

Mère Supérieure nodded wisely and comforted her friend. "You have shown me that letter that you have written to the government. I will take it and present it to the director for you; you should go rest in your quarters to better heal from the surgery, dear sister."

This pulmonary infection stifled Sister Denise's breath and robbed her of oxygen—soon, it would end her life.

When she had lain in her cot in that convent in France, she did not know what 'galloping consumption' meant, but it was what the doctor had said to her.

The head nun at her old convent had called the local doctor when she feared that the young girl would soon join her departed Jewish family. The hunchbacked physician, tottering in with a cane, came three days later. He knew that not many of the children would survive the cold spell that year.

The good doctor looked down over his reading glasses at the wasted little girl. "Consumption, my little one. Consumption you have now," *Docteur* Francois Tache said under his breath.

As he listened to her pubescent chest with his stethoscope, he shook his head in sorrow. Then he walked away to have a hot cup of strong tea in the convent kitchen as his payment. The hungry, orphaned child was left to be spoon-fed warm potato soup with bits of bread by sister Leblanc in her barren room.

It was only after the war, when Sister Denise was moved to live in Ireland, that she learned that she was infected with the dreaded tuberculosis: what the village doctor had called 'consumption.'

※

CHAPTER 7

Poor, Institutionalized, Working Girls

IF *Mère Supérieure* indeed threw herself out the fourth-story window of the chronic women's building, it would be her last act. Dramatic, she told Sister Denise, but effective, she hoped.

"The cancer is now in my bones, sister. You are still young, and that surgeon may have cured you of your TB. Then, after my death, you will be the new *Mère Supérieure.*"

The act would show Dr. Cartier, the medical director, and God that she was determined to save those poor, destitute orphaned children in this hospital, now forsaken by her God.

"When you go to meet our brave Doctor Gage, be sure not to let your rosary, or your skirt, drag in the snow and slush. He was kind to allow the meeting with you. And, my child, do not cough in his presence," *Mère Supérieure* ordered. She sternly pointed to the long, black habit with a rosary hanging from Sister Denise's waist and the heavy, silver cross around her neck.

Sister Denise acquiesced, as all nuns did when *Mère Supérieure* gave a directive. She avoided looking at the old woman and bowed her head in agreement. She vowed not to utter a word and worked hard to suppress a cough.

Now, she tried to sidestep the puddles of snow, frozen rain, bits of ice, and withered yellow, red, and gold maple leaves that were mixed into the black slush.

Sister Denise lifted her ankle-length, black skirt over her boots, which were laced well above her ankles. She tucked her rosary into her pocket and crossed herself three times.

She was one of hundreds of nuns from Europe, sent to work in all the Catholic—and even some non-Catholic—hospitals, residential schools, and private colleges throughout Canada after the war. Many were in administrative roles throughout the provinces, in charge of the wards and all the staff. They could be under the rule of a priest, or a nun superior, but were sometimes under the direction of a medical person.

In the mental hospitals like this one, the director called himself a psychiatrist; however, he was just a politically-appointed medical doctor, who was more of an administrator than a doctor.

What disturbed Sister Denise as she walked through the grounds were the very young, child-like girls working with older women. They raked autumn leaves onto their dirty, ragged skirts and cowered from the leering looks of the older boys and men who worked close by.

Institutionalized men with day privileges, who were known not to try to run away after being lobotomized, worked like zombies and sleep-walking robots. Sister Denise watched them sweep the walks and rake up the leaves into the small piles that were scattered about.

The little girl-children would fill their ankle-length skirts with the wet mass full of rot, stink, animal feces, debris, and worms. They would then trudge over to a wheel barrow, unload their foul-smelling burden, and start all over again.

She shuddered from the cold, but also in seeing that these children were undernourished, unkempt, dirty-faced, sad little girls with scraggly, matted hair. They all needed a bath, a healthy meal, some warmth, and hugs from a caring, loving mother.

"Such little children here, in this place?" she asked herself as she looked to see if Dr. Gage was down the hill waiting for her. A strong gust of wind came down from northern Québec and just blew her question away. She was certain that Dr. Gage would do something about these poor urchins.

If he wouldn't, then she and *Mère Supérieure* would send her letter to the provincial government and the newspapers; that and the suicide would surely make a statement, she prayed.

It was the uneven gravel pathway and the dirty slush that caused her to trip and fall to her hands and knees as she walked down the hill.

"Oh dear, I must not get wet and dirty before I meet the doctor," she prayed, and recalled the admonishing words of *Mère Supérieure* about keeping her skirts free of muck. She tried to push herself up and rise from her knees, but she was too frail and weak.

A young, very dark-skinned Indian woman in a long, shabby skirt with braided hair down to her waist swept leaves nearby. When she heard the weak gasp and saw the nun in the snow bank, she threw her broom down and came to her rescue.

"Here, sister, let me help you up," she offered as she grasped Sister Denise by her frail arms.

The two women struggled to maneuver their bodies off the gritty, icy pathway covered in snow. A lone, male orderly, in charge of the workers and standing in a heavy, warm parka and mitts, saw the two women and sped toward the pair.

"Get your filthy, red, Indian paws off this kindly nun, you grubby, stinking, redskin squaw," he shouted, and then pushed the Indian girl further into the nearby snow bank.

The orderly went to Sister Denise, who was then bodily lifted back to her feet by his powerful arms. She readjusted her shawl over her head and shoulders.

The man turned and spat a large gob of saliva at the young girl, who was trying to free herself of the snow where he had pushed her down.

The brute left, laughing, as the Indian woman, with tears streaming down her face, brushed the cold slush off her bare arms and cleaned her face of his spittle.

Sister Denise went to her, helped her back onto the pathway, and spoke softly to the brave, dark-skinned girl with braided locks as she waved the bully away.

"*Merci*, my child, for your help. Be brave, my child, and God bless you for coming to my aid. One day soon, you and your kind will be free once again, and be recognized as rightful citizens by the help of your leader, Riel," she said, with a strong French inflection.

The frightened girl stood still for a moment, but before she ran off to rejoin her team, she said, "Yes, our leader, Lafayette Riel, will free his kind; us aboriginals and the métis, sister. Thank you for your kindness."

CHAPTER 8

※

A Failed Attempt at Righting a Wrong

AS she watched the woman return to her work station, Sister Denise had a sudden flashback. She was still suffering from post-traumatic stress, and was sad and bitter, suffering terrible nightmares from what she had witnessed of similar depravity by men after the war.

Women, who had collaborated with the German forces in France, had lain with them for sex and money; later, they were called quislings: collaborators. After the war, they were called whores and stinking traitors, had their heads shaved in social embarrassment, and were often publicly stoned to death by the French townspeople.

She'd had to leave her sisters at the convent and be moved out of France in her early twenties, shortly after the war. Sent to Ireland, she continued to suffer from her nightmares. The devastating flashbacks made her stomach churn and her heart heave rapidly. She had never been able to talk about her traumatic experiences.

Her village priest in France had said that the move out of the country would dispel the night terrors. "It was God's wish," he had opined as he pushed her up onto the train for Cherbourg, and then the slow ferry to the Emerald Isle.

But the abuse that she witnessed at this asylum triggered her painful memories of what she had seen in Ireland. After two years, she had been happy to leave Galway and Father Joseph to be transferred to Canada.

She should never have allowed him to do those things to those young boys, to be so abusive to such children, and she chided herself for not talking to her bishop earlier.

She had been afraid to speak up—being of a lowly position at the Irish cathedral—about what she had seen when she had walked in on Father Joseph. He had been behind the altar, on his knees before the two naked boys with their pants down to their ankles.

She knew God would want her to put a stop to it. That was when she had made the trip to see the local bishop.

She was sure he would do something for those young boys. Surely, he would move Father Joseph. She didn't expect that it would be she who would be moved.

The bishop, an old, spent man, crippled and hideously bent over with a twisted spine, listened patiently and tapped his fingers on his desk, but never looked at her.

He kept his eyes focused on the large, wooden cross on the wall behind her as he spoke. "Coming from a country like France as you did, Sister Denise, you will be so much more comfortable in French Canada. You know their language. You know how to care for the ill as you did here, and the dry climate will be good for your consumption."

All Sister Denise could do was nod her head in fear and acquiesce with a simple, "*Oui.*"

"The institutions need you, in Canada, over there," the bishop added, pointing a twisted finger to the west while still not looking at her.

He stood up, said no more, and thus ended the meeting. He shuffled out of the room with his only faithful friend: his wooden cane.

He never mentioned Father Joseph, even once, or her complaints about him. It was just so much easier to move her, and not his friend.

He didn't need trouble just before his retirement to sunny Italy and the nursing home for retired priests on the Vatican grounds.

Sister Denise had been told at an early age at the convent to never express her fears, anger, or other emotions. She never did. She contained her suppressed aggression and hostility. Instead she had day visions, and night dreams, of such perpetrators being shot at with arrows.

At the same museum in Madrid, where she had viewed *The Madhouse* by Goya, she also saw the painting of Saint Sebastian. He was speared with multiple arrows, as depicted by the painter El Greco.

The curator on that visit had also explained, "Sebastian was martyred by the Romans for being a Christian and portrayed here in this painting in death. But he was saved by a kindly nun."

Thereafter in her dreams, and in daytime visions, Sister Denise would tie her offender, any abusive offender, to a similar stake and shoot poison arrows at him. She did this with that brute of an orderly from the snow bank.

She always prayed to God afterward to forgive her for having such vivid, intrusive, wicked thoughts.

Poor young children, she thought as she saw them sweep and gather up leaves on this cold, autumn day. She stopped to rest and watched as they were bullied by ruthless, psychotic men.

Those men giggled, called out to the girls, dropped their pants, and exposed themselves to the little children, even in the cold.

Those who saw Sister Denise also yelled out to her. They made other lewd gestures with their fingers. They laughed, pumped the handles of their rakes in a sexual manner, and held their crotch with the other hand.

She did nothing and quickened her pace. She crossed herself again and gave a silent prayer for their wickedness.

"And now here, of all places: in a mental hospital for the ill, where the children should be protected. Doctor Gage will do something about this," she said to herself.

CHAPTER 9

✳

Sterilization, Discrimination, and Hysterectomies

AS she stumbled along the path, Sister Denise prayed that Dr. Gage's rejection of the inhumane procedure of prefrontal lobotomies also included saving the poor, intellectually defective children.

Other than the imbeciles, idiots, and morons, there were many normal, orphaned children at this psychiatric institution. If any of the young ones were hostile, aggressive, ran away, or resisted such brutal employment, then they were punished by Dr. Cartier, the director.

He would order them to be deprived of food, held captive in the cold, freezing cellars, have their still-maturing prefrontal lobes slashed by the knife, or be sterilized. The older girls and women would be given a hysterectomy, a removal of their uterus, since he didn't want any pregnancies in his hospital. Such would cost money.

As to the dreaded prefrontal lobotomy, the scalpel, introduced through openings in the skull, was wielded by the famous neurosurgeon, Dr. Walters. Cutting the brains of such children was meant to make them docile and obedient in the hospitals.

Sister Denise knew that in this institution, as well as many others, there was an extreme bias against Orientals and any dark- or black-skinned patients, including the Indians. They were housed in the dark and dismal basements with the mental defects. Discriminated, they were secluded from the others. They were deemed to be unclean: sullied, filthy, and unworthy of the working white staff.

Some of the nursing staff called them the 'yellows,' 'chinks,' 'redskins,' or 'niggers,' and refused to take care of such patients. If forced to do so, they would immediately scrub their hands thoroughly up to their elbows after touching them.

Such patients had their charts labeled in bold letters on the front with vile, despicable, sexist, and cultural identifiers.

Women in Canada may have received the vote in the early 1920's, and even the Indians in the late 1950's. But the Orientals, mental defects, or any other patients in these kinds of institutions were not allowed to vote.

Dr. Gage's resistance to sterilizations and such heartless obliteration of the prefrontal cortex was well known to the director, Dr. Cartier. "You are simply ordered to keep your young, progressive, American ideas to yourself and mind your own business here," Cartier demanded of Gage.

Dr. Gage also had to stop lecturing the nurses that his American way was more progressive, more humane, and more medically advanced. He continued at the peril of being deported back to America by Cartier.

After all, he was just an American defector and a visitor to Canada, like thousands of others who were conscientious objectors. Cartier knew that Gage had moved north with the draft dodgers while the war raged in Vietnam.

As far as Cartier was concerned, Gage was a traitor to his country, a deserter: a yellow-bellied turncoat with a yellow streak down his back. He only tolerated Gage because he was bright, studious, reliable, hardworking, and well-organized.

The director saw him to be unlike the many other ignorant foreigners who worked at the hospital. Cartier had his favorite, despicable names for those foreigners: like Gage's friend, the Italian 'wop,' Levy; or the Israeli Jew, a 'kike;' the Puerto Rican, a 'spic;' the Oriental doctor, a 'chink;' and the Pole, a 'hunky.'

Sister Denise made it to the bottom of the hill and walked past the chronic women's asylum building. As the clouds dispersed, the sun warmed her frail body.

She stopped to catch her breath and watch patients shuffle out of the massive, stone structure and down the granite steps after their meager breakfast.

Breakfast at the asylum consisted of cold porridge swimming in watered-down milk without sugar. A slice of day-old bread was added, lathered with colored margarine—a dismal substitute for butter—and weak, black tea.

The women huddled together in rows of two; almost all of them were smoking hand-rolled cigarettes, since tobacco was freely provided to all the inmates. Cartier had recognized long ago that nicotine soothed the heart and brain of the savage beast and made them meek and obedient to his wishes.

Sister Denise watched the women as they walked down the path, giggling, talking to themselves, smoking, or shouting out to the men who were working on the grounds. Some lifted their skirts to the men raking leaves, making lewd and sexually suggestive remarks as they made their way toward the laundry.

Those working in the warm confines of the laundry were the lucky ones; they had grounds privileges, and could get away from the putrid, stinking, stale atmosphere of their crowded wards—for a few hours, at least. They would work in the warmth of the heated laundry building or in the kitchens, washing, cleaning, scrubbing, or ironing.

But at least comfortable, with the coming winter.

Sister Denise observed that some were in a rush to meet the men who were there with similar day privileges. The men carried loads of heavy laundry, lifted the bales of linen, or made the deliveries to the wards.

Some of the women occasionally had a favorite male inmate who protected them from the others. Many were easy pickings for the sexually deprived and frustrated male patients.

The women who were lobotomized, heavily sedated, or too feeble to resist the aggressive abuse simply succumbed to the harassment: the sexual groping or eventual penile insertions.

Many others were just happy to receive a few warm hugs and kisses from the belligerent brutes behind the massive laundry bins. The male nurses in charge were aware of the groping, heavy breathing, and squeals of laughter. They turned a blind eye.

However, some of those same male nurses or orderlies were also lucky; they had their turn as the day ended. Either with a willing female patient, or, otherwise, with a younger male patient.

A few of the women were not as lucky; some became pregnant and were forced to have an abortion as soon as their menstrual periods stopped. The nurses always knew when that was, and then the pregnancy would be confirmed by the visiting physicians who were on duty.

At the same time as the abortion, without their or their parents' or husband's consent, they also had their tubes tied. Their ovaries would be removed, or they were given a total hysterectomy. They never knew what surgery was performed.

Neither the public, nor the unsuspecting patients and their families, ever knew about the forced sterilizations, which Sister Denise had heard frequently occurred in many other such institutions.

Dr. Cartier openly lectured his medical staff on the matter. "We will order the abortions and the involuntary sterilizations. I do not tolerate spewing, babbling babies in this hospital. We are doing the world a great service by eradicating any future mental depravity, imbeciles, morons, and idiots."

He did, however tolerate the hundred or so little child orphans—normal young children. He had received a handsome stipend for each child from the former provincial Duplessis government.

Those orphans were all good workers, especially when they were hungry. But only if they survived the starvations, sexual abuse, pneumonia, tuberculosis, syphilis, and beatings by the more sadistic inmates or staff.

Many died of head injuries at the hands of brutal, psychotic inmates, or from fulminating skin infections produced by bed bugs or bites by hungry mice, rats, or hair lice, which caused life-threatening fevers.

Sister Denise saw many women who suffered severe pelvic complications after their forced sterilizations when she worked on the hospital ward. Antibiotics were not used on them, since such medications were expensive.

Such females were seen to be the wicked ones—sinful and forever damned to Hell, according to the staunch religious staff members. That included Dr. Cartier.

When Sister Denise and many final-year nurses listened to Dr. Gage's lectures on mental disorders, he was asked about hysterectomies.

"Good question that you asked, miss," Dr. Gage replied to the bright, dark-haired nurse sitting near the back. He moved back and sat on the edge of the table and added, "The term comes from the Latin, *hyster*, meaning 'the uterus.'"

It was a nun near the front, obviously appalled by such surgery, who asked, "So, why remove it if it's not diseased or cancerous?"

"Right. Well, for hundreds of years, maybe a good thousand, so-called physicians were convinced that women—who were called 'hysterics' then and still sometimes now—were neurotic or psychotic. The so-called doctors believed that their womb left the pelvis and traveled throughout their bodies."

"How ignorant is that, Doctor?" someone asked.

"Yes. They concluded that the wandering womb caused the hysteria: the emotional disorder. Hysterectomies were done on tens of thousands of women throughout the world."

Sister Denise stood to say that the class was over. "But no longer, Doctor Gage. Thank the good Lord, and thank you for the lecture," she announced and got up to lead the class to their wards.

Dr. Gage put his hand up to hold the nurses back for a moment. "You're right, sister. Actually, the last hysterectomy for that sole reason was last performed in the mid-west of my country." He hesitated for a dramatic moment, and added, "Just under five years ago, in the late fifties."

✳

CHAPTER 10

Cretins, Morons, Imbeciles, and Idiots

SISTER Denise walked past the patients who were called Mongolian idiots, morons, cretins, and imbeciles. They were a pathetic group of retards, often falling behind the others and tripping over themselves to keep up. As they struggled along, they desperately attempted to follow the basic instructions given by heartless older patients or orderlies ahead of them in line.

A nurse or orderly in charge of the group would shout out to them or push them to walk in a straight line to the kitchens and laundry rooms where they worked.

In 1927, the US Supreme court instituted compulsory sterilization, which was accepted in many other countries, including Canada. Ostensibly, it was 'for the protection and health of the state' to protect the eugenics and save the human race of defectives from the gene pool.

Sister Denise remembered the lecture from *Mère Supérieure* about those who were intellectually defective in the hospital.

"We refer to them as 'retards;' this word was after the Latin *retardo,* meaning 'slowed down,'" she explained as the class made notes.

Unfortunately, it was often the intellectually defective females who became involved in some sexual behavior quite unwittingly. The staff always concluded that these girls had sinned in some manner by having wicked thoughts of sex, or by being aware of 'carnal knowledge'; thus, it was those words that were written in their charts, according to the authorities.

It was when Sister Denise first came to work at the institute that she saw the words, 'For Unlawful Carnal Knowledge' in some charts, also written as F.U.C.K. in others. She became aware that those women were destined for sterilization for having lascivious erotic thoughts, and for indulging in sexual intercourse, often unwillingly.

She had read that in the Dark Ages of Europe having sex, or even having carnal knowledge, outside of marriage was legally unlawful. If someone was caught having such a sexual liaison, then the judge could sentence such a person to a severe fine, jail, or even hanging, especially if found to be homosexual.

The legal charge was 'for unlawful carnal knowledge,' or, simply written in the legal documents, F.U.C.K.

As to the abortions in mental institutions, the patient and their families might be told that the surgery was to remove an infected appendix or a bowel obstruction. The families were totally ignorant of the truth, and were just happy to have their child, of whatever age, out of their home and away from the ridicule of the community for being strange, different, or awkward.

Just last month, *Mère Supérieure* had lectured about the other retards while Sister Denise made notes from where she sat in the class room. She had observed that there were some Mongolian idiots in the chronic women's building on her wards. She had read that the Mongolian People's Republic in northern Asia had recently insisted that the term not be used anymore.

Those children, who looked like the children of the Mongol tribes, were the Down's syndrome babies.

The lecture continued. "The following classification, and the use of such wording, is used throughout the world. Cretins are those born as congenital, low-thyroid babies. These are the ones who were never treated with thyroid medication, however, as a result of it not being diagnosed properly.

"The idiots, as we refer to them, have the lowest possible IQ of all the retards: below twenty on the scale. The imbeciles are a step higher: twenty to forty-nine. The morons on the wards are just simple-minded, or 'feeble-minded', as our director often says.

"The word 'idiot' comes from the Greek for 'a private person;' as does 'imbecile,' for 'without a stick.' 'Cretin' is derived from French: 'A Christian, or God's fool.'

"The phrase 'Mongolian idiot' was coined after Dr. J.L. Down, a British physician. It then became known as Down's syndrome."

Thus, mentally defectives were classified in all other hospitals, as feeble-minded. The terms idiot, imbecile, moron, or cretin were always emblazoned, in bold letters, on the front of each of their charts.

Once the nurses or doctors saw that written as a definitive diagnosis on the chart, not much more was done, offered, or suggested as to treatment of any type. They would just be shuffled aside, laughed at, harassed, bullied, or played with sexually by the other inmates. Occasionally by the staff.

The female building that Sister Denise had just passed housed just under two thousand schizophrenics, manic-depressives, and other defective females. They lived and slept in packed quarters, with cots just six inches apart from each other.

There were not enough toilets, and even those available were always stained with feces, urine, vomit, and menstrual blood.

What the sister also saw, which disturbed her even more, was the substantial number of girl children. The 'Duplessis orphans,' they were called.

Dr. Gage had told Sister Denise in their earlier meeting, "This term is used to describe many hundreds of orphans, both boys and girls. They were hospitalized in various homes and institutions during the time that Mr. Duplessis was the premier of Québec."

Dr. Gage continued, "This institution received more generous funding from the government when our director accepted the orphans. Healthy orphans were thus intentionally diagnosed, quite by error, as being mentally unfit by local physicians and were sent to our hospital for 'treatment.'"

"Treatment?" she asked. "Whatever for? And for such young children?"

"Yes, sister. Most, if not all, the children were misdiagnosed by physicians, and many of the orphanages became 'psychiatric' homes. Such 'patients' were sent to mental institutions for 'treatment,' and such institutions received more funding to house the waifs."

Sister Denise wondered how, following such post-traumatic stress, abuse, depression, and unhealthy personal relationships, these children could ever fully, or even partially, recover.

※

CHAPTER 11

Working in the Institution

IN this hospital it was Dr. Jacques Cartier, who was not really a qualified psychiatrist, but rather a medical administrator, in charge.

Dr. Levy, like many physicians who had fled Europe after the war, came to work in the mental hospitals throughout North America; they were unable to find work elsewhere. Cartier was beholden to them, since they worked on the wards and accepted nothing but a paltry wage in exchange for freedom and the hope of a future in Canada.

Only a small handful would ever go on to become qualified psychiatrists. Levy was one of those and welcomed the employment and income to send to his family overseas.

Cartier also took all he could get for the poor children he employed, since the government paid him to save money from housing them in the community. Instead of boarding them in expensive orphanages, which was such an embarrassment in each community, they were sent to Cartier's domain.

As Sister Denise continued her trek to meet Dr. Gage that day, she sighed and stopped to rest. She had just passed the men's chronic wards building.

It was a three-story, gray, sandstone monstrosity: an identical twin of the women's building. No one, not even the director, knew exactly how many men were housed there. And no one really cared.

"Two or three thousand. More than the women, perhaps," *Mère Supérieure* had said to Sister Denise, a few nuns, and the first-year nurses. They were all introduced to the institution on their first day at the hospital in the early spring.

Mère Supérieure had marched out front, lecturing the forty young, bewildered, frightened young 'preemies,' as they were called: nurses in their first year. They huddled together as they passed the monstrous buildings. They wore sparkling white, starched uniforms, blue capes for warmth, white, polished shoes, and white caps.

"There … on the first two stories: we see bars, but not on the fourth-floor windows?" Sister Denise asked *Mère Supérieure*, pointing up to the top floor.

They had all stopped, enjoying the stroll that late spring day many months ago, with the azalea bushes full of red and pink blossoms. The trees were in full bloom, with robins and sparrows slowly returning north.

Mère Supérieure stopped her introductions and looked up. They all saw the pale faces of agitated, grimacing, fearful-looking men at some of the windows. Some were banging their fists at the third-floor windows, seeking release.

Others were trying to rattle the bars on the levels below, while some screamed or shouted obscenities to the nurses.

"No need. None try to escape by jumping out from the fourth floor," she replied.

Sister Denise had heard differently. No one cared if they jumped, and so some did.

She looked up to the top floor and saw a small patio with some unfortunate male standing there. He filled his lungs with cool, fresh air and tried to step further out on the small ledge.

Suddenly, an arm with a white-jacketed sleeve—an orderly—roughly pulled the man in by the neck and slammed the windows shut.

Today, on this late October morning, Sister Denise passed by groups of men brushing the leaves off the walkways with their makeshift brooms, which were made of long twigs cut from heather bushes and tied to broom handles.

They weren't getting very far, since the wind just blew the leaves back onto the pathway. They would just start all over again; they were in no rush. After all, they weren't going anywhere.

Not home. No place. Never.

In the distance, she finally saw Dr. Gage waving to her. He was smoking his pipe, as usual, and was bundled up in a brown parka and his gray, felt fedora to keep his head warm.

A young, healthy-looking, tall man, he walked back and forth and stamped his feet to keep warm. She saw him limping occasionally, with a larger boot on one foot.

She slowed her pace for a few seconds. She squeezed her rosary in her pocket and prayed that she could ask him about the little boys and girls. Suddenly she was afraid, hesitant. What if *Mère Supérieure* found out that she was speaking so forward with this doctor?

But she was pleased that she could go and rest soon in her rooms, and *Mère Supérieure* would confront Dr. Cartier with her documents.

Her first priority, she knew, was that she needed to recover from the pulmonary surgery to help cure her TB. She winced at the thought of having undergone that procedure some time earlier. At the time, she had wondered and prayed—would she even survive?

✳

CHAPTER 12

Surgery for Galloping Consumption

ALEXANDER Gage was very patient as he waited for Sister Denise and watched as she tried to avoid the black sludge and the slippery puddles. She dutifully held up her skirts, as she was told, to keep her polished boots dry.

He liked the kindly nun, but he already felt the churning in his gut with anxiety, since he knew that she was going to pressure him about the orphans.

"You are losing weight, Sister Denise," Dr. Gage said to greet her.

She humbly replied, "*Oui, docteur.*"

She was more emaciated with her chronic cough, and he was worried about her physical decline. But he saw that she had a good, strong mind, common sense, and a fierce, tenacious spirit. *A kind, spiritual nun*, he thought to himself.

He also knew that she had a very short projected life span. She had been hospitalized, briefly, on the TB ward at this institute up the hill. All such institutions throughout the world had a high incidence of TB due to poor hygiene, an inadequate diet, lack of fresh air, and the deplorable conditions of overcrowding.

The sister had been in isolation then, and had been given a pneumothorax, a surgical procedure for TB patients frequently done at such institutes. It was as a last resort.

Alex recalled that Sister Denise had been frightened when she was first told of the surgery two months ago. The visiting surgeon, Dr. Abercrombie, explained the procedure as Dr. Gage stood next to her bed. He gently held her sweaty, nervous hand as she listened.

"I know I have consumption, Doctor. A strange word for Tuberculosis. Is it not?"

Abercrombie smiled and patted her on the shoulder. "Many, many years ago, it was only known to be a disease that primarily consumed the lungs."

"And galloping? Like a horse galloping? Even more odd, Doctor."

"Yes, it is odd. Unfortunately for some patients, the tubercle bacillus leaves the lung and gallops throughout the rest of the body: into the bones and the brain. I'm sorry to say, my dear."

Alex could see her grimace at the 'my dear' description. Was it irreverent?

She said nothing about that. "Will it consume me, and race and gallop through me?" she asked fearfully.

Abercrombie knew that Alex had performed a spinal tap on the nun weeks before. He informed her that she had no spread of the disease in her spinal cord or brain.

Anyone suspected of the ailment was given a spinal puncture, since it was the easiest procedure to confirm any spread of TB into the central nervous system or elsewhere.

"Mental hospitals everywhere are endemic with TB," Abercrombie said, "perhaps due to poor ventilation, overcrowding, poor hygiene and diet, and lack of definitive treatment."

For the first time, Sister Denise smiled. "Yes, Doctor Gage assured me of my spinal tap results," she said, looking up at Alex.

Abercrombie was in a hurry to see the many others on the sick ward. "This surgery is a common treatment for TB," he said, and then explained, "That particular lobe of your lung, and only that lobe that is infected, will be collapsed, so it can rest and allow the lesions inside to heal with the added medications."

As Alex tightened his grip on her hand to calm her, she asked, "Will I be able to breathe, *docteur*? Breathe again?"

"Yes, my dear," the surgeon reassured her. "Air will be introduced through your chest wall with a large needle into the pleural cavity surrounding the infected lobe. That pleural cavity keeps your lungs inflated from the negative pressure in that cavity."

She turned her head away. Alex could sense her fear as her eyelids fluttered and beads of sweat dripped from her forehead.

The surgeon continued, "Changing the pressure in that cavity then collapses your infected lung, and it will stop the spread of the tubercle bacteria."

"I read about this in our library," Sister Denise explained proudly.

The surgeon then spoke to Alex as the sister listened. "Prescribe her the antibiotic streptomycin, Doctor, for the next several months. Then do a gastric lavage, a stomach sampling, to see if the bacteria are still in her body."

Sister Denise had been told that victims swallowed the bacteria as they coughed. It then sat in the stomach for prolonged periods, and could be assessed after the stomach was pumped out to get a sample.

Alex wrote the prescription into her chart and was kind and gentle with her as he wiped her forehead with a tissue. He listened to her lungs with his stethoscope, but through her pajama top only, since she was shy at revealing her chest.

A brief time following the surgery, she was up and insisted on walking about the small ward. She also insisted on being discharged after some improvement in her pain and her breathing was less problematic.

But Alex knew that it could be temporary if the streptomycin was not effective.

As Sister Denise stepped up to Alex on the pathway near the prison ward, he knocked the ashes out of his pipe exactly three times on the maple tree stump close by and put the warm pipe in his pocket.

He had learned early on to be methodical, obsessive in his behavior, and well-organized due to his lower limb deformity at birth. He had also learned that being obsessive was a healthy way of dealing with anxiety and anger.

He waited as she brushed down her skirt and patted out the damp creases. As she did this, she reminded Alex that this Tuesday morning, after the weekend, Riel, the Indian aboriginal, had to be examined on the prison ward by Alex.

"The director has written the order; the order for Riel to be slated for a prefrontal lobotomy, Doctor. I know you don't agree with that. Riel is a proud man: a leader of men, of his kind."

"Yes. A man of stature in his community of aboriginals: a leader."

"They, the others, they all call you an Indian-lover, since you are so kind to the likes of his race." She wheezed, apologized, and then suppressed a cough in her kerchief.

Alex shrugged it off. "I've heard those kinds of whispers before about my compassion for the aboriginals. I don't think that is a sin, is it sister?"

Sister Denise smiled, shook her head, and reassured Alex. She pointed to his boot. "Your ankle, Doctor. How is it in this weather?"

Alex simply nodded, but he tried to turn his foot such that it could be more in line. They plodded along together: Alex would escort Sister Denise to her warm, quiet rooms where all the nuns were housed so that she could rest.

He would meet *Mère Supérieure* later that morning to confront the director.

CHAPTER 13

Suicide—Or Was It?

THAT very afternoon, after Alex helped Sister Denise to rest in her quarters, he listened to her pleas about the Duplessis children. He agreed to help her.

He was pleased to have made that decision as he entered the chronic women's building, housing the sick ward on the top floor. It was a temporary clinic to house the children, since the proper hospital ward was full.

Mère Supérieure was waiting for him in the spacious doorway. She ushered Alex aside for a moment. "The older girl, the one who survived the attack, has partially recovered from the blow to her head. She is conscious now, *docteur*. She, too, is on this sick ward with the poor children. Doctor Cartier's orders."

Mère Supérieure was a small, wiry woman in her early seventies, and forever dependent on a cane to keep her erect. Her demise had begun soon after the amputation of both her breasts. A mastectomy to attempt a cure, but it was too late.

She held onto Alex's arm as they walked up to the attic, coughing because her cancer had invaded her lungs. The poor woman had much difficulty managing that height. Alex stopped between floors, and patiently waited until she caught her breath.

She pulled her black robe and a heavy scarf about her frail body, now weighing well under a hundred pounds.

When he opened the door to the attic ward and waited for her to enter, Alex was appalled at the dim lighting, lack of heat, and poor ventilation for the sick ones.

The windows were shut tight and covered in old, frayed, worn-out, filthy drapes from ceiling to floor. Alex doffed his fedora and took off his parka, hanging them on a peg at the doorway.

The suffocating room was filled with the stench of chronic malaise. Young children coughed blood-specked sputum into copper pots on the floor, the bedding was stained, and the mattresses sagged with protruding metal coils.

There were only a few children in their cots in the attic now, and those silently wept and cried out for their mothers. They were racked with fever from various childhood ailments, and some were just recovering from bronchitis, chicken pox, measles, whooping cough, or appendicitis.

Some of the adolescent girls had had their ovaries or their uteruses removed secretively, and now suffered from pelvic infections followed by pneumonia.

While Alex made the rounds with *Mère Supérieure,* he noticed that there was only one, young, first-year nurse on duty. She was bundled in her heavy, blue nurse's cape over her uniform to keep warm, and had very little experience in sick room training.

He walked to each one of his patients and listened to their frail chests with his stethoscope and felt their wasted bellies, scarred from surgeries.

"These children need to be better fed and better hydrated, nurse. Open the windows a bit and let some fresh air into this room. Also, turn the heat up. It's cold in here," he instructed the young nurse.

"We—sorry, Doctor, I ..." She hesitated, apologetic. "I was told not to open the hot water valves on the pipes. Doctor Cartier said it was too expensive, Doctor."

"Well, go and do so now, Miss Jannette," Alex ordered, looking at her nametag. He pointed to the valves on the hot water pipes in the distance. She respectfully bowed her head and scurried off.

Mère Supérieure, or 'Mother,' as she was known to the children, had left Alex to speak to Justine, who was in bed. The bed was against the wall, near the center of the attic room.

Alex saw that Justine was partially sitting up but still pale, wan, and sickly-looking.

He watched as Mother very quickly gave her something to put under her pillow. Alex presumed it was some religious token as an offering for a quick recovery.

Jannette returned. She had a warm, kindly smile.

"Please call in an orderly and get those beds cleaned up with fresh, clean sheets. Also, have lots of water at every bedside. Everyone here is to have three good meals daily," Alex directed, furious to see the primitive conditions.

Jannette gave a broad smile this time and ran to make the phone call. Alex could hear the hot water bubbling through the pipes surrounding the floor of the attic.

It was at that time that Dr. Cartier burst into the room.

Alex saw *Mère Supérieure* stiffen; she stood at attention in dutiful reverence with the director's presence.

As Cartier came close, the young nurse walked to her small station in obvious fear. Several children pulled their moth-eaten blankets over their pale faces in hiding.

Cartier was not a large man, but stocky and very quick on his feet. He did not wear the typical white coat of a doctor in a hospital. Instead, he wore an open-buttoned, woolen, blue jacket over a white, cotton shirt that partially covered his neck and scruffy black trousers.

Cartier's graying hair was slicked back from too much gel, which he also used on his sparse, black mustache. His nose and both ears were bursting with protruding, unsightly hairs. Alex always thought it strange that he wore slightly tinted glasses, even if it was evening or dark out, so no one could see his eyes.

"The windows of the soul," Sister Denise had once remarked.

Cartier didn't make any comment or recognition of Alex and brushed him aside. He only nodded brusquely at *Mère Supérieure* when she came to meet him. He muttered something under his breath and called her Bernadette; he always referred to her by name only, somewhat disrespectfully.

He looked at Alex and growled as he sniffed at the warming air now flooding the room.

He pointed at *Mère Supérieure* and bellowed out in anger, "I heard that you, um, wrote to the government, ah, or one of your nuns did, eh?"

Mère Supérieure nodded.

"I want, ah, to see that letter first, eh. Before you send it," he added crustily. He blinked rapidly, easily seen even through his glasses.

Mère Supérieure backed off slightly. Before she could answer, he gruffly took her by the arm and escorted her away from Alex and closer to the windows.

"Too, um, dark here, eh? Let's get some light. So, I can read what has been written by you, eh," he muttered, taking off his glasses, closing his eyes, and turning away briefly. He pulled her along to the windows.

As he did this, he turned to Alex and said in a harsh tone, "See to that, ah, young one there, in that last bed. Ah, examine his belly for me. Take that stupid nurse over there to assist you."

"He is still recovering from an appendectomy, Doctor Cartier. I'll check him over. He may have a bit of a fever," Alex replied.

"She is a kind and devoted nurse, *Docteur* Cartier," *Mère Supérieure* said, pointing to Jannette.

Alex left the two and looked to the end of the dismal attic to attend to the boy. He was sobbing and rocking back and forth in his cot.

As Alex did this, he walked past Justine and stopped at the end of her bed. "How are you today, miss?" he asked and then sympathetically added, "I'm sorry to cut your hair away, so we could attend to the slash on your scalp. The sutures came out cleanly."

Justine opened her eyes but put her hand up to cover the glare from the sun. It was just as Cartier fully opened the drapes on the window in front of her bed.

"Yes, that is acceptable, Doctor. Thank you; and my hair will grow back. I'm better today, and now awake, Doctor Gage," she offered in halting English.

Alex briefly inspected the scar on her head. "I heard that Celeste's father, Vittorio, came to visit you here, Justine."

"Yes, he was very kind, but also very angry, Doctor Gage."

"At you? Certainly not at you, Justine. You were very brave to shout out and call for help."

"No, Doctor. He said to me that he knows who it was."

"Who killed poor Celeste?"

"*Oui, docteur, oui.* He said it could be the other Italian working here. At this hospital. To get revenge."

"Revenge? For what? He shouldn't make accusations like that, Justine," Alex said, wondering where this was going.

Alex left Justine. *There is only one other Italian physician working here,* he thought to himself.

Alex didn't mention Dr. Aaron Levy's name to Justine, but presumed she knew.

Justine said nothing as she lay back and covered her face with a small, damp towel that Jannette brought her for greater comfort.

As Alex paused to absorb this news from Justine, he passed Cartier and *Mère Supérieure*, who were at the window near the ledge.

✳

Cartier opened the drapes even wider at the one large window where he roughly parked Bernadette. The nun was holding a piece of paper in her right hand.

"I need light, eh? To see what you have written, ah, to the provincial people in Montréal, Bernadette," he said, blinking rapidly and thrusting apart the grimy, old, stained-glass doors leading to the open landing.

One could step out through the doors, but only onto a small, concrete ledge. That ledge was hardly able to hold two people and was guarded by a wrought-iron rail only two feet high.

As Cartier opened the glass doors, he turned to Bernadette and pulled her closer to the edge, by her arm. He stood slightly behind her and pointed to the paper in her hand.

"Show me what, ah, what you have spoken of, so I can approve it to the ministry of health, eh, Bernadette," he said with contempt. He abruptly pulled the letter away and nudged her even closer with his body to the small, iron rail.

Bernadette faltered slightly, holding her cane for support. She was clearly nervous as to what Cartier was ready to read aloud in such a hostile manner and what he would say.

Cartier held the letter that he had torn from her hand and turned to look inside of the room.

He saw Justine, who was lying in the bed opposite him in front of the open, glass doors with her face covered with a towel. He turned further to see Alex and the young nurse, who attended to the sickly boy in the far corner.

Cartier then turned back to be with the nun and spoke gruffly at Bernadette to distract her. It was at that exact moment, as she cowered from his unbearable attitude—feeble and resting on her cane—that he raised his free left hand. He pushed her as hard as he could, over the rusted, wrought-iron rail.

She wavered slightly, and in a panic dropped her cane. She threw out her right hand and grasped Cartier's arm to save herself. As she did this, she tore at his sleeve jacket and teetered over the edge, losing her balance.

She looked him in the eyes as her frail body slumped over the rail, falling. Then in a second, she was gone.

Cartier stepped back and removed his glasses. He tried to hide his left arm with the tattered cloth hanging from his shoulder. He glanced over to watch her body, arms and legs askew, hurtle down the four stories to her death.

"My good God, she has jumped," he shouted out loudly, pointing to the void in front of him. At the same time, he forced the letter into his pocket and walked back into the room.

He appeared to be agitated and dramatic, yet cold and dispassionate, as he called out. "Look, she said she would kill herself. She did jump over, eh? She told Sister Denise and others that she was depressed, eh, would suicide. Poor woman."

✳

CHAPTER 14

A Witness to Murder

JUSTINE partly sat up just at the time that Cartier pushed the nun over the rail. She had raised her head from the pillow and pulled the towel from her face, feeling thirsty.

Justine had intended to reach over to take a sip of water from the plastic cup on her bedside table. As she did this, she locked eyes with Cartier as he turned back into the room, after he had pushed *Mère Supérieure* over the edge.

Cartier blinked and quickly put his tinted glasses back on. Justine, shocked and tremulous, recoiled and turned away in fear. She had spilled her cup onto her bed, and covered herself in her blanket.

Cartier said nothing.

However, Alex turned from his duty with the young lad and was startled with the shout. When he had palpated the boy's abdomen and covered him in his blanket, he looked to see that *Mère Supérieure* was nowhere to be seen.

He did hear a scream, or so he thought; it was the wail of a woman, somewhere outside: somewhere further down, far outside the building.

He told Jannette to see to the boy and rushed to the window. He pushed Cartier aside, just as the director secretly tore up the letter and put it back in his pocket.

"What happened, Doctor? You said she jumped? My God, why? Why?"

Cartier stepped back as he readjusted his glasses, agitated and hopping from one foot to the other. "Said she would, eh? Said she would. Suicide: she said she would, eh. Um, depressed she was. Dying with the cancer, she was." He shouted for all others in the attic to hear.

Cartier seemed out of control, hypomanic, moving about irrationally and talking gibberish.

Alex tried to calm him, but he was swept away by Cartier's arm. "I recall that she had been sad and withdrawn after her surgery, but she never threatened to act in such a manner. She still had work to do here, poor woman," Alex said as he went to the window ledge.

"Sister Denise can be the head of the nuns now," Cartier stated loudly. He walked away and out the door, still mumbling incoherently to himself.

At the window ledge, Alex was wary as he looked over the railing. He gasped to see the twisted body lying on the concrete walk down below, with legs askew and one arm beneath her body. The other arm was distorted at right angles from the fall.

He shielded his eyes from the sun and could see blood on the sidewalk below, spewing out from the fractured skull. Patients and some nurses huddled about. They cried and wailed from the dreadful sight. Someone brought out a blanket from the wards and covered the frail body.

Alex stepped back into the room and put his arm around the young nurse, who ran forward. Jannette sobbed aloud and trembled in horror at the imagined sight below.

Alex comforted Jannette and led her to her desk. "Are you able to continue here, nurse?"

She brushed her tears aside and only nodded sadly.

Alex left her and looked at Justine in bed. She sat up and motioned to Alex to come to her.

Alex came to Justine's bed and sat on the edge as she put her finger to her lips, indicating silence. "I saw him, Doctor," she whispered to Alex. She waited for some time to pass.

Alex couldn't hear her muffled voice and moved closer to the head of the bed. "Pardon, Justine? What? What did you say?"

Justine tried to sit up. Alex came to the head of her bed and helped her by raising her pillow, so she could be propped up.

"I saw him push her out the window. I saw it, Doctor. He pushed the poor woman over. I saw it. He knew that I saw him," she again whispered.

She was visibly frightened, and Alex could see sweat rolling down her cheek, her face red, and her heart thumping through her breast bone.

Alex came right up to her face. "What are you saying, Justine? You saw him push her? Push *Mère Supérieure?*"

Justine settled back into her bed: upset, clammy, wringing her hands, and searched for her water cup in the bed. "I'm scared. He will be after me. Don't leave me. Please. God help me now," she begged again and again.

Justine then rolled over slightly, put her hand under her pillow, and retrieved an envelope. She gave it to Alex.

"Here, she gave me this sheet of paper in this envelope. She said it was her real copy. She hid it with me. Doctor Cartier was not to know that she confided in me; she said that to me, she did."

Alex poured some water into her cup and put it in her trembling hands. He opened the envelope and read the official letter. The paper was neatly written: Sister Denise's original letter to the government, exposing Cartier and his corruption in dealing with the children.

Mère Supérieure's signature was also witnessed by her priest in town. Alex knew that Justine was now defenseless and in danger, although *Mère Supérieure* had also given him a copy of the letter much earlier that day.

He called Jannette over so Justine could hear. "I want Justine to have a twenty-four hour nurse with her, and near her, at all times. Just in case she goes back into a coma. I'll talk to Sister Denise to arrange it."

"*Oui, docteur,*" Jannette said as she tried hard to compose herself.

✳

CHAPTER 15

A Sweet Girl's Sweet Revenge

DR. Aaron Levy knew that it would be quiet, as usual, in the laundry rooms that evening. Only a few would be working that late. He had called the women's ward and already made certain that his favorite patient Euphemia, the moronic, deaf, and dumb girl, was working.

He knew Euphemia, and Euphemia accepted the good doctor and his weekly visits.

Soon after Aaron Levy had arrived to work at the hospital he had read Euphemia's chart. He had had to examine her for a bronchial condition. As he prescribed the penicillin, he read that she was a moron and was mute.

But being in a hurry, selfish, sloppy, and slovenly, he only read the front of her chart. It was her family physician's notes at the back that stated: *Euphemia has gonorrhea. Must be treated. Possibly even syphilis. Very promiscuous. Unable to confirm since she will be transferred tomorrow to the mental hospital.*

Aaron lit up and inhaled deeply, letting the ash fall on his desk. He let it sit there. He was pleased that it was a practical ward nurse who answered the office phone this time and at this late evening.

"Euphemia, nurse. I must write a question to her as to the town where she came from. She may be discharged soon with all the others," he lied as he licked his fingers after finishing his sugar donut.

"Yes, Doctor Levy. Our worker, Euphemia, will be working tonight. She is very simple-minded but is the best worker in ironing and folding the bed sheets," the evening nurse respectfully replied.

The path was the same one that Aaron had taken a few weeks ago, also on the way to the nurse's residence. It was very dark this evening, and he stopped for a moment and lit up again.

"Sorry that happened. It was an accident. An accident. Didn't mean to. Sorry," he muttered and walked on.

He flipped his glowing cigarette into the dry bushes and walked into the laundry building. He looked about and sighted his chubby, stupid quarry alone in the corner. She was obsessively folding bedding, which took time; most everyone else had left.

She was humming some silly tune to herself as she turned her head to find Aaron behind her. Alone in the corner of the laundry, she was far away from the other two workers.

The good doctor patted her shoulder to calm her as he gently pushed his pelvis into her buttocks.

Euphemia was one of a multitude of dim-witted girls working at the hospital. She was Aaron's favorite girl since she was silent and moronic.

He was her favorite doctor since she received a brand-new, shiny, fifty-cent piece for simply spreading her chubby thighs for him in the small linen closet next door.

Aaron gently maneuvered her into the adjoining closet where the laundry was stored. He lit up his vile, American Camel cigarette and looked out the door to make sure that the other two were still busy working before closing it. He turned on the corner light and led Euphemia to the table against the wall.

Effie, as the nurses on her ward called her, never spoke. She was deemed to be deaf at an early age from the dreaded childhood illness of German measles.

Her mother, of Greek origin, named her after the Greek saint, Euphemia, which meant 'soft spoken' or 'fair of speech,' since she never uttered a word, being deaf and of very low intelligence.

She, like the simple girls that Aaron had preyed on during the German occupation of Italy, never complained of his sexual assaults. They, like Effie, were just happy to receive cocaine, morphine, some lira, or other medicines that were unavailable but required by their family to survive in 1943.

Aaron talked, and knew Effie could see his lips moving. "I never harmed the poor girls in Naples when I gave them drugs, Effie. I never killed any of them for the services I provided with food, medicines, or drugs during the war," he whispered in her ear as he pulled down her panties.

He talked quietly to Euphemia as she mounted the table and spread her legs wide for him. *Maybe I could tell Euphemia about that terrible deed I did. She wouldn't tell anyone else,* he thought to himself as cigarette ash fell from his lips onto her thighs. He just kept on pushing.

"I didn't mean to hold her throat that long. I only wanted to scare her father, Vittorio, for what he did to my family in Italy."

Effie smiled vacantly as he finished what he came for. He was still talking, but flinched as he felt the searing pain in his penis when he pulled out.

Aaron waited until the burning pain subsided. He pinched his penis to get the foul discharge out and pulled a pillow case down to clean himself off.

Euphemia just smiled vacantly when she saw his lips moving, but she knew he was finished.

She waited patiently as he cleaned himself off with the newly-starched pillow case he had taken from the ledge next to her. She let herself off the table and bent down to wipe her genitals clean with the same pillow.

She straightened up and stupidly blew him a kiss, grinned, and accepted the shiny, fifty-cent Canadian coin.

She carefully, ever so compulsively, folded the pillow case back again and put it lovingly on the shelf. She smiled again, demurely, perhaps unknowing that she gave him something to worry about in exchange for fifty cents. Gonorrhea, known as 'the clap' or 'the drip.'

Aaron opened the closet door for Euphemia, shut the light off, and butted his cigarette out on the floor boards. He ushered her back to her isolated station. She returned to her duties, and Aaron was about to leave the laundry area.

He looked up to see writing on the wall, just above the doorway. It was a scrawl, but clear enough, and in dark, bold letters.

"It is not the healthy who need a doctor, but the sick. I have not come to call the righteous, but for the sinners to repent."

It was signed, *"J.C."*

Aaron's heart skipped a beat, and he felt it flutter uncontrollably for minutes. He read Jesus' biblical proverb again and again.

"It must be our director, Jacques Cartier, and not Jesus Christ. Putting up such nonsense, as usual, all over the hospital," he said out loud. Suddenly feeling the guilt in his burgeoning gut for his blasphemy, he then thought, *Does he know? Is he aware what goes on here? What I did?*

He crossed himself three times. Then, as he walked out the door, he lit up another cigarette for comfort.

He was startled to almost walk into Vittorio, his war-time compatriot from Palermo, Italy. He was on duty to walk the girls back to their wards, as ordered by Dr. Alex Gage.

Vittorio glowered at Aaron. He was certain he knew why Aaron was there. "What the fuck? You slimy wop. Were you into one of my girls here again, Levy?" He grabbed Aaron by the arm and pulled him aside.

Aaron struggled to free himself, but Vittorio was too strong: twice his size and had a powerful grip on his pudgy arm. So much so that his arm went numb.

He stammered and stuttered in fear. "Ah, no. Just getting my laundry that I sent last week."

"You slimy prick. I know what you were after. One of my girls. Just as I knew all about you in Palermo."

"That was then, *amico mio*. Long time ago," Aaron blathered as he felt his heart in his throat.

"Not so long ago when you used those poor, young girls for your own use, bribing them with drugs. Drugs and shit that you stole from the German army barracks and store houses, you fat prick. I know all about you."

Aaron freed himself of the grasp. He dropped his smoldering cigarette at Vittorio's feet and stammered, "Not like what you did. For that same army, for money. You sent my family to the concentration camps."

He turned and fled out the door, vowing on his mother's grave to kill Vittorio one day soon.

CHAPTER 16

Seeking Solace from Guilt

AARON almost ran out of the laundry building and into the dark pathways. Anything to get away from that Vittorio. Vittorio knew that Aaron was having sex with Gabriella, and Aaron knew he wanted her for himself.

Not that Gabriella would let Aaron have sex with her now. "Aaron, you've got the drip, the clap. Not with me," she said, knowing what gonorrhea looked like. She pointed to the oily puss dripping on her floor when he came at her with his pants down.

As he almost sprinted down the pathway, the howls of coyotes in the far distance and the hoot of owls in the nearby tree tops added to his burgeoning fears.

"I'll go and find my friend Alex in the hospital cafeteria. He is usually there having a bedtime snack," he said to himself hopefully as he entered the admin building.

Aaron had confided in Alex when they first met that he had escaped the tentacles of the Cosa Nostra mafia in Italy prior to coming to Canada.

"That slash across your cheek, Aaron? A war wound?" Alex asked, pointing to Aaron's unshaven face.

"Fuck no. The mafia. For stealing some drugs that I then sold. Bastards caught me one time only."

Alex had been clearly surprised by Aaron's appearance and demeanor when they first met. He was overweight, hirsute, and much shorter than Alex. He was forever smoking revolting cigarettes and eating sugar donuts.

His left eye was a glass blob, the product of an American sniper's wayward shrapnel grenade. He always carried a pocket stiletto, just in case. His wide belly was surrounded a few times by a long, silver chain, which then hung down to his left knee.

Aaron was sloppy and uncouth, but he was a good salesman for Alex in selling his acid blotters to the staff. The staff and his patients were never sure where Aaron was looking, since his right eye went one way and the glass globe floated in another direction.

Alex, sitting alone at a quiet corner table in the hospital staff cafeteria, welcomed Aaron when he came to join him after leaving the laundry room.

"You're sweating, my friend. What's going on?" Alex asked.

"I had a run-in with that Vittorio by accident. He said he would kill me for my love for Gabriella, my friend."

Alex finished his tomato, bacon, and cheese salad and pushed the plate aside. "Well, just be careful that neither he nor Cartier catch you screwing in Cartier's offices, Aaron."

Aaron lit up a cigarette, and Alex pushed the ashtray toward him. "I still very badly want to become a psychiatrist here in Canada," Aaron confided in Alex.

He ordered a coffee from one of the patients who worked there and added, "I can't write well, and could never pass those exams, my friend. Maybe you could write them for me."

Alex almost laughed out loud and shook his head in disbelief. "No way, Jose. No way; not possible. Listen, if there's a shit storm coming, then I want to know which way the wind is blowing, Aaron," he said, ready to leave.

"Sit. Sit, my friend," Aaron pleaded, holding him down. "No shit storm."

Some time ago, when Aaron had said he wanted to become a psychiatrist in Canada, Alex had only quickly explained. Now he reminded him, "Psychiatry, my friend, as a specialty of medicine, is only just being offered to medical graduates. There are only one or two universities in Canada that offer it, and it is mostly men who enter the specialty."

"I know I will have to go to the institute in Montréal, my friend," Aaron said shooing the patient away as she took her time and wiped the table clean after bringing him his coffee.

Alex relaxed. "You will need to spend another four years of training after becoming a qualified medical doctor, Aaron. You might have some trouble with the language."

Aaron brushed that off. "I heard about such a long time, *amico mio*. Still better than my life in Italy," Aaron replied, calling Alex 'his friend,' but bearing an underlying hostility toward him for other reasons.

"Some of those years will be spent in one of the asylums for training. Then you will have to write the qualifying exams. Very few actually get to work in the community, and psychiatry is still mostly 'practiced' only in the mental institutions."

Aaron listened to Alex, but his mind was elsewhere. He licked his fingers of the sweet that he sucked on from dipping his hand into the sugar bowl.

Alex got up to leave but wanted to admonish Aaron for butting his fag out in the sugar bowl. Instead he berated him, "Look, Aaron. You've been to the laundry. Those girls will no longer be taken advantage of. If I catch any staff fucking around there, I'll get them fired. So back off. That includes you."

Aaron blushed and stuttered, "Someone told you, *amico mio?*"

"I just know. And you've got the clap, so get on some penicillin," Alex said, lowering his voice. He wasn't going to reveal Gabriella's name as his source.

"I'll see my doc in town, Alex. Why do you call it the clap?"

"The clap or the drip. Pus drips—yuck—and clap from *clapier*, an area in bygone Paris full of brothels and whorehouses. Gonorrhea spread like wild fire from there."

Aaron listened, but hesitated and pulled at Alex's sleeve. He really wanted to tell Alex—no, he wanted to confide in Alex—as to his immoral actions.

He wondered if Alex had seen that hand-written adage of J.C.'s in the laundry room.

"Was it really Jesus? Or was it Jacques?" he wanted to ask. It was too late; Alex got up and walked away.

CHAPTER 17

LSD

WHEN Alex came to work at the hospital, he had learned from Aaron that he had been with the Italian mafia. It didn't take long before he willingly became Alex's conduit of selling LSD to the local staff and the wider community.

He peddled Alex's acid tablets, small blotters, and wafers, all impregnated with acid, for a small percentage. Vinny, Alex's landlord, was helpful: he put the packages together in his basement, also for a small fee.

Aaron received twenty percent of what he sold, each for ten dollars. All three made a hefty profit from selling the drug, which was not illegal, but also not easily available.

Aaron often scoffed at his paltry sum, and often chided Alex in a jocular but threatening manner. He complained to Alex, "Your Yankee *americano* wartime forces invaded my Sicily in the war."

"They freed your people of German occupation."

"They, too, screwed my drug money with the Germans," Aaron quickly reminded Alex.

With that facial scar across his cheek from a mafia blade as punishment for his cheating, Aaron again proudly explained, "I and my friends in the Italian mafia did well in supplying the Germans with marijuana, speed, cocaine, and heroin."

Alex was amazed at Aaron's courage at such a time. "No shit? That took courage."

Aaron nodded, very pleased with Alex's surprise. He dropped his smoldering cigarette into his near-empty coffee cup. "After all, they had nothing to do but sit around and use the drugs freely. Until you fucking Americans came and pissed all over my hard-earned lira."

Alex simply shrugged off the complaint and continued to use Aaron to help distribute acid. As a psychiatric resident in Boston, Alex knew that others in North America had been using LSD in the treatment of alcoholics. It was becoming a popular and acceptable form of therapy.

There was also another conduit for Alex for his profitable business. It was located at his 'clinic' run by his paramour, Christina. Her Casa Loma, a high-class house of ill repute, was just outside of Montréal, near the hospital.

Alex confided in Aaron, "This 'clinic' used to be occasionally raided by the police, because it was also used by a gynecologist to perform abortions. The well-known physician who provided the abortions was often arrested. Such abortions are still illegal in Canada."

"What happened to him?" Aaron asked, very apprehensive.

"The physician never denied his therapeutic assistance to any woman. If she desired the termination of her pregnancy, it was in that clinic, a surgically sterile setting, compared to the 'kitchen table' abortions performed by others."

"Those kitchen table abortions by doctors or quacks often cause serious pelvic infections or death, even in my own country," Aaron said.

"That's so, Aaron. This doctor who did the abortions welcomed me in my treatment of addicts. It gives the clinic an added semblance of authenticity and lawfulness," Alex confided.

Alex had heard that one of the registered nurses working at the hospital was also assisting this physician with abortions. Monique was her name, but their paths had never crossed. She worked at the clinic only in the evenings, after her daytime work at the institution.

Aaron was curious. "Where did this drug come from, my friend?"

"Albert Hofmann, working at a European pharmaceutical company, first produced lysergic acid in 1938. Twenty-five micrograms, a tiny amount, was like a few grains of salt. He accidentally consumed a small dose and had vivid hallucinations."

"It made him crazy? Insane?"

"Yes, but after taking a much smaller dose, he realized that it caused a calmness for himself and for anxious or nervous people. It was easily found in the ergot fungus, which readily grows on rye and other grains."

Aaron had some information for Alex. "I read that it was promoted by Timothy Leary in your country."

"That's right, Aaron. I met him in Harvard, where I took some of my training. There, LSD was first produced in a crystal form, but then into a colorless, odorless, liquid—like water. It was easily absorbed into paper blotters and sucked orally or drunk in a glass of water."

Aaron finished his apple pie for dessert and sipped on another coffee as they talked. "Where do you get it?"

Alex waited until another patient who worked in the staff cafeteria finished clearing their table. "I buy it from a pharmaceutical company in Montréal, my friend. Our director, Cartier, is a strong proponent of such treatments."

"But is too stupid to earn an extra income from it." Aaron smiled shrewdly.

Alex went on as they left their table and walked out. "LSD is becoming popular. I've heard it being called 'acid,' 'boomers,' and 'downers,' and that being on it can be called a 'trip.' At other times, a 'bad trip' can cause hallucinations, paranoid delusions, sweating, chills, tremors, and irrational, grandiose ideas. Some have become addicted and were convinced they could fly; they jumped off tall buildings."

"I hope that no happen for us, *amico mio*."

"No, it won't, as we use a very low dosage, Aaron. Unfortunately, I have heard of it used by some American clandestine government organizations, here in Canada. I wonder what they could think to gain from it?"

CHAPTER 18

Lafayette the Indian

TWO weeks later, *Mère Supérieure* had a simple funeral at the small chapel on the grounds. The bishop delayed the funeral to wait until the priest from Montréal returned from Rome to preside.

Sister Denise was proclaimed to be the interim leader of the sisters at the hospital but had to wait until she was duly appointed by Rome and the Montréal diocese, as the new Mother Superior.

Mère Supérieure's body was taken away to LaSalle, the village nearby, for burial.

After the funeral, Alex was pleased to have Aaron Levy with him when he would interview Riel, one of the many Aboriginals in the institution. "The director has canceled his ground privileges. He blamed him for the nighttime assault on those nurses," Aaron was too quick to tell Alex.

Alex stopped briefly and shook his head in wonder. "She told me he smelled of cigarette smoke. I examined the older girl after she was brought to the sick ward, Aaron."

Aaron said nothing, but unconsciously fingered his pack of cigarettes and pushed them deeper into his pocket.

Alex had met the Indian once, when he was admitted to the hospital. "He's a large man, with powerful shoulders and hands. He keeps to himself, is clean-shaven, and prefers his buckskin clothing to the hospital garb."

"I see that all the patients respect him. He bothers no one if no one bothers him, Alex."

"And he wasn't a big smoker."

Aaron thought fast. "I saw him light up, once."

Cartier hated Riel, because he was a leader of his people in the province and worked fervently to have parliament give aboriginals the vote throughout Canada. Cartier perceived him to be a threat and predicted that the Indians or 'redskins,' as they were called, would organize someday and govern themselves as a nation.

Cartier had diagnosed Riel as a psychotic, a hebephrenic: a type of immature, childlike schizophrenic. Many were diagnosed thus in such hospitals if no other cause for their unusual personality could be found.

Alex disagreed with Cartier's diagnosis, and was not in favor of prescribing anti-psychotic medications to Riel. Riel just cheeked the pills prescribed by Cartier and spat them out later.

Alex observed this 'cheeking of the meds' to be common with Riel. It was after the nurses handed out the prescribed pills and walked away that he pushed them into his cheek and then spat them into his hand.

This was a common activity, quickly learned by other patients. That was why Alex insisted that nurses wait until the pills were dutifully swallowed.

The two of them, together with nurses, had come to listen to Dr. Walters, the prefrontal lobotomy surgeon who would lecture that morning on the hospital ward.

"Why does our director think he is insane, Alex?"

"The *SQ*, the provincial police, said he must be crazy. They found him with a hatchet sleeping in the woods," Alex explained.

"I heard that he took down a small deer up in the hills, but on hospital property. Cartier said he was psychotic, and a thief to kill one of his deer on his property," Aaron said as they walked along.

Alex pulled a face and shook his head in disbelief. "He said that the land didn't belong to Riel, or the other Indians prowling about off the nearby reservation. This is Cartier's territory, he insists, and the deer are his."

They both stopped and looked up at the dark clouds looming over the river. Aaron pointed to a large flock of Canada geese, cackling noisily in a 'V' shape as they headed south again.

"It will be warmer for them." He sighed enviously and cupped his hands over his mouth to warm them.

"Aaron, it will be a sight to behold to see how the icepick surgeon copes with Riel when the time comes. I wonder who will win. Icepick surgeon! My God, what a handle to be labeled with," Alex said with a shudder.

He readjusted the zipper on his parka and pulled the fedora down over his forehead for warmth.

As they made their way to hear the lecture by the famous icepick surgeon, Aaron stopped and lit a cigarette. "Where did that name, the 'icepick surgeon' come from?" he asked, watching the cool breeze blow the smoke away.

"I heard about the famous Doctor Walters when I was in my third year of psychiatry in Boston, Aaron. Walters performed fourteen prefrontal lobotomies on schizophrenic patients at the mental institution just outside of Boston."

"What was the outcome?"

"Twelve survived the slicing of the front part of the brain with a scalpel. It was through surgical burr holes in the skull, as was commonly done then."

Aaron stopped and looked intently at his friend. "You are humming. A tune you are fond of, Doctor?"

"Oh, sorry. No. Just something from childhood. To tell you the truth, I was always in the habit of humming quietly to myself. It was just a nervous habit. I'm anxious that I must confront Walters and Cartier at some point soon to stop that surgical brutality."

They were close to the hospital ward, and the small auditorium adjoining it used as a lecture room.

"So? Why ever the icepick?" Aaron asked as he stopped to grind his cigarette butt into the gravel path.

"Walters lectured all the nurses, orderlies, doctors, and everyone else who would listen to him in Boston. He said that using an icepick was faster and saved the hospital the use of a surgical room and much money."

"Save money?"

"Yep. It was faster, and without a surgical team of anesthetists and nurses. But two died of hemorrhage in the brain, and one of infection later."

"But an icepick? How gross is that?"

"It is. Walters developed a sharp icepick, which he uses to puncture the brain from below and through the thin bone above the eye. He hammered his icepick up through that bone and into the soft underbelly of the brain."

"So, Cartier endorsed this idea to save hospital funds." Aaron scoffed.

"I'm working to get our government to abolish this practice. If I'm too late, then Riel and countless others will fall under the icepick."

"He's just a strange personality type: he is an Indian and prefers the woods, carries a knife, drinks, and has a hatchet. He likes his fire water, as the director called it. Maybe he has Korsakoff syndrome." Aaron added, stamping his feet and shivering as a cold gust struck them both.

"Maybe; I knew all about Korsakoff's psychosis. My mother was a heavy drinker and was prone to memory loss and paranoid delusions.

She was sure that the US government was spying on her; that's why she moved into Canada's far north, away from society."

Aaron added, "Korsakoff? It's the result of heavy, long-time drinking. Named after a Russian neurologist, Korsakoff. He found those alcoholic people to have a poor memory and confabulated—that is, told lies to fill in their blanks—and had false beliefs. They were delusional, Doctor. We saw many such disturbed ones in Italy. Too much *vino*."

Alex agreed. "There are many such patients here, Aaron. They will never recover."

The sun had risen in the north-east as a huge, red ball that late in autumn. It was too weak to dispel the early frost on the yellow grass or the mist rolling up from the St. Lawrence River as they both walked past the prison wards.

The low, austere building held prisoners who were deemed to have committed a crime but were insane and needed treatment as pronounced by either a judge or two psychiatrists.

They looked at the building. It had a flat roof, barred windows, and steel doors, and was partly built into the hill behind it.

"I was told that it was some cattle shed from two hundred years ago, later entombed in stone, and now one of our prison wards," Aaron explained, pointing down the frozen path to the grim structure.

Alex nodded. "So, I heard." He pointed to six men, shackled with irons, weeding a spent potato patch nearby. "Are they all still dangerous? Shackled like that? They were lobotomized. No need to shackle them now."

"All the other doctors bow down to Cartier. You, ah, you're the only one to put a stop to it, Doctor." Aaron said, looking at Alex with admiration. "You will take over one day, my friend; when we get rid of Jacques, that manic depressive idiot."

"I hope so, Aaron, but I'm wondering: how the Devil did you get here, man, from war-torn Italy?"

Aaron stopped, pulled out a donut from the bag in his back pocket, and gladly explained. "Myself, I escaped from the German *Gestapo* with many other Jews in Italy's north. Them and I, with hundreds of others, were in a rail cattle car outside of Milan, on its way to Germany and the concentration camps."

"My God. Aaron. What happened to you?"

Aaron wiped his brow and finished his donut. "I still sweat when I think about it. That train abruptly stopped as an American war plane strafed it, and the door was flung open. I and some few leaped out, and I rolled into a ditch," he said, needing to stop and catch his breath.

"Lucky you."

"*Si*. The guards on the train fired wildly as the train started up again. A Nazi bullet grazed the radial nerve in my left arm. It healed, but an American hand grenade and the shrapnel took out my eye later on."

"You were lucky; the others were not, but I see that your left arm is weaker and now hangs less strong."

"*Si, si*. Someone, and I'm sure I know who, told the *Gestapo* in Italy where all my Jewish friends and some family were hiding in Palermo and Naples."

"A rat fink collaborator, Aaron."

Aaron pulled out another cigarette. "They were in those cattle cars. I'll get that rat fink who works here, someday."

Alex had heard that it was Vittorio. Aaron and Alex had much in common, although coming from different countries. They were silently sympathetic to each other's deformities.

Alex looked at the heavy ring of hospital keys attached to the chain. "That chain, Aaron; why the chain?" Alex asked.

"Ah, *si, si*, my friend. It keeps my belly from twitching. From all that stress. Given to me by a German soldier. I saved him with a belly full of shrapnel, in Palermo," he answered, fingering the chain and taking in deep puffs.

"Lucky."

"That officer in the German army was grateful, but he probably stole it from some other Italian, the *figlio di puttana*," he added solemnly. He then explained, "Ah, sorry, what a son of a bitch, he was."

As they approached the massive doors to enter the building, the late morning sun shone through a break in the clouds. Alex looked at his Italian friend and pointed to the children working on the grounds.

"I was pressured from Sister Denise to do something about the orphans. But now, with the lobotomies, Aaron? It is too much for me, the pressure to act. After all, my tenure and residency in this country is dependent on Cartier, who already told me to mind my own fucking business."

Aaron nodded with an understanding glance. "Cartier said to me once that you are too aggressive, and a know-it-all. He said that you think that you Americans are so much smarter, and that you, my friend, want to make changes here at his institution."

"So, I heard," was all Alex said.

Aaron stopped and looked seriously at Alex. He waited as several nurses passed them on the path. "That good mother, *Mère Supérieure*, she did not jump. She was depressed for what she saw here, but she was pushed, I'm certain."

"I agree. She would not have torn Cartier's sleeve off his arm if it was suicide. She still had shards of the sleeve gripped in her hand. She wanted the letter to go out first; her only hope to help the children."

Aaron only nodded in agreement. Murder was too dangerous a subject now for him, after what he had to do for the mafia in Sicily. So, he changed the topic of conversation.

Aaron put his good arm around Alex to impart more news for him. "I agree. And those poor children here. I was told by Cartier's accounting assistant, my dear loved one, also from my country. Gabriella is her name. She is in the front office. She said to me that he pockets the money that the hospital receives from the government for those poor children."

Alex was not surprised but kept that information to himself. Only he and Gabriella knew that she siphoned some of that money to Alex by cooking the books. Alex would soon distribute the cash to the patients later for work that they did in the laundry, kitchens, and on the grounds. All without Cartier's knowledge. She was courageous to take the risk for those patients.

Alex looked at the engraved stone at the top of the landing to the prison building. It had ornate, Corinthian columns fronting the austere structure. The stone read, *"Bienvenue."*

"Yes, awful place to have a welcome sign in French, isn't it?"

Alex reached for his keys. "A strange, classical façade for such a dismal inner sanctum, isn't it?"

As they stared at the entrance, they spotted another placard attached to the large, stone prison facade. It read, in large, bold letters,

"Let the one among you who is without sin be the first to cast a stone."

A large *"J.C."* was etched below.

Aaron pointed to the placard and ground his cigarette into it. "Shit. It is Cartier again. He must be hypomanic, Alex."

"Or seriously depressed, my friend."

Alex felt sorry and concerned for his director but was unable to help him at this time. As he approached the great, wooden doors he pulled on the thin chain securely fastened to his belt. For the rest of the year, Alex knew he would be shackled to the large ring of ice-cold keys forever weighing down his belt.

Alex looked at the massive key made only for that ward. "I guess I'm not only the healer here, but also the jailer."

CHAPTER 19

Brain Surgery With an Icepick

AARON nodded in agreement with Alex's observation as he fingered his own set of rings with his good right hand. It held many large, brass keys attached to the long, silver chain coiled about his stomach and into his pocket.

The two waited as a group of nurses walked past them into the lecture room. Alex didn't mind sitting in, because he also knew that he might be asked about the surgical procedure in his qualifying exams in psychiatry.

Alex smiled at a nurse, a dark-haired beauty, who slowed her pace, turned at the door entrance, and winked at him.

Alex saw the twinkle in Aaron's eye as she walked past.

"She looks just like my beautiful young sister," Aaron said, wistfully.

"Indeed, a beauty. Gina, she calls herself on her nametag, Aaron."

"Sorry to say to you, my friend. She, my sister, was picked up by those same *Gestapo* Germans, ratted on by that pig, and she died in the concentration camps."

"Oh, so sorry indeed to hear, Aaron," Alex said as he put his arm around his friend in sympathy.

"*Si, si.* But this Gina is a look-alike to Gina Lollobrigida, the most beautiful Italian actress, Alex. I saw her movie five *multo* times, with

Humphrey Bogart. *Beat the Devil*, it was. Just ten years to this day, my friend."

Alex smiled at Aaron's recuperative powers: to lose his sister in one breath and gain a vision of Gina in the next.

They walked into the lecture room and were both on time for that late morning lecture. Alex looked about, waiting for the surgeon to talk on prefrontal lobotomies. He saw many nuns sitting near the back with their Sister Denise, and other nurses sitting closer to the front.

The room was also next to a small operating room, where Walters would perform his surgery when he returned sometime later that day.

Aaron, the Italian Jew, sat with his friend near the wall. He had to introduce the celebrated neurosurgeon, Dr. Walters, to the class. He was a Hungarian who had survived the Communist dictatorship in his country.

After the introduction by Dr. Levy, Alex placed his parka over his chair back and his fedora under the chair. Aaron joined him.

A young boorish Scot, by the name of Hamish MacDougall, sat behind Alex. He was a muscular, well-built bully who was known to push people around.

He nudged Alex in the back with his fist. "God help us," Hamish said, loud enough for those close by to hear, in his broad, Highlander brogue, "We've got an Italian wop, a Jew man who can't speak my Queen's English properly, introducing a bloody Hungarian hunky, who escaped Budapest in the late fifties. What next?" he asked, feeling so much more superior to others on staff.

Alex said nothing to the hostile bigot, but he felt Aaron squirm from the offensive comment. He lifted his weakened arm to rest on his left leg. The hair on the back of Alex's neck bristled.

"*Fica*. Pussy, in your language," Aaron spat out and motioned his head back at the smirking Scottish boor. He then stood up, turned, and smacked MacDougall on the side of his head with his good right hand.

At that critical time Alex was shocked; he recalled Justine's words after her assault: *"He called me a fica and said to be quiet or he'd kill me."*

He didn't have time to question Aaron about the word since nurses, and a few of the doctors, abruptly turned about to hear MacDougall yell out and swear. He hollered in pain as he held his head and protected his now-bruised and swollen eye.

He was ready to do battle with Aaron, but Aaron was faster. With the blink of an eye he moved his right hand into his back pocket. He withdrew his stiletto switchblade. He flicked a spring on the side of the switch blade, and the six-inch pointed steel knife sprung open.

Before MacDougall even batted an eyelid, Aaron quickly jabbed it an inch away from MacDougall's left eyeball, just below his hairline.

"Don't bother, *fica*, or your eyeball will feel the cold of this steel," he said. He ever-so-gently slid the point down the Scotsman's hairline, scraping the skin but not drawing blood.

Walters just stood there at the front, admiring the dramatic scene. Others close by moved away, fearing a bloody fight.

It was Alex who intervened and pulled MacDougall back. He said angrily, "Hamish, for God's sake, just sit down and don't do anything stupid, stupid. You'll lose an eye or your nose. It just won't look good on that handsome face of yours."

It didn't take long for Hamish to acquiesce; he slunk down into his chair while Aaron smiled and wiped the stiletto clean of skin fragments. He jammed the point into the arm of his chair and locked the knife back into place.

Walters guffawed something unintelligible. He wanted to settle the class back into his own drama on stage.

Aaron looked back to make sure MacDougall wasn't a threat anymore. He pointed to Walters, smiled, and said to Alex, "Yeah, he's ready to perform, my friend."

Alex grinned in agreement, still thinking of what Justine had said, and looked over the large class of nurses. Many were in their first or second year, with green or blue freshly-starched uniforms on Sister Denise's command. They wore similarly colored bands on their caps, indicating their year in training.

The thirty or so nurses with black bands over their caps, signifying that they were in their last year of the three-year program, were sitting together. They spoke in hushed tones about the scene with Aaron and Hamish that they had just witnessed. Gina turned and gave a sly wink at Aaron.

A dozen nuns sat stoically in the back rows with hands folded over their laps, not speaking and patiently waiting. The several doctors who were scattered about were all immigrants. Some were hoping to become psychiatrists once they learned English well enough to write the Canadian exams.

Most wouldn't make it.

The famous surgeon, Dr. Zsbignew Walters, sat on the large, wooden desk at the front of the stuffy, windowless room. He took his time lighting a fat Cuban cigar with a wooden match before starting.

Alex noticed that he had a perceptible tremor to his fingers as the flame flickered in his right hand.

"Parkinson's; and he will be operating with that tremor," Alex said to Aaron.

Aaron nudged Alex in the ribs. "God help those now dependent on his hands and failing eyesight."

Walters puffed, the cigar glowed, and everyone waited. Smoke engulfed the front row; the room lacked air. Walters buttoned his white coat over his wide frame, just able to envelope his large paunch.

Walters surveyed the large class over his heavy, bifocal glasses. He raised a photo of a bewildered-looking female patient with two gaping burr holes in her skull.

"The Hungarian Anglicized his name from Walzcenezcski to Walters," Aaron whispered.

"That was a clever idea," Alex agreed.

Walters was a short man, bald, with thick facial features and heavy, coke-bottle glasses. He had short, stubby arms and an overflowing gut. He wore a white hospital coat bedecked with specks of blood.

"Those blood splotches are his medals of honor, Alex," Aaron whispered.

Walters pushed himself off his desk with an audible groan. He walked between the rows of student nurses, who stiffened to let him pass as he extolled on the virtues of slicing off the frontal lobes of the brain.

Walters enthusiastically began his lecture. "Right here, right where my fingers are here, will two burr holes be drilled," Walters said in halting English, pointing to his own temples.

Walters spied the young, pretty, dark-haired nurse Gina, sitting near the front. Walters stomped over and stood hovering above her as she tried to make herself small and disappear deep down into her chair.

He suddenly leaned over, grasped her head, and pulled her cap off, which had been secured there by two bobby pins. It left her dark locks in disarray as she tried to smooth her hair back.

Surprised and embarrassed, Gina winced as he tapped her skull in two places with his two pudgy fingers, indicating where he would drill.

"This is here. Here will I, I and some surgeons, drill the holes," he said in halting English. He pounded her skull with his stubby index finger, which quivered slightly.

The embarrassed girl tried to turn away but was unable to free herself from his grip on her head. Gina blurted out, "My God, Doctor; how painful will that be?" She winced, and desperately tried to pin her cap back in place.

Walters ignored her question as thick smoke engulfed her and those nearby. Some coughed, choked, and spluttered as the room was filled with the stink of the pungent smoke.

Walters smiled at their discomfort as ashes fell on the nurse's starched uniform from the cigar stuck in his mouth.

"They would be just five centimeters above the eyebrow," the surgeon cheerfully lectured, as Cuban leaf surged out his nostrils.

The pretty nurse, now almost apoplectic from fear and embarrassment, had a severe coughing spell from the stench enveloping her.

As Gina attempted to clear the air, waving the stink about with both hands, other students next to her shifted away.

One got up and moved to the back, fearing she would be the next victim.

A young doctor gave a muffled cough from the back of the room as smoke drifted his way. He got up and walked out.

Alex flinched with visions of the scalpel being thrust into each hole in the pretty nurse's head. He remembered Gina as being the brightest one in his classes: an intellectual and a beauty.

"I will then deftly slice the frontal lobes from the rest of the brain, you hear me, causing sudden and irreversible apathy. But a cure, you hear me? A cure forever!" the brain man shouted in his heavy, European accent.

He turned and again held Gina's head in his paws. Alex again detected the tremor in his right hand as he gripped his reluctant victim.

A young nurse in her first year near the back gave an audible groan, grasped at her throat, and ran for the door. She only got part way when she heaved and vomited her meal onto an empty chair near the back. She then pushed herself out the door.

The surgeon stopped as the class turned to the back. They had heard the gurgle of gut heaving and the spewing of contents. Walters smiled, sucked on his stogy, and puffed out his chest.

He was very pleased with the response and the added stench now surging over the room.

"This, I tell you my friends, and I say, immediately produces a calmer patient." The man, who was a boor that could never make it as a qualified surgeon in Europe and was a poor example of a professor, preached on.

He then proudly added, "Your schizophrenic, it will be cured of delusions, and your aggressive patient, it will forever be submissive. We have such a one at this hospital, and he is one of your wild, heathen kind, too. An Indian, a redskin in leather moccasins made from the deer he killed."

Aaron nudged Alex. "That's Riel."

Alex focused on his notes, where he had written out a few of the surgical complications from the British medical journals that he subscribed to. They were not discussed by this arrogant oaf. Infections, seizures, paralysis, occasional idiocy, and periodic death. Bleeding in the brain was not uncommon, he had read.

The pompous neurosurgeon left the nurse and went to the desk, where he rifled through a tattered briefcase. He pulled out the worn-out, black-and-white, grainy photograph and presented it to the class, raising it high above his head. The photo shook with the surgeon's tremulous hand.

Walters added smugly, "Anyone here of you knows who is this? This woman, here?"

Students looked at each other. They all shook their heads.

He didn't wait. "It is the sister of the president, down in the south. She had the operation, and I tell you all, ah, that she was successfully cured."

Alex kept his mouth shut during such classes, but the elderly, balding doctor from Austria in the front asked, "What was the medical indication for this procedure, *Herr* Doctor?"

The surgeon looked over his thick spectacles in the direction of the obtrusive noise, hostile to the Austrian's use of the word referring to him. Hot ashes fell from his cigar onto the desk and burned a hole in his papers.

He blew the fire away as he glared at the questioner. "I am not a *Herr*, but a famous doctor, and not from your parts." Walters sneered and ignored the man. "That father, he was the famous Joe Kennedy—but you wouldn't know of him, would you up here? I had the pleasure of dining with him once, and he asked me for my professional opinion. Yes, you see, ah, Joe, I called him, he worried about his dull daughter."

At this point he started walking back and forth, huffing and puffing. He came to Gina again and stood before her. He unbuttoned his white coat in front of her and, slowly, in a perceptibly sexual manner, thrust his pelvis out for her.

Gina turned her head away as a pink blush enveloped her body.

Walters smiled, enjoying the girl's discomfiture, and walked away. "This simple girl, stupid and dumb forever, embarrassed the family with her ugly interest in boys."

He then added for good measure, "It was boys, such that was her vile interest. In wanting the boys." He looked at Gina again, leering.

A hush fell over the room, and a few nuns covered their faces with their hands at the sensual, carnal suggestion.

"Interest in the opposite sex gets your frontal lobes sliced," Alex said sadly to Aaron.

Aaron shifted in his chair and rose to see how the offended Gina was coping.

The surgeon continued. He was still on stage. He had another juicy vignette, and he raised yet another photograph. "Here, it is the Tennessee Williams' sister that you see now. She, too, was also cured by this modern technique," he added proudly.

Alex frowned, but kept quiet. The surgeon omitted the fact that both women had become confined to wheelchairs and required total nursing care thereafter.

He had cut too far back, and too aggressively, causing bleeding and near death. It rendered each woman devoid of all human qualities: an automaton, a zombie, in effect.

Alex had known about that terrible outcome, since he read about the results in the American Journal of Medicine and the letters to the Editor. He said nothing about that.

As the surgeon droned on, the tight, airless room slowly filled with cigar smoke from the front and the smell of acidic vomitus from the back.

"This Hungarian has been cutting and slashing his way through all the frontal lobes of belligerent patients, and others who were non-compliant, in mental hospitals across the country," Alex was reminded by Aaron.

"That's right, Aaron. Someday, he will get his due reward in Hell."

Walters had a quick additional comment, "But I, I, Doctor Walters, will use an icepick."

※

CHAPTER 20

Sister Denise Comes to the Rescue

ALEX could see that Aaron was disturbed by Walters harassing Gina in the front row. He was fidgeting, squirming, and fiddling with his silver chain. He stood briefly and watched Walters as he again singled out the nurse.

Gina desperately tried to avoid the sweaty paw as he grasped her head in one hand and brandished an icepick high above her shoulders.

"An icepick; it is a cheaper alternative to boring two holes in the cranial bones, it is. I say to you. A simple, sharp icepick saved paying for expensive scalpels, sutures, anesthetics, and busy, surgical staff, like all of you here," Walters, the icepick surgeon, lectured, still sucking on the half-spent stogie.

The poor, pretty victim wiggled, trying to loosen his grip on her forehead, and stuttered, "An ice p-p-pick?"

A terrified silence sliced through the thick smoke engulfing the room. Students followed the arc of the icepick he now brandished before them as it cut through the thick haze.

Walters loved the drama. He was on stage and in his final act. He bowed slightly and waited for the applause—any applause. But none came. He continued.

"I would bang my icepick, you see, with a wooden mallet. It would go into the much thinner bone above each eye socket, it would. That is, it is just under the eyebrows," he said.

He again used his stubby fingers on the same young nursing student's head, using her as a guinea pig.

He pulled Gina's head back and put his gnarled thumbs above her eye lids. The poor innocent pulled his hands apart and brushed tears away with the pain of his vise-like grip.

Gina buried her face in her hands as tears streamed down her face. She swooned and almost fainted over the nurse next to her, who tried to prop Gina up.

It was Aaron again. Alex saw him reach into the back pocket for his stiletto as he stood up.

"Don't, Aaron. Put it back, man. Put it back."

Sister Denise, sitting near the back, was faster than Aaron. She almost ran to the front, screaming at Walters, "My God help all those under your knife or icepick. You leave my nurses alone; do you hear me, Doctor?"

Aaron hesitated, but only briefly as the nurses and doctors all turned to see Sister Denise, with arms raised, threatening Walters with her fists as she confronted him at the front.

She pushed his rotund body away from the harassed nurse and said something very pointed to him that others couldn't hear.

With this brave encounter, Aaron left his place and ran to the front to help Sister Denise. He cradled Gina in his good right arm and then helped her back to her chair. Aaron then pushed Walters away from Sister Denise.

Walters slumped to his knees with the violent thrust, and before he knew it, Aaron was on top of him with his knee on his back. He again pulled out his stiletto, and was about to flick it open when Alex ran at Aaron.

Alex pushed Aaron away from the frightened Hungarian, who had dropped his cigar in the confrontation, burning a hole in his white jacket.

"Don't, Aaron; put it away, man. Put that knife away. They will fire you and send you back," he shouted.

But it was Sister Denise who pulled Aaron off Walters.

"You, as a doctor, should know better than to be abusive with your pelvis or harass any of my good nurses with your icepick. Shame on you, and God help you," she said as she helped Walters up.

She found his cigar and handed it to him. "Here, you will need this to calm your tremor."

A few in the audience stood up and gave a muffled clap as Walters sneered and slowly raised his corpulent body. He took his cigar and walked away. He was again pleased with the reaction, but not the attack on his body.

He spat at Aaron and walked to the desk. He put the photos away.

Sister Denise helped Gina rearrange her uniform and her hair. She clipped the cap back on the nurse's head and gave her a hug. "Be brave, my dear, and don't let anyone abuse you," she said, loud enough for other nurses to hear, pointing to Walters.

The lecture, and act one, was over, and the curtain came down on the pathetic stage.

Walters walked back and forth, shaken. He sucked on his black Cuban and mumbled something as he pointed at Sister Denise. He waved his grotesque weapon at Aaron, and then at his captive audience.

Alex tried to pull Aaron back to his chair, but Aaron left Alex and went back to Gina. He gently took her by the arm and ushered her out, with Sister Denise following. He closed the door after them but remained inside the room at the back.

Many nurses said something to Sister Denise in adulation and gratitude as she passed by. Some even patted Aaron on the back.

Walters had composed himself and had a parting speech for them. "Instead of employing a costly operating room with nurses and doctors, I do not do so, as I say to you. I do not use up valuable doctors' time. I do not burr holes through the thick skull of imbeciles, as you have here. I save hospitals much money. I use a sterile icepick; I do all that with no anesthetics. Well, maybe just some sedative," he shouted, and stomped out.

He was finished. Everyone waited.

At this point, Aaron walked to the front again. He turned to the anxious group, who talked in muffled tones about Walters, Aaron's attack, and Sister Denise's courageous action.

"Doctor Walters has surgery at a hospital in the west. He will return here over the next few weeks for his famous procedure on several of our patients," Aaron said with his Italian accent and poor English.

Alex made his way to the back as everyone walked out past him. He avoided the thick mess of porridge, milk, toast, and tea on the floor.

Then Alex walked out with Aaron, zipped up his parka, and pulled the fedora over his head. He was shaking his head in dismay from what he had just heard from Walters' lecture.

He stopped for a minute to light up a cigarette that he had received from Aaron to calm himself. Aaron blew on the tip of his own Camel and watched it glow red as he covered his head with his toque.

Aaron turned to his friend. "I read in the journal of neurology that in your United States about forty thousand people were lobotomized by now, Alex."

"Yes, Aaron; the exact numbers are difficult to ascertain in the reports from various countries, but in Great Britain many thousands, and in the Nordic states over nine thousand. Some are young children, and many are mentally retarded."

"God bless their poor souls," Sister Denise added; she had stopped to hear the atrocious statistics. "Here in Canada, many thousands have fallen under such a knife and icepick. By the time you and I leave this place, the icepick man will do his evil work many times over," Sister Denise said to Alex pointedly as they all left the lecture room.

"Not if I have something to say and do about it, sister."

"God bless you," she answered, and made the cross with her fingers.

"Your breathing is much better, sister. No more cough," Alex remarked, looking at Sister Denise as she wrapped her shawl around her head and shoulders.

"Much better, Doctor. *Merci*, since you doubled the streptomycin antibiotic for me," she said with a broad smile. She hurried off to catch up with the student nurses.

The two young doctors started the short climb back up the hill to the chronic wards. Aaron, breathing heavily from smoking and climbing the hill, spoke between puffs.

"Stalin, the dictator of Russia, slaughtered millions in his country through starvation and the death camps. Even the heartless barbarian that he was had outlawed the procedure years ago."

"Yes, he said it was too barbaric! Too bad Walters didn't go east to Russia, after Hungary."

Aaron readjusted the chain to support his arm after the debacle. "Now, my friend, it is up to you."

CHAPTER 21

Casa Loma

THE nurses on the wards were still abuzz with the Walters debacle, Sister Denise's courageous act, the young nurse's endurance, and Dr. Aaron Levy's brave rescue. After that ruckus, Sister Denise had stopped her group of nurses and nuns outside the building to say a prayer. Alex waited and listened while she asked God to forgive Walters.

After the short prayer, she stood on the steps and sang *Nearer, My God, to Thee*, a heart-rending tune that everyone chimed in for, Alex included; it was one of his mother's favorites.

It was that next weekend that Alex and Aaron had a few days off from hospital duty. Aaron needed more money for his recent sexual liaison with one of his girlfriends, Velma, in the Montréal brothels. She was the only one who accepted his drip—or the clap, as she also called it.

The old Jeep of second-war vintage that Aaron had bought in Montréal was roadworthy after a lube and oil service at the hospital garage.

Aaron drove to pick up Alex from the room he was renting from the Vinny DaCosta family early that Saturday morning in November. Dark storm clouds drifted in from the north.

Aaron needed the triple amount of money that Velma demanded because of his drip, and Alex needed the nimble fingers that Christina provided.

Alex maneuvered himself into the front seat and held on for dear life to the headrest. He pushed aside the Playboy magazines on the seat, which was also littered with gum wrappers, soda bottles, and stale cigarette butts. He pulled his fedora down hard over his forehead, so it wouldn't fly off.

Vinny had also welded in the roll bar, just in case, but it was devoid of any other safety features.

"Seat belts, Aaron. You also need seat belts in this thing you call a vehicle," Alex said as the Jeep rumbled along. Since it was devoid of springs or shock absorbers, Alex was jostled up and down, sideways, and back and forth.

"Like a all the Jeeps I rode for you Yankee fuckers in Italy after the war." Aaron laughed.

The floor was littered with empty cigarette packages, Pepsi cola bottles, old socks, spent condoms from sex with various whores in Montréal, and old newspapers. Alex shoveled all that aside to make room for his feet.

"Hard on my back and spinal cord, man. This old jalopy is full of crap. Clean it up."

Aaron could care less and blurted out, "Fuck yeah, my friend, but I need more dollars. Aaron is piss-poor, man. Someday, new shocks, when I get a better percentage from that dope you sell."

Alex bit his lip and didn't respond; he only held on tighter as the Jeep flew over deep potholes and ruts in the gravel road. At times, it almost became airborne. Alex pointed the way, along the highway bordering the mighty St. Lawrence.

Alex looked at Aaron. "Piss-poor, Aaron? How terrible is that?"

"An old saying. In my Europe hundreds of years ago, those who were tanning leather used urine in the tanning process. The uric acid is a good tanning agent. Poor people living near the tanneries pissed in a pot and then sold it to the tanners for a paltry amount."

"So, they were called 'piss-poor'? Interesting."

"Yes, my friend. And if they were so poor they couldn't even afford a urinal pot in their bed rooms, then they 'didn't have a pot to piss in.' They were the poorest of the poor, Alex."

"Poor people, Aaron. Like those in our hospital."

It only took an hour to get to Christina's 'summer cottage', as she euphemistically called it. All the local and provincial politicians, police, and other government officials who visited Christina's beautiful young girls there knew it as Casa Loma.

Alex pointed to all the magnificent homes they passed along the riverbank. "The upper-class in Montréal and throughout eastern Canada have cottages on the thousands of Québec lakes and along the St. Lawrence River."

"They are mansions in effect, and a pleasant escape from the summer heat of the cities," Aaron said.

"We're almost there, Aaron," Alex said, pointing to Casa Loma in the distance.

Aaron had a different name for this mansion. "Christina's whore house will have a few of the river captains and the local mayors in tonight, Alex. Should be good for sales. They buy that acid shit you sell to get a better hard-on; but you keep most of the lira for yourself," he said, honking the horn in anger.

"Fuck off; it's what you sell and then spend on those whores, or your dark beauty, Gabriella, Aaron. Christina's beautifully appointed Casa Loma is a high-class house. Of ill repute perhaps, as we used to call them in the deep south."

Aaron cheered up with the vision of money. "She should have a large package of cash for us, Alex, since business has been good these past few months," Aaron said as he calmed down. He turned on the windshield wipers as a mist came down.

As they drove along the highway, Aaron pointed to the truck that whizzed by, heading back to the hospital. "That's Vittorio, Alex. Must have just left Christina's. Motherfucker."

"She told me the last time we were there, Aaron. He wanted the shit he gets from that drug trader, Bruno, to have Christina sell it for him."

"Bruno and his family, including that fucker, Stanislaus, run the drugs to Canada from the Caribbean and the States in his shit scows."

"She said that it was too risky for her. Prefers our acid and speed pills," Alex announced, relieved.

"Be careful, my friend. He is, how you Yankees say it? Volatile? He said he would kill you, or get Bruno or Stanislaus to do it, if she didn't comply."

Alex pulled the tarp over himself to keep warm. His gut heaved and churned with the threat. "Did you bring your stiletto with you, just in case? For protection?"

Aaron turned sideways and patted his back pocket. "*Si, si.* But Christina, your own beautiful courtesan, chooses her customers carefully, and Vinny will be there in case of trouble with the sailors. I know that you give her thirty percent, but I deserve more now, my *amico*."

Alex again didn't take the bait; they could see the 'cottage' in the distance on a hill overlooking the St. Lawrence. "Get rid of more to the staff, and I'll bump it up a bit for you. Why do you refer to Christina as a 'courtesan,' Aaron?"

"In my country long ago, the intelligent, beautiful, and mature women, like Christina, were originally the couriers for our nobility."

"You're kidding? Couriers?"

"*Si*, the kings, dukes, and other nobles couldn't trust their servants or the riders who delivered information or money to other nobles across the lands, so they used these beautiful women. The women traveled in style and in safety."

"They were well protected. Fortunately," Alex said.

"They slept with the wealthy: confided in them. Then used them to transfer money and important messages to others across their realms."

"They were hookers?"

Aaron shook his head. "No, no, my friend. These women were very high class, intelligent, credible, and very discreet service ladies. They became the most reliable couriers: trustworthy. The word came from 'couriers of the court:' messengers, or courtesans."

"Interesting. I know that she passes messages from the mayor of LaSalle, and from other politicos, to the other underlings in government or to land developers. They, in turn, pay her handsomely for the information. She returns the favor with her young girls and takes a nice percentage for the discreet service."

"A modern-day courtesan, and protected by her friend, Theodore: a cop from Montréal."

Aaron maneuvered the Jeep and pulled into the spacious grounds of the mansion. A number of valet drivers were patiently waiting beside the parked limos for their passengers. They were smoking and talking, drinking good wine offered by Christina, and waited for their political bosses to leave Casa Loma.

"The French in Napoleon's time did the same, Aaron. The 'Let them eat cake' lady who was guillotined and the Japanese geisha girls were all the same. All were beautiful courtesans," Alex said.

Aaron agreed as he looked out for his favorite girl, hoping she was still there.

Alex got out and took his loaded briefcase full of LSD with him. That same briefcase would soon hold a generous sum of cash in return.

First, he would deliver that substantial amount of acid wafers, vials, and blotters loaded with liquid to Christina.

Casa Loma was a large, three-story wooden structure, fronted by spacious verandas and supported by grand Doric and Corinthian marble columns. Christina rented out her basement to Alex for his 'clinic,' where he treated the addicts.

He squinted as the new coat of white paint covering the manor gleamed in the sun that came out briefly between the parting clouds.

The house overlooked the wide expanse of river as it flowed by this early winter. Christina had inherited it from her wealthy Spanish second husband whom, it was said, she had slowly poisoned with arsenic.

She had confided in Alex that she had, in fact, done him in with arsenic because he was so sadistic. He was a sexual pedophile, a pederast preferring anal sex who often beat her during his drunken rages.

Christina had Casa Loma painted white, she explained with tongue in cheek, because "It signifies purity and virginity to the men who like to come here, Alex."

With blue trim and with two elaborate turrets, Casa Loma had an opulent garden covered in a variety of colorful red and yellow maple trees, bushes, and summer annuals. They were now fading and dropping off in the bitter cold and stormy nights.

Christina was eagerly expecting the delivery, and so she was standing and waving to her dealers, blowing kisses from her front balcony. She carried an umbrella for the two men since the rain clouds were threatening again.

Alex was always pleased to see her and more pleased with her kind, sexual services to him.

This service she freely delivered with her deft fingers and with her beautiful, full lips. Not so freely, however, as he had to first deliver what was in his brief case before she obliged in turn.

After all, business was business.

She took a few steps down the front stairs in her high, four-inch heels, and Alex thought that she must have been a beauty in her youth; she was still a striking woman in her early forties, at least ten years his senior.

Christina was tall, trim, and fair-skinned, with flashing bright eyes and firm, ample breasts that he worshiped. Alex knew that she took after her blonde, Swedish mother, whose painting she had on her bedroom wall.

But she was also wily and cunning, like her recently-departed, darker, Algerian-French father. *If there ever was a femme fatale,* Alex thought, *then it is Christina.*

She used her beauty to entice wealthy politicos and business types at the Casa Loma. Alex quickly recognized her dangerously seductive powers in manipulating men—except for Alex, who played her game. This added to his private income with the drugs he provided, and he gladly received sexual favors in turn. It was a mutual partnership that worked very well.

This occasionally included the periodic playful whipping, which he often looked forward to.

Her lashes to his bare buttocks were a good-humored, erotic game for both of them. This sensual experience he had learned from his witch of an aunt, who occasionally spanked him for being naughty. As it happened, he found this always produced a powerful erection for him in his early teens.

This in turn, was often admired and enjoyed by one of his young female cousins in auntie's basement rooms.

These teasing lashes by Christina also relieved him of the guilt he felt for having exciting, carnal thoughts in his youth. It was after he listened to the sexual activities as a youngster with his mother's paramours in the adjoining rooms of their squalid apartments above the pubs.

Alex and Aaron met Christina as she walked down the oak steps from the front veranda. Today, despite the cool weather, she wore her low-cut, sleeveless, almost diaphanous, sweater, which she knew Alex liked.

She opened the umbrella, covering Alex and Aaron under its shelter, and gave each man a warm hug.

As she did this, she could feel the rising quiver in Alex's groin, and slipped her hand down. "Is that a pistol you're carrying? Or are you just happy to see me, Alexander?"

"Just happy to see you, my dear."

"I see you're ready for me, Alexander. I'm ready to play with my favorite instrument and use my new cat-o'-nine-tails on your muscular backside," she quietly cooed into his ear.

She let Alex gently caress her left breast through her sweater as she slipped her tongue across his lips.

"I always rise early, every morning, Christina. A new cat-o'-nine-tails?" Alex asked with a grin, slapping his fedora hat against his thigh to shed the few snowflakes and rain water off the brim.

He could feel the blood rushing into his groin and the fullness in his crotch already with the idea of the game they lustfully played.

Aaron passed his keys to the valet to park his vehicle and said goodbye. He left quickly to find one of Christina's pretty great, great daughters, Marianna. One from her very great grandmothers, from two or three centuries ago, was one of the *filles du Roi.*

Aaron had explained to Alex that one of Marianna's great, or even greater, long-time grandmothers was one of the last remaining *filles du roi,* or 'daughters of the king.'

"Where did you get that idea, Aaron?" Alex had asked on their last Casa Loma trip.

"I read. Took European history in college as a boy. I tell you, that King Louis the fourteenth was worried that the English might take over French Canada, since they were fast settlers building on the fur trade."

"When was that?"

"It was over three hundred years ago. The fur traders, trappers, and French men colonizing Canada had no women in this country, apart from the Indians."

"So, he brought over the women?"

"*Si*, my friend: he sent over to Canada more than seven hundred young girl orphans, street girls, and other singles throughout France who wanted marriage. He wanted to keep his men happy and working."

"How could they afford to travel, Aaron?"

"They couldn't. The king recruited the seven hundred or more between 1665 and 1675, provided transportation by coach, and then shipped them over in the holds of ships. He gave them a financial dowry, a house, and a marriage contract."

Alex laughed. "A contract for marriage? No kidding."

"*Si*, some of those contracts were still held by men here, in Québec, after their marriage. Vinny, your landlord, told me he has such a one. Interesting, but outlawed recently. No longer valid, *amico mio*."

"Did it work? They married, these girls?"

"Yeah, but it was a difficult life. They lived in the woods, and they were not experienced in farming, traveling by canoe, or portages over hostile Indian land. Some died: slaughtered, infections, pneumonia. But they produced *multo* children."

"So? Are you going to marry Marianna? She's quite young for you: barely sixteen. You like them young, eh, Aaron."

"Ah, Fuck no. Seventeen, though. She wants a French man, not a wop like me. I do well for her with my right hand, and fingers that no man could do such ecstasy for her roused, magnificent mound," he answered with a lecherous grin.

"You use the condoms, I hope. That penicillin for your drip may take some time to work."

"She insists on it, as does Christina."

"Good for you, Aaron. That takes a lot of skill, which many men don't have, or are unaware of that small, critical organ. But you still have Gabriella?"

"*Si, si.* But Gabriella won't let me fuck because of that drip. Marianna accepts me still but knows that I will marry Gabriella soon. She is, how you say it? Broad-minded."

Alex didn't like that of Aaron but said nothing about his waywardness with women. Gabriella was a beauty, faithful to him, and deserved better.

Christina pulled Alex along as a light mist enveloped them. She, too, was in a rush to experience another comfortable acid trip with him in her bedroom. First, she would exchange the money for the contents he held in his briefcase.

"Come, Alexander, to my boudoir. We can relax for a few hours," she said hurriedly, pulling him up the steps through the massive, glass doors, and then through the spacious living room.

"Aha, said the spider to the fly." Alex laughed, but accepted the gentle pull. They passed through the living room, where several wealthy men from Montréal were in various stages of undress. They caroused, drank, smoked, and laughed with young, beautiful girls who were stark-naked and sitting on their laps.

Alex admired a young, dark, Oriental girl, now half-naked. She straddled the ex-mayor of LaSalle, who was impotent on the couch, panting in ecstasy. She desperately tried to get him erect, but without success.

The mayor paid Christina triple for her; she was sought after by all the men for her agile, athletic body, long legs, and firm breasts.

Bruno, a shaggy, Russian ape, butt-naked and displaying his disgusting, hairy ass, was on top of Babette, another small, nubile, Vietnamese girl in the corner. She dramatically screamed French curse words at him and pounded away at his hirsute back with her small fists.

That hysterical effect only got Bruno more excited. He huffed and puffed loudly.

Babette turned away from Bruno, smiled, and winked at Alex and Christina as they walked up the staircase.

"Shit, Christina, I should pull Bruno off that girl. I fear that he is too sadistically brutal with her," Alex said, holding Christina back.

"No, Alex, she is one tough drama queen: the kind Bruno likes. She's a strong one, and loves his cruel ways," Christina explained as she pulled him along.

Multiple small, one-inch square blotters had been sucked dry and were now scattered about the carpet. Other blotters were waiting on nearby tables.

These blotters provided the recipients with an acid trip. The LSD provided a more excitable sexual orgasm, gladly delivered by Alex and Aaron on periodic weekends.

In another corner, a gramophone was playing "La Vie en Rose" by Édith Piaf, the famous French chanteuse. It was a song about bliss, cheerfulness, and a world seen through rose-colored glasses.

The mayor of LaSalle, Boudreau, was now walking about in his long, woolen, winter underwear. He spat out his acid-soaked blotters onto the floor and sipped on gin and tonics instead.

Boudreau patiently waited for a blissful trip so he could get an adequate erection. He then used it, if it developed, on one of the girls and paid a very high price to Christina on arrival at the door for the experience. In cash.

Bottles of Canadian rye whiskey, Labatt beer, and cheap gin dotted the tables throughout the large, ornate room along with cans of ginger ale, 7-Up, Coke, and tonic water. Large, silver ice buckets were scattered about and loaded with expensive champagne bottles.

Cigarettes and good, Cuban cigars were scattered about the room near large ashtrays. All of this filled the space with acrid smoke, hilarity, and ecstatic, playful, sexual screams.

Alex marveled at Christina's thoughtfulness for her clients and the girls in having large fans blowing out the stench through the nearby open windows.

Scattered about were plush chairs, sofas, original paintings on the walls, and bouquets of fresh flowers on all the tables.

As he looked down from the top landing, Alex extolled, "Christina, you've spared no expense in making your clients comfortable."

"If they got half of this cheerfulness in their own homes, I'd have been out of business long ago," she said, laughing. She waved to one of her elderly clients from Ottawa, a respected politician in the opposition party, making out on one of her sofas.

She blew him a kiss just as the hand of one of her pretty, nubile girls assisted his ejaculation into a condom. It had been dutifully provided by the same girl, which Christina demanded to protect them from STDs, sexually transmitted diseases.

Alex pointed to all the spent, sucked-dry blotters, which went for twenty dollars each. "A nice percentage to you, Christina. I'm pleased to add to Édith Piaf's blissful world, seen through rose-colored glasses," he whispered to her.

She smiled and nodded in agreement. "Don't worry about Vittorio. Aaron told you, I know. I don't want that pathetic cocaine shit that Bruno and Stanislaus sell to Vittorio."

Christina left Alex and ran down the staircase. She pulled another old man, a retired police officer, off the sofa and away from one of her young girls, whom he had fondled.

She berated him. "No fucking until you pay me first, in cash, as expected at the door, or else fuck off out that same door."

"*Pardonnez-moi, ma chérie,*" he quickly apologized and tore up the check that she gave back to him. He again apologized and then gave her five newly-minted one hundred-dollar bills.

"I'm not your fucking darling, but cash only from now on," she spat dramatically, embellishing the theatrics. She counted the money and then escorted the man and his girl into a plush, elaborate bedroom.

She went to the gramophone and loaded six more long-playing records on the machine. Christina then sprayed the room from a bottle of her favorite *eau de parfum*.

"I hate the stink of all those cigarettes in my house. But all those fuckers like to smoke after they've finished fucking," she said to Alex as she rejoined him.

He inhaled the scent of the perfume, as it wafted through the area. She was smart. She knew that it seduced all the men to a higher pitch of sexual excitement.

Thus, they spent more of their money. And made more for Alex.

CHAPTER 22

Christina, the Courtesan

THEY both walked into her bed chamber hand in hand, and Christina snapped the lock on the door. Alex, now in the bedroom, relaxed after all the stress of the hospital, the added responsibilities, and subtle hints from Gabriella about Aaron's nighttime activities in the laundry rooms.

Alex would put a stop to that very soon.

But now at the Casa Loma, Alex had no obligations or duties. He was just a very willing participant. After all, now he didn't have to do much, plan ahead, or prove himself.

He quickly doffed his heavy, winter jacket and smartly hung his shirt on the chair back with his fedora. Pants, socks, shoe, and his boot went under the bed. Orderly, neat, and tidy, as usual.

As he watched Christina take his briefcase to her desk, he admired not only her physical beauty, but also her great willingness to help other women in the province.

"Christina, I heard that you refused to service some of the police and a few politicians who came to Casa Loma. They were the ones who were hostile to the gynecologist who performed illegal abortions here and in Montréal."

"So?"

"That could cut some of our fancy income," Alex said with some hesitation. He feared being too critical of her, as she could turn on him, also.

Christina opened the briefcase and smiled at the contents. "Those bastards often jail my gynecologist friend. He helps women and young girls who don't want a pregnancy and saves their lives from those pricks who butcher them."

"I know you, and Vinny's wife Mamma D, also organize the women in Montréal and in Ottawa to march against parliament. To make abortions legal; so good for you."

"Right. And Katarina—Cartier's wife—and my daughter, too. As is your Sister Denise, now that she has put on some weight, and is strong enough to march with us."

"I didn't know that Sister Denise was so active," Alex said, surprised.

Christina only nodded, smiling as she fingered the LSD wafers and liquid. As Alex mulled over these unselfish qualities in her he asked, "Should I have a shower first, Christina?"

Christina stood back, smiled, and looked him up and down. She liked what she saw in his mature, athletic physique, and shook her head. "Fuck no, Alexander. I like the smell of a real man, and not that shit cologne that some men use."

She emptied the contents on her desk and then walked to her wall safe. She dialed the numbers, clicked it open, and filled the briefcase with a large amount of cash.

"You took your usual percentage?"

Christina winked in agreement, and then dramatically shed her own top and stepped out of her skirt and high heels.

"Of course," she answered, and put his newly-filled case on the floor. She seductively massaged her breasts to excite the nipples, adding, "How is your poor ankle in this wintry weather?"

He stood up and took off his boxer shorts. "More tender, but it will get better once you massage up high, higher up." He laughed, holding himself in his hand.

Alex had heard her sad story, once confided in him as a psychiatrist. It had occurred when they had first met, and while she was under the influence of acid. She tearfully explained that she had been sexually abused by her older neighbor as a young girl.

"He stank of that shit cologne while he fingered me in my own bed. It was after his parents visited my family downstairs," she explained as they lay together in bed on their first visit, months ago.

"You didn't tell him to fuck off?"

"Fuck no. He was bigger and older, and he came into my bed after I turned the lights out. He said he would cut me up and feed me to the hungry wolves howling in the woods if I told on him."

"Sorry to hear, Christina. You poor girl."

"I was only fifteen then, but very mature for my age. I could hear them. I still hear them, the howling, if I take too much acid, Alex."

"Sorry. We won't do that again. No liquid anymore. It's too strong; just the blotter," he reassured her.

"It's all right, Alexander. After he diddled my clit with his hand, and then his tongue, he had me spank him; but only after I had my climax. He said his mother used to give him spankings that got him very sexually excited."

Alex grinned, as this was just like his own adolescent story. "Some mother, she was. She was sadistic, and he became masochistic. You encouraged and promoted that in him," Alex had said, not berating her. He was thinking it was time to roll over onto his stomach.

The memory led him to ask, "What happened to your neighbor, the perv? Did you get back at him?" He watched Christina put on her leather outfit and leather boots and pull out the new whip from her desk drawer.

"Sure did," she said as she playfully pounded her fist on his shoulder and buttocks, getting him excited with the thrashings. "When I was older, I told him to take me into the woods. I played with his dick and said we could have some sex in the bushes for a change."

Alex knew that she would get revenge. "Did he go for that?" he asked with a questioning smile, looking up at her.

Christina slapped the whip in the air a few times to get a feel of the new cat. Alex could hardly wait.

She whipped him a few times playfully and explained, "He did. And I did him in, the motherfucker. Hit him on the head with a rock and rolled him down into a ravine."

Alex felt himself totally fade away with such sweet revenge. "Holy shit, Christina. What happened to him?"

"Prick died, I guess. Cops found him dead. Bad accident, they said. He was devoured, partly: by those same wolves." She massaged Alex's partial erection to get it up again.

"Jesus, Christina. You're one tough lady, but a very smart woman," Alex said. Christina just smiled and went down on him, to get him ready once again.

The oral sex worked, but the whipping on his bare buttocks with her new cat-o'-nine-tails was even more powerful. Alex vowed to himself never to cross her in the future as she finished the playful whipping.

After the brief sadistic play, she stripped off her leather costume and moved into bed with him. As they lay in bed naked, she sprayed a whiff of body lotion on her neck, just as he liked.

This aroused him more, and she then added more lotion on her hands as she stroked him methodically.

"You still won't enter me, Alexander? You just want my hand?"

"Sorry," he said as she fingered his genitals after the playful sadistic game.

"Don't be. I understand; I know that you're quite obsessive and have a fear of getting gonorrhea or syphilis from any woman."

"Yep, we talked about that, and I don't trust the rubbers."

"Not that I have such venereal disease, as I always insist on my men downstairs using condoms, and I don't fuck around."

"I know."

"I get regular medical check-ups from the nice gynecologist who visits my girls here."

Alex knew that she had an ample supply of Sheik condoms of various colors, sizes and shapes, in her bedroom table drawer.

"I was too obsessive about cleanliness from an early age. Saw too many with GPI at my hospitals."

"GPI?" she asked.

"General paresis of the insane. It is a horrendously slow, but eventually fatal, disease. Horrible to see how such patients suffer so much after being infected with syphilis. Our mental institutions are full of such patients."

"From syphilis? Where did it come from?" she asked as she continued to stroke him lovingly. He was never in a rush, and enjoyed the slow, rhythmic manipulation.

They both waited for the small dose of acid to take effect, sucking on the wafers.

Alex was unable to contain himself as they talked, and he caressed her breasts, but finally let go. He inhaled deeply just as he exploded into her warm hand.

She held his face against her warm breasts until he started breathing again, which took several minutes. He gasped for air and breathed in the euphoric fragrance as he lay on her breasts.

Temporarily exhausted, he continued. "Syphilis? Who knows? Syphilis has been around for thousands of years, with the Roman armies spreading it throughout Europe. Napoleon's troops and the whores, cooks, and women who accompanied the armies also spread it throughout the countries he invaded. It spread like wild fire."

"Poor women. And men, I guess," she said as she spread his semen over her breasts and abdomen. She rubbed the fluid in gently over her tight abdominals, adding, "The best body lotion ever."

"Poor women, indeed. The men came home to France, and then again into all the other countries they invaded, after the battles. They then infected their wives and spread it to the rest of the whore houses they frequented."

"Why is it called general paresis? Insanity?"

"The spirochete, the syphilitic bacteria, invades the brain, the spinal cord, and all the nerves, causing paralysis. The brain turns to mush and causes hallucinations and paranoid delusions—that is, false beliefs."

"And so, it made you insane, crazy, and cognitively impaired, but also paralyzed? Therefore, general paresis?"

"You got that right."

As they lay together, Alex slowly, deftly, maneuvered his left hand over her mound of pubic hair, down to her inner labia, and into the genital lips.

He found her clitoris, which was already erect from earlier tender manipulation of his caresses and her own excitement from being the playful sadist with the whip.

Christina had her eyes closed and kissed him deeply with her tongue. He continued to gently stroke her pubic area as he sucked on her tongue, which she liked. She then went into a spasmodic convulsion, with thighs spread wide open, and then grasped his body with her long legs and rolled on top of him.

He held on to her tightly, warmly, until she revived, and then she rolled onto her back.

Christina reached over to her bed table, sat up in bed, and lit a cigarette. "Fuck, that was a good one. Thank you, my sweet. You do that the best."

Alex smiled. "Pleased to be able to help. *Merci,* also. That semen, full of protein, keeps your beautiful belly nice and hard, Christina," he replied, taking her cigarette for a quick puff.

"*Oui,* my love. I use it whenever you come on my breasts and stomach. Why the whip, Alexander? Where did that playful masochism come from for you?" Christina asked, interested.

"I used to throw darts at my aunt, at a dart board I set up, in her basement room. She was sadistic to me, emotionally. One night, when I was a young kid, she came in and caught me with a photo of her on the dart board. Gave me a licking with a leather belt: a spanking with my pants down."

"Oh, you poor boy. Just like that perv who came to my bed."

"I guess. I was still young and had my first great erection with her belting me and blew my load. It was very powerful, Christina. Never had it again that strong until you, my love."

Christina was pleased to hear that. "I read that masochism relieves guilt and anger in men and some women. It gives women in that highly dependent state the ability to fantasize about sex, tied up maybe, without having to work or get involved."

"That's so. They just find it exhilarating, keeping still, and they can only get off that way: helpless but ecstatic. It is a freedom. An independence." Alex nodded as he played with Christina's breasts. "Sadomasochism was coined by the Marquis de Sade, who wrote about the practice of sadism. Thus, the name."

"And masochism, Alex? Where did that word come from?"

"Also, by another therapist, Sacher-Masoch, who then wrote about masochism. Came from his name. A long time ago, they called it a perversion, but nothing is a sacred perversion anymore, Christina."

She let him snuggle at her breasts, knowing that was what he liked. "You are also worried about gonorrhea. Gonorrhea does the same, I guess, to the brain, like syphilis?" she asked as she inhaled the Philip Morris cigarette, a brand that she liked and kept at her bedside table.

"No, not the brain, Christina. Gonorrhea does infect the uterus and other female organs, causing havoc with sterility. It could also cause trouble for the male prostate, giving the man a painful discharge from the penis."

"Bruno is still on penicillin."

Alex scoffed; he was mistrustful of the Russian. "Bruno, the captain of that stinking scow full of cow manure, docked close by. He is now fucking that pretty young Dauphine girl downstairs. He was lucky to get a shot of penicillin."

"They caught it soon after he was infected, in the cheap clap houses that he frequented on the docks in Montréal."

"And thankfully before coming to your Casa Loma."

"Yes. And finding Dauphine. But I insist he still use the condoms."

"Careful with Bruno. That asshole is a moron, devoid of intelligence and a compulsive fire setter if provoked."

Christina acknowledged. "He pays double, and on time now. Be careful of his cousin, Stanislaus. Vittorio deals drugs with both those two pricks."

Alex nodded; he had heard that before. He took a tissue from the box on Christina's table and wiped himself clean of lotion. She handed him a soft washcloth to clean himself better as he got up and pulled on his pants and buttoned up his shirt.

He watched Christina wash herself with the warm, soapy washcloth she always kept in the basin of hot water by her bed.

"Why don't we get married, Alexander? I would be good for you," Christina said as she squatted down to wipe her thighs.

Alex almost broke into a laugh but thought quickly of the value of Casa Loma. *Would I still have to give her a share of my profits, if we were married,* he wondered.

"Are you kidding, Christina? You and Babette are a good team in bed already. Without me."

Christina motioned to her bed. "I have a king-size bed here for the three of us, my darling. Babette is a wee little thing and doesn't take up much room."

✳

CHAPTER 23

Ménage à Trois

IT was only in his brief, one-time, wildest sexual fantasy as an adolescent that Alex thought about a *ménage* à *trois*. He had read at that time in his uncle's books on sexual disorders that it translated from the French as a 'household for three.'

"I'm not sure I could handle, so to speak, two women at the same time, my sweet."

Christina was amused by his boyish wit and charm as she slowly, but tantalizingly, dressed. "I read in some magazine that your very famous psychoanalyst, Carl Jung, insisted that his wife and he sleep with one of his teenaged patients. She was a Miss Toni Wolff, as I recall. The three did have a three-way for many years."

"Fuck no! I never heard that or read about it before." Alex laughed, looking under the bed for his boot.

Christina had another zinger for him. "Well, how about the Brit's famous Horatio Lord Nelson, who was in bed with a lady, Emma Hamilton, and her husband. Well, that is, until Horatio was killed five years later."

"The guy up on the statue in London's Trafalgar square, looking out to sea? Not the famous Lord Nelson?"

"You bet, sweetie. The one and only."

"I didn't know that one. But anyway, Christina, those sexual three-ways take up too much energy. I can't juggle three balls in the air, never mind satisfy two active women fucking in one bed."

Christina came to Alex and stood in front of him, spreading her legs. "Oh, I could. And you and I could have sex one night, maybe with the whip, while Babette watches. Then you and Babette, she is using the whip on you another night, while I watch."

"A lot of watching. Not fond of watching. I like the action."

She continued, "Then you watch as Babette and I make hot, passionate love on the third night."

"Christ, Christina, as the good lord said, I would need to rest on the forth night."

Christina laughed as she lifted her skirt up to her hips. "That was on the seventh day, gorgeous, is what He said," she replied, crossing herself three times as good Catholics do.

"Let me give it some thought, but thanks for the offer," Alex replied. He knew that having a profitable and lucrative business with Christina should remain as it was.

He did not want to spoil it all with a marriage, or a three-way bed partnership. Especially with Babette, who was an unknown number in the troika.

Alex finished dressing and whistled the tune from "La Vie en Rose" as Christina paraded about, still half-naked without panties or shirt. She jiggled her breasts in front of him as he finished dressing, dramatic like a strip queen on stage, with long legs and a firm butt.

With her skirt up, she pushed her pelvis with her curly pubic hair in his face. She massaged his face with her naked pelvis to entice him further, possibly into a marriage, he surmised.

As she squatted in front of him, Alex ran his hand up her thigh and playfully poked a finger into her vagina.

"Very nice, Christina. How long have you and Babette been bed partners?"

Christina let the finger sit there for a few seconds, and then withdrew from Alex. "Three years. She was a ragamuffin, homeless on the streets after both parents were killed in a car accident. I found her in a bar, hooking."

"Nice young girl. I've observed that she's dyslexic, poor thing, can't read," he said as he picked up her photo on the bedside table.

He admired Babette as a nubile sexually attractive nineteen-year old. "She must be well under ninety pounds soaking wet," he said, smiling.

Christina laughed as she poured more hot water onto a cloth. "I have a tutor teaching her how to read and how to deal with her bad lisp, also. Indeed, poor thing."

He liked that obsessive habit of hers: cleaning herself with the wash cloth. He didn't ask her more questions about her lesbian partner, as it was none of his business, he decided.

Christina stiffened as she heard screams from below. "God damn, Alexander. I must see what the fucking ruckus is going on down there. Monique, my daughter, has a young Catholic girl in one of the rooms. We might have to help her with the abortion."

"Abortion? Really? Vinny told me about that. A nurse working at our hospital helps that Montréal physician with the abortions," Alex recalled as he tied up his boot.

"He does it here also, my love. Monique assists him at his clinics in town, but he's in jail again."

"Good for her," Alex agreed. He took his case and opened it to confirm the amount of cash. He jammed it into her other large, metal safe in the corner of the room.

"It'll be nice for you to meet my daughter," Christina said as she brushed her lips against his at the door.

As Christina finished dressing, they both heard more squeals and loud, boisterous swearing from the level below.

"I'll bet it's Bruno again."

"I hope it's not that big asshole Bruno. He may have taken too much acid again, and drinking my good champagne at the same time."

※

CHAPTER 24

Bruno, the Russian Bear

ALEX heard Babette, the petite Oriental girl who was also Christina's lover, wail downstairs. He hurried down the elegant stairway to the living room, following Christina.

"That fucker, Bruno, has the poor girl in a headlock. He's carrying her about the room, stark naked and welded to his hip," Christina yelled to Alex as he rushed into the room.

Alex feared the worst. Bruno had overdosed on acid and a bottle of Rye whiskey and had thrown a full bottle of champagne against the wall. The combination was disastrous: he was having a bad trip.

Aaron Levy had dashed into the melee from a side room, but his girl, Marianna, was too frightened, and had locked herself in.

"Aaron, get the intramuscular sodium amytal ready. Hurry, man," Alex shouted as he pointed to the kitchen. He always had a supply of fast-acting barbiturates in the cupboards, ready for such an occasion.

Aaron tried to respond as he pulled on his pants with a condom still hanging out. It was while Aaron was in that act of dressing, unbalanced, that he was knocked down by Bruno rushing past him.

Bruno was naked, a large, brawny ape covered in black body hair from head to toe. He stank from sweat after multiple acts of sex with Kitty, and then having tried the same with Babette.

The girl cursed using all the French swear words ever written and was in a terrified frenzy as she hung upside down. Bruno easily held her torso wrapped about his body by one hairy arm. He pushed aside someone wanting to help with his burly other arm.

Babette was dragged about the room, kicking and screaming. In his wild, agitated state, Bruno again slammed into Aaron as he went to the kitchen. He bowled him over into a large, potted plant, spilling its contents everywhere.

The room had emptied of girls and clients, since Bruno was now acting like a raging bull in a china shop. He shouted, cursing his mother, Russia, the Tsar, and Stalin. He was completely irrational as he responded to his vivid hallucinations.

"Fire, there's a fire in these here shit houses, and Bruno, he is burning up," he shouted, partly in English, some in French, and much in Russian. He blamed Babette for setting him ablaze.

Alex and Christina were no match for the psychotic lunatic, but they both tried to calm him. Christina helped to free Babette as Alex pulled him apart from the hysterical, screaming girl.

Boudreau peered out of his room where he had first escaped and ran into the chaos to help. He dove at Bruno, grabbed his ankles, and started to pull at his legs to try to topple him down.

Bruno roared like a bull moose in heat and simply swatted them all away like pesky flies. Suddenly, he again grabbed Babette and threw the girl down on the carpet.

He jumped on her and again attempted to enter. His sexual excitement was a combination of adrenaline, acid, rye whiskey, beautiful Babette, and the monstrous surge of male hormone, testosterone.

As Bruno pumped himself into Babette, he groaned and cursed in Russian. Babette shrieked in terror in French.

It was Aaron who came to the rescue, shouting in Italian with syringe in hand.

Before Aaron could act, Bruno missed the introitus, the vaginal opening, and let go all over poor Babette's thrashing legs.

Babette still pounded her little fists at Bruno and tried desperately to free herself of his massive, corpulent body. He had her small body locked in a tight hold with both his legs around her.

"Damn you, Bruno, I told you to put on a French safe first," she squealed.

Aaron had dropped the intramuscular shot when Bruno thrashed about violently against the four who attempted to subdue him. Aaron, thinking fast, reached into his back pocket and retrieved his stiletto.

Alex and Christina grabbed both Bruno's arms. Boudreau had him by his legs and tried to pull him off the girl.

Aaron, with a deft swipe of the open blade, jammed his stiletto hard into Bruno's massive backside.

His rump went into spasm, and he let go a massive surge of wind. Aaron backed off from the vile odor and waved his hands to clear the air.

"Good shot, Aaron," Christina yelled, pinching her nose. Bruno, at first uncertain who was defiling his anus, shot straight up into the air. The steel point went through the fleshy side of his right buttock, and out again near his hairy asshole.

With that, Alex picked up the syringe, already loaded with sodium amytal. Christina, in the meantime, had been thrown to the ground by Bruno's sudden levitation, with the stiletto still up his buttocks.

In that brief moment, the young girl freed herself and quickly rolled away.

"Hold him for a minute, Aaron," Alex shouted, as he plunged the amytal into Bruno's left buttock. He emptied the contents of the syringe into the beefy flesh.

Bruno's body contorted as he yowled aloud; his backside shuddered violently with the violation. With that convulsion, Alex fell back and was unable to withdraw the syringe.

Babette, rescued and more composed, quickly took a potted amaryllis plant, still in bloom, from a nearby table. She held it dramatically over Bruno's head and said three Hail Marys to her dear Jesus. Once she finished asking for forgiveness, she smashed the red, ceramic pot onto Bruno's cranium.

This violent act seemed to quell the beast in Bruno. Still partly conscious, he turned and sat up on his knees. He looked about, bewildered, with the stiletto still up one side of his buttocks and the syringe stuck in the other side. As the earthy contents of the pot dripped down on his head he shook, convulsed, and, sedated, fell face-down on the carpet.

Aaron breathed a sigh of relief and withdrew his knife. Alex pulled out the syringe, and then all four jumped on his hirsute, foul-smelling body.

Gradually, Bruno succumbed to the shot. He discharged another massive fart, followed by some foul-smelling liquid feces that spilled out onto the floor.

"Fucking yuck-ity yuck, what a stink," Christina yelled as she turned from the foul stench.

By then, the room had quieted down, and some of the guests returned, including the girls.

Alex called out to the girls, "Get him cleaned up and roll him into the corner, with a blanket to cover him, and let him sleep it off."

One of the girls brought in a pail of water and a mop, held her nose, and shoved it up Bruno's buttocks. She swished the mop about, and then cleaned Bruno's thighs of feces. Another girl brought out the Hoover and vacuumed the floor.

The mayor of LaSalle, Boudreau, rolled Bruno into the corner and covered his body with a blanket. The mayor, still naked, pulled on his pants, brought to him by a girl, sighed in relief, and went back to his room.

Alex checked Bruno's pulse; as he hoped, it was still palpable. "I hope the bastard doesn't die from all the alcohol, acid, amytal, and violence bestowed onto his body," he prayed. "The overdose and shock could kill him."

"Maybe not such a bad thing, Doctor," Babette said as she helped Alex turn him on his side in case he vomited; that way, he wouldn't aspirate his stomach contents.

Babette cleaned her thighs of Bruno's semen and pointed to him. "He'll sleep it off," she lisped, exhausted with tears running down her face.

Christina went to Babette, gave her a warm hug, and asked if she was hurt. "I don't want this fucker in my house again," Christina said as she wiped some of Bruno's feces off her own legs with a towel.

Babette reassured Christina that she was not injured. She went to Bruno and pulled his blanket up. She held her nose and sprayed Bruno, and then the whole room, from the bottle of *eau de cologne* on the table nearby.

"You go upstairs, rest, and only be the receptionist from here on. No more fucking around," Christina whispered to Babette.

"*Oui*, my *chérie. Merci, merci*," Babette replied thankfully. She spritely ran up the stairs, with a towel wrapped around her body, to Christina's bedroom.

Christina watched her bounce up the staircase, and then pulled Boudreau into the corner, away from the group.

"Lafarge said that the property fronting the river will go up for sale next month. Buy it. It's cheap now, before the vultures from the Ottawa parliament hear about this. They want to develop that land as a park."

Boudreau had found his shirt and rifled through his pants. "*Merci*, Christina, for this message. *Merci*," he said with a twinkle in his eye. He reached into his pocket and gave her a large wad of bills.

The room slowly calmed, and everyone was pleased to hear Bruno snoring loudly in the corner. It was time for Alex and Aaron to return to Christina's boudoir, count the money in the case, and give Aaron his percentage.

"Good for Christina," Aaron said once in the room. He pointed to the wad of bills, sufficient to choke a horse. "As a courtesan, she gets well-paid for passing messages back and forth between police, land developers, and government officials."

They both watched as Christina took off her clothes and slid into bed next to naked Babette.

"To sooth her anxious nerves," Aaron said to Alex as they both walked out.

✳

CHAPTER 25

The Pyromaniac

AFTER an hour, the chaos at Casa Loma had settled down. The weather was still cool and damp, with clouds hanging low, as Aaron and Alex went out to Aaron's Jeep. Alex put his case in a strong box securely chained to the back seat and covered it in a tarp.

Inside Casa Loma, Bruno had scattered his blanket about as traumatic nightmares and paranoid delusions slowly receded from his psychotic brain.

He walked about looking for other girls, and then, with ultimate rejection and fatigue, he yelled out that he was ready to leave.

He lit matches and threw them about with shouts of, "Fuck this, and fuck that, and fuck all of you."

A few of the clients slowly gathered their belongings and walked out, searching for their valets. They feared a further donnybrook now that Bruno was up, vile tempered and threatening to torch the place.

Christina pointed to Bruno as Alex walked back in. "That fucker will pay me triple for what I lost as my clients piss off," she swore.

"And double to me, with my loss," Alex added, watching his business evaporate into the slight drizzle of the cold, late-afternoon air.

Aaron heartily agreed as he opened the door. "The girls were happy just to clean themselves up and count their hard-earned wages."

Alex rested with a coffee and cheese crackers as he watched the girls also go into the kitchen for a late brunch. They started to preen themselves for the evening ensemble of important guests that were expected to arrive for the weekend soiree.

Christina always had a few attractive, female soloists singing in skimpy, seductive garb on the weekend, as well as a piano player. She charged double to entertain her political guests from Montréal and Ottawa.

Christina blew kisses to all her departing visitors and closed her front entrance doors. She went into the kitchens.

Quite soon, she came out carrying a large tray of French onion soup, brie and soft gruyere cheese, a bottle of wine, crackers, and duck pâté for Alex and Aaron.

As they sat on the couch and ate the hearty meal, she looked at Alex. She motherly dabbed some leftover warm, melted gruyere cheese from his chin.

"You'll have to help me with that abortion on the young black girl in the back room, Alexander."

Alex paused. He had to think about that. "What happened to Monique, your daughter? She was doing it."

"She phoned. She's busy in town. Helping a different gynecologist with another poor girl. Too bad. Poor young teenager."

Alex sipped on the wine and thought of his answer. "Shit, Christina, I don't do abortions. It's still illegal, and I could go to jail."

Aaron agreed. "Like what happened to your friend, that other, infamous gynecologist recently."

Christina had a worrisome look. "In jail again he is, but a light sentence this time, since all the women in Ottawa and elsewhere are marching on parliament to change that law. Your dark-haired East Indian girl, Rani, was leading them."

"Rani? Who lives with me at Vinny's house?"

"That one. Brave and determined to change that punitive law."

"Vinny told me his missus, Cartier's lady Katarina, and several of the nuns with Sister Denise are also raising Hell in that march."

"And my daughter, so I might need a doctor close by if she bleeds, Alexander," she said, looking him in the eye.

She always referred to him in his full name when serious or sexually playful.

Alex didn't blink.

She nodded to Aaron and offered him the duck pâté. "*Non*, my *chérie*. Don't look at me, sweetheart. You get well paid, and I'm not going to your prison and back to Sicily. Fuck that," Aaron said as he spread the pâté on a cracker and swilled it down with a glass of red wine.

Christina shook her head in dismay as to how she would cope. She called over one of the girls to clean the tray and return it to the kitchen. "Well, just be close, both of you. Just in case."

"How the dickens did you get involved in this, Christina? With that doctor doing abortions here and your daughter assisting?" Alex asked.

Christina helped the girl tidy up and picked up a few scraps of crackers, spilled onto the carpet near Aaron.

Christina perked up. She was glad to hear that Alex was interested. "I met him through Monique, some months ago: before he went to jail."

"Kindly lady, your daughter."

"My beautiful daughter is a kind and devout woman, a Catholic, and with many mothers has also marched on the parliament buildings with him," she said, hoping Alex would still help her.

Christina spied Bruno, still at the entrance. He was lighting cigarettes, one after the other, with wooden matches.

He would watch the glow of the match and then snuff it out with his bare fingers.

"At least he uses sterile techniques, and his women don't die of infections, or bleed to death from those fucking kitchen table abortionists."

"I agree. They couldn't have cared less and were just interested in making money. I saw them in *Napoli*," Aaron piped in.

Christina got up and shouted at Bruno to get out of her house and never come back.

Bruno gave Christina the finger. He bent over and dropped his pants and shorts to show her his ass. It had a huge bandage that Babette had taped on both buttocks. He straightened up, dressed, and stomped out.

Christina sighed, tired from the day's work. She continued her story as she finished her glass of wine. "This very special obstetrician and gynecologist is a Polish Jew, who was in Dachau, a German concentration camp during the war. He survived."

"No one else did. Not my family and friends," Aaron said wistfully.

Christina put her hand on Aaron's left, withered arm in sympathy. "Came to Montréal and was horrified to find so many women dying from abortions."

Aaron had other information. "I heard he did vasectomies on men. He cut the vas deferens, the tube taking sperm from the testicles. Sterile after that. Worked well, but he got into some shit over that, also."

"The Catholics were angry that he gave their women pills and intrauterine devices to stop pregnancies, and then the vasectomies."

"Got the Pope's nickers up," Alex said, as he waved to Bruno as he walked out. He still looked about for one of the girls.

"I decided to help my daughter and the good doctor and offered Casa Loma as a temporary clinic for free. Until he got out of jail."

"Good for you. So, is the black girl in the back room a Catholic?"

"No. Just a young kid who worked in the old quarter of Montréal. Left work late at night and was hit on by three white guys."

"Injured?"

"Fucking well raped by one of them. The other two fuckers held her down while the bastard did the dirty on her in the back alley," Christina replied in disgust.

Aaron patted Christina on the back in admiration and told Alex he was going out for some fresh air. "I need to smoke a joint, calm down, and see what Bruno is up to."

Alex asked, "Parents wouldn't help her?"

"No father around: left the girl and mother destitute. Mother is a hooker working the docks. Lisbeth went to the hospital clinic, and they told her she must have the baby."

"How did she get to you?"

"Lisbeth was found by her roommate in her bed after she had slashed her wrists. Monique met her in the ER of Montréal General, where she teaches part-time as a psychiatric nurse. She told Lisbeth that she would help her through that doctor's clinics."

"And your daughter sent her here. So, what do you do? How do you get rid of the fetus?"

Christina got up and told one of her girls to stand at the door and welcome the new guests in and make sure Bruno didn't come back. The young girl did so and offered each a glass of champagne and some chocolates as they arrived.

"The doctor taught me how to sedate Lisbeth and give her a pill that would dilate her cervix. She should be ready by now. I use a small spoon, a curette on a long handle."

Alex was amazed at her audacity as she spoke. "I insert the spoon into her vagina, through the dilated cervix, and curette, that is, scoop, out the fetus from the uterus."

"And the fetus?"

"Pack her with some gauze, and she'll be fine. Blob of fetus goes in the furnace."

Alex wanted to ask what she charged for the service, thinking how he could make some extra money. He put that thought aside.

"Good for you, and that Lisbeth met Monique. I'll be here for a while if you really need me, in case she starts bleeding."

"She's a healthy, strong, young lady, and will stay the night," Christina said. She got up to arrange the rooms for her new guests.

Alex was ready to have a rest on the couch and wait for Aaron, who wanted to see his girl again.

He was jarred out of his reverie when he saw the front door fly open. Aaron ran back into the room, shouting. "Fire. The west wing veranda is on fire, and the wood shed next to it. Must be that fire setter: fucking arsonist, Bruno," he shouted again. He pulled the fire alarm on the entrance wall.

Christina turned with the shout and immediately went into action. All the girls ran into the living room. Some of the guests started to leave.

Three of the girls mobilized the kitchen crew to start the pumps. They all pulled out fire extinguishers to be ready.

Alex pulled on his parka and donned his fedora. He rushed out to assess the damage and see what the fire was doing from the front steps.

The groundskeepers and valet drivers were already dousing the west veranda with water pumped up from the river.

Alex found Aaron, who helped direct the staff with water hoses onto the wooden veranda to his left. The fire still smoldered, with periodic spouts of flame bursting through the wood shed between the wooden floor boards.

"Had to be that asshole, Bruno, with his matches, Alex," Aaron shouted. He looked about for the Russian oaf.

Alex pointed to a dark, overgrown bush area close to the river's edge, just past the smoldering veranda. The sun was setting. "There he is. He's got Babette in a fucking neck hold again, for Christ's sake, Aaron."

Aaron started to run in Bruno's direction. Alex followed.

"She was just outside, by herself, having a quiet smoke," Aaron said, pointing to Babette.

They both moved toward Bruno, but cautiously. He was unpredictable, and they feared for Babette. He had his pants down and tried to manipulate himself against Babette's bare buttocks. As he had done before.

Bruno had her in a vise-grip with his left hand around her neck. He was forcing himself into her thighs.

"Let her go, Bruno," Alex shouted as the two reached him in the grove of bushes. Others in the gardens were afraid to approach Bruno. Someone called the police and fire trucks.

"Fuck off or I'll strangle her. She set my ass on fire, and it's still burning," Bruno shouted at them.

"Let her go. It wasn't Babette, and we won't harm you, Bruno," Alex yelled again as Babette cried out in desperation.

It was Aaron who took matters into his own hands and brought out his stiletto.

"You don't stand a chance with him," Alex yelled. He took the knife away from Aaron and ran at Bruno.

As Alex came at the brute with the stiletto open, Bruno turned and stuck out his leg. Alex slipped on the slush of snow and mud and plunged into the nearby thicket.

Bruno guffawed heartily at the intruder's plight. He then threw Babette to the ground. He turned her head in his burly arms and snapped her neck.

"Serves you right, you fuckin'muffdiver, fucking that Christina instead of me," he gloated as Babette gurgled her last breath.

Alex tried to regain his balance but reared back, aware that Bruno could do the same with him. Babette had dropped to the ground, lifeless, in the cold grass and muck.

Bruno then gave out a howl like a wild banshee, pulled up his pants, and attacked Alex.

Alex struggled to get up and tried to make a move toward Bruno. Bruno was twice Alex's size, and despite wearing his heavy parka Alex was faster. Still more agile even with his lame foot, he stepped away.

As Bruno charged once more, Alex made his move: he stuck out his good leg and tripped him. He then jumped on Bruno's back, with the stiletto at his throat. Alex had a good hold on Bruno with the knife at Bruno's neck.

Some of the drivers were shouting at them. A few tried to get closer, but feared Bruno's wrath. They turned and saw that several police cars, with sirens wailing, had already moved onto the grounds.

But it was Christina who ran in to help, with Aaron close by. She saw her young lover lying dead on the ground and Alex on top of the big ape's back.

Christina was beside herself. She yelled at Bruno and charged him with her fists flying.

With this distraction, Alex eased his hold on Bruno. Bruno took advantage of this and easily flipped Alex over. He started slowly throttling him.

With his other fist, he slammed at Christina as she came to him. He easily knocked her down. Others, hoping to help but fearing a vicious attack, backed off and shouted for help as the police cars moved in.

Alex tried to free himself of Bruno. He wanted to help Christina to pull her away, fearing that Bruno would soon kill her.

Bruno, however, was only interested in killing Alex. He recalled that Vittorio wanted him out of the way, and this was his chance. He continued to strangle him with one thick arm on his neck, shouting at Aaron to stay away.

"Bruno, let him go. We won't hurt you," Christina shouted as she stumbled to help Alex. Alex was gasping for breath, and slowly turning blue. Bruno moved his head away as Christina approached.

As Alex was slowly succumbing to the strangle hold, it was the shot from a rifle that caused Bruno to let go. That heavy crack, somewhere in the distance behind Alex and Christina, ended the struggle.

Alex saw the bullet zinged over him and split Bruno's head in two. "Holy fuck," he shouted as he threw his body over Christina to avoid any other bullets coming their way.

Aaron was beside him, also holding Christina down in protection.

Alex rolled away with Aaron's help and pushed Bruno's body from his. Some of Bruno's brains and blood spattered his face red.

He and Christina turned and looked at the police man, who ran to help them. He still held the rifle, ready to shoot if Bruno stirred.

"Good shot, Theodore. Good shooting," another policeman said to the marksman.

Theodore went to Bruno and kicked him over, face up, to make sure he was dead.

Aaron pulled Alex away and gave him his handkerchief to clean Bruno's brains and blood off his face. He then went to Christina, who sobbed wildly, cradling little Babette in her arms.

Storm clouds filled the air; the rain had turned to a light snow that fell on the group. The police brought stretchers to take Bruno's body and also that of poor Babette's.

"We were after that fire-setting arsonist, but he always got away. He escaped on those shit scows back up the river," Theodore said as he helped his mate roll Bruno's body onto the stretcher. He added, "I had to wait until Bruno turned away from you there to get a clean shot, and not hit you."

Alex was shivering in the cold and visibly shaken from the ordeal. Holding his neck—which had been twisted in Bruno's grip—and still taking in gulps of air, he pointed at Theodore. "Good idea, Theodore. Thanks for that, man."

Theodore gave a thumb's up as one of the policemen tried to help Christina. He tried to pull Babette's body from her tight embrace.

"No, I'll take care of her, where it is warm. In my house. Come there," she said as she shivered in the cold. She carried the body away through the light, falling snow.

"Let her go for now. Let her grieve," Alex said, holding the officers back. He readjusted his heavy coat on his shoulders and found his hat in the bushes.

One of the girls came to help Christina. She put her own jacket around Babette's body and carried her back to the house.

Alex tried to comfort Christina. "Take a sedative; we always keep them in the kitchen. I'll be back soon. Call me at any time, and I'll come quickly," he said with tears welling up in his eyes.

Christina accepted the warm hug that Alex gave her and told one of her girls to get an ice pack for Alex to put on his neck. With tears streaming down her face, she solemnly took Babette from the other girl. She carried her lover's body into the house.

Once the fire was out, the fire chief made his inspection. He declared the house habitable.

Alex and Aaron got into the Jeep and drove off in despair. "Keep that ice pack on your neck Alex. I'll drive carefully to not jar you, *amico mio.*"

"*Grazie*, Aaron."

Aaron aimed his Jeep back up the road toward LaSalle, and then the hospital. "Why did Bruno set fire to the house, Alex?"

Alex pulled the tarp over their heads for warmth. He yanked his hat tight over his own head as the snow slowly drifted into the Jeep.

"Angry bastard. Some call these fire-setters arsonists, as the police did, but he's not an arsonist. Arsonists create fires for insurance purposes, or to kill those in the house for whatever reason."

"This prick enjoyed the scene as he watched the fire."

"Right. He's a pyromaniac."

Aaron slowed down as the road slippery with sleet. "I've heard that word. Latin, *pyro* for fire."

"Yeah. They're brain disordered, possibly early brain injured. Simple, and like playing with matches from an early age. They are obsessive and compulsive, with an irresistible desire and impulsive pleasure in observing fires."

Aaron slowed his Jeep on the corners. "Fuckers, they are."

"Maybe so, Aaron. It appears that they get some sexual pleasure, a high feeling, from the flames, the heat, and the thought of planning more fire-setting in the future. But not for monetary gain."

"I read that they yearned for their mother's warmth in childhood."

"Maybe. That's what the analysts say. You can find them in the crowd later, as they watch a fire and often sexually play with themselves."

"*Si, si.* Masturbating, with a joyful expression on their face, in ecstasy. Like Bruno."

Alex nodded, and told Aaron to slow down to avoid potholes in the road. "I read that's how the police identify them now. They get plainclothes cops, often women, to go into the crowd. They will search about to find such an ecstatic, orgasmic man, usually playing with his genitals, on the edge of the crowd."

"Then they can arrest him, I guess."

Alex held on to the roll bar with one hand and his ice pack with the other as the Jeep was tossed about. "I guess that was what that cop, Theodore, was talking about." Alex said as he readjusted the cold compress to his neck.

"Not an arsonist, Alex?"

"No. Maybe Bruno could be in this situation. They usually start fires in revenge or for wanting to teach someone a lesson. Thrill seekers also do it for money, and are criminals. Being caught adds to their excitement. Planning the fires is pleasurable, and thinking they are more clever than the police."

"Well, this is one that the cops got."

"I wonder what will happen to that gynecologist now, Aaron. And Christina, with her lover now dead? I'll call Christina often. That gynecologist? I'm sure he'll get out of jail soon, what with all the pressure on the government by those protests and the women marching."

"He was brave to try and change the laws in this province," Aaron said as he slowed down near the DaCosta's home.

"Yep. And he will continue to operate his abortion clinics, together with all the doctors he trained. He is dedicated to doing the right thing."

"Just like you, my friend. Just like you," Aaron replied, pulling in front of the DaCosta's, where Alex lived.

✳

CHAPTER 26

Katarina

ALEX called Christina every day to see how she was. When she reassured him each time, he told her he was greatly relieved as he massaged his neck, a chronic reminder of his near death at the hands of Bruno.

He knew she was a lady with stamina, resilience, and strong faith, and was not prone to suicide. She knew that he would recover from his stressful, traumatic, neck disorder.

"I'll still run our profitable business, and very efficiently, too," she said with confidence on the phone.

Alex felt the relief. "The grief will be better once you get over Babette's funeral."

After Alex returned from his weekend at Casa Loma, he was standing in Cartier's office on his ward, having been summoned from his usual duties. He discarded the cold pack, since everyone was asking him about the injury. He hated hearing such concern and having to answer such questions.

In the office, he read Riel's official committal papers; it was signed by two outside psychiatrists, handed to him by Cartier.

Such papers would legally keep Riel in hospital until he was cured by the lobotomy.

"Glad to see him as you wish, Doctor Cartier. We'll put him on chlorpromazine, the newest of tranquillizers, to start with," Alex said smartly, wanting to impress.

Cartier tapped his fingers on the papers. "This will keep ah, Riel here, in this hospital," Cartier ordered. "We do this in this, um … country, maybe not how you do it where you, ah, come from; but it is the law here, eh?" he added.

He took off his tinted glasses and cleaned them with his tie. He avoided looking up at Alex. He was blinking rapidly, which was a bad tic of his.

Alex was concerned as to the legality of the certificates, so he read them carefully. One paper was signed by a local physician, who was a close friend of Cartier's. Another psychiatrist, who had just graduated under Cartier's mentorship and was obliged to Cartier, had signed the second document. Both signatures declared Riel to be insane.

Alex thought that such lack of independent opinions was unreliable. He wanted to tell Cartier that those psychiatrists were probably advocates on Cartier's behalf and not impartial. But he feared Cartier's wrath.

Cartier guffawed, angry still about the idea of medication for Riel. "Pills? Won't work. You Americans always think you're smarter, eh? He'll have the prefrontal lobotomy, eh? We must fix that um, red man with pigtails once and for all. For poaching and sleeping in the bushes on my land."

Alex wanted to tell Cartier to fuck off, but he was dependent on Cartier for his career at that point.

He made his ward rounds after that uncomfortable meeting and went outside.

"The rising sun is burning the fog and cold air aside," he said to himself longingly, thinking of the warmth in the deep south.

He coughed to get the grime of the filthy wards and smell of human waste out of his throat.

Alex scanned the horizon and stood outside as he rested his aching foot for a moment. He looked south to America, and wondered if any of his friends in medicine, who were now in Vietnam, had survived the unpopular war.

He marveled at the St. Lawrence River, flowing far below him in the distance and rushing out to sea.

The gloom and desolation of these buildings as they front the waterway remind me of the lyrics to "Cry Me a River." It is a sad song I often heard in the bars where my mother worked in the south, Alex thought wistfully.

Alex watched and listened to the freighters incessantly blowing their fog horns as they struggled to inch their way into the port of Montréal. It was several miles further up the wide river. Other rusty vessels and old scows and barges were captained by tough, rough men like the recently-departed Russian bear, Bruno.

They slowly passed by, laden with timber, refined smelter products, and animal carcasses. They gladly allowed the river to swiftly deposit them into the yawning Atlantic.

Alex trudged up the steep incline toward the administration building, where he was to meet Dr. Cartier again later that morning. Cartier had the lower floor for his offices, but the upper stories held those patients who had ground privileges and were most likely to be discharged soon, once they recovered.

For their work on the grounds, these few hundred inmates, men and women, were given a paltry ten cents daily for their services. Alex had arranged for this with the head nurse of the female wards, Nurse LaGlace. Everyone else knew her as the 'Ice Queen.'

"This is from your own pocket, Doctor?" Alex had heard LaGlace ask with a questioning smirk. He gave her the cash each week for her to distribute.

"It is. Happy to do it," he said.

But he didn't tell her that the thirty cents came from Gabriella.

Gabriella hated Cartier for being so cruel to the children. She had lost her very young daughter to the war in Sicily and would do everything she could for the poor orphans at the hospital.

So, she altered the books, and took the money out of Cartier's account. She knew that he had pocketed the funds for housing the young children.

"Cartier is too absorbed with his own demons, and his other problems with Katarina, to ever check his accounts," Gabriella told Alex weeks ago when they had boldly concocted the plan.

Gabriella met each of the men and women who worked in the kitchen, laundry, and gardens to add to the stipend, and gave them several additional dollars per month.

Alex had a wicked smile as he explained to Gabriella, "We've opened the store in the hospital repair garage, unknown to that prick, Cartier. It was with the aid of Vinny, my landlord."

"I thought so. Vinny runs the garage and Cartier never goes there," Gabriella replied, handing Alex more money.

Alex, together with Vinny, Gabriella, and Aaron, sold sweets, cookies, chocolates, cigarettes, and personal goods to the patients and made a profitable sum in return.

As he walked up the steep steps to enter the Admin building, Alex slowly dragged his left foot, which was aching from the cold, damp weather. As hard as he tried, he couldn't keep up with the young, fleet-footed nurses. They scampered up the steps and were all bundled in their clean, blue, woolen capes. Such capes were clasped by a small chain at the neck to hold them as they ran up the walkway.

Despite his slight limp, the nurses still gave the new doctor at their hospital—a handsome one at that, without a strange accent like the Europeans—sideward, coy glances and smiles.

Alex arrived at the top of the Admin building and again had to rest his leg. The bright, exterior, marble walls and grand Corinthian pillars were a sheer contrast to the drab interior wards of all these three-story, red brick monstrosities present throughout North America.

When Alex reached the top, he came face-to-face with Katarina standing in the doorway.

Those who worked with her as a volunteer on the wards knew her as Katie. But it was Katarina to Alex, in deference to her husband, Cartier.

She was a young, blonde, Russian lady, apparently married to the director, but no one was quite sure of the dubious arrangement. Katarina was in her mid-to late-twenties, with very soft, blue eyes, natural blonde hair, and an ample bosom.

"She has long, slim legs; a real knockout with that flat belly and goodly figure," as Aaron had described her to Alex one day.

Not that Alex ever noticed as she walked by him on the wards. She always smiled at Alex and greeted him with some Russian salutations that he never understood.

She would walk past and swing her hips tantalizingly while she carried old, worn-out books and magazines. They were for patients on the wards.

Alex had met her before, at Cartier's home on the grounds, when he'd had a cocktail party for the new doctors that summer. He found her to be a cunning little vixen: suggestive, dramatic, and a seductive hysteric.

Despite all that, a real 'blonde bimbo,' as had Aaron said then while they both watched her mingle with her guests.

On this day, as the nurses scurried past, she saw Alex approach the building. She waited for him at the top of the steps, close to the door and under the grand facade.

From the steps, she and Alex watched Sister Denise stand far below on a large, broken-down tree stump.

Alex was surprised with her renewed vigor as she encouraged many patients to gather about to hear her sing. As she got ready with her favorite tune, she announced for all to hear, "Everyone is welcome to come to the chapel on the grounds. It is open every Sunday and some evenings for prayers."

She handed out simple pamphlets inviting those with ground privileges to join her for prayers. It was then that she sang out the inspirational and rousing tune, "Amazing Grace."

It was with such intensity that all those who gathered were spellbound by her singing of the words.

As they both listened from the top of the steps, Katarina whispered, "What are those words, and where did they come from, Alex?"

Alex, impressed by her curiosity, explained, "Aha, Katarina; good that you ask. They were written by a sailor, John Newton, who became a clergyman in the late eighteenth century. He felt the remorse, the guilt, after transporting slaves from Africa to America for the Royal Navy in those years."

"Not very nice, Doctor, to do such."

"Yes. His ship was almost lost in a storm off Ireland. He was saved, and he prayed and asked God for forgiveness and redemption. He was saved by God's mercy."

"So, Sister Denise now sings?" she asked as the sister's voice reverberated off the walls of the nearby buildings.

"Amazing Grace, how sweet the sound
That saved a wretch like me
I once was lost, but now am found
Was blind, but now, I see

T'was Grace that taught my heart to fear
And Grace my fears relieved
How precious did that grace appear
The hour I first believed

Through many dangers, toils and snares
We have already come
T'was Grace that brought us safe thus far
And Grace will lead us home."

"Yes, she sings for forgiveness for the lost souls of the young orphaned children here. To be saved from death and despair. Her words are so prophetic. She tries so hard to stop the buses from bringing more children to this God-forsaken place, by lying down on the road with other women from Montréal and the villages close by."

"I and some nurses here do that, *da*. Sorry, I mean, yes. The buses turn back. A young nurse, Monique, helps the sister, as I now do with other ladies," Katarina said.

"So I heard, but your husband is not pleased, Katarina."

Katarina shook her head and added, "Very frankly, Doctor, that same Jacques Cartier, is not my real husband." She emphasized the word 'real' in halting Russian. There was a suggestion in her tone that she was, therefore, available to him.

She whispered again something in Russian to Alex as nurses appeared. She gently pulled Alex aside into a small area near the corner. It was away from the nurses, and they entered the building.

Shit, Alex thought, as he accepted the gentle, but firm, tug, *This blonde floozy will also want something from me, for sure.*

Alex felt that he had to be polite to the director's 'wife,' or mistress, and accepted the gentle pull.

"I must tell you, so you can protect your patients, kindly Doctor," Katarina immediately announced. She spoke with a Slavic intonation and strong accent to her voice.

"Protect? Like who?" he asked, now interested.

She was cradling a small doll in her left arm, also with blonde hair, partially covered by a blue, woolen shawl.

"I must say this to you. As to your patient, I was told that she is your patient. It is Juanita who said this to Katie. That Jacques uses her in her room, on her ward at night times," she said in a muffled tone.

As she spoke, she raised her voice on the last syllable at the end of each sentence. Alex had observed such 'up speak' in the southern States, quite commonly and usually always by women.

Alex felt uncomfortable with such information and was prepared to walk away. "Look here, Katarina: Juanita has many delusions, and one is that J.C., Jesus Christ himself, uses her. Please don't spread rumors about the director," Alex said, trying to be angry.

Katarina didn't flinch from his rebuke. She smiled, and again insisted, "*Da*, yes she is, as her nurse told me, delusional. But your prophet, J.C., who died on the cross is not the one who abuses her. It is our very own J.C., your Jacques Cartier. He is the one who will be … how you Americans, say it … be crucified, one day?"

Alex looked at her mistrustfully again. "This is dangerous information you're spreading, Katarina. Gossip is bad," he said, frowning but still interested.

Katarina, unperturbed, persisted. "Katie will say only to you, um, eh…" she hesitated. "When I was with Jacques, in France where we met, his head man, the hospital director, was there. He fired Jacques for the very same reason."

"They kicked him out? Out of the country?"

"*Da*, we had to leave that country, or he would go to prison for his needs with other women in that hospital."

"He told me he was the hospital director there, in France," Alex said.

Katarina furtively looked down the steps and away as a nurse opened the doors and passed by. She reached into her pocket and opened her palm.

"No, he was not so. Not a director there. You see what he eats for breakfast and nightly meals, Doctor," she said as she offered her hand. It held several large capsules.

Alex cupped her hand in his and looked at the yellow capsules. "It's lithium, Katarina. Lithium carbonate?" he asked with a quizzical look.

"Jacques, he needs such medicines; ever since his wife went into the mental institute over ten years ago somewhere; Katie knows not where. She had cut, um, sliced, he said to me, her wrists. He told Katie he needs more from the drug man in the town."

"It's called the pharmacy." Only manic-depressives needed lithium, but Alex said nothing.

Katie pocketed the yellow capsules and shrugged her delicate shoulders.

"Is he strange, or does he do any unusual things, like odd behavior at home?"

"No. Well, ah, um, he hangs banners in the house and sometimes outside. Sayings of our Lord, Jesus," she said, embarrassed. Her face turned a rosy pink.

"I've seen those about the grounds."

"*Da*, yes. My Jacques, he sends me to the drug man. I refuse, but he hits me if I refuse." she said in her broken English, worried.

She lifted her sleeve to reveal a recent, large bruise on her left arm, just above the elbow.

Alex looked at the bruise, still engorged with blood and susceptible to infection. "You must see a doctor, Katarina. That could get infected. Go see a physician, in town, when you go to the pharmacy."

Katarina had more information. "Yes, the nurse said so, also. He said he will harm me, but I will kill myself first," she said with a tear running down her cheek.

Her tearfulness looked genuine to Alex, and not a theatrical dramatization. "You must get some help, Katarina. Speak to your doctor in town," he offered, more sympathetic.

"Thank you, kind doctor. Katie saw that you are a kindly man to your patients, here. I know that you stopped the use of straightjackets, not like in my Russia ..." she trailed off as other nurses came up the stairs.

Alex backed off slightly.

He had been told by the head nurse, LaGlace, that Katarina had developed a strong bond with Juanita. Katarina read to her almost daily from old magazines and Readers Digests from years ago. LaGlace said it calmed the fear inside Juanita while she was in the padded cell.

Katarina saw that Alex was uncomfortable. She turned as her eyes misted over again. She dabbed another tear away.

Katarina tucked her old, tattered Readers Digest volumes under her arm and looked at Alex seriously. She lowered her voice again. "Katie is leaving Jacques. She is moving back to Russia very soon, when she has money."

Alex had nothing to say about that. He pointed to the little blonde doll, tenderly held by Katarina. "The doll? Your doll from childhood? Cute."

Katarina beamed with the question and Alex's interest in her now. "No, *nyet*. My baba in Russia sent it to me. She said for Katie to pray every night to have a baby with the doll down there," she answered, spreading her knees apart slightly in expression.

"Interesting. Does it work?"

She laughed. "Katie prays, but Jacques only wants other women," she answered, looking for some response in Alex's face.

"Yes, well, you must talk to your husband about that," Alex said in earnest, trying to be professional.

He feared that he had already said too much. *If she tells the chief, and quotes me, then shit will hit the fan for sure.*

Katarina smiled and patted Alex on the shoulder. "Katie, uh, um, maybe Katie, she says too much. Sorry. But Katie must tell you again. Juanita said to Katie that she will one day kill that nurse," she said, but turned away with a guilty look.

"That nurse? Miss LaGlace?"

"*Da*. For letting that happening, what he does to poor Juanita."

Alex shook his head and readjusted his scarf under his parka, feeling anxious with that information. He pulled the fedora tighter on his head as a strong wind struck him in the face. "Highly unlikely. She has no weapons in that padded cell."

Katarina thought about that for a minute but said no more. She walked away, down the steps, and left Alex outside the door.

CHAPTER 27

A Strange and Hostile Confrontation

ALEX watched Katarina's trim body walk down the steps, quickly dismissing any thoughts that he had of her. He wanted to talk to Aaron's woman, Gabriella, about the money and their risk in her fudging the accounts.

Just as Alex turned to the entrance, Cartier opened the door to leave the building.

Cartier, surprised to see Alex standing there and Katarina just leaving, gave Alex a withering look. He said nothing, but only bit harder into the stem of the glowing pipe between his teeth.

"Aha, come. I'm off for some, ah, tea," Cartier said.

He grabbed Alex roughly by the arm and pulled him along. Alex grudgingly submitted and allowed Cartier to drag him down the steps. Cartier was shorter than Alex, stocky and strong, but he walked quickly with a heavy stoop, as though he carried a mighty burden on his shoulders.

Today, he was bundled in a winter coat, and his silver hair flowed from under his cap, which just covered his ears.

Cartier stopped, readjusted his tinted glasses on his nose, and sucked on the pipe firmly clamped in his jaws.

He glared at the sun, now high in the sky on that winter day, and stared at Alex. "You were talking to my wife, eh? What did she tell you? The nurse, LaGlace, told me you, ah, opened up one of the wards. You didn't ask me first. Why?" he asked, frothing at the mouth.

Alex's shoulder muscles tightened, unsure of which question to answer. He avoided the first one. "Well, yes, sir. Most of the women had full privileges, anyway. You had agreed. Remember?" Alex said.

Cartier had obviously forgotten but appeared to be thinking quickly. He turned and sternly jabbed a finger into Alex's shoulder. "Look here, it's a radical idea. I don't want trouble with, ah, ahem, elopers. They throw themselves in that lake over there," Cartier growled.

He suddenly stopped and rudely turned Alex about. He pointed to the large body of icy water in the distance, now covered in a thin wisp of snow.

"I'll make certain they are not suicidal, sir."

Cartier got back to their walk and looked somewhere far beyond Alex's left ear. "Make certain. We pulled out two last year, near, ah, near death. It's a bad stain on the hospital, and on me. Isn't it, eh? Are you listening?"

"I am sir, but I'll take full responsibility of my wards, sir. Your neck looks injured. A bad fall, sir?"

Cartier snorted and covered the red mark on his neck, now bereft of a bandage, with his woolen scarf. "What did you learn from that redskin, ahem, Riel, that Indian, he calls himself?" he asked abruptly, changing the conversation.

The marks were that of sharp fingernails. *Katarina's, or Juanita's?* Alex wondered. "Only that Riel appears lucid. No evidence of delusional formation."

"Aha, you see: you missed it. He is good at putting one over on you. You are not as smart as some say you are." Cartier chortled.

Alex kept his cool and changed the subject. "I see that you ordered a larger dose of Seconal, the bedtime hypnotic, for Justine, sir. It may be too strong for her, since she was in a coma, Doctor Cartier. She is just getting over her pneumonia."

Cartier abruptly turned to look at Alex face-on, venom dripping from his lips. "She gets restless at nighttime. Irritable, and still very confused. Needs to be rested. It will calm her," he answered very firmly, not appreciating his orders being questioned.

End of discussion.

All Alex could say was, "Very well, sir. I'll see the young boy who had the appendectomy tomorrow, late morning, after I finish my ward rounds. Maybe he can be discharged, and I'll check up on Justine, also. See how she is. Maybe move her back to the nurse's wards."

Cartier sucked on his pipe to get the embers glowing again. He waited. "So, what did you learn from that red savage who poaches on my land? He has a filthy squaw in the hills."

Alex wanted to tell Cartier that his nose was dripping but let that go also. "I didn't know that. Obviously, a very well-bred native. Not educated, with our schooling. But he has good common sense, and appears to be wise, in his ways."

"I'll see him over the next few days. He's not educated. Stupid."

"Well, I've met some highly educated people, but some of them weren't very smart, sir. I've seen many who have very little schooling but are street-smart: wise and clever. Riel has his wits about him."

"Bull. Still a wild Indian," he said, finally wiping his nostril with his sleeve.

"But street-smart, sir."

Cartier looked displeased. "I told you, I'll see him soon. You also transferred him into the, ah, men's building. Are you crazy, ha, just like him, eh?" he yelled out. He laughed, pleased with the comparison.

With this unprofessional and inappropriate squawk from Cartier, a nurse walking by glanced at Alex.

Alex gave a discomfited smile in return to the nurse and backed away slightly from Cartier. "Doctor Levy agreed that he could be on his ward and not in the jail wards, since he works to escort the nurses home at nighttime. I told him he must stay, sir, with the committal papers. He laughed and said it would be warmer there than in the woods," Alex said as he tried to smile at Riel's remark.

"Levy? That Jew wop? Stay away from him, you hear? He visits my accountant, and has no business with her," Cartier shouted. This time he seethed with rage and was almost apoplectic.

"Well, we cross paths occasionally, sir," Alex lied. "Wop? Why are they, the Italians, called that?"

Cartier softened. "With Out Papers. W.O.P. When they, and all those like, ahem, ah, harrumph, Levy, came through immigration at Ellis Island in New York, they had no proper visa or papers. The immigration officers just stamped W.O.P. across their forms, 'without papers.' That was it: calling out, 'here's another wop,' to the medicos behind them, to examine them for TB," he replied. The lecture calmed Cartier down.

"Interesting, sir."

The director changed moods abruptly again. He reverted to Riel, once more. "Still, a troublemaker. He wants the Métis nation to be, ah, free, and have rights like us white men have. Another communist, eh? A red commie. Like Helmut, the doctor we have here from Germany. That Kraut."

Alex bristled with the racist remarks, but hesitated and felt that he should defend Riel. "Much like our past president, Abraham Lincoln, wanted to free slavery in my country, sir. Now we have Martin Luther King. He wants equal rights for the blacks."

Cartier attacked again. "He's another troublemaker. Maybe, like you. There was no mention of your father on your application form. Was he a doctor, eh? Like me?"

Alex wavered. How much should he reveal? "Well, I never knew him, really. Left me, early on."

"And your mother?"

Again, Alex hesitated. "She lives in the north, somewhere in this country. An alcoholic, unfortunately."

"Aha. So, is that why you went into, ah, psychiatry? To treat the old lady?" Cartier asked, smirking.

Alex wasn't going to get into a pissing war with Cartier and answered in a joking way. "Doubtful, sir. I liked the hours. Unlike surgery," Alex answered with an uncomfortable laugh.

"Learned nothing from that wastrel father of yours?"

"Not much. But my mother was a school teacher when sober. Taught me to be reliable, honest, trustworthy, and to do unto others as I would have them do unto me. Help those in need. Sir."

Cartier didn't pick up on that, and instead pointed to his boot with the stem of his pipe. "Your limp, I see it slows you down, *mon ami*. None the less, you are still, ah, one of my best students," Cartier said as he tried to relight his pipe in the cold breeze.

"*Merci.*" Alex replied, surprised to receive the first and only compliment from his boss. He didn't tell Cartier that he saw an orthopedic surgeon in Montréal who was going to correct that left foot soon.

The smell of brie cheese and garlic sausage, plus the stink from Cartier's soggy pipe, struck Alex squarely in the face. Did he smell rye whiskey on his breath, that early in the day?

The pipe was lit, smoldering in the wind. "Nothing like a good smoke," Cartier explained, as he inhaled deeply.

"I heard you lived in Paris, sir. Must have been nice."

Cartier finally smiled. "Ah, you heard, eh? Well, an esteemed position, outside of Paris, in fact. As the director, ah, of the largest institution, there."

Alex tried to look impressed but recalled Katarina's words earlier.

Cartier had more to say. "That man, King, wants equal rights for the blacks in America? And that Jane Fonda, that Hollywood woman. Also a peace activist. Indians and the Métis half-breeds need to know their place."

Alex let that pass. "The White House was under siege, sir. My friends and I were in Washington last year, opposing the war."

Cartier wasn't interested. "My library has my latest book on psychosurgery, published in 'sixty. I'm one of the leading, ah, authorities on physical treatments for the insane. Read it."

"I'd appreciate that, sir. Look forward to reading it."

Cartier laughed inappropriately; his mood had changed abruptly, from a somber one to one of hilarity. He pulled out a stick of Juicy Fruit gum and stuck it in his mouth.

Alex again recalled Katarina's lithium capsules and the sudden mood change for Cartier. Alex wondered if he had a duty to ask Cartier about his illness and need for meds.

Cartier stopped partway up the hill and looked at Alex's oversized boot. "Your army down there, across the border: it drafted you, bad foot and all? It must be desperate for doctors, in Vietnam."

Alex brushed off another insult and simply answered, "Yes, sir."

"Canada was wise to keep out of that mucky muck. I heard that you are giving your wages to patients who work here, but a paltry sum indeed."

"A pittance, sir, but something for them to work harder: in the kitchens, laundry, and in the gardens of your hospital, sir. Like that man there," he said, pointing to the sweeper and trying to suck up to his boss.

"Unprecedented," Cartier sneered and spat the gum out.

"Yes, sir. It is new here. If it's a novel act, that is new, and you're right. It's unprecedented, sir."

Cartier wasn't sure if Alex was putting him on with that explanation. He turned toward him and had a vile parting shot.

"Look here. You, um, better toe the line here, or I'll get rid of you, like I did with that hunky of a Pole who gave me back-talk. I sent him back to Warsaw, and by Christ, I'll send you back to your country. To be with your black friends and that Martin Fucking Luther King." He swore at Alex and stomped off.

Alex, shaken by the sudden, inappropriate vitriol, stopped for a moment to compose himself. He took some deep breaths, and in that split second, he suddenly had a vision.

He saw Cartier's face on that dart board he had set up in his auntie's basement room when he was a youngster. He pictured himself tossing huge, pointed darts at the facial profile. Cartier's nose was the bull's eye.

Alex shook off the image and started walking slowly again. He wasn't worried so much of ending up in Vietnam, or for being a draft dodger. No, he was more worried about being back in America, and in prison after saving his mother from her brutal rape. And for what he had done to her alcoholic rapist. He and his mother never heard of that body being found.

He trudged on, worried and humming again to calm himself.

Alex was livid with Cartier for his belittling and pompous attitude. He was also stunned by Cartier's mercurial emotions, rages, and his need for lithium carbonate, a very potent but effective medication for manic-depressives.

He'd better not do audits on his accounting files and fire Gabriella for cooking the books, he thought to himself with a wide grin as he fingered the cash in his pockets.

He had one up on Cartier.

158

※

CHAPTER 28

A Most Pleasant Surprise

ALEX was still worried about Cartier's threats of deportation back to America. If that happened, he feared that any evidence he could give in court if charged of saving his mother from the rapist would not hold up with any judge or jury.

"For what I did to that pervert, and now this prick calls me a trouble-maker," he muttered as he slowly mounted the steep steps to his office.

Cartier began to consume his thoughts as he dragged his foot up the incline. His left foot ached daily, and he feared further surgical correction. His wry neck, or traumatic torticollis, was in periodic spasm, and his gut churned so much so that he avoided food. His recurrent diarrhea became bloody at times.

Alex was desperate to receive a healing touch for his bottled-up anger, and then his guilt for throwing darts at a mentally ill man. It became an overwhelming obsession as he dialed Christina's number from his office phone.

He was in a deep funk and was grateful that Christina was available and glad to see him that evening.

When he arrived with his briefcase, Christina welcomed him with open arms. She dusted the snow from his jacket in the foyer and pulled him into the large room.

They sat in the living room, drinking hot tea and eating cheese scones, while Alex warmed himself before the open fireplace and talked about his anxieties and obsessions.

Christina listened and didn't interrupt him as he unloaded, and then it was her turn. After a long, sympathetic conversation about her loss of Babette, Christina reassured him that she was sufficiently recovered. It was then that he explained again his confrontation with Cartier.

"With all that hostility, your poor ankle must be so painful, Alexander. And in this heavy snowfall. You are limping even more, you poor boy," she said, rubbing his legs to warm them further under the blanket that she had used to cover them both in.

After eating and drinking, she helped him up the grand staircase to her bedroom. The exchange of acid and money was quick and easy. As usual.

She hugged him again and soothed his nervous, pent-up energy. Then quickly stripped down, and just as quickly helped him to undress.

"Just come to bed and lie down beside me to keep warm. I have a blotter for you, but I had some acid earlier, so I'd better not take any, my sweet," she said. She massaged his ankle with her warm toes as she stroked his genitals with her nimble fingers.

Alex sucked on the blotter and let the soothing feeling of the LSD take effect. It calmed his pent-up anxiety, his throbbing headache, and the gastric pangs flooding through his gut.

As Christina held him warmly, he bent down and gently suckled on her left breast. They lay naked, tightly wrapped into each other's bodies.

It wasn't long for the acid to calm the obsessive rantings in his brain enough so that he could send her into a wild spasm as she achieved orgasm. She waited to catch her breath, and then skillfully manipulated his genitals.

She slowly and methodically took her time as he, in turn, massaged her breasts.

Once he was spent, exhausted, and in a state of bliss, he lay his head on her breast and murmured, "I'm sorry about your loss, my love."

Christina said nothing and just let him fall asleep with his head on her breasts, breathing quietly and snoring gently.

Alex suddenly awoke with Christina next to him. It was the door opening to her bedroom that had stirred him. He was surprised, as very few had the key to her boudoir.

He was even more surprised to find Christina's new bedmate, Jasmine, a dark beauty, standing beside him. Alex recalled, from previous visits, that she was a mulatto.

"She had a black father from French Guiana and a white mother, a Methodist missionary in South America," Christina told Alex last month.

On this occasion, Christina sat up in bed when the girl walked in. "Welcome, Jasmine. Please join us. You must come and rest after cooking all day in the kitchen, my sweet."

Alex was astounded by this novel state of affairs. He watched this beautiful, young girl seductively glide out of her apron, and then her dress and underwear, and nimbly slip into bed next to Alex.

She pulled the covers over the three of them but didn't say a word as she pressed her beautiful body against his.

Alex wasn't going to berate Christina for so quickly forgetting about Babette. He was too overwhelmed by having two beautiful women on each side of him.

"Christina, I recall that we talked about a *ménage* à *trois*, but this is not for me," he said. Jasmine had already moved down his body and was ready for an oral encounter.

"Let's just try it, Alexander. You will like my Jasmine," she said as she began to kiss him and caress his chest and abdomen.

Christina was more aroused as she watched Jasmine remove the covers and fondle Alex.

Alex pulled Jasmine up and away from his genitals. "Sorry, ladies. You are both beautiful, but this ain't for me. Maybe some other time," he said, moving across Jasmine's body and out of bed.

He was too obsessive about disease, but Christina already knew that.

Christina covered Jasmine in the sheets and said, "I understand, Alexander. Jasmine does not feel rejected. She only works the kitchen. It is okay, my sweet; she is clean."

Alex felt reassured, but still too restrained and prudent. "Thanks, for that, Christina. Thank you for seeing me. That was most helpful," he said as he got dressed.

Christina insisted on helping Alex with his boot and encouraged him to follow through with the orthopedic surgeon she had found for him.

"Please come again, and soon, as I may need your help with a certain matter as to my new lover here," she said, pointing in Jasmine's direction.

Alex finished dressing and thanked Christina for her time and therapy. He said *adieu* to Jasmine.

What will she want from me the next time? he wondered as he patted his case full of cash and left.

CHAPTER 29

"Murder," She Wanted to Cry

IT was that very next morning, before lunch, that Alex felt obliged to see young Albert—the boy who had the appendectomy in the attic sick ward.

He felt very much better and more relaxed after the soothing, therapeutic encounter with Christina. He rushed back to the hospital wards after sleeping in late.

He still felt the stir in his crotch as he thought of Jasmine. The young, lithe, very attractive, sweet, dark girl. It was that soft, honey-colored hue to her skin as she stripped down that moved him.

Alex put that thought aside as he met Aaron outside the women's building. Aaron told Alex that he had watched over the little boy every day, and he had recovered.

"He can be transferred back to his ward, which now has heat on the first floor thanks to you, and be with his friends," Aaron said, and then added, "Justine, she is free of that coma, my friend, and should be transferred also."

Alex agreed, but called out to Sister Denise, who was just leaving the wards to accompany him and see Justine. "*Oui, merci*, Doctor Gage. She is so much better and can help me with the new class of students who have just arrived," she said in gratitude.

Sister Denise buttoned her winter coat over her nun's habit and tucked a toque over her head to keep warm. Alex did the same with his parka and slipped on his fedora, which now sported a new feather on the side.

"Nice hat, Doctor Gage. A fedora? Why do you call it that?" Sister Denise asked as they walked along the path to the building.

"Fedora? Well, at the turn of the century, the famous actress, Sarah Bernhardt, was on the New York stage. She was playing Princess Fédora Romanoff, who was a bit of a cross-dresser."

"The hat became popular then?"

"You're right, sister. It replaced the expensive beaver top hat and the bowler and was much cheaper for the ordinary man. But it was also preferred by the gangs of New York. Made popular by the tough guys in the movies like Frank Sinatra and Humphrey Bogart."

"Interesting; it looks good on you. But come now, Doctor, you're not an ordinary man."

Alex just smiled at Sister Denise and said nothing about the compliment.

Once in the building, they both hiked up the stairs to the attic. Sister Denise was not at all breathless and had a renewed vigor since her lungs had responded so well to the medications after her surgery.

Alex enjoyed the exercise of climbing up the steps, limp and all. He unlatched the doors and they both walked in.

Alex stopped to look around as Sister Denise went off to see the young nurse in charge. He took off his hat and parka and laid them on a bed close by.

The room was warmer, and light was streaming in through the open windows. A slight, cool breeze wafted in.

As he looked about, he saw that Justine's bed was empty.

She must be washing in the lady's toilet. And where is her special nurse today? he thought to himself. He called out to the young nurse in the corner, who was busy charting at her desk.

Alex looked about at the clean beds with water jugs on tables close by as he walked toward the nurse's area. He hoped to find Justine there.

The young nurse was always on duty and slept with her patients in the attic. The nurse was near her desk, and waved to Alex when she looked up as he approached.

He hurried to see her as he walked past the three young ones, who were still coughing in bed. They were now covered with their warm blankets and had water at their bedside tables.

There were some old magazines and children's books for them to read, which Katarina had brought for them.

He approached the desk, and but couldn't recall the nurse's name; this nurse was new. He looked at her nametag.

"Claudette? You are new here? Where is the other, older nurse who was in charge?"

"I am, Doctor. I came here to nurse at this hospital three months ago, although I am new to this ward. The director sent Janette away and made me stay here," she said almost apologetically.

Alex scratched his head, wondering. "Doctor Cartier? Why did he do that? But, sorry, yes; you do seem very competent and well-organized. Good for you, Claudette."

"Thank you. I am a quick learner, and Sister Denise supervises me almost daily here. I hope it is to your agreement."

Alex nodded. "Yes. Of course. The children are recovering and will soon be discharged. We will close this ward, since the hospital sick ward has been expanded and is ready."

"I will look forward to that."

"Is Justine in the bathroom? *Comment ça va?*" he said with a smile. He was pleased to speak some of her language, albeit in broken French.

Claudette put her charts down on her desk and stood, as nurses always do when a doctor is present. "*Bien; merci, docteur. Et vous?*" she asked, very politely.

"I am well, Claudette. Thank you. Justine? Where is she?" he asked. He motioned her to sit down as he took the empty bed next to her desk.

"She is fine, *docteur*. Bathing herself in the hot water that we have now, thanks to you."

"She can leave now with Sister Denise, who is attending to the young ones," Alex replied, pointing to the young children whom the sister helped to dress.

Claudette was silent for the longest time. Alex waited; perhaps she was sad to lose her position here after such a time. He stood and put his arm on her shoulder in sympathy to console her.

"*Oui, docteur.*"

"Doctor Cartier told me that he ordered extra barbiturates for her at nighttime. So she could rest better," Alex said.

"*Oui, docteur.* But he added a double dose for her. I saw him put the capsules in her mouth when he visited earlier, last night."

"That was too much. I told him so."

"*Oui, docteur.* I thought so, also. With respect."

She then pulled Alex further away, into the darkened recess of the attic. "Please, I don't want the sister to hear, *docteur.*"

Alex followed the gentle tug on his arm. "What is it, nurse?"

Claudette hesitated and looked about to see that no one was close or watching. "I saw him, *docteur.* I saw him. He didn't know I was here, in the dark corner."

"Saw who, Claudette?"

"It was dark. Late last night, and only the partial moon coming through those closed drapes," she said.

She didn't look at Alex as she pointed to the drapes, now ajar.

"Saw him? Who?"

"Doctor Cartier."

"Pardon, Claudette? Doctor Cartier?"

Claudette waited. It was a long pause.

"I know that it was him. I saw him try to use the pillow over Justine's head and face. It was very late, at nighttime."

"A pillow? Over Justine?"

"*Oui*. He took the pillow from the bed next to her. Held it over her face. He did it as she slept so soundly from the pills."

"My God. Are you certain, Claudette? Certain?"

"I saw him. I am certain, *docteur*. He thought I was sleeping in my bed, as the covers on that bed are heavy from the cold and in a heap."

"He didn't see you?"

"He thought the cluster of covers was me," she said, blinking rapidly. She spoke in hushed tones, with lips quivering. She pointed to her empty bed, so that Alex knew where she rested.

Alex couldn't believe his ears. He waited. He sat Claudette down on the bed, beside him.

"Claudette, are you sure you weren't dreaming? You were asleep?"

"*Non, docteur. Non.* I couldn't sleep. I was sitting there at my desk, in the dark, praying for Sister Denise to be well, and my own father, who is ill with the cancer."

"Sorry about your father, Claudette."

"He didn't see me. I know it, for certain, in the darkness."

"Darkness?"

"Not so. With only the moon. I saw him. I coughed loudly. He looked in my direction and then saw me.'

"And the pillow?"

"The pillow, he put it back after I waved to him. He left in a hurry. I waited. I wanted to tell Sister Denise that there was an attempt."

"And?"

"I went to my patient and awoke her to see how she was. Justine, she was drowsy, but well. I gave her water to drink. She fell back to sleep. She was well."

"And? Sister Denise?"

"She came in the very early morning to make rounds. I didn't say anything to her about that," Claudette explained, looking to Alex to see if she had done the right thing.

Alex reassured her. "You did well. Claudette, you are certain as to what you saw? Certain?"

"*Oui*. I am quite certain. I was awake, and it was dark, at night. But the moon, it shone enough. Not dreaming, *docteur*."

"Good you told me."

"What should I do? I am certain I saw it. I am afraid, please ..." she trailed off.

Alex waited. Cartier would deny everything, and just say that he was making rounds, often wandering about at nighttime.

He must be going through depression after the news that Katarina was leaving him. And then he also had to get rid of the witness.

He tried to reassure the girl. "For now, Claudette, nothing. Do nothing. Leave it to me. I'll remember what you said. Do not be afraid, and we'll keep this to ourselves for now. Okay?"

Claudette nodded in agreement. "Should I tell Sister Denise?"

"I don't think so, Claudette. Leave it with me. We will move Justine soon. She will help Sister Denise teach the undergraduates. You were very brave to tell me."

"*Merci*, Doctor Gage. You are very kind to me, and to the poor little ones here," she said. She looked at the young children sitting up, ready to leave.

"If anybody asks you about that night, then just tell them that you were sleeping in your bed. You have the right to rest at nighttime. That you saw nothing."

"*Merci*. I shall do that. *Merci, docteur*."

Alex told her that he had to see the little boy and transfer him soon. "I'll think about all this and how to handle it. Have no fear, Claudette.

You did well and are safe here; and you will be safe on the new medical ward. I will see to it."

"I will work closely with Sister Denise?"

"For sure," Alex said, reassuringly.

Alex waited. Claudette raised herself to her full length, which wasn't much. In a show of gratitude, she took Alex's hand in hers and held it very briefly. She tried to smile.

Alex put his arm partway around her shoulder, but not too warmly, as he feared any misinterpretation.

He walked away to see how the boy was doing, and to examine the three girls still there before discharge.

He couldn't think or decide what to do with Claudette's information. After all, she had been tired, it was dark, and maybe she was in a dream state. She was in prayer, and perhaps had some religious vision.

That's what Cartier would conclude.

I wish Justine hadn't locked eyes with Cartier on that dreadful day with Mère Supérieure, he thought to himself as he prepared to leave the ward.

It was ironic that Justine survived the attack on the grounds but was almost murdered in the hospital ward. *She would have been, if not for Claudette,* Alex thought as Sister Denise approached.

Justine had finished bathing and was dressed in her graduate uniform.

"Put on your cap with the black band and dress warmly, Justine. You will assist me from now on in teaching the other nurses in the classes," Sister Denise said as she helped Justine wrap her scarf about her and don her heavy coat over her shoulders.

Alex arranged for the other children to be moved. He discussed a new position for Claudette, and Sister Denise agreed.

CHAPTER 30

"How Are You, Mother?"

IT was that very next morning that Alex felt obliged to call his wayward mother. He would do so after meeting with Sister Denise, officially the new *Mère Supérieure*.

Alex called out to *Mère* Denise *Supérieure*, as was her new title. She was just leaving the wards with Justine.

"*Bon jour*, Doctor Gage. As you can see, my pretty Justine is much better now, and can help me with teaching the students," she said in gratitude.

Alex breathed a sigh of relief. Justine was safe now.

He left the two and went to the ward on the first floor, where he had a sparse office. It held a simple metal desk with two drawers that were so rusted and twisted that they were useless.

Two unmatched plastic chairs and a grubby, tin waste paper basket were the only other objects. The room smelled, since it had not been used for years. Alex threw open the window to clear the stale air.

The early morning sun ushered in a fresh, but cold, breeze. He had a son's duty to call his mother, to reassure her that he was still alive and find out if she was also.

He did so and waited patiently for the dial tone to connect. Once she answered, she didn't wait for the pleasantries, but immediately scolded him, as usual.

"You'll be murdered in that country as a draft dodger. Safer in Vietnam," she shouted, but ended with a giggle. There was a loud burp into the phone.

"The odds are much better at this hospital, mother."

He had hoped to find her sober this early in the day, but that was too much to hope for. Alex wanted to know more about his father.

He recalled her earlier stories. "It was easy for your father to pick me out with my French accent, Alexander, baby. He was such a handsome brute. A French-Canadian, and we had a lot in common at first," his mother had told Alex as a young boy.

She drank her mint juleps as she talked and laced up his special boot before he went to school. Young Alex wasn't sure what he heard with her slurred speech and her giggles so early those mornings.

"He was fascinated by the dark-skinned Creoles in our south, Alexander baby," he recalled her saying. For some unknown reason, she always laughed as she talked, as though everything was a joke.

As it happened, Alexander later discovered that all they had in common was the French language. Plus lots of sex, which often awoke him, and the jugs of mint juleps in her rooms.

Articles in the psychoanalytic journals that he read later in life convinced Alex that his mother was an immature borderline personality disorder. Complicated with alcoholism, an addiction to barbiturates, and an early head injury.

Alex knew she was currently teaching at a small school in the northern wilds of Ontario. Garth, her fifth 'husband,' a geologist, lived with her in a seedy trailer park. He had been hired to find a copper deposit for the Radisson Mining and Smelting Company.

"Russia will nuke us," she had told Alex when they lived in New Orleans. Therefore, she had moved as far north as she could—with a banjo player. He left her penniless after he took an accidental overdose of drugs and died.

It was not long after that Garth found her as a needy woman in a local bar.

On this cool morning, Alex stood at the window and watched the sun slowly rise in the east. "Mother? How are you?" he asked again.

His mother never replied to questions like that. With her usual 'tee-hee-hee,' she answered, "Alexander, baby, is that really you? How thoughtful of you to call. I told you, don't call me 'mother.' I'm far too young to be a mother."

He waited while she lit her cigarette. "Okay, okay, Francine, calm yourself. Listen; this time, I need to know about one of your boyfriends. Surely one of them is my father."

There was a long hesitation. Alex heard the clink of ice cubes falling into her glass. He knew that she had forgotten how many boyfriends she'd had, especially in New Orleans.

"Alexander, sweetie, are you using the oil of wintergreen on your ankle every night?" she purred sweetly and chuckled.

"Yes, Francine, and the Epsom salts in the foot bath like you told me. Listen, try to concentrate."

"Well yes, my sweet. Well, I remember one of them as a tough, rough man, Alexander baby. My, my, he was well built: powerful and handsome." She hesitated. "And above all he loved every, and I mean every, woman he ever met on Bourbon Street."

"A loving man, Francine," Alex added, sarcastically.

She ignored that. "But he was very gentle in bed, and knew how to please a woman, Alexander dear." She hesitated and chuckled. "So sorry, Alexander, but you know what I mean."

Damn, he thought, *not again. The details of her sex life with so many men are something that I don't need to know.* But at times, as a teenager, he would peep through the key hole to see what was going on next door.

"Okay, okay, mother, I don't need that kind of information."

His mother cupped her hand over the receiver and whispered, "To answer your question: well, he left when I had you. I was destitute again."

"Auntie said it was you who left, for 'another loser,' as she put it."

There was a long silence, and a few minutes later, Garth was shouting in the distance. "Who are you talking to? Get off the fucking phone. It's costing me money, numb nuts."

Alex squirmed. "Tell him it's my nickel. I'm paying for the call. What was his name, mother? Maybe I can trace him now that I'm up here."

The speaker was muffled again as Francine shouted, "Oh, shut up and drink your coffee, lover boy." She chortled.

"Pardon, Francine?"

"No, no, not you, Alexander. He's still sober, but into coffee now: an addiction to caffeine." She whispered into the phone. "His name? I doubt it, darling boy. He kept changing it because of the red coats. The police. I'll tell you he went by the name of Provencher."

"Provencher?" he asked, writing that down.

"That was only once. When he lived with me, he changed it to Gagnon, since he feared the red coats up north. I became Rene Gagnon for a brief time."

"Sounds nice, Francine, musical. So, I became 'Gage' from Gagnon," Alex said, sarcastically again.

She laughed, swirled the ice cubes in her glass, and tried to suppress a coughing fit. She took a deep drag of her cigarette. "He had a mother who was still living then."

"Where?"

"It was in the Gaspe area. Southern Québec. She was in LaSalle, I think."

"Thanks, like the town nearby. Keep well and watch that liver of yours."

It was with some hesitation that Alex then asked, "Francine, have you heard or read anything about that pervert? You know, on the riverbank in New Orleans?"

Alex heard the quiver in her voice as she answered. "Nothing, Alexander. Nothing. You saved my life, you did. The fast-flowing river took his body out to sea. Nothing. Nobody. Nobody never found him."

"Thanks, Francine. Good to hear," he answered.

"You won't forget to use the Tiger Balm on your foot, will you?"

"It smells. Are you working, mother—er, sorry—Francine? Drinking? I heard the ice cubes in your glass."

"Heavens no, sweetie. Orange juice. I organized the AA group I started up here, and Garth is the president."

"Wow. No kidding. Good for you, Francine."

She had more to say and proudly announced, again with a childish laugh, "And I'm teaching K to three, full time. Good money. Almost as much as you, sweetie. Gotta go."

The phone went dead. Alex had to sit down after that and digest his mother's astounding recovery and rehabilitation.

Maybe Garth was not so bad after all.

❋

CHAPTER 31

A Therapeutic Torture Chamber

AFTER that bizarre phone call to his mother, Alex felt more hopeful for her recovery. Still preoccupied with that conversation, and thinking of Jasmine and what could have been, he didn't pay attention to where he was walking.

He carelessly turned right and down an extra flight of stairs into the basement of the building.

At the entrance to the cellar, he was confronted by two huge, steel doors, supported by rusted metal hinges. They screamed for lubrication when he tried to open them. The steel doors creaked and groaned, resisting any movement.

Intrigued, he pushed harder, and as they reluctantly opened he peeked inside to find a massive, cavernous hall.

He gasped to see the enormity of the immense basement room. Looking up, he saw the cellar had large, metal light shades, devoid of light bulbs. They were suspended by wires from very high, lofty ceilings.

As Alex's eyes became accustomed to the dark, he stepped back in horror at the sight and took in a quick breath of the dank, musty smells.

The room was virtually vacant except for several enormous, white, badly stained, cracked, porcelain bathtubs. They were in the middle of the room but were scattered about without any semblance of organization. Along the side of the room were other dull, black, filthy metal tubs.

All the tubs had gigantic water spouts for hot and cold water, and all were connected with very long, rotting, rubber hoses running into rusted wall faucets.

"My God; a water treatment room for poor souls. They suffered from mental illness. From a hundred years ago," Alex blurted out to the rats milling about.

He rubbed his eyes to get the grunge out as he tried to focus in the dim light. He carefully walked through the cement dust, kicking mice aside to the humongous tubs.

Mice, ants, flies, silverfish, spiders, and large, menacing rats scurried away as he plodded along. A few feral cats slunk about, chasing the mice for an easy meal.

As he walked, he stirred up the heavy layer of gray concrete dust from a hundred years ago. It filled his nasal passages and left him coughing as spider webs loaded with rotting flies hung on top of him from the ceiling.

He held his nose; the stink of putrid pools of water on the floor that had filtered in from cracks in the walls rose to fill his lungs as he walked through the filth.

Alex sneezed and blew the grime from his nose. He went to the outer walls seeking light and air, coughing as he plodded along. All the basement windows along the three sides were cracked, large enough for cats and mice to scurry through the openings.

He threw open a window, letting in the freezing air, and took in a few gulps of fresh air.

He walked back to the center of the room, holding a handkerchief over his face and pushing aside grotesque spider webs from his fedora. Beside each tub was a large, metal chair with straps to bind the poor, wretched patient in.

A pulley system above each tub was used to lower the chair, with its victim, into the hot water or into a freezing cold tub.

He had read about such primitive therapeutic measures from centuries ago. It was used throughout Europe and the Americas and was depicted in paintings of the old British Bedlam mental institute.

The system was devised to plunge helpless psychotics into very hot or ice-cold water in hope of curing the disturbed mind of hallucinations and delusions.

Alex cautiously gripped the edge of a tub to look in. He suddenly heard, and felt, something behind him. He jumped up, thinking for a split second that it was a phantom from the past, seeking retribution, vengeance, and freedom.

Alex abruptly turned and shouted out, "Jesus Christ!"

It was Aaron Levy, the Italian Jew, behind him. "No, my friend. Not Jesus Christ. Only me."

"Well, thank the good Lord it's you, Aaron. Scared the shit out of me."

"So sorry to scare you, Doctor Gage. I was a using this room for group therapy," he said in his thick Italian accent, as he pushed away gunk dropping down from the ceiling lamp above.

"My God, Aaron. Thank God it's you. I found this torture chamber by mistake. What are you doing down here, in this God-forsaken basement? How cruel was this treatment?" he asked.

Aaron patted his friend on the shoulder with his good arm to calm him down after the fright. "You, ah, are right, as our almighty Lord abandoned these God-forsaken patients. They struggled to survive such cruelty in this here torture basement."

"Indeed, it was, my friend."

"See here, the patient would be strapped into the chair, and then lowered into the enormous baths full of hot or cold water," Aaron said proudly, having read of the history. He whispered softly, as if the insane dead might still be listening.

"They would be tossed into those tubs faster than you could say 'Jack Robinson,' my friend." Alex whistled.

"Who? Jack? He worked here, Alex?"

Alex gave a slight chuckle, mimicking his mother. "No, he didn't. Jack Robinson was the executioner in the Tower of London hundreds of years ago. He was the fastest and most agile with the ax in beheading. Very famous for his quickness. Never missed. Very speedy. Everyone asked for him only."

"And so, faster than you can say 'Jack Robinson,'" Aaron repeated. They both laughed.

Alex nodded in agreement but tried to compose himself. He was glad to have a sane, living soul next to him in this Hell-hole. "I've read that the steaming-hot water was to send blood to the brain to purify the body of evil, psychotic spirits. If that failed, and it did, then they were plunged into the ice-cold water in the next tub. It was supposed to recharge the depleted nervous system. But it wouldn't, Aaron." Alex shook his head in disbelief at the cruel attempt to treat the insane years ago.

"Some of them never survived the intense temperature changes," Aaron reasoned.

"Yes. Many died of pneumonia afterward in the cold cellar."

"I saw such a picture of such a hospital, called St. Bonifazio, on a painted canvas in Florence. It was depicted by a painter, Signorini, in the mid-nineteenth century. It depicted a room in the insane hospital's women's ward, where the poor souls were treated, my friend."

As Alex stood there, muscles tense and cold sweat beading on his forehead, he heard water gurgling down the sewer pipes in the corner of the clammy room. It sent shivers down his spine and a twinge in his neck.

A lone seagull cried in the distance, and the room went dark. A passing cloud had covered the north window that Alex had just opened, bringing down a torrent of rain.

A shudder swept through his body as he leaned over one of the damaged tin tubs. It was scratched and heavily dented inside. Most likely from the hands, fingernails, and feet thrashing about.

All limbs had sought freedom. But in vain, since they were shackled.

Alex stood up and away from the tub. A rat squealed in agony somewhere in the dark corner. The pitiful thing had been caught by one of the feral cats.

"Good God, Aaron, I think I just heard the wail of a deranged soul. It cried out as it struggled for air after being plunged into the deep bathtub."

"God never had anything to do with such inhumanity. It was a rat, my friend."

Alex gave a sigh of relief. He looked to the doors and thought of escape. "Man, how can you work in this awful place, this rat-hole of a dungeon?" Alex asked. He pointed to rusted chains fixed to the walls, with leg irons strewn about. They would hold the insane until their turn came to be treated.

Aaron remained passive, as always, and only replied, "Quiet and peaceful it is, my friend. Silent."

"I guess the smells don't affect you after your head injury in the Italian campaign."

Aaron nodded in agreement, and he walked to the corner near a window. "I heard that you visited Christina and helped the alcoholics with your acid therapy at the Casa Loma again."

"Yes, Aaron; she is coping with her loss, and we are still doing well with her business and our percentage."

As Alex watched, Aaron left and maneuvered twelve chairs into a circle. Hundreds of flies swirled upward, seeking the only beam of light as a ray of sun briefly broke through the stained windows.

Alex buttoned his white coat against the putrid dampness and yanked his fedora further down. He wiped his brow with his coat sleeve. Waving his hand across the room, he asked, "Aaron, did you have such awful places in Italy?"

"All a these mental hospitals are the same, Alex. Red brick, three-story buildings with immense wards. Each held over five thousand long-stay patients, here or in Europe," he replied, obsessively arranging his chairs in concentric circles.

"The same in Italy and throughout Europe?"

"The architects of these monstrosities unfortunately overcompensated. They constructed *bella ultimo* palaces to house the mentally ill."

Alex joined Aaron where he was setting up his group chairs. "*Bella,* shit—beautiful they weren't," he said, tapping the back of a chair three times and resetting it obsessively in concentric rows, exactly four inches apart.

Alex's friend had another piece of history, now that he was pleased with his chair arrangement. "These were popularly called Bedlam, after the old *grande* Bethlem Hospital in London, dating back to 1247."

"In those days, the public paid a fee to help support the hospital financially. They brought their lunch and were entertained by the psychotic behaviors and disjointed ramblings of the patients," Alex added as they both walked back through the room of empty tubs.

Depressive Levy was a storehouse of historical fact, with more detail than Alex needed to know for his exams. "Chaos was rampant prior to medications, and no *dottore*, no doctors. The public, they would jeer at the patients. They would be naked and confused, raving about Christ and the Devil. They would jump out at the leering *pubblico*, much to their delight at Bedlam, in 'ye olde' England," he told Alex.

"I guess there was no such thing as proper treatment was there, Aaron?"

"I wanna tell you, Alex: none. In those days, only herbs, tonics, hot and cold baths, and God, if he was present at all. But pneumonia, syphilis, starvation, infections, and freezing cold would finally end their hapless survival. Very few survived, indeed."

"Look there, in that corner, Aaron." Alex pointed to rows of wooden benches.

"*Si, si.* There were no baths or showers in the wards at that time. Fifty patients at a time would be marched down here. Men and women separately. Clothes would be put on the benches and they would be herded against the wall, naked, and sprayed with hoses as a bath. Once a month by the orderlies. So, it was then, my friend."

"No one had any semblance of privacy," Alex said, horrified.

"And so, *amico mio*, during such naked times men found each other and sought out any shred of human warmth through an encounter. They would seek an opening, be it oral, anal, or, if possible, vaginal on occasion. Women, too, would seek simple human warmth by lying together in bed through the nighttime."

"I see that the staff, at times, would say or do nothing, knowing that such behavior was not uncommon in the hospital. But they knew not to allow the children to be abused, Aaron."

"*Si.* The staff would usually turn a blind eye to any such lustful activity and self-gratification, single or group."

"The staff too would be attacked. Some even killed by patients."

"God almighty. Poor souls, indeed. Let's get out of here," Aaron said, pulling Alex along.

They walked past the large boiler room, fed by enormous gas furnaces that would heat all the buildings through the hot water systems. Their institutions was manned by dozens of engineers, mechanics, boiler makers, gas fitters, plumbers, electricians, cooks, and ancillary staff to sustain them.

They walked out of the sordid basement, pulling their parka hoods over their heads to cover themselves from the rain.

"Raining cats and dogs, my friend," Alex remarked as they walked along in the downpour.

"No dogs, here, Alex. Some cats, maybe."

"Ha, Aaron. That's an old saying from the time of our poor Bedlam days. Stray cats died on the rooftops, and poor dogs died of starvation in the gutters. In the heavy rains, the streets were awash with these dead animals."

"Aha, so it rained cats and dogs."

✳

CHAPTER 32

An Ill-fated Confession

"BUONGIORNO. Come, I'll buy you a coffee, Aaron." Alex laughed as he mimicked his friend in faulty Italian as they plodded along.

"Coffee, it's a free here, Alex," Aaron replied seriously. Live cigarette ash fell on his jacket and burned a small hole in the cotton.

As they walked up the hilly path, Alex whistled the tune of "Twist and Shout."

"Ah, *bella, bella,* Alex." Aaron said, as he waved to one of his chronic male patients.

The man stood rigid, a side effect from the tranquillizers. He talked to himself, in the bushes just off the path, and in the light drizzle.

As they both neared the administration building, Alex stopped. He looked up at the flag pole. He saluted the Canadian flag as it waved in the strong wind.

Aaron looked worried. "That's a red ensign, my *amico.* It will soon be replaced by the maple leaf, if this new prime minister, Pearson, gets his way."

"I guess you don't like changes, do you? As for me, I'm grateful to Prime Minister Pearson. He welcomed us draft dodgers."

"And us poor wops."

"But I fear that Cartier might send me back to the States, as he ranted, raved, and threatened me recently."

"He won't. Not just being a draft dodger, my friend. Many are here. That man, he needs the help of bright men like you."

Being a friend, Alex thought he could confide in Aaron. He needed to tell someone the real reason he feared returning to America. He hoped that a confession might absolve him and give him some peace of mind from his underlying guilt.

"Look, Aaron. It's not that. It's because I did something, not too long ago. To save my mother. From certain death, I feared."

Aaron put his only good arm around Alex as they walked along the path. "We all do something stupid, from time to time, my friend. What was it?"

Alex hesitated, but continued since Aaron was a good friend, or 'amico,' as he often called Alex. "It was while a drunken hobo and I sat on the riverbank outside New Orleans talking. You know, in Louisiana, America. Just before I came here."

"Aaron knows. The wide Mississippi River."

"Yes. My mother was down by that river. She was drunk and with her boyfriend. He was an abusive pervert," he said. He took his time, hesitating again.

"Yes? So? People, they do that. I used to fuck my girlfriend on the banks of the Arno. It was outside of Florence, before the war."

Alex took a deep breath and continued. "Yeah, well. This drunken sot suddenly rolled over onto my mother and tried to fuck her. She yelled out, but he clobbered her with a vicious punch. He started raping her violently."

"My God almighty! What did you?"

"I didn't know what to do, Aaron. That vagrant drinking beer next to me told me to help her. She was screaming. I heard her screaming, Aaron. My God, I still dream about her screaming for help."

"You do? What did you do then?"

"Aaron, this man had a Swiss army knife and gave it to me. So I ran down and jumped on the rapist. I pulled him off and jabbed my knife into his side. I was beside myself. In a frenzy."

Aaron listened intently. He appeared thrilled to hear the grisly story as he lit another cigarette. "What happened?" he asked as he stood in rapt attention with fumes belching out his nose. He looked at Alex, totally absorbed.

Alex opened his parka; they were under the cover of the building and he was in a sweat. "I don't know. She got her hands on his neck. Throttled him. My knife in him, maybe into his kidney, put him in shock."

"I saw many like that in the war."

"He had a coronary. Died. I didn't mean to injure him. Just to scare him off. He died, Aaron."

"Good for you. You had to save your poor *mamma*. All *mammas* are good to their boys."

"Yes, I had to save her. He would have killed her," Alex said as his eyes misted up in grief, but also in relief.

"The police? Did the police come?"

"No. My mother recovered and sobered up quick enough. She pushed him off. I helped her, and we rolled him down into the river. The tide quickly swept his body out to sea. Into the Atlantic."

"It was good for her, and you. There was a witness? No witnesses?"

"I went back to the drunken sot up onto the bank. My mother took off. The body disappeared. That hobo said good riddance."

"That man was not worth to be alive."

"Thanks, Aaron. My good friend. *Graci.*"

"Well, my friend. Have no worry. It was done to save a good woman. Your *mamma*. Your deed is safe with Aaron. I killed many during the war in Italy to save others. Like your *mamma*," he declared. He crossed himself twice and flicked his still-glowing cigarette in the bush.

Alex remained quiet after that but felt somewhat relieved. Finally, he added, "My mother, she was still confused from the sour gin. She made hooch in her bathtub."

"That's like piss. Yuck."

"But she was sober enough to tell me never to talk about it. And I haven't seen her since. I still phone her from time to time."

Aaron gave out an audible sigh. He again patted Alex on the shoulder as they walked into the building. He wanted to change the subject, to help Alex forget about his trauma.

"You did well, my friend. Now, never talk about it, forget it."

"Thank you for listening. I feel better about confiding in you."

Aaron swept his hand over the rolling plain and the lake below. He diverted the attention from that scene and explained as he looked across the fields. "You know, Alex, this hospital was built on farm land. It is outside of the small town of Verdun, miles from Montréal. The first psychiatric patient was admitted in 1890."

Alex was pleased to get off that subject and talk of something else. "It was a long time ago, Aaron," he said, still nervous as they stood in the entrance.

"Right. It produced howls of protest from all the farmers nearby. They were convinced that the patients would infect their livestock. They said that all their cows would go mad with insanity from the hospital patients."

"My God; now, in the early sixties, it has nearly five thousand patients. The cattle didn't go loony." Alex finally laughed.

As Aaron and Alex looked about, they heard the occasional wail of a lonely seagull and hawks feasting on rotting carcasses in the bushes. Other rodents, rats and mice, scurried about, seeking safety from the feral cats. They were fed by the patients, and soon became their only friends.

Aaron stopped for a minute. He was in serious thought, with his good arm on Alex, and held him tight. His face lit up with a sudden, wild idea.

"Listen my, ah, friend. The exams in psychiatry are coming soon, and Aaron is poorly prepared. I will fail those finals. I have poor English, and will fail, my friend," he repeated. He emphasized the word, 'friend,' again and again.

"Keep at it, Aaron. Study hard. You can make it."

"No. He can't not. But you can for me. You can write them for me. I can give you my ID. You can enter the room, with so many others, and write them for me."

"Piss off. No way," Alex was incensed.

Aaron laughed. "Only the written, that is. I might get through the orals, I am sure, if you do the written ones. For Aaron, your good friend."

Alex was aghast at the thought. "Aaron, you are fucking bastard; that's illegal. I can't and won't do that. No way."

"Ah, yes, my friend," Aaron said. Then he stuck the knife in. "Yes, we all do something illegal, don't we? Even to save our dear *mammas*."

"Bugger off for even asking me to do that."

"Ah, think. About helping your friend, now. You will do this thing, for your good friend. For certain. *Carpe diem, carpe diem*, my friend."

Alex was dumfounded with the threat. He came face-to-face with Aaron, and spat out, "'Seize the day,' you said? Asshole. Up to your old, Sicilian, mafia tricks, again, are you? You will have a short life span."

Aaron didn't budge an inch and didn't back away. "You are threatening your *amico*?"

"No. Not me. Keep acting like that and someone else might," Alex replied. He wavered, and thought that he could smash Aaron's face in, but declined. He feared the stiletto in Aaron's back pocket.

Aaron abruptly walked away and waved to Alex with a thin smile on his lips. He turned and gave Alex the finger, then walked down a few steps into the basement cafeteria for a free coffee.

Alex filled his pipe with tobacco; his hand was unsteady with the threat of exposure. *I did a stupid thing to confide in Aaron,* he thought to himself.

He lit the pipe to calm himself; the match flickered with his trembling fingers, and he wished he also had some acid in his pocket.

"What an asshole!" he said again, but not exactly sure who he was referring to. Was it to himself, since he had talked too much, or to Aaron?

For as of now, Aaron had some incriminating information over Alex.

CHAPTER 33

Captivating Monique

"There is only one happiness in this life, to love and be loved."
George Sand

ALEX, still in a state of panic, relit his new pipe just to warm his hands again as he walked up the steps into the building. He unlocked the door with the large, metal key hanging on a ring fastened to his belt.

He was out of the freezing wind and rain, but into the stench of his foul ward, occupied by depraved humanity. He had left orders to have the wards cleaned better: scrubbed and vacuumed with new beds and linen.

Such changes took time.

Once in his office, he hung his parka in the closet and put his fedora on the hook. Looking in the mirror, he slapped his head with the stupidity of inadvertently creating his own inner madness by talking with Aaron.

"Idiot! Moron! Imbecile!" he said, looking at his image in the mirror.

He locked his office door and slowly made his way into his very own Bedlam, housing over a hundred females in that one, single ward.

Alex slowly strolled down the long, bleak corridor toward the nurse's station. As he passed three padded cells, he looked in on Juanita, housed in one of the rooms.

The peephole was a slit in the door, but Juanita knew someone was watching her. She quickly combed her fingers through her thinning hair and moved into the middle of the small, tight room. She began her bizarre dance for the peeping Tom.

As Alex peered in, he found his patient completely naked. She was dancing slowly and held a blood-stained pillow tight to her body. Her dance partner.

As she wheeled about, she bounced off one heavily padded wall and onto another. He heard the babble of a garbled tune. She laughed at her own song, one only she could understand.

Alex recalled Aaron's advice. "Juanita's favorite trick is to piss, vomit, or shit into a cup, or wrap some shit in paper, and hide it under her bed. When you're off-guard, she'll fling it at you. I always let the nurse go in first," he had advised as he showed Alex around on his first day.

As Alex left Juanita and her 'dance partner,' he tapped on her door to say goodbye and thought to himself, *I'll get rid of these padded cells soon, as I did with the straightjackets.*

He walked to the nurse's station at the end of the long, poorly-lit hallway and looked up at the drab, neon tubes precariously suspended on rusting wires. They periodically flickered and went out, never to be replaced.

The partial lighting produced an eerie glow: they shone a dim light along the filthy, barren corridor with tarnished floors.

The grimy walls of the hallways screamed for a coat of paint and lacked the hygienic and sterile qualities of a proper modern hospital. The wooden floorboards creaked under Alex's weight as he trudged along.

As he looked down, he saw them stained from ground-in fecal material, menstrual blood, sputum, urine, and human bile juice, or gastric acid. It left a mottled stain that he couldn't avoid as he walked along.

An old woman was on her knees, picking at festering sores on her belly. She had stripped down naked and played in a pool of urine next to her.

Alex gently raised her from the floor, took off his white coat, draped it around her, and led her to her room.

Her room had twenty beds so close together that he had trouble maneuvering through the maze to find her cot. As she sat down on the bed, the rusted springs creaked.

She handed him a few bits of toilet paper as he put her on her bed. "These coins are for you, Doctor," she said with a vacant grin.

Alex pulled a thin sheet over her. A nurse was called, and Alex ordered a penicillin cream for her infected scabs.

As he walked out, three patients descended on him. One poor soul looked like one of the trio of witches from Shakespeare's Macbeth; like she belonged sitting around a boiling pot on the camp fire.

Another was partly naked, with a hospital gown opening in the front. The third was rambling incoherently.

The student nurse, who responded to his call, led them away.

Alex went back to his office and retrieved a fresh white coat from his closet. He banged his new pipe into a large, metal tray to empty the hot coals. Alex had bought the expensive pipe, the famous Italian Stromboli, when he was in Montréal. He liked the rough ridges on the bowl that made it cooler to the touch.

Depressed with what he had seen and what he had confessed to, he walked back into the corridor, slowly dragging his left foot, and stepped into another patient's room. An orderly was cleaning a large area of liquid fecal matter from the floor in the corner.

He looked in the mottled, lead mirror and adjusted his blue and white polka-dotted bow tie. He combed his black hair, slicked back with a dab of Brylcreem.

"Brylcreem, a little dab will do you. Brylcreem, the gals will all pursue you." He laughed at his own feeble attempt at some humor to cheer himself up. He hummed the popular tune played on the radios again to quell his anxiety.

He licked his finger to smooth back the pencil-thin mustache, newly grown to add some maturity to his youthfulness.

Once he was satisfied with his doctor's white coat, hanging neatly over his almost-six-foot frame, he ventured out into the corridor again. He tried to keep his left foot from dragging, as this gave him a peculiar gait, with the foot making a slight circular movement as he shuffled along.

Alex continued down the long hallway as a patient pushed a rotary polisher over the floor boards. She was oblivious of Alex walking toward her.

He moved away before she ran him down. "You're doing an excellent job, miss."

She turned her machine off. "This is my special privilege, for good behavior. I'll be discharged tomorrow, Doctor." She smiled meekly. "But I do have some pay for my work to spend at Mr. DaCosta's grocery store."

Alex patted her on the shoulder and walked past. He wasn't going to tell her that he and Vinny had set up the store in Vinny's hospital garage, where the patients could spend their monthly 'wages.'

Alex would recoup his take, and Gabriella's disbursements, less Vinny's small percentage.

Just before the nurses' station, he found one room with a note pinned to the wall. *"Patient recovering from convultions. High tempatur."*

He stopped, took out his pen, and corrected the spelling. He peered in. Lying in bed was a young woman. She was highly sedated, with her blankets pulled down to her knees.

The room was drab: paint had peeled off the walls, and it stank of human wastes. The linoleum floor was torn and grimy.

Alex was appalled to find, standing over the patient, the same male orderly he had met a few minutes ago. He was dark, large, muscular man with his hair tied in a bun on his head. The bun was strung together with an elastic band and partly hung down his back in a ponytail.

He had his back to Alex, but Alex could see him feeling his patient's large breasts with his right hand, which was heavily stained with nicotine from smoking.

"What the Hell are you doing?" Alex shouted as he stormed into the room.

The man, startled, turned. He quickly covered the patient with her bed sheet. He made for the door, nudging Alex aside. "Ah, nothing, nothing. I was just checking her pulse."

"Like Hell you were. You were feeling her up," Alex said. He pointed to the obvious bulge in the man's trousers and tried to hold him back to get his name.

The male orderly, stronger than Alex, pushed him aside and bolted out the door. Alex shouted for his name just as a student nurse entered upon hearing the commotion.

"That orderly, nurse; what's his name?"

"That man, he is from the laundry room, *docteur*. I know his wickedness," the nurse replied with a strong French accent.

Alex looked at her nametag pinned to her starched, white blouse. "Give me the pervert's name, Monique. I want him fired."

The small hospital badge on the white uniform, signified a graduate registered nurse. She pulled out a small black pad, wrote the order down as to what had occurred, and answered, "Immediately. I will inform Nurse LaGlace."

To his astonishment, he realized that it was Monique, Christina's daughter. It was she who used the Casa Loma to perform abortions while the gynecologist was in jail.

He watched as she gently covered the naked woman in bed. "I have heard of you, Monique. You're Christina's daughter. Nice to meet you at last," he said, and offered his hand to her.

"*Oui*, Christina told me how great you are to her," she replied. She smiled and took his hand but held it for longer than the usual handshake.

"Great, really?" he asked. He blushed with the comment, as Christina often used that word about his sexual prowess while in her bed.

"In so many ways," was all she said as she saw his face turn red.

Her genuine warmth, and Madonna-like smile, was a welcome sight for Alex. "You're a registered nurse?" he blurted out, stupidly. He already knew the answer but had to change the awkward conversation.

"*Oui, docteur.* I graduated last year, but wanted also to have the psychiatric experience," Monique replied. She had a twinkle in her eye, clearly pleased to meet her mother's paramour at last.

Alex was quite smitten with this beauty. "Good for you. As a qualified nurse, could you help me with the pregnant women on my chronic wards? I want them all in one area, so they can care for their babies and not be separated anymore," Alex suggested. He gently touched Monique's bare arm below her sleeve.

Monique moved slightly into Alex to let his warm hand sit there a second longer. "*Oui, merci*; I would look forward to working closely with you, *docteur*," was her simple reply.

Alex turned his attention to the woman in the bed, who was stirring. Alex felt her forehead and checked her pulse. "Her pulse is steady, and the fever is down," Alex said as he wrote a note in her chart.

Monique took the chart from Alex, documented her temperature, and nodded to her patient in bed. "She was attacked, late at night. Almost raped but fought well against the phantom."

"Phantom?"

"Some man. A patient he must be. Jumped her from the bushes as she walked from the laundry. She worked late into the night, *docteur*."

"Poor woman. The police told me about that happening here."

"She scratched his neck."

"Good for her. Did she recognize him?"

"*Non*. Said he wore a black hood over his head. Smelled of smoke."

"All the patients smell of smoke, Monique."

"*Non, docteur*; not any male patients out that late at night."

"I agree. I'll make sure an orderly escorts all these women working late at night, hereafter."

"Thank you, *docteur*. I will tell all such women never to walk alone," Monique said as she straightened out the bed.

Alex looked at the nurse as she smoothed the patient's hair back. Monique was petite and fair, with short, curled, blondish hair. She appeared to be just slightly younger than his age.

"That orderly, he won't work here anymore. I'll see to that. Who is he?" he assured Monique, who nodded gratefully.

He thought of asking her about her abortion clinic but left that for an evening visit.

"His name? Vittorio. Vittorio Battista, *docteur*. Be aware, as he is a danger to us all," she almost whispered, as if she thought the walls had ears.

"A danger? To us all, Monique?"

Monique looked around. The patient was sleeping soundly. The room was empty. She pulled Alex away from the door. "He, Vittorio, is the eyes and ears for our director. No one, not even you, cannot fire him; he is protected by our director, his overlord and boss. He informs on us all, and will do so on you, also. Be careful."

"*Merci*, Monique. *Merci*. Thank you. I'll be careful, but where will Cartier send him now? I'll make certain he is not on my wards."

"Ah, yes. Back to the laundry rooms, where he does what he wants with the young girls there. He is passionate with Gabriella, Doctor Cartier's accountant. She, like Vittorio, is from Sardinia the Italian island. Or perhaps Sicily; I am uncertain."

"Yes, I know it. But Doctor Levy told me that Gabriella, I think her name is Gabriella Verdiccheo, is Levy's girlfriend. They almost live together, and Doctor Levy told me they are to be married soon."

"Yes, Doctor, Vittorio is a very jealous man and hates Doctor Levy. They do not live together. He wants Gabriella for himself. You must warn your friend. He is mad, murderously insane with jealousy, and said he would kill Doctor Levy if he finds him with her. He is a pervert."

Alex looked at Monique warmly, and thanked her for her information. "How do you know all this, Monique?" he added, interested in her varied knowledge.

Monique hesitated for a moment and feared to divulge her secret. "The others here, they all speak a different language. I can understand French, Spanish, Italian, and some German. I hear them talk, but I pretend not to."

Alex laughed at the courage and intelligence of this young woman. He told her so. She returned a warm smile as he added, "I'll deal with Vittorio. Director's friend or not."

"*Oui, docteur. Merci.* God have mercy on his wicked soul, *docteur.* He will meet the Devil soon enough," she said firmly, and went to her patient again.

"I won't tolerate any abuse of patients. Please write that up in your daily rounds for your head nurse, Miss LaGlace."

Monique looked up after making another note in her pad. She turned her head to listen to Alex humming a tune. "*Oui, docteur.* That tune you are humming. What is it?"

Embarrassed by the unconscious revelation of his anxiety about Aaron's threat and now her warning about Vittorio, he answered apologetically, "Oh, sorry. Elvis Presley's 'Don't Be Cruel.' Sorry."

"Don't be. I love Elvis. More so his 'Blue Christmas' and 'Jail House Rock,'" she answered cheerfully. "They are my favorites."

Alex noticed she had beautiful hands and nimble fingers, like Christina's. He suddenly had a brilliant idea and a way to see more of this beauty. "As a registered nurse, you and I will make ward rounds every morning, to treat those patients with medical illnesses on my wards."

Monique gave a slight curtsy, and ever so gently took Alex's hand. She moved him away from the bed; her patient had opened her eyes and asked for water, so Monique had to attend to her.

Alex let the warm touch linger there as he left. He made a mental note to see Monique for an evening date, quite soon. Perhaps he could stop the weekly visits to Christina, he thought, now that he could see more of Monique.

And get off the acid blotters that he had become reliant on.

Once Monique attended to her patient, she returned to walk with him to the nurse's station. At first, she walked quickly, since there was work to be done. Alex tried to keep up with her but faltered; he had tied his boot on too loosely, and it held him back.

Monique hesitated and stopped. "Oh, sorry, Doctor. Your foot must be hurtful this morning."

Alex, embarrassed, turned away slightly. "No, not hurtful physically. It's been a kind of yoke for me, a burden. A cruel, inhumane bondage. Not to be able to keep up with you," he stammered.

Monique didn't waver for a minute, and ever-so-quickly took him by the arm. "Doctor Gage, you must never be uncomfortable or embarrassed with your birth ailment. You must have been very courageous to achieve what you have. And to do what you have accomplished here so far."

She wanted to say more but feared he might think she was too brazen or too forward.

Alex was so overwhelmed by such compassion that he turned to hide his eyes as they teared up. He looked straight ahead, and all he could say was, "Thank you, Monique," as they slowly walked away down the long corridor together.

⁕

CHAPTER 34

Riel's Sister, Beatrice

"Love one another with brotherly affection."
Romans 12:10

OVER the next few days, Alex was always glad to see Monique on East Three, one of his chronic women's wards. It also now housed his six pregnant patients.

"Karen became pregnant by her husband. A quiet visit in the bushes on the grounds last spring," Alex told Monique as they made rounds.

"I heard that Karen's husband was very pleased."

"It is their first child. The other two women were from male patients in the laundry room. The other two from the kitchen hospital staff, maybe."

Monique knew about Charmaine as they came to her bed. "By Jesus himself, as Charmaine cheerfully whispered to me yesterday."

On the insistence of Alex, they were now all bedded off in a corner of the ward and under Monique's supervision. The other two hundred long-term psychotic women were scattered about in a labyrinth of over-crowded beds in the rest of that ward.

"Martha has severe postpartum depression, and I don't want her to kill her baby. She can nurse the little girl but put her on round-the-clock supervision," Alex explained to Monique late that day.

Monique made the rounds with Alex and made a note of the order. "She is better with the new antidepressants you put her on. She now cares well for her newborn, *docteur*."

He reviewed Martha's meds in her chart and left after he arranged a weekend date with Monique. She had inherited the long legs and firm breasts that he liked, just like Christina's.

Alex had finished his ward rounds but talked to Fournier, the head nurse. He wanted to reduce the number of beds on her ward. "After we discharge patients who are improved and prescribed the new medications," he explained as he saw Riel walk in.

Riel pushed a cart through the door with a load of fresh laundry. Riel saw Alex leaving, smiled, and gave a halfhearted salute. "Your shipment is in. In with your partner," he said to Alex quietly. He left to sort out the laundry onto shelves in one corner of the ward.

Alex wasn't going to thank Riel at this time for the machine-rolled cigarettes that he received through Riel's reserve. That reserve straddled the Québec/American border, and the superior-quality cigarettes were made in the US.

Thus, it was easy to smuggle cigarettes into Canada. He sold them at Vinny's shop, and it nicely added further to their income.

Patients were happy to spend their few paltry dollars in Alex's 'canteen.' Vinny would be there to sell them candies, chocolates, women's toiletries, men's grooming aides, and some groceries. The bestselling products were the cigarettes provided by Riel.

"Mister Riel has a thriving business; he used to sell his cigarettes to the teenagers in our country at half the government store price," Vinny once told Alex.

"Mr. Riel, if you can supply Mr. DaCosta the same quality of fine-rolled cigarettes, he will buy them from you," Alex offered last month when he had transferred Riel from the prison ward to the open wards.

Riel was only too pleased to do business with Vinny and Alex. His long-distance transportation costs across the country, accomplished using semi-trailers, would be much less, and his profits much better.

Everyone was happy with the financial arrangements. Alex was happy to be able to send some of those profits to his mother. She used the money to buy winter clothes for the school children and paid for a warm, nourishing breakfast when they came to her school. It had been Monique's idea, when Alex once confided in her.

As Monique attended to her patients later that same evening, Cartier came to the ward. Cartier had transferred Beatrice, Riel's aboriginal sister, to this chronic ward under the head nurse, Fournier's, care.

All the lights were dimmed, and patients had returned from their dinner in the basement kitchens. Monique saw that some patients were already in bed, while others snored loudly in their chairs where they sat.

Doctor Gage did well to insist that the kitchens provide a better-balanced diet, with more meat and vegetables, Monique thought. Some of the patients had already gained weight and were sleeping soundly.

However, she knew that Cartier was not pleased with the added expense and had told Doctor Gage just that.

Cartier abruptly called to Monique. "Bring me Beatrice's chart, nurse," he shouted as he stood and watched Beatrice, the obese retard, in the corner.

Riel was still busy sorting out bed sheets and towels. He then picked up the dirty laundry from corners in the room.

When Riel heard the shout, he came out of the corner with his loaded basket. He saw Cartier as he leered at his dull, moronic, mentally ill sister.

Monique brought the chart for Cartier. Suddenly, she and Cartier were startled as Riel moved quickly and swung his laundry basket into Cartier where he stood near the nurse's office.

Riel stood there face-to-face with Cartier, defiant, glowering, and threatening. "Riel has warned you. You stay away from my sister; she is ill in head and body," Riel snarled.

Monique stood her ground but was fearful of the menacing look on Riel's face.

At first Cartier took a step back, but then he became incensed. "What are you doing here, red man?" he asked as he violently kicked the basket aside and came at Riel.

Monique quickly stepped in between the two combatants. "He works in the laundry room now, *Docteur* Cartier. He also assists in cleaning here," Monique said.

She tried to edge Riel away before a fight started. Several patients had become agitated with the commotion and moved away.

"Who gave him that privilege?" Cartier yelled again. Spittle flowed from the side of his mouth.

"Doctor Gage did so. He asked *monsieur* Riel to be there, in the laundry. To observe any abuse and to escort the nurses back to their residence after dark. For safety," Monique answered without hesitation.

Cartier abruptly grabbed the chart out of Monique's hand and swore. "That redskin monster is not safe to be out on the grounds." Cartier pointed at Riel.

Riel heard that, turned, and bristled in anger. He took a step toward Cartier.

Nurse Fournier ran into the office, ready to call security. One patient started to cry. Others cowered against the wall as they recoiled from the angry shouts; they could see a fight brewing.

Cartier stepped behind the laundry basket for protection.

It was Monique who took charge again. "*Monsieur* Riel, let me take you to visit your dear sister. She waits for you over there," Monique said.

She took the man by the arm and pulled him into the corner.

Riel, at first surprised, resisted the girl half his size. He hesitated but agreed.

"*Madame* Fournier will bring you both a cup of tea," Monique added.

She escorted him away and sat Riel down by his sister. She motioned to Fournier to get tea, who was only too glad to do something useful.

Monique left brother and sister to sit together and talk. Fournier brought two chipped mugs of warm tea as they sat there in the near-darkness, with Riel holding his sister's hand.

Monique continued to dispense pills to every patient as she watched the couple out of the corner of her eye. She could see that Riel was stroking his sister's thinning hair and talked softly and soothingly to her.

Cartier stomped into his office, clearly still furious, with Beatrice's chart in hand.

Fournier, now in a sweat from all the banter and several patients sobbing and babbling incoherently, tried to busy herself. She boiled more water and made more tea as she gathered cookies from an old coffee tin for Cartier.

After some time, Monique encouraged Riel to leave. "It is time for your dear sister's nighttime sedation, *monsieur* Riel."

Riel stood, bent down, and smoothed the sparse hair on his sister's head, and then kissed her on the forehead.

Beatrice took the small, paper cup from Monique, with three different-colored pills, and quickly swallowed them.

After that, Riel went to Monique and put his arm on her shoulder. "Riel thanks you, kind nurse. My sister, she has the Devil in her head. Please, keep her from harm's way and that man," Riel whispered.

He nodded toward the office and then pointed at his sister as tears welled up in his eyes.

Monique said she would, and gently eased him and his basket to the door. He waited for her to let him out, since the doors were locked for the night.

Monique had finished her chores and saw that Cartier's office door was open.

Cartier, meanwhile, returned to what he really came for.

CHAPTER 35

A Most Profane Act

CARTIER had read Beatrice's history when she was admitted some months ago. He read about her sexual delusions—that is, her false beliefs. She was convinced that the Devil had entered her body through her vagina and anus.

As he read this, he could sense the power surging in his loins.

He reveled in the fact that her sexual fantasies were rife with gross, sadistic bestiality. Her daydreams and night terrors of whipping fantasies especially excited him.

He smoked his pipe, and drank his tea brought to him by the head nurse, the ever-so-obliging Fournier.

The nurse, Monique, walked past his slightly-ajar office door. She had busied herself with arranging medication for the morning staff, but from his office he could tell she watched Beatrice get ready for bed.

Fournier, also in her office, turned the copper kettle off, and passed the pot of tea and cookies to Monique, gesturing for her to bring them to Cartier's office.

Monique did so with the tray. She politely excused herself as she knocked on the door, briefly waited, and walked into his office.

Cartier said nothing and just pointed to his desk for her to set the tray down. He then sat back and sipped his tea. As he looked up at

Monique he wiped a tea stain off his desk, scowled, and closed the chart.

Cartier rolled his chair away from his desk and riffled through the tattered chart again. Monique said nothing as she took the empty tray and prepared to leave.

Cartier sat back but was startled as Fournier rushed in. She pushed Monique aside and muscled her out the door. She carried in a plate of ginger snap cookies.

Cartier hated Fournier, a heavy-set woman with a mustache, which she had neglected to shave that day. He looked at her and saw her to be simple like her patients.

She wore a page-boy haircut, with a stained uniform lacking her nurse's cap that night.

"Knock first, next time. I may be busy," he growled, and pushed the plate away.

Fournier wasn't fearful of the director. "Riel's sister is diagnosed as a Mongolian idiot. All the better for us," she said with a sadistic smile, and pointed to the chart in Cartier's hand.

She knew why he was there. He also knew why she had asked him to transfer her to this ward. And what she did with the retarded young girls.

Monique stopped outside the door, listening, when she heard Cartier's question.

"Have you taught her how to lick yet, Annette?"

Monique heard the words, "*Non*, you always come when I'm on duty, and she is only for you, my director," Annette Fournier said mockingly.

Monique came closer to the door. It remained ajar.

"The late shift is what you prefer. I saw to it. You can do whatever you please with your harem of female idiots at such a time, Annette."

"*Oui*, director."

Cartier bristled. "You will call me 'Doctor,'" he shouted. His hand trembled, and the tea spilled again onto his desk.

Fournier didn't flinch. "Having her here was part of your pleasure. In defying her brother Riel, that big Indian," she added.

Cartier backed off. "You know I turn a blind eye to you and those younger cretins that are here just for you," he said.

"I gladly return the favor by having a plump one for my director, ah, I mean, doctor."

Cartier finished his tea and pushed his chair aside. With the squeal of the chair on the floor boards, Monique scurried away.

Cartier walked out with Fournier. Monique busied herself with cleaning and restocking the medication trays. She watched out of the corner of her eye.

Fournier escorted Cartier through the ward. Words were not spoken; not even a glance between them. Both came close to the bed that they were after.

Beatrice was sitting alone on her bed, almost catatonic, slowly rocking back and forth. Saliva dribbled down her chin as she gradually became sedated from the bedtime medication.

Cartier inhaled deeply as he came close to Beatrice. Monique heard Fournier whisper, "A younger woman's scent is nice to inhale, is it not, Doctor?"

Doctor Cartier didn't respond.

"You remember our *Docteur* Cartier, Beatrice?" Fournier asked the simple girl.

Cartier pushed Fournier aside. He sat beside Beatrice and put his arm around her.

Monique, as she calmed another patient close by, saw Beatrice wince and try to pull away. Cartier tightened his arm around his victim.

Fournier smiled with the aggressive act. Beatrice was hunched over and isolated: passive, dull-looking, and mumbling to herself. She started to play with a small Raggedy Ann doll, stroking its thinning, red hair and kissing it from time to time.

"She sits there, like all the other fat farm cows." Fournier said in halting English. Monique passed by and took an old woman in the next bed to the toilets.

Cartier nodded in agreement. He left Beatrice playing with her doll. He talked to a few patients, giving the semblance of a ward round. Monique returned and remained busy as she applied antibiotic ointment to a woman's ulcerated leg. It reeked of decaying flesh after she had returned from a weekend with her family.

The room was austere, filled with wooden cots and metal springs, which creaked under the weight of obese women, now snoring loudly. A few miserable souls made their way to three cracked toilet bowls. They were stained with fecal material and menstrual blood, standing open against the wall with only a tattered curtain separating each stall.

Privacy was nonexistent, but Monique knew that she would get her Alex to make changes soon.

Cartier shouldered an ancient hag aside as she pled for her discharge. He returned to Beatrice. He spoke to her kindly, took her by the hand, and pulled her up.

Beatrice cowered like a cornered animal. She pulled her doll tightly to her chest. Cartier stopped and looked around to see where Fournier had gone and saw Monique.

She was busy fixing a bed cover across from his office and gently soothing a patient's anxiety about her electric shock treatment in the morning.

Fournier returned after settling another patient into her bed after her toilet. "That one, she is from the east. She is a simple French girl, my director. She knows nothing and very poor in English." Fournier smirked and pointed a dirty, gnarled finger at Monique.

Cartier nodded. He was pleased to see that she was a student nurse in psychiatry, with a different uniform, and obviously from another hospital.

Cartier and Monique looked at each other. Monique gave a slight curtsy; Cartier turned away and walked into his office as Fournier followed.

"My office at night: don't you use it for your nighttime pleasures. Lock the door," Cartier said to Fournier in English.

Last week, he had walked in on her as she sat in his chair.

At that time her fat, naked thighs were spread apart, devoid of underwear, which she held in her hand. A young, dimwitted girl was on her knees in front of her. Her face was deep in Fournier's crotch.

It was late evening. Fournier put her finger to her lips as the girl continued. "Yes, Doctor, shush, I am near to it," Fournier whispered in ecstasy, just at that critical time.

Cartier closed the door then and waited patiently. The girl wiped her face and pocketed a few precious coins provided to her by Fournier.

Fournier readjusted her skirts and pulled up her underwear as Cartier waited.

At that time, Cartier had then walked her out of his office once Fournier was finished.

"And those amphetamine tablets. Stop taking them from my desk drawer," Cartier now added to her sternly. But he was secretly pleased. She was now addicted to the speed medication.

Fournier was much more compliant now, dependent on him for the tablets that give her a rush. In turn, for the favor, she brought Beatrice to him whenever he wished.

"They, those tablets are free for you from the drug reps, Doctor," Fournier reminded the director.

On this occasion, with Monique in the ward, Cartier said nothing as he moved Beatrice over to his desk and opened his drawer to see the bottle of pills. He knew Fournier replaced the small, white speed tablets with aspirin.

He allowed this to happen. He often rewarded her with more bottles of Dexedrine, the brand of amphetamines the drug reps provided.

This evening, Fournier waited with Beatrice placidly standing near her. Cartier passed such a bottle to her, plus a small, two-dollar Canadian bill.

Beatrice just stood there and talked to the Devil in her soul, dutifully waiting in his office.

Fournier took the bottle and the bill. She was in such a hurry that she forgot to close the door in her rush to consume one of her happy pills.

As Fournier left, Beatrice stood meekly in the middle of the room. She held her pathetic doll and scanned the ceiling. She murmured to herself and quietly laughed to some inner joke that only she knew.

She easily acquiesced as Cartier, his back to the door, brought out his stethoscope. He lowered her cotton housecoat and untied her hospital gown.

Beatrice stood there, rigid, with one hand at her side; the other was clamped to her little doll companion. She looked straight ahead. Earlier that night, Monique had tied back her sparse, graying hair in a tight bun. She was devoid of makeup, which gave her a wretched, forlorn appearance.

Outside the office, Cartier heard Monique complete her rounds of medication; the tray on wheels squeaked as she pushed it past his door.

Cartier placed the cool silver cup of his stethoscope to the dark, warm, aboriginal skin of Beatrice's breasts. Beatrice shivered and gave an audible sigh.

"Be calm; this is to make you well, my dear woman," Cartier whispered in her ear as he listened to the rapid breathing.

Her pendulous breasts heaved with the stimulation and caress of Cartier's hands. Beatrice wheezed, "My devil is here with me, Doctor."

Cartier moved the cold cup over her naked breasts and mocked her. "You have black hairs covering your nipples. Did the Devil do that? Bad, bad, bad girl that you are."

"*Oui, docteur,*" Beatrice simply agreed.

Cartier felt the massive breasts. He was pleased to see that the nipples reacted. Sweat rolled from her armpits and fell on Cartier's hands. He continued to massage her excited, beating chest.

Beatrice stood there and bit her lip. She grasped her ragged doll firmly and started to hum to herself again. It was in her native tongue: a tune her mother sang to her in childhood, at bedtime.

Cartier spat into her ear, "Hold your gown high around your waist, good woman."

Beatrice did as she was told. He palpated her abdomen with one hand and then felt her buttocks with the other.

She stood there, passive and obedient.

"This is just a routine examination, Beatrice; stand still and be quiet like a good girl," Cartier said in a hoarse voice. She could hear his breathing becoming rapid as his hand passed further down her thighs.

When he fingered her genitals, it was only then that she flinched.

Monique was about to ask Cartier if he needed assistance with Beatrice. She wanted to interrupt what she was witnessing in his office, to save her patient.

She moved her tray closer and peered in the door, half open, and saw Beatrice standing naked from the waist up. She hesitated, but decided to simply watch, and make a mental note of what she observed. *She would speak to her Alex of this and perhaps write to the College of Physicians of such abuse*, she thought.

Cartier turned the desk light down to a soft glow. Beatrice crouched over his desk with him behind her.

"Now, Beatrice dear," Cartier said speaking slowly in French to her. "Those demons: I'm going to cleanse you of them. But you must keep this kindly treatment to yourself. I am the doctor in charge here, and I will rid you of the Devil with my belt."

"*Oui, merci beaucoup.*" She nodded gratefully.

He pulled her gown up over her head as she stood. He made her bend over his desk even more and raised her body to expose her buttocks. Then he snatched her doll away from her and threw it on the floor.

He took off his leather belt and whipped her a few times. She didn't stir. He waited. She didn't complain. He repeated the whipping. She said nothing.

He lowered his pants.

She stood there slightly bent over, murmuring softly as his naked body met her backside. He pressed his naked loins against her buttocks and entered her thighs.

To his surprise, she turned her head and pleasantly whispered, "Ah, *docteur,* your Beatrice is feeling better, she is."

Beatrice remained bent over his office desk. He turned her head away, so she couldn't see him. The room was darker: the lights were dim. He could hear the rubbing of him between her thighs. He was pushing hard.

When he was finished, he wiped himself with her gown. He was rough as he pulled her head back by her hair. "Promise again not to tell anyone of this new treatment," he insisted.

"*Oui, merci, docteur.*"

Cartier slapped her hard across the head. "You're a stupid woman, so don't forget. It's just between you and your doctor."

"*Merci beaucoup, docteur,*" Beatrice said again as she massaged her head from the slap. She bent down and lovingly picked up her doll from the floor.

Cartier helped her dress and tied her gown at the back as he led her out.

Monique was near the nurse's front office with her head down, cleaning her tray.

All the other women were already in their cots. The lights from the nurse's office cast a shadow, as the heavy snores moved across the crowded ward.

As Dr. Cartier left the ward, he waved to Fournier. He smiled to see her lead a stout, young girl into the laundry room. There she would use one of Cartier's two dollar bills to pay for services soon to be rendered.

Monique saw Fournier turn and give a wide grin as her director left. Cartier looked about before he closed the door. He didn't see Monique where she watched from the bed she was making, for one of her patients, who had finally returned from the toilet.

Monique had to make notes on each patient as to their behaviors that night in every chart in her office.

This now included detailed notes on Cartier's visit with Beatrice, but for her eyes only, and only in her private journal.

For now.

✳

CHAPTER 36

A Sad, Pathetic Story

MONIQUE had a final duty to perform before her night shift was over that night. She was instructed to administer an intramuscular injection of ferrous sulphate to some of her patients. That included Beatrice.

Three patients were chronically anemic from iron deficiency. It was Dr. Gage's orders, and she was more than pleased to assist the good doctor.

Monique completed her notes in each chart and then prepared a small tray. It had sterile gauze, needles, alcohol swabs, and three vials of the red liquid that contained the iron preparation.

She walked to one patient and shook her gently, since she was still awake. "This is an iron supplement. It will cure you of your low hemoglobin, the result of years of excessive menstrual bleeding, Ophelia," she told the young woman in French.

She did the same with another. Beatrice was one of those three women with a very low blood hemoglobin count. It was due to a poor diet when living on the reserve.

Monique went to Beatrice and sat on her bed. She had just returned from the examination with Dr. Cartier but was still awake. This was unusual for Beatrice, as she should be drowsy after the nighttime sedation.

Beatrice seemed more uneasy, anxious, and unsettled, but said nothing. She was lying on her back with the blanket pulled up to her chin, and she clutched her raggedy doll with dirty hair made of red yarn to her breast.

Monique filled the syringe with the red liquid and then tapped it to release the bubble of air. She smiled knowingly as Beatrice shut her eyes tight. She often avoided the sight of the large needle.

Monique gently asked Beatrice to roll over. She nudged the girl's arm aside as she tried to protect her large buttocks from the impending attack.

Monique shone her flashlight at Beatrice and spoke softly, quietly in French. "Do not be afraid, *ma chère*. It is time for your injection again. This will give you some nice, rosy color to your lovely cheeks. It will cure your Raggedy Ann doll, also, and give some color to her hair," she said to her patient.

Monique brushed her patient's hair back and put the doll on the pillow, next to her head.

Beatrice reluctantly obeyed and turned over onto her side as she clutched her doll. The nurse pulled up the blanket and raised her patient's gown to expose her rump.

Monique heard the rapid succession of tiny pops emitting from the rectum. She turned her face until the putrid stench passed by. Her patient said something apologetic but passed more wind again.

Monique fanned the stench away with both hands, waited patiently, and then proceeded. She pinched the buttock muscle to insert the sharp needle.

As the light from her flashlight shone over her patient's backside, she was horrified to see the red marks outlined on her flesh.

"Beatrice, *ma chère*," she gasped. Monique saw the raised red welts across her buttocks. She turned her more to expose her rump.

"Who did this to you?" Monique asked knowingly. She had been uncertain of what little she had observed in the darkened room of Dr. Cartier's examination, but now she knew. Still, she wanted a verbal answer from her patient.

Beatrice buried her face in her hands and remained silent. She squirmed and kissed her doll's head on the pillow.

Monique demanded an answer. She used the gown to clean away whitish tracks. These she recognized as spent semen, the ejaculate still between her patient's thighs.

Her patient's buttocks went into a spasmodic contraction as the fleshy cheeks stiffened. Her back muscles tightened with the abrupt question.

In a hushed tone, Beatrice quietly replied, "Ah, *oui, mademoiselle, mon docteur. Le bon docteur.*"

"The good doctor, Beatrice? You mean our Doctor Cartier? In his office nearby, over there?" she asked, pointing to Cartier's office door.

"*Oui, oui,*" was the timid reply.

Monique looked about. Cartier was gone. Fournier was still preoccupied in the laundry room. She looked at her watch and took out her journal and ball point pen.

She marked down the time, the place, and the conversation she'd had with her Beatrice.

Riel's cautionary words suddenly filled the air around Monique, "*Keep her safe, and keep her from harm's way, please.*"

"Beatrice, can you write your name, *ma chère?*"

"*Ah, oui*" was the simple but proud response.

Monique had her sign the notes and witnessed the signature. She then gave her the injection. She cleaned Beatrice's buttocks of sperm with a towel from her tray, covered her patient, and tucked the sheets in around her neck.

She pushed the doll under the bedclothes next to Beatrice, who quickly grasped at the doll and immediately started to snore.

Monique sat on the bed and looked at her written words and Beatrice's signature, duly witnessed.

She then looked up through the window to the starlit sky. She prayed to her god and asked for guidance.

The Ice Queen

IT was a few days later that Alex was back at the hospital at eight in the morning. He found Monique pensive and preoccupied that day.

They had spent the night before in his car, enjoying each other's bodies as they parked near the river. He was grateful to Monique that he no longer had to visit Christina to relieve him of his obsessive anger and frustrations.

She, in turn, was grateful to him for the pleasures he provided with his gentle kisses and his wandering fingers. She reminded him that she would remain virginal until marriage.

They went to an outdoor movie. It was a cool night, with bright stars in the distance. But they had no trouble keeping each other warm under a blanket.

Alex questioned her about being contemplative and absorbed that morning on the ward. She gave him some lame excuse about her concerns as to her mother's ongoing despair.

Alex was still hesitant. "Is it about me, Monique? About us and what we did at the drive-in?" he asked anxiously when they had a quiet moment, waiting to meet LaGlace.

"*Non, mon ami.* Not at all. It was very nice," she answered with a blush and then went about her duties.

There was work to do, and Alex finally turned his attention to the large common room at the end of the hallway. Many patients were vacantly staring at the small, scratchy, Electrohome television set. It had poor reception with its bent-wire antennas and was suspended from the ceiling in one corner.

They all sat idly, twirled their hair, fiddled with a skirt, or picked scabs off their arms and faces.

Today, the television featured the *Red Skelton Show* in grainy black-and-white. No one was laughing at the comic. He paraded about in his clown's uniform with a large, scooped out orange for a bulbous nose.

They were all heavily sedated, or still recovering from electroshock therapies, and in a state of confusion. Their memory disorder was the result of that morning's treatments.

Alex went to the nurse's office. He knew that the women had to be stimulated with activity and mobilized into some useful action. He would make the changes soon; as soon as the carpenters came to make the toilets private.

Once in the office, he pulled out Juanita's chart from the wooden file box and read her admitting doctor's notes. Juanita had been readmitted last month, after setting fire to her neighbor's house and roasting the neighbor's cat in her own oven.

"God ordered me to cleanse the neighborhood. The cat signaled that the world would end, and the Russians were coming," she was quoted in her chart.

The head nurse, LaGlace, was behind her desk. Alex disliked LaGlace, even before he learned that 'glace' in French meant 'ice.'

LaGlace was not pleased with Alex since he started making rapid changes to all the wards.

She was in her late fifties and had that frigid bitterness about her. Her pursed lips lacked color, her teeth were clenched tight, with several missing, and she wore a constant, rigid scowl on her face.

Alex looked at her that morning, sitting behind her desk. Her large, muscular body was sheathed in a heavily-starched, white uniform. Over her gray hair, severely pulled back in a taut bun, was a small, white, nurse's cap.

The Ice Queen remained seated behind her desk, cold and dispassionate, which showed her obvious disrespect for Alex as he entered. Nurses on all the wards always stood whenever a doctor entered a room. They often brought the doctor a cup of tea and a cookie.

Not LaGlace.

"Is Juanita getting some exercise in the padded room?" Alex asked LaGlace.

LaGlace didn't look at Alex. "Actually, no, and it is Doctor Cartier's orders that she remain there. On her recent discharge, she became pregnant again. She had an abortion by some quack. That made her psychotic again, Doctor."

"Juanita suffers from chronic schizophrenia. Quacks and other strange ducks don't make people psychotic, Miss LaGlace," he answered so the other nurses in the room could hear and learn something.

LaGlace grumbled something under her breath and in anger thumped her lead pencil on the desk for effect.

Alex disregarded the bang of the pencil, which lost its lead point with the force of the blow. Alex loved a good argument but decided to drop the subject with the 'Ice Queen;' he needed her agreement if he was going to make changes on her ward.

Any minor changes he had already ordered were too slow for Alex. At least LaGlace had agreed to give the paltry coins to those who worked, which Alex offered as a reward.

Alex looked at Monique as she entered the room. "What is Juanita yelling about now?" Alex asked. He pointed down the hall to the padded room.

Before Monique could answer, Alex heard the grumble from

LaGlace. "She's shouting that Jesus had intercourse with her last night. Poor woman has decompensated with delusional projection, you hear."

"Christ, not again," Alex said under his breath. He recalled again Katarina's remarks about her own J.C., the director, entering Juanita's orifices, and not the sacred Jesus.

Alex changed the subject and pointed to the common room full of women who were highly sedated. "We need to get all those patients active on a daily basis, Miss LaGlace. I also want some female nurses, on your orders, in the men's prison ward. They will have a more calming effect on those poor men."

LaGlace pushed her chair back and leaned forward. "Really? I can't believe what I just heard. You already ordered a daily walk for my patients. Also, some social worker is to come to my ward to mobilize them. My nurses have better things to do," she shouted at Alex, emphasizing that it was her ward.

Alex didn't blink. "We will start tomorrow. I'll pull two aides off the open ward in the other building to help your nurses, and also get an occupational worker here to activate the patients."

LaGlace slammed her fist down on the order book on her desk. "I heard you opened those doors when I was away. Indeed, most of them will elope."

Alex held his own. "We'll also start group therapy, and a physical exercise program. Let's get those patients walking, and running, and talking to each other about their problems."

"What? What is that?"

"They can help each other. This will take some of the pressure off the nursing staff," Alex said quietly, but firmly.

The three student nurses now in the room dropped what they were doing and stared at Alex. No one ever told the Ice Queen what to do.

Alex raised his voice for others to hear. "There are patients here who have open privileges. I'm going to transfer them to the open ward." Alex said, looking LaGlace in the eye.

LaGlace pushed her chair back. She leaned over her desk and stared angrily at Alex. "Doctor Cartier must be told, and surely he won't approve," she scolded.

One nurse closed the chart she was completing and walked out, fearing a crisis. Alex put his chart back in the box, reared up, and put his hands on LaGlace's desk.

"I did, and he does. End of discussion. Now, let's go see Juanita," Alex said, ending that argument.

LaGlace wasn't ready to end it. "Truly, my patients are at risk coming back from the laundry, where they work at night."

"At risk from what?"

"One of your perverts, actually. That big Indian, I'm sure. Jumps out and rapes my patients. Murdered one."

"Can't be him. I heard it was a different man, with a black hood over his head. I now have Riel escorting the women together, with the help of other men who have privileges. They are to walk in groups from now on."

LaGlace snorted, put her reading glasses on, adjusted her cap, and snatched Juanita's clinical chart from the box.

A deafening silence filled the room and lasted a few seconds. LaGlace resorted to what she did best.

She continued her lecture, raising her voice. "You can read my notes later, Doctor. This Juanita has imagined wish fulfillments due to unsatisfied impulses of hate and hostility, producing a splitting of the ego."

Alex was unimpressed with such psychobabble, which he had already heard from psychoanalytic therapists in Boston last year. He let it go.

He knew that LaGlace picked up such analytic rot from old text books in the hospital library, which were outdated from the last century.

A graduate nurse locked the medicine cabinet after dispensing pills and looked at Alex. "Juanita told me she's a clairvoyant. Foretells the future, she does. She said your president, ah … Kennedy, I think … will be shot quite soon, she said."

"Shot? Assassinated?" Monique asked fearfully, now looking at Alex for a remark.

The Ice Queen got in another parting shot. "Yes, indeed; like that other Yankee of yours, Lincoln."

"President Kennedy won't be shot. He's the first Catholic in the White house and will serve two terms; I'm sure of it," Alex said as he lit his pipe. He was pleased to have eye contact with Monique.

LaGlace reminded Alex, "You have to examine Juanita physically, actually. She will have her lobotomy soon, so make sure she's free of pneumonia. I don't want any complications for Doctor Cartier, or any delay for Doctor Walters, the surgeon, do you hear?"

"I hear," Alex replied. He and Monique followed LaGlace as she stormed out the office and down the hall to see Juanita.

LaGlace quickly marched down the hallway, ahead of Alex and Monique. She pushed aside one, and then another patient asking for medication changes, discharge, or day passes.

"Doctor Cartier increased her anti-psychotics last night. Up to three hundred mgms of chlorpromazine, daily," she said, without looking back at Alex.

"That's a chemical lobotomy in itself. At least it's reversible, unlike a surgical lobotomy," Alex said out loud for LaGlace to hear.

"Yes, Doctor, but her religious, persecutory delusions were set in her youth, causing the splitting of the ego."

"I doubt it, Miss LaGlace."

"You heard me?" she added.

"I do, I do. Perhaps a hearing aid would help you, Miss LaGlace," Alex offered seriously and in a caring manner.

LaGlace smirked as she found the right key for the door of the padded cell.

Alex turned and whispered to Monique, "I wonder why she's such a cold character?"

"I suspect she wasn't breastfed long enough, if at all," Monique answered with a twinkle in her eye.

With all three standing at Juanita's door, LaGlace turned her attention to the small peephole in the door.

"Pardon? Speak up, Doctor," LaGlace said, turning abruptly and causing Alex to step back into Monique.

"Nothing, just talking," Alex replied. His right elbow grazed Monique's right breast—the one he loved to caress at the drive-in. He apologized, but Monique only smiled and pressed his hand with hers.

As they approached the padded cell, Monique whispered in Alex's ear, "Be careful with Juanita, as she is a danger to us all. She very much hates our head nurse, here. Saves broken pieces of cups and said she wants to kill her."

Alex recalled Katarina's words about Juanita wanting to kill LaGlace.

LaGlace unlocked the padded cell, but suddenly a fight broke out down the hall. LaGlace turned to see one woman with her hands around another woman's throat.

"She is turning blue, Louise. Let her go," LaGlace shouted, and ran after the screaming banshee.

Alex was glad to see the last of the Ice Queen, so that he and Monique had a moment alone.

"Is there a problem between us, Monique?"

"*Non.* We will talk this weekend, my sweet. Don't worry, as it is a concern I have and will tell you then. Not about us," she said. She pressed his hand again and walked away to help LaGlace.

Alex turned to face Juanita's padded cell. It had a wooden door reinforced with long, steel plates. *Even a raving psychotic couldn't budge it,* Alex thought as his hand touched the cold plates.

There was a small hole carved into the rough door, which allowed a caregiver to look in before opening the door. Just in case the patient was violent.

"This slit in the door allows the only breath of fresh air to enter the room," Alex said sadly.

Both nurses returned from the melee down the hall.

CHAPTER 38

The Attack on the Ice Queen

ALEX saw Juanita through the tiny peephole, pacing back and forth. She was partly naked, and held a ragged, gray blanket over her shoulders to cover her wasted breasts. A torn pillow sat in the corner of the room.

Her metal bed was partly covered by a thin, bare mattress. It was full of holes, which allowed the metal springs to spike through.

Alex would rid the hospital of padded cells soon.

LaGlace unlocked the door. Alex stepped back to let her walk in first. Monique followed.

Alex looked at the plaster peeling on the one wall and the padding torn off the others by some raving lunatic. He shuddered that a human being would be imprisoned in such a primitive cell.

"This dampness chills the very marrow of my bones," he said as he buttoned his white coat and turned up the collar.

"This room faces west, toward the river, so the sun barely filters in," Monique added. She looked up at the small, barred window. Multiple cobwebs, laden with dead flies, hung just below the window and the ten-foot-high ceiling.

"The dry plaster is just dangling from the ceiling, with a frayed wire holding a naked light bulb," Alex said pointing up.

"A fire, waiting to happen," Monique added, shaking her head.

LaGlace partly deaf, shouted out, "What about it? Surely this is not one of your fancy hotels in Miami, Doctor, actually? Do you hear me?"

Alex smiled, unfazed. "I've never been in one of those fancy hotels, Miss LaGlace. But we will get rid of padded cells like we got rid of the straightjackets."

LaGlace snorted loudly but said nothing. Alex marveled that LaGlace could talk with clenched teeth, her lips puckered and hardly moving. It was just like the ventriloquist he saw on the Merv Griffin TV show last year.

"Not a hotel, Doctor. This is a hospital. You hear?"

"Nor should it be a hotel, but we must make it warmer and cleaner. Let's get some carpenters and painters. Get her a good bed and some fresh air in here, Miss LaGlace."

LaGlace ignored the order and shouted at her patient. "You will be punished for tearing the pads off two of the walls, Juanita," LaGlace threatened. She pointed to the deep scars in the thick pads screwed to the walls.

Alex pulled out his notebook and made an entry to talk to Cartier about the squalid conditions. He looked at his patient, who was now sitting up in her bed.

Juanita was a petite, South American woman who had probably been quite attractive before being ravished by schizophrenia. She still had clear olive skin with unkempt, straggly, thinning, gray hairs and large, black eyes.

There was a frightened look on her face. She sat up, looking far off somewhere into the distance, beyond the confines of her cell.

"This room smells of urine," Monique said as she pinched her nose from the stench of acidic vomitus and urinary stains. They were deeply embedded in the heavy mats, now scattered about the floor and nailed to the door.

"My, my, a bit squeamish, are we?" LaGlace said sarcastically.

"We have to clean this place up, Miss LaGlace. Very unhygienic."

"Surely, we didn't have smelly hospitals like this in your America, Doctor?" she quickly added.

"Well, some were, but we cleaned them up in the past few years," Alex replied.

Juanita laughed. The Ice Queen scowled. Monique looked uncomfortable.

Alex approached Juanita, wanting to talk with her and assess her psychosis better, but remained slightly apart from her bed.

Juanita continued to cackle, possibly at the previous remark by Alex. Alex thought it was some inner voice. Perhaps it gave her instructions. She dropped her hand searching for something under her bed.

Alex recalled what Aaron said about Juanita. She would hide a pot under her bed. Always let the nurse go in first, he cautioned Alex, since she splatters everyone with her urine.

He saw it coming, and he quickly stepped back. Juanita found the metal pot full of last night's urine, spittle, nose drippings, and feces. She threw the contents at the three visitors.

"Watch out," Alex yelled. He and Monique were quicker on their feet than LaGlace; they both sidestepped the volley.

LaGlace was not so lucky.

The putrid muck hit the front of her newly-starched white uniform. It slowly slithered down her waist and off the hem, onto the floor.

"I'll punish you for this, you old hag," LaGlace shouted. Venom dripped from her lips, and fetid human waste slipped down her skirt.

LaGlace grabbed the pot and threw it in the corner. Alex could see that Juanita was not quite finished yet. She had hidden something else in her blanket. She turned sideways on her bed to search again.

Monique, too, was on guard and pointed at the blanket. She backed away and pulled Alex with her. LaGlace was too preoccupied with the assault on her uniform to look at Juanita.

LaGlace swore in French and bent over to shake the sticky slop off.

Only Juanita could hear God's voice instructing her, *"She is the vile one, Juanita. The one who must be sent to the devil for her evil work."*

"Yuck. Not a very nice thing to do to your nurse, Juanita," Alex said.

Monique still grasped Alex by the arm and pulled him back to the open door. She went to LaGlace to pull her away. She was too late.

Juanita hooted and cackled like a wild banshee. She jumped off her bed. She had rolled her flimsy blanket around her arm and danced naked in the cell.

LaGlace was still preoccupied, cleaning off the slime with a bed sheet. That was when Juanita made her lethal move on LaGlace.

Alex watched in horror as Juanita deftly brought out a small paring knife from her blanket. Alex moved forward to protect LaGlace, but he was too late.

Juanita jumped onto LaGlace's back. With her left arm, she circled LaGlace from behind and quickly used the knife in her right hand to forcefully jab it into the other woman's neck several times.

With that act, she severed the right side of the nurse's exposed neck.

When Alex saw how spritely Juanita was jumping off her bed and attacking LaGlace, he made his move. He quickly pushed Monique away as he ran at Juanita.

She still had her nurse in a death grip.

He didn't make it. It was too difficult to reach Juanita, who had pulled LaGlace into the corner. She was protected by LaGlace's body in front of her, and had already accomplished what she wanted to do.

Alex saw the right carotid in LaGlace's neck spurting like a geyser. It was so violent that Juanita's face was covered in blood as she bent over LaGlace.

The nurse's head was partially decapitated on the right side. Her eyes bulged out of their sockets. Her head fell forward. It was no longer supported by her right sternomastoid neck muscles, as they were also severed.

Juanita gave a simple vague smile. She quickly composed herself, pleased with her action. She simply let LaGlace drop to the floor and then went to her bed.

Alex grabbed LaGlace, who immediately went into a violent, spasmodic convulsion. Her brain was devoid of blood. Her head reared back, sucking in air as her diaphragm contracted. Her arms and legs thrashed about in the traumatic seizure. Her bladder emptied.

Alex couldn't hold her as she dropped to the floor. "Quick, Monique, get some help for LaGlace and call the surgical ward. Urgent."

He tore strips from the bed sheet and tried to stem the flow of blood as it spurted from her neck.

This attempt was impossible, since LaGlace was still convulsing. Her back contorted into a rigid spasm. Her lower body flailed about as the contents of her bowels spilled out on the floor.

The room quickly filled with nursing staff as they heard Monique yell for help. Horrified by the gruesome scene, one young aide fainted outside the door.

LaGlace lay comatose on the floor. Her convulsions had ceased, but her body continued to spasm, twitching and gasping for air. The blood drained from her face as Alex tightened his grip on her carotid, again in vain.

As Alex tried to stem the flow with blood-soaked hands, two nurses tried to help. Slipping on the messy floor, they finally placed LaGlace on a stretcher brought in by an orderly.

Monique calmly ordered the nurses, "Be sure to put pressure on that side of the neck only. Perhaps she will live. Take her to the surgical ward."

Alex watched LaGlace be taken away. He turned to hear Juanita calmly talking to herself, serene and composed with a blissful smile on her face.

Juanita was huddled in a ball, slowly rocking back and forth in the corner of her bed. She was peaceful, tranquil.

Monique went to Alex and washed the blood from his hands with a soaking wet towel she had found in the rooms next door. "Come, my love. There is nothing else for us to do here," she said, pulling him away from Juanita.

She feared another attack.

Monique pushed Alex out the door. She then went to Juanita, who was now quiet, composed, and at peace with herself. She covered her nakedness in the blanket that had fallen on the floor after the assault.

"The nurse will bring you your medication, Juanita. To make you feel better, and then you can go to sleep." She brushed Juanita's hair back from her swollen eyes. She saw Juanita's weapon still on her bed where she threw it.

She picked it up, wrapped it in a small towel, and left.

Monique and Alex were left alone in the corridor after locking the padded cell. A few nurses scurried about, talking about the attack.

Two orderlies arrived with buckets of water and mops to clean the padded cell and hallway of coagulated blood and human waste.

"How did she ever get that paring knife?" Alex asked one of the third-year nurses.

The girl shrugged her shoulders. "We don't know, sir. She did work in the kitchens briefly, washing dishes, Doctor."

Monique confirmed the nurse's observation. She gave the nurse the paring knife, wrapped in the towel. "Destroy this weapon with the towel, nurse. Put them into the garbage and the incinerator. We don't want it back in the kitchens."

The nurse took it. "*Oui*. I will."

Monique led Alex away from the huddled group, who were still talking about the attack. She squeezed his hand, smiled, and said, to comfort him, "This weekend will be warm, perhaps. Maybe there is a new movie at the drive-in. Call me, Alex."

Alex, clearly still anxious about the attack on LaGlace, said he would.

He called to the same graduate nurse who still had the towel and knife in her hand. "Please give Juanita an intramuscular of one hundred mgms of chlorpromazine as soon as you can. Get her some clean blankets and tell the nurses to be extra careful today."

※

CHAPTER 39

Vinny DaCosta

AT the end of that horrific day, Alex knew that the prognosis for the Ice Queen was poor. He was happy to return to his new home with Vinny and Mamma DaCosta, the best ravioli chef in the country.

He had first met Vinny when he drove onto the mental hospital grounds with his half-ton truck on his first day in Canada. It was after a long journey from Boston, and he was exhausted.

He was one of hundreds of draft dodgers who were in the long queue at the border leaving the States, and he was thirsty and hungry.

Once on the hospital grounds, he discovered that his right front tire was almost flat. A nurse, walking to her ward, saw that he was in trouble. She pointed to the deflated tire. "Maybe you can drive it to the hospital garage, right over there. Mr. DaCosta can fix it for you."

She directed him to a large, two-story wooden building nearby. Alex slowly maneuvered his vehicle into Vinny's garage.

He looked about, and found the garage full of hospital trucks, lawn mowers, late model cars, mangled bicycles, and an ambulance on blocks. It was waiting for new tires and an oil and lube job. Vehicles were all scattered about, outside and in, waiting for repairs.

Vinny was the mechanic in charge, and he had several male patients who were his assistants. Alex pulled his car up to the entrance of the large, open doors. He found Vinny underneath one truck, repairing the rear axle.

Vinny rolled himself out on the trolley as Alex introduced himself. He looked at the flat tire and then at Alex with his boot on his left foot. "Too bad, but I see you got two flats there, young fellow," he said. He laughed at his own joke as one of the aides, covered in grease, also guffawed.

Alex accepted the joke as he usually did and told Vinny he needed a room. It was then that Vinny suggested that his wife, simply called 'Mamma,' had a clean room for him in the town close by.

He assured Alex that she was a good cook, and Alex could live with them for that year. Alex immediately liked the man, cynical and with a wry sense of humor. He made the deal right there and then.

Months later, he drove to the small town after Juanita's attack on LaGlace, to where the DaCosta's lived. The sun was setting, and it was a cold afternoon as he listened to the news about President Kennedy sending more troops to 'Nam.

He sucked on his pipe, like a soother to quell his fears, and also some guilt: the remorse for friends in 'Nam who may never return, the guilt and anger after Aaron's threats, and remorse for the attack on LaGlace.

Alex laughed out loud when the radio announcer played "Crazy" by Patsy Cline, last year's hit on the music charts.

"How appropriate for work at this place," he said to the announcer. He sang along, "I'm crazy for trying ..."

As he sang out of tune he drove into the small town of LaSalle. Vinny DaCosta, a retired Korean War vet, had a traumatic head injury from the war, according to Mamma D, but he was a good listener.

Alex always felt relieved of his angst after working all day at the hospital and talking frankly with Vinny. He quickly became a fatherly figure to Alex, who was lovingly fed by Vinny's wife, Mamma D, a motherly cook he'd never really had.

Alex discovered early on that Vinny also suffered from shell shock from the Korean War.

As a youth, Alex had never had the warmth and the homey style of a house that existed in the DaCosta's large, two-story wooden building. It was clean and comfortable, with a screened-in veranda circling the front and the east side.

The screens were new, and the house had a fresh coat of white paint with blue trimming. The veranda floor was covered in bright, yellow linoleum and was Vinny DaCosta's favorite hiding place.

Now shining in the setting sun, the house was a pleasant contrast to the dark and gloomy mental institution and a peaceful sanctuary for Alex. It was aglow as the pale rays of the yellow, setting sun struck the white frame that late in the day.

At first, he found the master of the house, Vinny, to be stupidly amusing. He often spouted out various philosophical reflections, political rants, xenophobic, racist, sexist, homophobic, and chauvinistic views about all and sundry subjects.

But Alex learned quite quickly that he was full of interesting inside information about all the staff and the intricate goings-on at the hospital. He was also very willing to rent out part of his garage as a commissary, adding to Alex's income.

Whenever Alex came home, he found Vinny sitting in a cane-backed chair with his feet propped up on three empty beer cases. He was forever smoking his vile, Canadian Sweet Caporal cigarettes and chewing on pumpkin or sunflower seeds. The spent seeds were gingerly spat on the linoleum floor close to his dog, Claudius.

That made it slippery for Alex as he maneuvered around Claudius, Vinny's guard dog, who lounged at Vinny's feet.

Vinny, quite opposite in character to Alex's obsessive cleanliness, would drink and smoke, scratch and burp, cough and spit, belch and fart. This latter release often forced his dog, Claudius, to slink further away with each foul discharge.

As Alex closed the veranda door behind him, he found Vinny in his usual chair. "What are you watching on TV, Vinny?"

Vinny didn't look up. "An oater; you know, an old western with Randolph Scott," Vinny muttered while he cleaned his ears of wax with a wooden match stick. He then picked at his teeth with the same stick, watching Randolph shoot up the saloon bar full of bad guys with his pistol.

Alex accepted Vinny's handshake, scratched Claudius on his neck, and commiserated with Vinny as to the near-death of LaGlace, of which Vinny was quickly aware.

Alex found his small bedroom on the second floor to be clean, with spotless sheets. But not very private or sound-proof.

Due to the thin, plaster wallboard, his sleep was often interrupted by Vinny's snoring, Mamma D's groans from an arthritic hip, and her belching from too much spicy ravioli. Or from their son's squeaky gramophone on the other side of Alex's room.

If it wasn't for the snores, the pumped-up music, or the smells of marijuana smoke drifting in, then it was Paulo's erotic groaning and his bedmates sighing and squealing during their noisy sexual liaisons.

The current bedmate was the other roomer in the house, Rani: a mature, attractive, East Indian girl who had the room down the hall.

Rani was also a resident in psychiatry, but in her second year at Montréal General. She was very determined to succeed and become a professor in the department of psychiatry at the university. She was occasionally taking practical lessons at the mental hospital but was enrolled at the General.

And she preferred to sleep in Paulo's bed.

Alex felt sorry for Mamma D, a kindly, portly woman with a large, soft bosom, full of hugs and kisses; so unlike his own emaciated, alcoholic, vacant mother. Mamma D didn't get much help from her husband, Vinny, who believed that all housework was woman's work.

Paulo treated his mother unkindly. He smoked dope and drank beer in his room and rarely came down except to eat.

"The acorn doesn't fall far from the tree. Like father, like son," Alex said to Paulo that day when he walked into Paulo's room late that afternoon.

Such a cliché about the acorn was beyond comprehension for poor Paulo. He only grinned stupidly and considered it a compliment.

As to Mamma, Alex liked overweight Mamma D as soon as he met her. She spent all her time in the kitchen, and obviously had never missed a meal in her life.

There was always a small Philco radio playing in her kitchen and a tape player.

"Dean Martin is my favorite," she proudly announced as soft background music played: "Come Back to Sorrento," "That's Amore," "Grazie, Prego, Scusi," "O Sole Mio," or "Santa Lucia."

One day, Alex pointed to the potted plants on the kitchen windowsill. Mamma D watered them daily, including the few tomato plants nearby.

"Lordy Lord, those are Paulo's special plants, Alex; but goodness gracious, they don't produce much flowers," Mamma D said. She worriedly stirred the damp soil with a kitchen fork and added more water.

Alex didn't have the heart to tell her that they never would produce tomatoes or flowers. Paulo would clip the leaves and smoke them in his room whenever Rani would make a visit.

After two weeks of eating pasta, Alex's pants had to be let out one inch. Still, he wasn't going to insult Mamma D's meals.

"There must be thousands of Italian men going to their graves prematurely. They didn't want to insult their wife's cooking," Alex once said to Rani, who nodded wisely. She preferred to cook her own curried dishes in her room in an electric pan.

Vinny, on his days off from the hospital, always wore long, Stanfield's underwear, washed clean by Mamma, and buttoned up to his neck. His blue, wool toque, worn in the wintry weather, came down to his bushy eyebrows.

A heavy lumberjack's shirt covering the Stanfield's, was open, revealing tomato sauce stains from yesterday's meal. The Stanfield's also served as pajamas.

Vinny was much taller than his wife, with a round, chubby face, short, thick arms, and an ever-increasing beer belly. But still tough and muscular.

He had a smile on his unshaven face, as though he knew some deep, dark secrets. Which he always did. Vinny kept his mouth shut, but his ears open, at the hospital.

"You did well to give those laundry girls an escort late at night, psycho man. That cooled that Jack the Rapier off, and to keep his pecker in his pants. He's going to throttle some poor woman again if you don't catch him," Vinny offered, as he picked his teeth with the wooden match.

"It's Jack the Ripper, Vinny. Sergeant LeBeouf and the *SQ* will get him, Vinny. We'll catch him."

Vinny, today clean-shaven with serene facial features that radiated tenacity and vigor, had some more gossip for Alex.

"The dictator's wife will be moving back to Russia one day, sooner rather than later, Doc."

"So, I heard, Vinny. The word is director, Vinny. Director."

"I don't think so. Know what I'm saying?"

At his boarding home after work, Alex often rested in Mamma D's warm kitchen. The days in mid-December were shorter and colder, and the evenings chilly, but the kitchen was a welcoming haven.

His mouth watered at the smells of pasta as it simmered on the new Tappan electric stove. Vinny bought it through the Hudson's Bay catalogue, and it featured the oven at eye level.

Just right for short, chubby Mamma.

Mamma D gathered up the laundry, stretched out on a rope next to the warm stove. Vinny had just finished watching the end of a John Wayne movie, *Back to Bataan*, on the front room TV.

The two men eagerly sat down to dinner.

Alex's mouth watered as the plump woman put a piece of garlic bread, smothered in margarine, on Alex's plate. The plate already overflowed with an excess of homemade spaghetti, also suffocated in garlic pesto sauce.

"Where's my dinner, woman?" Vinny sneered, looking at Alex's plate.

Vinny took the last drag of the short butt and methodically flipped it into the sink.

Mamma D smiled warmly as she piled his plate full of pasta from the pot on the stove. "Hell's bells, I kept it extra warm for you, Vincent dear; keep your shirt on, gosh almighty."

Vincent could hardly wait as he dug in. He dropped his fork and, with a mouth full of spaghetti, muttered, "I seen by myself, I did, that your head honcho goes sideways. Know what I mean?"

Alex wiped his chin of sauce. "Sideways?"

Vinny made a twirling motion with his finger and pointed at his head. "Yeah, you should know, being a big psycho doc. Your boss goes coo-coo, bonkers, from time to time; you know what I'm sayin'? Nutty as a fruit cake. Nutso."

"Maybe, Vinny. maybe."

"I seen him. Babbling away once, late at night. Came while I was fixing his old, two-door Ford. Likes the ladies on the idiot wards, I'm told. His brains are hanging there, between his legs," Vinny said, grabbing his crotch.

Alex just listened as he ate his spaghetti. He tolerated Vinny and wasn't going to get into a discussion or argument with him.

"I never saw him that way, Vinny," he lied.

"Well, I did. It's a *Looney Tunes* place, doc. It's a potpourri of deranged zoo-manity. That killer there is like that psycho, Jack the Rapier, I says again. He goes for the lonely, psycho girls only, or some nurses." He pointed at Alex with his fork dripping in sauce for good measure.

"Good gosh almighty, Vincent, the word is 'humanity,'" Mamma D said as she put another veal meatball on Alex's plate. Mamma D turned down the small Philco television set on the counter. It showed clips of the Jack Paar show.

Mamma D clucked as she put her hand on Alex's shoulder and massaged his neck gently.

"Heavens to Betsy, you're very courageous to work there, young man, by gosh, almighty, for sure" she said.

Alex leaned into the thick paw.

Vinny washed the pasta down with a glass of homemade red vino. This home-made hooch Alex savored only once, but later rejected, fearing blindness. It reminded him of the bathtub gin his mother drank.

Vinny sucked the juices off one finger at a time.

"This good young man gets good pay for a good day's work, woman. I hears good things about him, I does."

"Darn it all to dickens, don't you mind my Vinny, Doctor," Mamma D said kindly. "He was shell-shocked in Korea. He was with the United Nations peacekeeping force, he was, but he knows everything that goes on there at your place of work. By golly."

Alex sliced into the meat ball as he watched Mamma D tie a bib around Vinny's neck. She lovingly dabbed the juice from his chin with her apron.

Mamma D dutifully went to the windowsill on Vinny's brusque command and brought the pitcher of wine to the kitchen table.

"It's a fine kettle of fish, Vinny. Remember now, the new rules in this *La Belle* Province of Québec are changing now for the better for us ladies."

"Bullshit."

"The government is passing a new law, and you have to respect us ladies now. A wife is no longer obliged to obey her husband. Remember?"

Vinny sneered and threw his hands in the air. "I voted against those commie, pinko, socialist Liberals. Country's going to Hell in a hand basket with those fem's rights."

Mamma D again massaged Alex's shoulders and explained. "The law in this province said that a husband must provide everything for his wife with a written contract in his hands. Now the law has changed. Dog gone it, she can have full legal property rights for the first time, by golly, and no more written contracts for us gals."

Vinny sopped up some pesto gravy with his garlic bread and countered. "Horse shit. All those fem frogs have conjugular obligations to their husbands, like it or not. You also," Vinny growled.

He looked at Claudius near his feet, who looked up and seemed to nod in agreement.

Mamma D winked at Alex and replied, "Holy mackerel, the world is changing, Vinny. Ain't no more so. No more written contracts, like before," she insisted.

Vinny smacked his lips, slurped his wine, and lit up a Philip Morris cigarette. He pushed his chair back from the table and changed the uncomfortable conversation from the argument that he was losing.

"Those poor Indians are still at the bottom of the totem poles. Riel. He believes that idiots like his sister and cripples like you are nearer to God. Are special in this world." Vinny chuckled, pointing to Alex's foot under the table with his fork.

Alex didn't mind such stupidity coming from a guy like Vinny, who was now his business partner. "That's what I heard, Vinny. Lafayette is a big guy. Native French. Indian, with moccasins, braided hair, deer-skin jacket, and all those beads, but a gentle soul, really," he said, looking at Vinny and giving him a sly wink.

"Yeah, yeah, I know that half-breed. He helped me with a truck motor once at the hospital. Strong as a mule. He just lifted the front end for me."

"Strong, but a gentle soul, Vinny," Alex offered.

Vinny made a fist and took a swipe at a fly feeding off his stained bib. The insect evaded his closed fist but continued to hover as Vinny reached for a deadly weapon under the table.

Mamma D picked up her husband's empty plate and put it in the sink. "It's okay, Vinny. The Honeymooners is on TV; your favorite show. Toddle-off away now, from here. Now take your smoke like a good fellow, gee whiz, and go watch the boob-tube," Mamma D insisted.

She helped Vinny up and untied his plastic, yellow bib from around his scruffy, unshaven neck that he had missed with his razor.

Vinny picked up his fly swatter from under the table as he blew smoke out his nostrils. It was El Toro preparing to do battle with the pesky intruder.

He smashed the helpless fly where it rested on the kitchen counter. Its last meal was a flake of cheese. Its fatal error was washing its face with its two front legs.

Vinny gave out a loud, "Ha, Gotchya." He washed the blue, rubber flap of the fly swatter in the kitchen sink. It was loaded with recent kills and sticky carcasses from past fallen combatants.

A spider crept across the window sill. "It's okay. I'll get it, Vinny." Alex took a glass tumbler and edged the spider into it with a piece of paper. He opened the window and dropped the spider outside.

Vinny snarled at being deprived of another kill. He walked out. "That Riel, he'll throttle the dictator someday soon."

"Why, Vinny?"

"For messing with the squaws in that place. 'Specially with Riel's poor sister, Beatrice: a simple soul," Vinny replied as he slammed the window shut.

Alex thanked Mamma D for the dinner, said goodbye to Vinny, and went to his room. He closed his door behind him, lay on the floor, and did forty pushups. Still sweating, he lifted his home-made barbells while doing sit ups.

Finally, he took his shoes off and wiggled his toes. He gingerly massaged his crippled foot. It ached at the end of each day, made worse in the cold, freezing weather of Québec.

After filling a bucket with hot water and Epsom salts, as his mother insisted he do every night, he felt the soothing effect on his ankle.

As he sat there, soaking his foot, he looked forward to meeting with Monique soon and going to the drive-in again.

✳

CHAPTER 40

A Disaster on the Lake

A week later, in very late November, Alex left the building and his female wards to have a pipe after lunch with a group of smokers. "It's unusual to have a warm day for a change," he said to Aaron, who joined him.

"The natives here call it an Indian summer, my friend, but it's late this year. Warm for a few days, we pray to God."

Alex left the devious Aaron, unzipped his parka, stuffed his fur hat into his back pocket, and walked away. The warming sun tried its best, but the wind blew strong, cold gusts from across the lake, close by.

"A dark storm, it is still in the distance. Will hit us soon," Riel warned, smoking one of his cigarettes as he pushed his laundry basket along the path. It was full of fresh bedding for the women's ward.

Someone in the crowd that gathered shouted that they could see a canoe in trouble on the small lake.

Riel pushed his basket off the path and pointed far into the distance. "Two women: your kind, they seem. They are trying to paddle to the shore," he shouted to the group.

Aaron cradled the sun from his eyes with his hat and stomped on his cigarette. He peered into the distance and tried to see what Riel was pointing at.

"You have the eyes of an eagle, Riel," he said in awe.

"Those two, she and her, shouldn't be out there, them women. Those waves and that strong wind will tear that canoe apart," Riel shouted to the group.

Others heard the shouts. Several nurses, orderlies, and a few patients who had ground leave gathered near the shore.

The rays of the sun came out for the last time through the dark clouds, and the wind picked up. The group followed Riel, who left his laundry cart. They moved closer to the edge of the lake, shouting out to the two women.

They watched in horror as a strong gust rocked the boat and tipped it over slightly. Icy water gushed over the edge.

"Those two young women are in big trouble," someone yelled.

Alex could see one girl trying to stand up. She waved her arms at the group and shouted for help. It was a foolish move; it caused the canoe to tip over, spilling them both into the frigid waters.

Alex watched in horror as the girls held onto the edge of the canoe and screamed for help. They both flailed desperately in the freezing lake.

"She tipped them over," Alex shouted. He took one of the nurses next to him by the arm and told her to get help.

"One is already going under the waves, with only her arms above water," Riel shouted. He threw off his heavy buckskin jacket and ran to the edge of the water.

"I'll call security and get a boat out there," a male nurse said as he ran back to the wards. The wind picked up and spewed a cold mist over the excited, worried crowd.

Alex knew help would arrive too late. He was a good swimmer in Florida, but dared not try in those freezing waters, and with his lame leg.

"Run for it, Lafayette. Now is your chance," a few of his friends, the Métis who had ground privileges, shouted to Riel.

"Don't do it, man. They'll catch you, lock you up, and throw the key away forever," Alex said pointing, to the prison ward.

As Riel vacillated, Alex felt he had to do something. He threw his parka on the ground and began pulling his shoes off. It was the boot that delayed him.

The girls, splashing about in the waters tried to get back onto the canoe once again, but in vain.

As Alex struggled with the laces on his boot, the shouting on the lake stopped.

"The boat is awash, and the other girl has gone under," someone yelled. Drops of rain began to slap at the company of helpless onlookers.

"The other is trying to hold her friend's head above the waves by her hair," an orderly close by shouted to Alex.

Monique was now next to Alex. She had run down to the lake with other nurses from the residence. She fell to her knees beside Alex and pleaded with him not to try the rescue.

"Wait for the boat," she begged.

"Too late. Hypothermia," Alex shouted over the howling wind. As Alex unbuckled his boot he saw Riel from the corner of his eye. The big man hesitated. He looked to the forest for a few seconds, and then scanned the lake.

"The rescue boat. There is none coming," Riel said. Alex could see the anguish on the Indian's face as he waited a split-second, trying to decide to make a run for it.

Before Alex got his boot off, Riel pulled off his heavy sweater and kicked his moccasins away. He pushed Alex away, brushed aside the large group now gathered at the lake's edge, and ran into the freezing waters.

"It's our good friend. It's suicide to go in there," his Metis comrades, huddled together for warmth, yelled to each other.

Monique grasped Alex's arm. "That is my roommate out there. It is her day off, and she wanted to canoe again. She went with Miss Katie. Please, God, help him get there in time," Monique prayed as she watched Riel run into the rising waves.

"Katie? You mean Doctor Cartier's wife? It doesn't look good, Monique," Alex said. He put his arm around the girl and put his parka on again.

"I told them not to go out today," she said. She crossed herself and prayed quietly.

Alex felt her body shaking violently, both from the freezing cold and the tragedy unfolding. She turned her head into Alex and away from the tragic scene, fearing disaster. He took his parka and wrapped it around Monique.

Alex held her as they watched Riel wade into the water waist-deep and start swimming with powerful strokes toward the boat. He had never seen such a strong swimmer, even in the Olympic trials held in Florida years ago.

Cartier had heard the commotion and the shouting through his open window. He came out of the Administration building and ran to the lake's edge.

The disturbance had patients and staff looking out at the frightful scene from every window in the nearby buildings.

"No one can survive such freezing waters," Monique said next to Alex, as he put his shoe and boot back on.

"He's going to make it, Monique; have faith. He's almost got to them," Alex said pointing to Riel.

Riel had reached the capsized canoe and was holding one girl above the waves by her arms. Thunder rolled from the black clouds in the distance, and a bolt of lightning clapped across the lake.

A shout went up from the large group.

"He's pulled one onto the overturned boat. He's bringing the other one to us," Cartier said. He was standing next to Alex. "Is it Katie? My Katie?" he asked as Riel came close to shore.

"Riel is pulling one girl and holding her head above the water," Monique said as Riel scrambled ashore.

Riel, still holding the girl next to his body for warmth, stumbled as he cut his feet on the shale on the beach.

Others waded in and helped to pull him and the girl to shore. One picked up the girl and carried her to safety.

Cartier pushed through the crowd around Riel. "My Katie; you left her there, Indian. We'll get a boat out there for my wife, the other one that you left, you stupid Indian," Cartier growled in disdain, with spittle flowing down his chin.

Cartier was agitated and emotionally out of control, with no regard for Riel's heroism.

Riel didn't look up as he heard the contemptuous remark from the director. He continued to massage his frozen feet and pull black leeches from his legs.

"Me and this one is alive. That one, she will be dead soon. Her lungs, they are full," Riel said as he pointed to the canoe. He had laid the girl down as nurses covered her in blankets.

They all watched as the canoe slowly drifted further away in the strong wind.

Monique left Alex and rushed to the unconscious girl. "She's breathing. Thank the Lord and thank you," she shouted to Riel, kissing her small cross around her neck.

Riel was sitting on the shore, rubbing his arms and legs. Monique pushed the crowd aside and started to apply first aid to her roommate.

"My wife. It's Katie out there. My God, do something," Cartier pleaded with Riel, then again added with contempt, "Get back out there, red man."

Riel stood up, looked at Cartier, who was frothing at the mouth, and, with some hesitation, waded back into the frigid waters. "That one there, she might be with us yet," he said as he pointed to the boat.

With that, he again jumped into the lake and swam out against the rising gusts of wind. It brought sheets of rain and a spatter of snow onto the group.

Nurses bundled the rescued girl in blankets and took her in to the hospital wards. Monique followed as she turned to watch Riel, with powerful strokes, swim near to the boat for a second time.

Alex stood, helpless, as Riel flipped Katarina onto his stomach to keep her head above the waves. He rested briefly to catch his breath. Then he swam back with difficulty, often being lost in the waves, even with his powerful back stroke.

Cartier was beside himself, running back and forth, confused and agitated. Lost and bewildered in the turmoil, he was now dependent on the Indian that he so despised.

Several rushed into the water to meet Riel as he began to flounder and crash against the rocks with Katarina on his chest. A strong wave forced his shoulder against a sharp boulder, causing him to cry out in pain as he passed the girl to the others.

Riel struggled to stand as others waded in and pulled Riel by his arms ashore. They brought the girl, Katarina, into the huddled group. She was ice-blue, not breathing, not stirring.

"Help that one quickly, men," Cartier commanded. He pointed to Katarina and disregarded Riel.

Alex turned Katarina over onto her chest as black water and weeds gurgled from her mouth. Two male nurses, together with Alex, then took turns breathing into her mouth.

Alex, exhausted, did all he could to get the slimy muck out of Katarina's mouth and clear her airway. "She's coughing. Maybe, just maybe," he said after two minutes of pressing down in quick bursts on her chest.

Alex smiled for the first time as he received pats on his back as he watched Katarina cough, splutter, and choke. She opened her eyes, gasped for breath, and said something in Russian.

Three orderlies threw their white coats over her. They carried Katarina, breathing and crying, to the nearest building.

As the gale began to lash stinging sheets of water against the thinning crowd, Alex went to Riel. "We've got to get those blood-sucking leeches off you, Lafayette. Those scratches could get infected also," Alex said. He pointed to the deep cuts on his shoulder from the rocks. "You were amazing to save those two women, Lafayette."

Cartier didn't follow his wife to the hospital ward. He seemed dazed: he mumbled incoherently, anxious, and walked about in circles.

"He must be traumatized," Alex said to one of the remaining nurses. "Take him into that building and get him warm," he ordered. "Keep an eye on him."

Cartier brushed the girls aside and just stood there.

The big man, Riel, sat shivering on a fallen tree stump. Tears ran down his face with relief and gratitude that the crisis had ended without loss of life.

Others came over and said things to him in admiration. They patted him on the back and marveled at his bravery.

Riel remained huddled over as he squeezed the water from his long braids. He wiped the blood from his scarred feet with a towel that someone gave him.

"Get a blanket around the man. Hurry," Alex shouted as he put his parka over Riel's shoulders.

One of the guards found a heavy blanket and wrapped it around Riel. He brought him his moccasins. "You're lucky to survive that freezing water, Indian man."

"The Devil wasn't ready for me yet. Our God still has work for me to do. Lafayette is sorry for the poor little one, but she will live.

250

Lafayette's sister drowned in a river, many years past. I couldn't save my dear little one then," he murmured sadly.

"That was a brave act, Lafayette. You should get a medal for saving those women," Alex said putting his hand on the man's frozen shoulder.

Riel said nothing. He sat there, pulled on the frayed string that held something from deep inside his shirt, and grasped it tightly.

Two orderlies wrapped Riel in more blankets as he blew stinking water out his nostrils and slapped his arms to warm his body. He slowly got up and followed them to the hospital ward. Riel stopped and looked back at Alex.

Alex nodded and gave a thumb's up sign. Riel frowned and shook his head, downcast. He turned toward the forest with a yearning look, and then raised both hands to the darkened sky in surrender.

"I'll see you on the medical ward, Riel. Monique will help you with your injured shoulder," Alex shouted.

As the group disbanded, Alex took Aaron, who had returned to join the commotion, by the arm and up the hill, together with Cartier.

"We might give him some extra privileges. He deserves our gratitude. Both those girls would have died out there. He could have taken off in that confusion, but he didn't," Alex said as he helped Cartier up the small rise.

"Privileges? Like what?" Cartier snorted.

"Well, maybe no more shots in his backside. Extra tobacco and work in the laundry, where it's warm, on a more regular basis," Alex suggested.

"We'll see. We could use a strong back there," was all Cartier would say.

Alex and Aaron watched Cartier walk away. Aaron turned to look at Alex. "So, my friend, you will do it? Write my exam in psychiatry for me, your friend? The examination in the New Year, in Montréal."

Alex reared back. "You call me a friend? To ask me as a friend to be charged with an illegal act. A fraud, and when discovered, I'll be accused and sent back?" Alex said, jabbing his finger at Aaron's chest and staring him in the eye.

"Ah, yes, still my friend you will be. For Aaron will not call the police in New Orleans with what you did. Aaron, he found the newspaper at the Montréal library from your city. It was all about that drunk. The one they found in the river. You know the one, my friend."

Alex was aghast with this information. "They found him? I don't believe you. You are making this all up."

Aaron smiled, a wicked, knowing smile. He pulled out a Xeroxed copy of a newspaper clipping from the Orleans' Daily Herald. It was dated and underlined.

Aaron showed it to Alex as they stood out of the snow and sleet, under the cover to the steps leading to the snake pit, where they met for Aaron's group meetings.

Alex scanned the paper clipping, the wheels turning in his mind. Alex grappled with the date on the clipping to the time of saving his mother, from rape.

"Now you believe? His jacket, it was hung on a tree branch in the river. Didn't save him from the ocean. Died. I have the name of the bum you were sitting with on the bank. I will phone him to confirm what he saw."

"Bastard. You are a fucking bastard, Aaron. You did a lot of digging. Now what is your plan, and what do you propose to do?" Alex asked, knowing full well what it was. But he needed to hear it so that he could prepare his next move.

Aaron looked away as if deep in thought, but he already had a plan, and a purpose. "Simple, my friend, simple. I have a friend in Montréal with the Italian mafia, an *amico*."

"Fuck you and your Mafiosi 'amico's.'"

Aaron snickered. "He will fashion a false ID for you with my name and close enough facial features. You know, to get you into the room."

"Fuck you, Aaron. I repeat, what a motherfucker of a bastard you are."

"We have time, my friend. Think about it. I have this man's address and phone number in Orleans: the bum you sat with."

"You do? Lots of digging, you prick."

"He became sober, an upstanding citizen with an acceptable position now. In the governor's office, in the post office department. The police would like to help solve a murder," Aaron said.

He patted Alex on the back and walked away with a smug look on his face.

"I say again, fuck you, you bastard."

Aaron stopped and looked back. "And I say again, grow some tits and go fuck yourself. Aaron will also tell Cartier what Gabriella and you, and Vinny, does with his money." He laughed and walked away.

Alex stood there, digesting the turn of events and regretting the day he befriended that Italian wop.

His heart was thumping and his body sweating in the cold. He needed to talk to Monique, or maybe Vinny, about his dilemma.

He decided on Monique, but when Alex arrived on the sick ward, he found Monique telling the other nurses about Riel's courageous act. One girl was already gently rolling up Riel's buckskin pants to deal with the black leeches on his legs.

"Oh, I hate those black suckers," she squealed, trying to pull one off. Another nurse brought hot tea and warm towels for Riel. Monique quietly took over.

"Don't pull them off, Yvette. Use your finger nail at one end and gently pry it away. It will let go slowly. Do it slowly and carefully, so it won't break his skin, and use some salt on them. They hate salt," she ordered.

While the nurses cleaned Riel's arms and legs, Alex could see that Monique was busy, and there were too many people around to talk.

He busied himself checking Riel's back and chest. "You're clear of them, Lafayette. The shoulder has a gash, but it will heal with time and a bandage," Alex reassured the big man.

Monique bathed the shoulder wound and red blotches from the blood suckers on Riel's legs and arms with peroxide and alcohol. She wrapped another warm blanket around him as he drank hot chicken soup from a plastic cup.

"We all owe you much in gratitude, Mr. Riel, and we will be forever in your debt," Monique said as she gave him a hug. She held him in her arms for some time.

"No one has been so kind and called this man 'mister' before," Riel replied, leaning into Monique for warmth.

Alex nodded, confirming the praise. "Have a hot meal, warm up, and stay here for a while, Mr. Riel. You did well to save those women," Alex said, emphasizing the word 'mister' again.

"Use the salt on those leeches, nurse." Alex reiterated. "It was used widely hundreds of years ago for that same reason. But also to pay the serfs in wages instead. They had no money," he explained to Monique.

"Salt? As a wage, Alex?"

"Yes, Monique. Salt was very hard to get and a sought-after commodity for the poor people back then."

"The French called it '*sel*,' Alex."

"That's right. We got the word 'salary' from that practice. A reward for work done."

Riel listened to the explanation and smiled for the first time. He said, "None of us gets out of this short life alive. I do not fear death, but only fear being there when it comes."

Monique laughed at the quip. "We shall all take loving care of our hero," Monique said, holding Riel's arm and taking him to the kitchen table for a hot dinner. "No more salt, Mister Riel. Maybe a good salary for your courage one day."

Alex watched as the petite nurse escorted the man, twice her size, away. He watched as she ladled more soup into his cup, and then she sat beside him on the bench.

Alex's heart warmed at his kindly Monique. They would meet on the weekend and he could tell her of Aaron's threats.

That evening, Alex called in to the sick ward to ask how Riel was feeling. "He had another meal after we got him from the hospital. His favorite. The cook had some venison and fried three steaks for him."

"Give him some salve for the cuts on his feet, nurse."

The nurse laughed good-heartedly. "Riel used some chicken grease he got from the cook. It worked better, Doctor."

"I'll have to get some of that stuff," Alex joked.

"He's dead tired and snoring in his bed now," the nurse was glad to report.

It was the very same nurse who had taken the kitchen knife from Monique and destroyed it after the attack on LaGlace.

She told Alex about nursing LaGlace on the sick ward. "She is brave, trying to walk, but will be in a wheelchair forever," she explained sorrowfully, then stating that LaGlace was her close mentor.

※

CHAPTER 41

Paulo and Rani

ALEX had placed LaGlace on permanent disability. The left half her body was paralyzed, she was confined to a wheelchair, and her speech was incoherent. She no longer impeded progress on Alex's wards.

Alex was pleased with Cartier agreeing to his suggestions about Riel after he had saved Katarina's life. Katarina told Alex soon after the canoe trip that she was leaving Cartier and returning to Russia, where she would be safe from his physical and sexual abuse.

Cartier was in hiding, apparently depressed and holed up at home. Katarina said to anyone who listened to her that her Jacques was just ailing. That's all she would say.

With Cartier out of commission, Alex hired psychologists, occupational therapists, and social workers. He wanted to mobilize the chronic patients with group therapy, work-related activities, and individual counseling.

And Riel, the savior, was granted extra privileges.

By the end of December, the discharge of healthier patients was progressing. Cartier went into a deeper psychotic depression after Katarina decided to return home to Russia.

At least Cartier was out of Alex's hair, but Aaron's threats were still hanging over him. It was like the Damocles sword, forever suspended above his head.

He had read Cicero a great deal while in his aunt's basement rooms and had his uncle's books available to him. Cicero, the Roman poet, said that those in power are in peril, as he himself felt at that time.

The story went that a Roman statesman was jealous of the king. This statesman wanted to sit on the throne for a day, just like his king, and experience the ultimate power of the crown.

The king agreed, but when the man sat there, the king hung a sword above his head. It was strung above his head and dangled there only by a horse's hair.

The man became isolated, agitated, alone, and overwhelmed by citizens and underlings who constantly demanded and wanted something from him. He soon realized that power was fragile: it was very lonely at the top, and simple virtue was sufficient for a happy life. Thus, it was the threat of the Damocles sword hanging above his head, so to speak, that changed his mind.

It was Vinny, who never demanded much from Alex, but told him about LaGlace being suicidal after becoming paraplegic.

"I repaired the wheelchair for Clarice, doc," he told Alex one day.

"Clarice?" Alex answered, thinking hard of who that could be.

"Yeah, doc. You know, LaGlace. Clarice. In a wheelchair forever and a day with her paralysis. She's depressed, doc. Talked about life not worth living."

"No, I never did know her first name, Vinny. Sorry to hear, Vinny. I'll get our psychologist to visit her," he said in earnest.

Alex was also astounded that Juanita was now calm, quiet, and less paranoid: she wasn't hallucinating or delusional. Was it the attack on LaGlace, or Cartier no longer visiting Juanita? *Or maybe both*, he wondered to himself.

Alex was looking forward to the weekend with Monique when he got home late that Friday. He came across Vinny's son, Paulo DaCosta, in Paulo's bedroom. He was a hunk of a fellow, and usually at the local 'Y' gym working out, and rarely in the house.

He was in his early twenties, and on this Friday, he had just returned home from clubbing seal pups to death off the coast of Newfoundland. The fur was highly prized in Europe, and Paulo came home with a large bank roll each time.

As Alex walked past his room, he found the door open. Paulo was lying on his bed reading the latest Playboy magazine and playing with himself under the covers.

Paulo sat up and called Alex in. He showed the magazine to Alex. "Jayne Mansfield, the blonde bombshell." Paulo laughed, showing Alex a scantily-clad Jane. He jumped up, tore out Jayne's photo, and pinned it on the wall.

"My pa said you was here. You know, I just read an article in this here Playboy. Like, about marijuana and intelligence," Paulo said, holding his crotch as he grinned at buxom Jayne.

Jayne was leering down at him from above his bed.

"Not a good mix, Paulo. Pot and the IQ."

Paulo only smiled vacantly. "Say, you're a head doctor too, aren't you, like that Indian babe next door, Rani?"

He rolled over and opened his bedside table drawer. Paulo pulled out a pistol. He pointed it at the other naked Playboy girl, Marilyn Monroe, pinned to his wall, and said, "Bang, bang. But I still like to give that Rani a wham bam bang in the you-know-where. Know what I mean?"

Alex stepped back as Paulo waved the pistol around. "Yep, I think I know what you mean, Paulo, but you shouldn't smoke pot or play with guns. Both are bad for you, man."

"Do you think so?"

Alex stepped aside from Paulo brandishing the pistol. "Yep, a patient of mine died. He smoked that stuff, too. As did his wife," he said seriously.

Paulo put the gun down and looked worried. "Really? Died from smoking this shit?"

"Well, actually, no. Not from smoking that shit. From a big argument as they both smoked. His wife shot him."

"No shit," Paulo said, perplexed by the vision, but pointed to Rani's room. "Are you into the yellow sari yet, doc? She's, like, a nympho. Always wants something in return. Like, if she puts out, then she wants something from you to put in. Know what I mean, pal?"

"Yeah, I guess I know what you mean, buddy. She's a nice girl. Worked hard to get into medicine and then psychiatry. Not many women in this profession yet. Very bright young woman."

"No shit?"

"Be careful, Paulo. Her father may be after you with a shotgun if you knock her up."

Paulo fell back on his bed, laughing and holding his side with the guffaws. He kicked off his snake skin Cowboy boots and turned back to reading Playboy.

Vinny told Alex later that Mamma D took Rani in like she was the daughter they never had but yearned for. Rani loved Mamma D but, "She never took to me," Vinny said. "Didn't go for my sense of humor, my missus told me."

Vinny continued, "Rani was the youngest girl, and had five brothers living in Vancouver on the coast, with very traditional East Indian parents. They found a husband for her. An arranged marriage to a wealthy man when she turned twenty."

"Sometimes these marriages work out very well, Vinny," Alex tried to explain. He started to elaborate, but Vinny cut him off. "Piss off. Not with overweight, short, Chandran, her man with a huge beard and three youngish children from his recently departed wife."

"No shit, Vinny? So, she's married? Here in Québec?"

Vinny spat out the last of his pumpkin seeds onto the veranda floor. "No, not here, or any other place. She told me that he was decent enough, but stupid, and didn't know how to satisfy a woman. He only wanted babies from her."

Alex watched Claudius lap up all the seed slobber loudly and fart as he did so. "So?"

Vinny booted Claudius away. "So, she ran away and came here. Been with us for four years. Got into med school here, and now she is a nutcase cracker: like you, my boy."

Alex smiled at Vinny's vocabulary, and didn't mind the insulting language. "But her parents live in Montréal, Vinny. She told me."

"Yep. They were disgraced by Chandran's wealthy friends. So, her father opened up the Delhi Curry Palace in Montréal. He now has ten restaurants throughout Québec and Ontario."

"Wow. Best thing they ever did. Thanks to Rani, I guess," Alex said, moving away from smelly Claudius.

Mamma D was shouting that dinner would be ready in a few minutes.

Alex got up and asked Vinny, "What's in the bag, Vinny? Sunflower seeds? As usual?"

Vinny opened the bag. "No, smart ass. For you." It was a large, paper bag full of dollar bills sitting beside him.

Vinny turned off the TV. "So, how are all the goof-balls? I fixed the fire truck's engine today. You got lots of them there pyromaniacals in there, plus the lady who set fire to some building." Vinny said to Alex.

"Yeah. An accident, Vinny. It's pyromaniacs," Alex said, tired as he dragged his foot across the floor. Chubby Claudius, Vinny's pooch, was stretched out near Vinny, grinning at Vinny's joke and guarding the empire.

Vinny took the last drag on a soggy cigarette. "The head honcho is more loco now that his Russkie blonde is going. In a shit-hole depression since Mère Denise got all those fem women to lay down on the highway, helped by our Rani. Stopped the buses from bringing children to our hospital, they did."

"I heard that Rani was one of those women, Vinny."

"Yes sirree, sir. Her brothers own all those buses that bring the children here. She got them to tell her what days they transport those kids here so that the women can put up barricades and stop those buses from coming through the gates."

"Wow. Good for Rani."

"The dictator is out of a lot of moola now."

Alex sat down on the stack of beer cases to rest. "Mamma did well to help out by canvassing the town ladies to join them as well, Vinny."

"You bet she did, with a copy of Mère's letter to the parliament in Ottawa to get the children back into their communities."

Alex got up, since Mamma D was shouting again from the kitchen. "The women, and your missus, made it happen, Vinny. Cartier had to give it up. Poor man is in a severe depression now with all those losses."

Vinny was not that sympathetic, and only spat his toothpick out and came up to Alex. "By the PS, my boy, we made a bundle this week with the fags Riel delivered," he whispered in Alex's ear through his cupped hand.

Alex took the grocery bag full of money that Vinny handed him and gave Vinny his share.

At this point, Mamma D was shouting again that the tortellini was on the table. Vinny finished his beer, and Claudius and master slowly ambled into the kitchen.

When Alex walked in to the kitchen he was surprised to see Rani, the young, attractive, East Indian girl, sitting at the table. Alex had never seen much of her before but admired her for her courage in stopping the buses.

Rani was often away at the university in Montréal taking classes or visiting her parents or helping cook in the Curry Palace for her father. Or sometimes holed up in Paulo's room for the evening. Alex could hear them through the thin walls sighing, moaning, and loudly squealing in orgasmic ecstasy late at night.

Alex had discovered from Vinny that she wanted to be in charge of the psych ward at the General Hospital in Montréal. Alex was sure that would happen one day soon.

Alex pulled out a chair and sat next to her. She had short, jet-black hair and dark eyes, a petite young woman of medium height with a long, prominent nose and high cheek bones. She looked stunning in her beautiful and colorful sari.

Paulo came into the kitchen, filled his plate with spicy tortellini pasta, smothered it in pesto sauce, and went to his room. He sniffed the air, sneezed from Rani's powerful perfume, and blew his nose into his shirt sleeve. He demanded, "Hurry up, Rani. We gotta go, lady."

Alex looked down at Claudius, who was sniffing at Rani's very high heels. He smiled to see the dog's erection after getting a whiff of her overpowering perfume.

"Claudius! God almighty, you should be ashamed of yourself. Get away from Rani," Mamma D shouted and kicked the dog from under the table.

Vinny chortled, but pointed his glass of wine at Rani. "You shouda' been one of those Florence Nightingates or whatever. We need good nurses here, not feminized doctors."

It was Mamma D who stepped in to quiet things down. "Oh, glory be my Lord, shush up, Vincent. Be kindly now to the nice doctor," Mamma D scolded.

Rani slammed her fork on the table and went right up to Vinny. "You know, Vinny, we are only young once; but you, you Vinny, will be immature forever," Rani growled.

She poked her finger at Vinny's shoulder and walked out in a storm, taking her plate with her.

Vinny rolled his eyes to Heaven and looked at Mamma D sitting across the table. "She's touchy, touchy, missus. Must be on the rag: that time of the month." Vinny scoffed and put his partly-finished plate on the floor for Claudius.

Alex eyed Claudius coolly as he snuggled up to Alex's foot. He wasn't fond of dogs, and dogs didn't take to Alex: they were always sniffing at his lame foot and the boot.

"Why call him Claudius, Vinny?" Alex asked, looking at the dog who was now devoid of his erection after the kick.

"Claudius? We had a break in five years ago. He is a good guard dog. He's a killer, just like that Roman emperor, Claudius. Named the pooch after him."

"Really?" Alex gave an amused smile as he finished his meal and put his plate in the sink, rinsed it, and put it in the cupboard.

Claudius sat up when his name was called out, passed a large supply of wind after devouring the spicy tortellini, and crept away from Alex.

"Yeah, he's a good guard dog. Pisses on the porch though, and farts all over the place. Has bladder incompetence, poor little bugger."

Alex fanned the air with his napkin. "He's overweight, Vinny. Maybe that's why he's incontinent."

"Bladder trouble, just like his master. Know what I'm sayin? But when in Rome, do like them Romanians do, I always says," Vinny laughed.

Alex smiled and looked at the dog, spread out beneath Vinny's legs now. "Where's his nametag, Vinny? Should have a nametag on his collar."

Vinny pointed the fly swatter at Claudius. "Nametag? Shit, he ain't got none. Poor bugger can't read."

Claudius wagged his tail and pulled himself from under the table, agreeing with his master.

After that uneasy dinner and messy tit-for-tat row between Rani and Vinny, Alex had his coffee in his room. He opened his book on Psychiatry to study.

It wasn't long before Rani walked in without knocking. "That Vinny should be on my ward. I'd be the first to order the lobotomy on him," Rani said. She was still seething about his remarks; she had likely heard the last ones on menstruation as she left.

Alex smiled, but he had enjoyed that banter between the two of them. "Wow. Sexy outfit, Rani," Alex said with a whistle, for she had changed out of her sari. He pointed at her mini-skirt revealing bare thighs as she walked to his bed. She wore a low-cut blouse, exposing what Vinny referred to as a "well-stacked babe."

Rani was bathed in a heavy perfume and body lotion. The room was flooded with the strong perfume. Alex watched her breasts jiggle, and one almost popped out of the meager blouse as she bent over.

Rani sat down on Alex's bed and crossed her legs. "You men are all the same, right? Wanting a fast poke in the hay. But you can have it anytime with me, big boy," she said with a chuckle.

She maneuvered herself closer and pinched each breast higher and closer together.

"Hard not to, Rani. I mean, it's all hanging out," Alex teased, adding, "Be careful how you dress, Rani. Lots of psychopaths out there that you'll be treating."

His eyes settled on her open blouse again as she bent over to pick up one of Alex's books on the floor, close to his bed.

"Like what you see, Alex? I can handle those character disorders. Have no fear," Rani said as she looked up to see him staring down.

"Beautiful, Rani; they're both beautiful, but no thanks. Be careful, though. There are lots of weirdoes in those bars that you and Paulo go to. He's not the brightest candle on the cake, and Paulo's a chip off the old block."

Rani pushed her breasts back into her bra and looked at Alex's book case. It was made of a few bricks and two planks of wood.

"Jesus, Alex these are all on genetics, neurobiology, and the brain. How come you're reading British psych journals? Heavy stuff, this shit."

"Found most of them in Montréal. The Brits are front-and-center in this kind of research. Medication and brain biology. It's the future, Rani," Alex said, fanning away the pungent perfume with a medical journal.

"You've got the balls, mister, to make all those changes on the wards. Look here, I see that you've got an occupational therapist on the wards now. What else, fucker?"

"Some wards are getting a new coat of paint. Windows are to be open, new toilets, and no more padded cells."

Rani could see that Alex wasn't responding to her sexual dalliance. She became more professional. "I agree. With the new meds, chlorpromazine, those psychotics are now much calmer: like a baby. All your patients are in exercise programs and running around outside freezing their balls off in the freezing air. What for?"

"Healthy body, healthy mind, Rani."

"Lucky for you Cartier agreed, big boy. He's not around much."

Alex let that pass. "He seems to be preoccupied, Rani. Not focused on his work, and he goes away somewhere for days on end."

"Vinny's right this time. Said he's depressed. Probably in some whorehouse now that Katie is leaving."

"I'm worried about Cartier."

"You're lucky he's out of your hair."

"Maybe, but I've always been lucky, Rani."

"You've got to be good to be lucky, and lucky to be good, fella."

"You were good to get into psychiatry. Smart, intelligent, and wise to want to change a male-dominated profession. Good for you. We need more women to help the mentally ill."

"I'm working on it," she said proudly. "The prof said I could be in charge of that psych ward if I made a good presentation to the class on the treatment of a character disorder."

Alex nodded. "Good for you. Where are you going, all decked out like that?"

"Going out for a beer with Paulo. Want to come? Maybe you and I can have a quickie in the back seat," Rani teased, laughing.

"Ah, no thanks, Rani. Got to study with the exams coming up soon. Be careful with Paulo: he runs with a tough crowd and selling that dope."

"Exciting fucker, he is. I agree, not the brightest, but a good fucker. Not much excitement around here, otherwise."

Alex picked up his pipe, filled it with tobacco, and pointed to her short skirt. "Attractiveness can be a liability in this business, Rani. Predators—including a lot of patients that you will be treating. We have others, too; many around here, like the orderlies, will spot you a mile away in that outfit. Be careful, and don't take any risks."

Rani came to the point as to why she came to Alex's room. "Riel already told me something about himself. He comes from your part of the world, Alex. And don't worry, I can handle those fucking creeps who want to screw a dark pussy."

Rani looked ravishing in her very high heels and short skirt, all ready to go out with Paulo. "Riel, though? He's a gentle soul."

Rani strapped one of her pumps on tighter and pointed the other shoe at Alex while sitting at the foot of his bed. "Yep. Lived with a French woman in the south. Said he was married to her."

"Really, you got a lot of history out of him. I heard that you were sitting outside the lab when he was there for his blood work and chest x-ray after his fall at the lake," Alex said, admiring her trim ankles.

She saw his gaze and stretched her slim leg out further, exposing her bare thighs. Was she wearing panties? He thought not.

"But look, mister voyeur, let's get back to Riel, and not my legs or my pussy. I was waiting for the x-ray film to dry to see if he cracked a rib. He said his best time was being married to some French woman."

"French? In the States?" Alex asked. He watched her dab her lips with bright red lipstick. Then she brought out one breast at a time and painted each nipple with her lipstick.

Rani put her breasts back in and nodded as Alex reached for a box of matches on his plastic bedside table. "Yep. Not really French, like from France. Somewhere in the deep south, he told me," she said. She hooked a few bracelets onto her wrist.

"He likes to tell stories, Rani."

She shook her wrist and jiggled the jewelry pieces into place. "He said they liked to drink together and party."

Alex flinched as he recalled what his mother had told him about his father but let that pass. "The guy could be dangerous with a beautiful woman like you. Always have someone close by, and only see him on the ward."

"Can you delay his lobotomy and give me a chance with psychotherapy?"

Alex laughed out loud. "Psychotherapy? With Riel? You're kidding. Anyway, it's up to Cartier, Rani, not me."

"That pussy-seeking pervert? He was kicked out of France. I heard he wanders the women's wards at nighttime."

"That's not acceptable if it's true, Rani. Don't spread false rumors about the man," Alex chided, seriously.

"That's what a head nurse on East Three told me. She's a lesbian and came on to me when I had to examine one of her ill patients."

"East Three? Riel's sister is there."

"That Lessie said Cartier visits at night," Rani said. She smoothed her skirt down, ready to leave.

"Have a nice time, but be careful, Rani. As I said, Paulo runs with a tough crowd."

"Yeah, well, I can change him too."

"Doubt it, Rani. Take care, you hear? You better tighten up your seat belt, Rani. You're going to have a bumpy ride hanging around with Paulo."

Rani howled with laughter. "Good one, but I hear that there's a cute French nurse taking care of you. Fucking at the drive-ins."

Damn, no secrets at this hospital, Alex wanted to say. "Vinny tell you that?"

"Fuck no. Not Vinny, that squirt. One of the orderlies was parked next to you at that movie place. Your windows were all steamed up. Could see bugger all but heard plenty."

"I'll have to change drive-ins." Alex laughed.

"Do that, Alexander. Much quieter further away," she said as she walked out the door.

Only his aunt, and Monique's mother, ever referred to him as Alexander, he thought as he watched her walk out.

※

CHAPTER 42

Where is Paulo?

AFTER Rani closed his door, Alex fell asleep. He was exhausted from dueling with Rani and reading a dull, British journal on statistics of the mentally ill.

It was midnight when he awoke to the loud wails of Mamma D and the banging on the doors downstairs.

Shit. Vinny must be in a drunken stupor again and fighting with his missus. Alex groaned. He pulled on his pants and found a shirt in his closet to wear. He fastened his boot on and tied the laces up on the other shoe, rubbing the sleep out of his eyes.

A flashing red light drew him to the window. "You're in big trouble now, Vinny. The local *gendarmes* are here," Alex shouted, as he then made his way downstairs.

In the kitchen, he found Mamma D sobbing uncontrollably with her head folded into her arms on the kitchen table. Claudius was at her bare feet, licking her toes as she cried and prayed in Italian to Jesus and all the blessed saints she could recall.

Vinny was talking to three policemen in his long, winter underwear and wearing his bright, red toque. The back flap of his Stanfields was half-open, revealing a rather unpleasant sight.

Rani was at the kitchen sink, crying with Mamma D. They both took turns sobbing hysterically. Alex looked at Rani, who was holding her sweater, which was blood-soaked, in her hands.

She stopped wailing to run the hot water tap and vigorously scrub her hands and try to get the blood off her sweater.

Alex watched as Rani ran about with only one high heel on. The left heel had broken off, and so she waddled about on one foot.

"What happened, Rani?" he asked as she wiped blood stains off her sweater and held onto the broken heel. Alex looked around. Paulo was missing. "Where's Paulo?" Alex asked, now fearing the worst.

Rani dried her face and threw her sweater on the floor. Her black, shiny hair was wet from a light snowfall that night, but it was also splattered with dried flecks of blood.

As soon as she saw Alex next to her, she flung her arms around his neck. Alex held her closely, but very quickly she picked up her sweater and took him by the arm. She dragged him up the stairs, away from the crowded kitchen, which was slowly filling up with policemen talking to Vinny.

"Rani, talk to me. Where's Paulo?" he asked again when they were partway up. She only wailed and cried louder, and forcefully pulled Alex up the stairs in her panic-stricken state.

With Rani on his arm, they both stumbled in to Alex's room. Alex closed the door, and Rani immediately fell on his bed and buried her face in his pillow.

Alex knelt down beside her. "I can't understand what you're saying, Rani. Talk to me, woman," he pleaded. He moved his pillow, which now had wet snow and red splotches of blood, away from her face.

He cradled her face in his hands and gently turned her over.

Rani threw her arms around Alex again and looked up in terror. "I left Paulo downtown, you know. He was in a local cabaret, drinking with a bunch of his frigging druggy friends. Then I went out for some samosa and coconut chicken. I was hungry."

"Alone? In that area?"

"Yes, by myself, Alex. Then, then, he picked me up at the Old Calcutta restaurant. You know, to drive me home, right?" she said.

She continued to talk in small spurts and gasp for breath in between. She pulled a towel that Alex gave her around her body, covering her breasts.

"Is this Paulo's blood in your hair, Rani?"

She sat up, wide-eyed, and furiously combed at her hair with her fingers, drying her head in the towel. "We were driving home. Downtown, downtown. Paulo saw a frigging car following us. He shouted at me to duck down. He said that he forgot his gun, for fuck's sake."

"Good for him."

Rani reared back and looked at Alex incredulously. "Shit. Maybe not, dumb-dumb."

Alex let that go. "Yeah? Go on, Rani. Go on," Alex repeated. He picked out small, sharp bone fragments from her black tresses. "These must be pieces of Paulo's skull."

With that, Rani pushed Alex away. She went to his bathroom and brought out a roll of toilet paper. "He told me that it was some of his friends. They followed us. We stopped at a red light, and the same frigging car pulled up beside us."

Alex waited patiently this time. He watched as she unrolled a wad of paper, soaked it in the sink, and dabbed at flecks of dried blood on her face. She walked about the room, somewhat more calm and composed, as she combed her hair and looked at the residual bone pieces in her hands.

With a groan and a large "yuck," she almost puked and threw them on the floor. Smelling her fingers with her nails encrusted in blood, she gagged again.

Alex waited as Rani again left Alex and went to his sink. She opened the taps full force.

"Tell me, for God's sake; is that Paulo all over you?"

At first, she didn't answer, and instead took off her bra and plunged it into the sink. She tried to wash it of blood, but finally gave up and just threw it in the corner.

She turned to face Alex. "Paulo rolled down the window. He started talking to the two guys in the other car. I mean, this guy started shouting at Paulo, for fuck's sake. You see, they were both arguing about money."

Alex went to his closet and put his sports jacket around Rani's naked shoulders. "What happened then, Rani? What happened?"

"Paulo began swearing at both of them. He said he wasn't going to pay them. What an asshole."

Alex already knew that.

As Alex buttoned his jacket to cover her nakedness, she walked back and forth, tremulously dabbing at her tresses.

"So, what happened then, Rani? Settle down, girl. Tell me what happened," he asked, fearing to hear the words but knowing that Paulo must be dead.

He pulled her over to a chair, sat her down, and knelt beside her. He used another wet towel to clean the specks of blood from her neck. He held her hands to stop them from shaking.

She took Alex's head in her hands and looked into his eyes. "Suddenly, this prick pulled out a pistol. I mean, really. A fucking big friggin' Luger. He fired two shots right into poor Paulo's head. At point-blank range, man. It was fucking awful."

"Jesus. A pistol? At point-blank range? He shot him?"

Rani shook Alex's head as though he was stupid and brainless. "Yeah. Shot, stupid. With a big, be-Jesus, fucking gun, stupid. Bang, bang. Just like that. Jesus Christ almighty. Look, the other car sped off."

"Rani, I told you he was trouble." He was sorry to berate her at such a time.

She ignored that. "Paulo fell forward on the steering wheel, and onto the horn." She put both hands to her ears. "That bleeping, friggin' horn, it kept blasting away in my head. I can still hear it."

"My God, woman, what did you do?"

Rani looked at Alex as though it was another daft question. "I was screaming, man. Friggin' screaming my head off and yelling with Paulo's fucking oozing brains splattered all over me."

"What a nightmare. You're shaking, Rani. Deep traumatic stress, girl. Take some deep breaths. I'll find some barbiturate pills to calm you down."

Rani pushed Alex aside and went to his sink again. She opened the cupboard above the sink and ransacked the few bottles that were there.

She found the bottle of barbiturates. She took out a capsule and swallowed it with a glass of water.

She turned to Alex. "He's been killed, right? Shot. He's dead: kaput, *finito*. Fuck, the trunk had a garbage bag full of money." She gurgled as she gagged on the capsule.

"Poor Paulo. His mother is in hysterics. She's probably fainted. Vinny said he knew who did it. I'll go down. You stay here," Alex said. "By the way, did you bring the bag home?"

She lay on his bed and waited for the barbiturate to work. "No. The cops confiscated it, with the car."

"Damn. Too bad. Here's a blanket. I'll be right back, Rani. You just rest and let the Seconal calm you down."

He took a few pills and put them in his pocket. When he went downstairs, the kitchen was chaotic with the police and Vinny.

Another policeman, bundled in a fur-lined parka, stomped the snow off his feet in the hallway after he came in.

While the policeman made notes and talked to his comrades, Alex found Mamma D on the sofa. She rocked back and forth, sobbing.

"You're white as a sheet, Mamma D," Alex said.

She was doubled over in a fetal position, calling out Paulo's name over and over. She tried to be brave, and blurted out, "God almighty. The fat is in the fire now, Doctor."

Alex agreed, but straightened her out on the sofa and pulled the blanket that Vinny brought for her around her body.

He then went to Vinny, who was very calm in all this craziness and pandemonium. He was sitting on a kitchen chair with his toque pulled down to his eyes and was still wearing his long underwear down to his ankles. He sucked on a cigarette and stroked Claudius, who sat beside him.

One policeman was on the phone speaking in French and occasionally pointing to Vinny. Another officer came to Vinny and scratched Claudius' belly when he rolled over with all fours in the air.

"We got a good description from the Indian lady who was with your son. We brought her home and we know who the killer's car belongs to," he said to Vinny.

The kitchen was full of smoke as all the cops had also lit up. They talked in hush tones to each other, so Mamma D wouldn't hear.

Alex got Mamma D a glass of water. "Here, take these two Seconal pills I got for you," he offered. She quickly gulped them down.

"Rani told me they were arguing about a hefty sum of money. Paulo said he didn't have any," Vinny said to one policeman.

The officer was taking notes. Vinny scratched at a red sore in the opening to his back flap.

"We might have an idea who they are, Vincent," Dominique, one of the policemen, said.

"I have a damn good idea who they are, Dominique. One is a wop, mixed up with that frog. The other slant-eyed prick is a chink. Both in cahoots with their leader, that Israeli kike with the Russian mafia whores from Montréal," Vinny said, cursing under his breath.

One policeman was writing as Vinny swore. "Kike? How you spell that, Vinny?"

Vinny ignored that and went to the fridge and sliced up a salami sausage and rye bread. He put it on a plate with a few garlic pickles and opened some beer for the police officers.

Vinny chewed on the salami and pointed at Alex with a sausage. "You're a doctor. She's all upset and historical. Do something," he said to Alex, motioning to his wife.

"She'll be okay; not hysterical at all but grieving, Vinny. She'll be asleep soon."

After a few minutes, Mamma D was snoring loudly from the sedative, lying bent over on her side on the sofa.

Vinny kicked Claudius away as the dog stood up on his hind legs, eyeing the salami on the kitchen table.

The police left. Vinny took out another Labatt's beer from his new Amana fridge. He turned on the Sunday morning rerun of *I Love Lucy* as a distraction.

Claudius rolled over to be closer to his master, and they both watched as Ricky Ricardo sang the opening number.

Alex patted Vinny on the shoulder. "I'm sorry for your loss, Vinny. Paulo was a nice guy."

Vinny looked up with misty eyes. "Yeah well, an eye for a wop's eye and a tooth for a chink's tooth, I say. They'll get it from yours truly, here. Soon," he said, going to Mamma D.

Alex followed. "Take it easy, Vinny. Slow down and let your police friends do their job. That's what they get paid to do."

Vinny stopped for a minute and looked at Alex. "Yeah, well, no one could do shit for Gabriella when she called the cops. That prick, Vittorio, was smashing her head against the wall in the Admin offices. He was screaming that if she continued to see that wop doctor, he would kill them both."

"You mean Doctor Aaron Levy, the Italian who is courting Gabriella?"

"Courting? Shit no. He's in her pants every day. Even on her desk in the Admin building now, since the head honcho isn't around anymore in those offices."

"Aaron has the clap, Vinny. He's finally on penicillin, but she still won't have sex with him. She told me."

"Well, I walked in on them one time fucking away on her desktop." He thought for a second. "Well, maybe a hand job, it was. Probably. Yeah, but she told me he wears a Sheik."

Mamma D stirred awake and chastised Vinny. "Gosh almighty, darling. Don't talk that way to the young doctor. Shush up and help get me to my bed now, like a good boy."

Alex told Vinny to do just that; but before he went, he asked, "Vinny, you called one of those guys a "kike" to the *gendarmes*. I know how you refer to some as a "chink," and I know what a "wop" is now, but a "kike"? What is that?"

Vinny looked at his wife, who was comfortable enough, and took Alex aside. "Listen up now. A "kike" is a Jew from Israel. When they left Palestine in the late nineteen-thirties and came to America, the immigration officers on Ellis Island asked them to sign their name on the document. Got it?"

Alex hesitated, shrugged his shoulders and replied, "No, not really, Vinny."

"Okay. So, some couldn't even write their names. So, the officer told them to put down an "X" instead, the simple cross. The Jew said he couldn't, because the cross was in reference to their Jesus, who died on the cross, and it was sacrilegious."

Vinny kicked Claudius to get him out of his way. He moved to help Mamma D get up.

Alex was getting impatient. "So? So what, Vinny?"

Vinny held up a minute. "So, the Jews signed the document with an "O." The officer looked at it and said, 'What's that?' So, the Jew said it's a kikel, Hebrew for the letter 'O.'"

"Oh. I get it now."

Vinny explained that the officer couldn't pronounce that word, so he turned to the medical doctor behind him, who would then examine the immigrants for TB, and shouted out, "Here comes another kike."

"No kidding, Vinny?"

"Yep, kid. No kidding."

"Not nice, Vinny. Not nice."

But Vinny had already left.

✳

CHAPTER 43

Students at the Asylum

WITH trouble in the DaCosta home, it was now no longer the safe haven for Alex. Mamma D was depressed and praying almost daily in the local church. Vinny was stomping about, planning revenge, with Claudius following. So Alex spent the last week of December and the first week in January sleeping in the Admin building.

The Admin building had consultation rooms to admit new patients and extra rooms for relatives from out of town who might want to visit overnight. It also had the private offices for Cartier, Gabriella, and *Mère Supérieure*.

There was a heavy pall over the DaCosta home, and Christmas was hardly acknowledged. Alex's Christmas season was celebrated on the wards, which were festooned with seasonal streamers. A small gift was given to all patients who didn't have family at Cartier's expense. Christmas trees were decorated at the entrance to all the wards, also at Cartier's expense.

There was extra turkey for everyone, and Alex made sure that Christmas music resonated throughout all the wards. Many patients went home for the holidays that week.

Mamma D was depressed, often crying all night from the loss of her son. Vinny was agitated all day and threatening retaliation. Claudius smelled trouble and followed Vinny underfoot. Rani was supportive and caring to Vinny and Mamma D.

Alex left.

"I'll be away for a while, Vinny. I need to study where I can have some peace and quiet," he said to Vinny. He had gathered up his books, three blankets, a pillow, and his toiletries that day.

"It's okay. I get it."

"Where's Rani?" Alex asked, pointing to her room upstairs.

"The Indian queen is visiting her parents in Toronto for a while, doc. She'll be at the hospital clinic seeing patients there. I'll really miss that fem."

Vinny was quite sincere.

Alex said goodbye to Mamma D as she came downstairs and kissed her on the cheek. She whispered to Alex at the front door, "On my word, Vinny will get rightful revenge. You know, for Paulo's murder for sure, by gosh almighty, Alex."

"Look, let the police do their thing. You're depressed enough without having to worry about him now."

Vinny returned with beer in hand. "Watch your back in Admin. That hunk, Vittorio, is out to get Aaron and you for doing business with Christina. He thinks Aaron got revenge for what Vittorio did in Italy."

"I think he also knows that Gabriella cooks the books for us. I'll remember your warning, Vinny. Thanks."

Alex thought of confiding in Vinny as to Aaron's threats. He needed to get it off his chest and just relieve himself of all that angst.

He decided to let it go. After all, Vinny had enough to worry about.

After Alex settled in his temporary office in the Admin building, he had work to do that morning. One of his duties was to usher twenty medical students around the wards. They came in bunches from the medical school to get a glimpse of psychiatry in the mental hospital.

Part of their training was also to have them observe the dreaded ECT. Juanita would be their clinical case for that day.

Alex reluctantly asked Aaron's help to lecture the students. He would sooner punch him in the face than ask him to assist, but he put that thought aside for another day. After all, Aaron was a storehouse of historical fact on mental hospitals, and Alex would have to bite the bullet this time.

The students were on time at 9 AM. Alex greeted them, told them not to be frightened, as they obviously were, and outlined the agenda for the morning.

Leaving the Admin building, the students stopped periodically to listen to Aaron. He thrived on teaching the students that day. He didn't make eye contact with Alex.

Aaron stopped periodically and gave them the usual lecture on the evolution of mental hospitals.

He pointed to the massive, red brick, four-story chronic women's building, now looming in front of the students. "These a, buildings here, they were copied after the insane asylums of England and France. Usually called 'Bedlam.'"

"Bedlam?" someone asked.

"The word Bedlam, my friends, came from the old original Bethlem Royal Hospital in London centuries ago," he reported.

Some students scribbled furiously in small notepads as they trudged through the heavy snow toward the chronic women's building. Another winter storm was blowing down from the north, and the students were anxious to enter the warmth of the wards.

Aaron continued as they walked up the stone steps. "Pneumonia, bronchitis, and other infections were prevalent in a, those a, places, my friends. Syphilis, small pox, and TB also," Aaron said. Alex listened while he shivered on the frozen steps.

Finally, the group entered the building and stopped at the entrance door of Alex's ward. One bright student at the front of the group asked, "Doctor, I read about GPI. Do you still have people suffering from syphilis here?"

Aaron nodded wisely as he opened the door to LaGlace's former ward. This door was no longer locked, since Alex declared that ward was to be open in the daytime.

"Many are admitted with general paresis of the insane, or GPI, a common term for the terminal phase of syphilis."

"Do they become psychotic, Doctor?" one student asked, feeling self-important for having used the term.

"They are openly insane, with delusional and hallucinatory behavior. They defecate and urinate anywhere and everywhere. It is because their neurological system was destroyed by the syphilitic bacteria, the spirochete, after many years of the infection," Aaron lectured.

One of the students was interested in law and the criminally insane. He asked, "Are there many here under court certificate as being insane at the time of their crime?"

"There must be thousands across North America who are incarcerated under the M'Naghten rule," Alex explained. The group stopped to make notes.

He continued. "It stated that a person who committed a crime must know that he was doing wrong. Daniel M'Naghten was delusional—that is, paranoid—and convinced that the British Prime Minister in 1843 was doing him harm. He shot the wrong man by mistake, who died soon after."

"What happened to him?"

"The jury ruled that he was insane, and he lived out his life in the Bedlam institute. Thus, the M'Naghten rule has been used throughout many countries."

"They are all in locked wards, Doctor, I hope," a smart-ass said with a smile on his face.

"Most are, but some have been lobotomized or heavily tranquillized and can have an open ward with privileges, albeit carefully watched. They could be in remission—that is, free of their psychosis."

"Like those who suffer from syphilis? Doctor Gage, shall we?" Aaron added, gesturing to the open ward door.

Alex filled his pipe and lit a match. He warmed his hands on the hot bowl, full of Amphora tobacco coals, and added, "Good question. Let's go in, and we'll show you what syphilis really does to a person. Although it can be cured with penicillin now, if caught early enough."

Aaron smiled at Alex for the first time. It was not a warm smile, but a smirking, scornful grin. "The doctor mentioned Bedlam for M'Naghten. The first asylum, the Hospital of St. Mary Bethlehem, the old Bedlam, was originally founded as a priory, a convent in 1247 in London, England. The first records of such admissions were dated from then."

"Were relatives allowed to visit those poor people in those days, Doctor?" the young female student asked.

Aaron looked at her. She was dark, perhaps Italian. "The public ah, they were invited to visit the hospital as a form of amusement. It was not out of support, or empathy. The hospital needed their entrance fee to financially support it."

"They paid to be entertained?" the girl asked.

"*Si, si.* Good question. The people would bring their children, chairs, and food for themselves. They would have a picnic as they sat and were duly entertained," he said, winking at the female student.

He continued, as the girl blushed. "Patients would walk about naked, confused, and raving about God, Christ, and the Devil. They would jump out at the paying public periodically and scare the onlookers. It was a circus, but it made some paltry pennies for Bedlam. The fee kept that asylum in money."

As they walked along, a curious student asked Aaron why he had left Italy and come to Canada.

Aaron, at first hesitant, explained. "The pope in Rome opened the monasteries to the Jews to save some. I thought it would be safe there, in Rome."

"Were you married, Doctor Levy?"

"Fortunately, yes: to a Catholic lady. God bless her, but Mussolini outlawed such marriages between Jews and Catholics in 1938. But that early marriage was lucky for me. We were hidden by the Christian underground in convents and in the monasteries by the monks."

Alex knew that he was burdened with the guilt of having survived while his thirty other family members had gone to the gas chambers. Alex had heard from Gabriela that Vittorio had collaborated with the Germans and exposed many of those Jews where he and Aaron lived in Italy.

Aaron turned away. His eyes watered. "My wife, she died on our voyage across the Atlantic. Of the tuberculosis."

A sad pall flooded over the group as Alex moved them along through the women's ward. This morning, there was a small class of female nursing students who would join the medical students. Three occupational therapists, whom Alex insisted be hired by the hospital, would also attend.

They joined the medical students once they were all gathered on the ward.

"We will now witness ECT, electroconvulsive therapy," Aaron announced.

Alex stayed back for a few minutes as the students followed Aaron into a small ECT room.

He saw Monique bandaging a patient's head who had been cut after an argument. "How do the nurses find the open ward now, Monique?"

"They are behaving themselves, *merci*. There are fewer fights, and the ladies are smiling after the group therapy. Many are wearing some makeup. They are washing and bathing more in the showers and have a greater respect for themselves with the clean, private toilets."

"Cartier didn't like the idea at first."

"*Oui, docteur*, so I was told. The girls are happy that our director of nursing and Mère Denise insisted in renovating the bathrooms."

Alex lowered his voice and pulled Monique aside. "I'm looking forward to seeing *The Music Man* this weekend at the movies with you, Monique."

Monique looked around and whispered, "*Oui*, I love that Buddy Hackett and Robert Preston. They each have a nice smile like you do, Alex," she said lovingly as they parted.

Alex caught up with the students in the therapy room, who were waiting for Juanita and several other patients to have their treatment.

Aaron expounded, "Juanita will be first today. She should have responded to the older treatment of Insulin Shock Therapy, but now we use electric shocks to cure her."

One student asked in disbelief, "Insulin?"

"Yes, insulin. Patients suffering from schizophrenia and manic-depressive disorders would have up to fifty insulin coma treatments here, and in my country also, before the war."

He set up the apparatus for electroconvulsive therapy.

Another student blurted out, "Fifty, did you say, Doctor?"

Alex intervened, since Aaron was busy connecting electric cords into the machine. "Insulin coma was provided daily, every morning for several weeks, until the patient recovered. It was still used up until the late fifties in mental hospitals," Alex said as the group showed interest and disbelief.

"Why a coma, Doctor?"

"To produce a convulsion. We knew that, for some reason, a convulsion of whatever kind was curative. It was observed for centuries that those who were mentally ill and had a blow to the head or an infection with a fever, and then had a convulsion, got better."

Someone asked, "Insulin, like for diabetics?"

"Yes, insulin was given intramuscularly, and the patient went into a gradual diabetic coma. The diabetic coma was so severe, with the brain deprived of sugar that the patient eventually had a grand mal seizure."

"For how long?"

"This convulsion might take two hours to develop, but it was the convulsion that was healing," Alex said.

"Insulin, Doctor; why insulin?" one asked.

Aaron interjected, "It was safe and easy to correct afterward. The patient would sweat profusely, gradually become unconscious, and have the required convulsion."

"How did you get the patient out of it?"

"Sugar in water was sent down the patient's esophagus by a tube to revive the patient quickly."

"Fifty times in a diabetic coma; did they all get through it?" another student asked curiously.

"No, a few never came out of the coma. Some needed other forms of treatment. Some just never recovered and stayed here forever."

Juanita seemed oblivious to her visitors as they slowly drifted into her room. She had her own room now, since all the padded cells had been closed by Alex's orders.

Monique looked under her bed, satisfied that her metal pot was empty.

The students pushed their way into the confined space, but several just stood at the doorway. The walls of the room had been painted. The bed was new, with clean linen, and the floor scrubbed spotless.

Monique, cheerful and welcoming to the anxious crowd, pointed to the clean walls and bed. "Doctor Gage, he has ordered all such rooms to be clean, *mes amis*," she explained as she sat next to Juanita, who was becoming agitated.

"It's okay. You'll be okay, Juanita. Settle down; these are medical students, learning to be doctors to help people like you." Alex said.

"What is her prognosis, Doctor?" a student asked.

"It's difficult to say. She didn't take her medication when her relatives took her out for Christmas. She then relapsed from all the excitement, and with Christmas wine and whiskey," Alex said with a heavy heart.

✳

CHAPTER 44

The Dreaded ECT

ALEX was grateful that insulin shock and coma was no longer done.

"It was a very traumatic procedure, for patient and staff alike. It was very staff-intensive, with many nurses and doctors checking each patient quite often. It took many hours to have an effect," Aaron expounded.

"Also, it wasn't as therapeutic as ECT, and even this procedure is less required now that medications are available," Alex explained to the nervous group.

The students watched as a nurse busily cleaned the electrodes.

"I hope I won't have to revive those students who might faint like last month," a grad nurse said quietly to her friend.

The nurse pointed to the waiting room next door, full of apprehensive women. "Ten patients today, Doctor. The youngest is eighteen. Suicidal Sally is on again for another set of treatments."

"Yes. Unfortunately, the last nine did her no good," Alex said, putting the electric tongs, attached by wires to a black electrode machine, on the bed near Juanita. "Juanita is first, and we'll have to hold her down gently because of her arthritic hip," Alex added worriedly.

"A special room hereafter will be set aside on each ward for shock treatments, and Doctor Gage will have an anesthetist available in case of emergencies. The anxious patients will be escorted into the treatment room one by one," Monique said to the group as she checked the electric box.

The group looked at the small, black box, capable of a jolt like a lightning rod.

Alex pointed to the box. "This will transmit the electricity across the frontal lobes of the patient. She will be held down by two strong nurses or the orderlies," he said as he explained the procedure.

The only emergency equipment in the room was an oxygen tank with a black, rubber mask hanging at its side.

He looked at the nurse in charge and nodded. He was ready. So was she, as were the others beside Juanita's bed.

The students looked more nervous than Juanita. Juanita wore a white, cotton hospital gown, which was too big for her frail body. "My hip, Doctor. It was still sore after the treatments last year," she said.

"Juanita, you must stop spitting out your pills once you're discharged," Monique said as she pulled the gown around her body and covered her emaciated legs with a blanket.

Monique checked Juanita's blood pressure and wrote it down. Alex seemed satisfied with the numbers.

"We'll be careful," he reassured Juanita.

Juanita's gown was smoothed out by Monique as she stroked her forehead to calm her. Alex put jelly on the two metal tongs to get a good electrical current across her forehead.

He clamped the instrument, which looked like the tongs that could pick up a twenty-pound block of ice, onto her temples.

The two orderlies on each side held her shoulders and hips firmly into the mattress. One nurse pushed a rubber mouth guard into Juanita's mouth.

Juanita gagged and pushed the mouth guard out with her tongue. "Juanita please, keep it in. It's so the few teeth you've still got won't break with the convulsion," Alex said, pushing the guard back in. "You will feel much better when this is over."

Alex held her jaw in a tight grip with his left hand. He held the tongs across her forehead with his right. Alex nodded to Monique.

She pushed the button on the electric box. A one-half second of current flowed across Juanita's frontal lobes.

Alex heard her lungs go into a spasm as her head jerked back and her mouth opened wide, seeking air. Juanita's eyelids swept back, and her eyes rolled up into her head. Her jaw muscles shuddered, and her teeth clamped down on the rubber guard.

The students gasped as her frail body jerked into a violent, spasmodic contraction. The convulsion lasted for over a minute. All the muscles attached to her skeletal frame contracted. Alex held her jaw tight against her head as she turned blue.

He put the oxygen mask over her face and pumped air into her lungs. Slowly, she started to breathe again. The nurses and the orderlies tried to keep her body from gyrating off the bed.

One student quickly left the room. Another turned toward the wall, the blood drained from his face, as he held on to his mate. The nurse whispered to the orderly to catch another, whose knees buckled.

Aaron escorted one pale student out to the hall.

After the seizure, they quickly rolled Juanita over onto her side so that she wouldn't vomit and inhale her own gastric juices and aspirate.

"Okay, you can move her over onto the stretcher. Check her hip," Alex said nervously. "Give that fellow this waste basket, just in case," Alex offered as he heard a young man retch, clamping his hand over his mouth.

The students slowly recovered as they whispered amongst themselves to dispel their anxieties and compare notes.

They stepped back as Juanita was wheeled on the stretcher into the recovery room.

Alex cleaned the heads of the tongs with a cotton swab. "Juanita will have eight more treatments, three times weekly. Hopefully, it might help."

If not then she'll have the lobotomy, Alex knew, but kept that to himself.

That one treatment was enough for the students. They filed out quickly while Alex stayed to complete the treatments.

Alex had one more duty to ask of Monique, who remained behind. "I heard you'll be on East three next week, Monique. Could you help with Nanette: she is psychotic. I'm worried about her going into labor soon, with twins."

Monique came to the door where Alex was waiting alone. "*Oui*, yes, of course. Jeanne, who just had her baby, is fine, and the little one is suckling well, Alex," Monique said, pressing his hand.

"Thanks to you."

"You have been very brave to establish that department with all the resistance against it. I love you more for all your kindness to these poor people," she added.

Alex straightened up, feeling ten feet taller, and thanked her for her support. They both walked out together as Aaron escorted all the students down the hall.

Now the students were to see the rooms and nurse's office, where they would have a lecture on medications. Then, they could sit in the common room to observe the patients.

"Soon, my friends, this treatment will be much improved. Doctor Gage is working with the general hospital in town and the anesthetic department. He wants to have muscle relaxants to be given intravenously to the ECT patients. It is to reduce the muscle contractions and stop any fractures," Aaron said, pointing to Alex, who rejoined the class briefly.

"Sounds like a great idea," a student offered somewhat sarcastically.

Aaron looked at the young man, but only nodded in agreement. "Also, an anesthetist will be present in case of emergencies, and a better, mild, sedative will be given to calm them down before the treatments."

The female student asked in all seriousness, "Who ever found or discovered such a procedure, Doctor Gage, and how?"

Alex took over the lecture. He looked at the girl's name tag. "Good question, Laurie. A couple of Italians, Cerletti and Bini, in the late nineteen-thirties, experimented with electricity for many reasons. They jabbed people who had uncontrollable spasms with electric wires to try and cure the tremors."

"I read that electric currents were used long before then, Doctor. Egyptian physicians, and others later on, used electric eels to try and cure nervous maladies."

"Yes, but by accident; they found they could produce a convulsion in dogs, pigs, and other animals by passing the current across their victim's frontal lobes."

The group was interested: they made notes, and all were in rapt attention. "Poor dogs, to be treated in such a cruel manner," Laurie piped up.

"I agree, but the manager of the local abattoir, located just outside of Milan, asked them to find a way to slaughter animals faster, with less blood, by using their electric jolts."

Laurie shook her head in dismay. "Why at the abattoir, where they kill animals anyway? That's one reason why I don't eat meat. Yuck."

Alex chuckled. "Yes, many are vegetarians now. The manager said it was too messy. Blood all over the place, he complained. He wanted the doctors to do it faster and more humanely."

"Did they?"

"Well, they strapped down some pigs and jolted their brains with the current. Unfortunately, all they found was that the animals just had convulsions. They didn't die, and instead ran off squealing."

"Bad luck, doc. So, they gave up?"

"Not quite. They were very discouraged. Then, later, they thought maybe, just maybe, they could cure mental ills with a convulsion. It had been known for centuries that anyone who had a seizure due to a blow or fever from an infection was cured of their insanity for a while. So they went to the local asylum outside Milan, and they tried it on a few chronic, insane schizophrenics, who were in the long-stay wards at that hospital," Alex explained.

He paused for the dramatic effect and sucked on his pipe for a minute.

Everyone waited until Laurie asked again, "So? So, what happened?"

Alex tapped his pipe on the step and refilled it. "After three or four treatments, those severely ill men were cured. They insisted on going home. And they did."

"Good for them," a student at the back whispered to his buddy.

"After that, the next treatment was done in 1938, in Italy, but it was all delayed due to the war. Started again in 1946. No anesthetic, no muscle relaxants, no nurses, no oxygen mask to help the patient breathe."

"Just wires to the head bone, Doctor? Wow," someone asked.

"No, they used an ice tong; you know: those tongs that pick-up blocks of ice. The tong was then padded, oiled, and placed just over the temples. Then the doctors administered a jolt of one hundred and ten volts for about two-tenths of a second."

"That's what we practice still, but we will use an anesthetist to sedate the patient and watch his breathing and other vital signs. It's so much safer now," Aaron added.

The group of students were left to wander into the common room.

After the brief lecture, it was Laurie who took Alex aside once they were alone. "Doctor Gage, I just wanted to say that this has been difficult for me, but I wanted to thank you so much," she said in a soft, low tone with a quiver in her voice.

"You're welcome, Laurie, but for those historical lectures?"

"No, Doctor, no. It was because of my brother. My brother was ill, suffering from delusions of grandeur. He believed he was President of America, and a king at other times, walking about with a bed sheet as a toga just like Julius Caesar."

"Sorry to her about your brother, Laurie."

"Thank you for your kindness. He was admitted here. It was you who treated him, Doctor Gage," she confided. She seemed fearful to be talking about a relative so close to her.

Alex shook his head, trying to recall the history. "When was that, Laurie?"

"Earlier, in September. My brother Charles said you were new here. He said you were very kindly to him. It was this very same treatment that we just witnessed that cured him."

"Good to hear."

"Also, my parents were so grateful to you for phoning them often to tell them about his progress."

"Well. Thanks for telling me. I hope he is well and do give him my regards."

"I will, Doctor Gage. I will. He has gone back to college to be a vet. He always loved animals, dogs especially. Chuck was my kid brother. I raised him from childhood, since Mom had to work."

"I recall talking to your dad."

"Yeah. He is in a wheelchair. Multiple sclerosis and disabled. Mom brought home the bacon, but not for me," she said, giggling.

"Ouch. Sorry to hear, Laurie. You did well to care for Chuck. Well done. Congratulations."

"Oh, thank you. No one ever said that to me," she said with her eyes misting up. She added, "My parents and I are indebted to you for being so kind to him. Bless you," she repeated, with a tear in her eye. Her face turned red. She took his hand, pressed it warmly, and walked away.

Alex watched as Laurie joined her classmates. She was wiping a tear away and blowing her nose in a kerchief. He relit his pipe and was ready to make ward rounds with Monique.

However, Aaron was waiting for him until they were alone. "So, my friend, I need you to go and have your photo taken by my friend. He will come here and take your picture. You know, to be put on my ID to let you into the exam room, my friend," he said, emphasizing 'my friend' twice.

"I sure as Hell won't, and don't call me friend, Doctor Aaron Levy," Alex said, emphasizing his name.

Aaron smirked and, with a dramatic flourish, brought out the newspaper clipping. He pointed to the name of the new mail administrator, whom he would call if Alex didn't agree.

"Sure, you will, my friend; I am so certain you will, friend. Oh sorry, I mean Doctor Gage." Aaron scoffed and put the papers back in his hip pocket.

Alex watched Aaron turn on his heels and slowly walk out the massive doors, leaving them open for the cold breeze to blow in on Alex.

Troubled, with his foot aching in the dampness now coming through the open door, Alex stood there for the longest time.

He thought of what his options might be.

✳

CHAPTER 45

Gabriella

THAT week, Alex continued to read and make notes in his small room at the hospital. He was anxious but forced himself to study.

The next day, back in the Admin building again, he met Gabriella, Aaron's girlfriend, in the hallway. She held a stack of accounting papers, to be filed away.

This day, unlike in the past, when she was always cheerful, she looked morose. She was a pretty, dark, Sicilian girl: "well-proportioned," as Aaron once said.

This day, she had her head down, sorrowful. She stopped to talk with Alex and pulled him over to a small recess in the hallway. Away from visitors milling about.

Alex was surprised to see the bruise on her right eye, even though it was starting to fade.

"Hello, Gabriella. My goodness, what happened to you?" he asked, concerned. He pointed to the discoloration on her face. "Who hit you? Was it Doctor Levy?"

She hesitated for a moment. She wanted to talk. "No, Doctor Gage. I've heard nice things about you, and I want to tell you that Vittorio said he would kill you. It was for moving him out of the wards and into the laundry rooms. He is dangerous, Doctor. Be careful, please."

Alex had heard such warnings before, from Aaron. Vittorio threatened to get Bruno, or his brother, to kill him over the drug trafficking with Christina.

One time, Vittorio had Aaron by the neck and threatened him also, for seducing Gabriella away from him. He called him a *figlio di puttana*, an Italian son of a bitch.

"Yes, thank you. *Grazie*, Gabriella. *Grazie*, but was it he who struck you?"

Gabriella put her hand up to cover her eye. "No, no; not Aaron. It was Vittorio, but some time ago. I am healing," she said. She turned her head to hide the bruise.

"I'm sorry to see that. Why did he do this to you?"

Gabriella started to walk away. She was fearful, maybe that she had said too much. "He wanted to take me away to his rooms in the city. To force me to live with him. He has a gun, Doctor. Be careful."

"I will, but you be doubly careful, Gabriella. Doctor Cartier doesn't come here much anymore?"

"He is upset. Like over the children who are now gone. Was your presentation to the provincial authorities difficult?"

"Only partially, because I couldn't speak French. The Premier of Québec insisted that I bring an interpreter. So I did. I also showed him *Mère* Denise's official letter again, about the little children working here."

Gabriella was impressed, and quickly grasped his hand and shook it rapidly. "Like, well done, Doctor. The government has agreed, and is sending all the children back home, or to their group homes, in the cities. Many are in foster homes or adopted out."

"And all before Christmas, too. We have to teach some of the patients to now work in the laundry, kitchens, and gardens, but it was worth it."

"The director. Like, he's not here much anymore. Angry at you. But, like, there is still much money he's not, like, aware of," she said with a forced smile.

"Good, we can still disperse it to those patients, Gabriella. You won't get into trouble?"

"He's oblivious of what he has in his accounts. Like, no problem-o," she said, and walked away.

He watched her leave. His concern was the possibility of Cartier being one of the oral examiners, if he ever recovered from his deep despair.

Cartier was rarely seen at the hospital anymore, after Katarina had left him and emptied his bank accounts.

She had returned to her Russia.

※

CHAPTER 46

Vinny's Risky Plan

ALEX returned to the DaCosta house and prayed that Vinny and Mamma D had quieted down after two weeks. Rani was about more often, cooking, cleaning, and helping Mamma D.

Alex was restless on the couch in the Admin building, and the nights were cold in late January, so he came to his home to help as Rani had to go back to Montréal.

On a Saturday morning a few days later, Alex had a day off. He woke from a short nap to hear howls from the kitchen.

"Damn. Same thing I heard from Mamma D after Paulo's murder. What now?" he said as he went downstairs.

He found Mamma D in tears again but coughing. "From a bronchitis," she reassured Alex, who expressed concern.

"Listen," she howled. A small transistor radio, sitting on her kitchen table, had the news on.

"What is it, Mamma D? Did Vinny have an accident? Is he in hospital?"

"Oh, my Lord no, it's Rani, for gosh almighty. The police just called. They said she, and for goodness sakes, was in the hospital. Badly bruised after being attacked. Maybe raped, good Lord."

Alex's mind flooded with visions of Rani in some alley. She could have been accosted by the addicts she liked to treat in the out-patient's clinics at the hospital in town.

Alex had a second thought. "Was it Lafayette Riel? He has been transferred to a group home, on Rani's insistence, and he was living near Rani's hospital clinic."

Vinny heard the loud wailing and bounced into the kitchen, cigarette dangling from his mouth and Claudius trailing behind.

Then Mamma D told him the bad news.

Vinny pounded his fist on the table with such force that the cutlery and plates spilled over. Claudius slunk under the table, trembling, and pissed on the floor.

"Who would do that to our Rani?" Vinny shouted. The veins on his forehead exploded into a dark blue, and his face went chalk white.

"Do they know who did it?" Alex asked as he put his arm around Mamma D and sat her down, turning the radio off.

"Lordy lord, some man with a pony tail. Left his guitar in her office."

Alex knew immediately. "Oh my God. It was Riel. I told her not to see him at that clinic, wanting to do psychotherapy with him. Damn her. She told me that he played his guitar for her."

"Yeah. I remember: tits and ass, tits and ass, not good for Riel," Vinny yelled out. He mopped his head with his sweaty bandana, and then cleaned up the dog's urine with the same headscarf.

"Don't swear, Vinny." Mamma D moaned. She took the sopping wet bandana and rinsed it in the sink.

Alex sat down next to Mamma D. "It was Riel, alright. They'll find him. He was living near the hospital, waiting for the results of his lab tests after his shoulder injury."

"Don't blame yourself, doc. You can't shut the barn door after the chickens are out. Look, do you want me to get him for you?" Vinny said, strutting about the kitchen. He flexed his biceps and pointed his fingers, like a loaded pistol, shooting here there and everywhere.

Alex shook his head and gave Mamma D a clean napkin to wipe away her tears.

Vinny guffawed and lit up another vile Philip Morris. With that soother, he snorted like a wild bull. Blue smoke came out of his flared nostrils.

"If they jail him, then I can get in and I'm out before they know it. All the coppers at the station know me real good. A couple of pops in the side of the head, and it's over. I'll use the silencer," he said, pacing the room.

"Shush, already, Vincent. Golly gee. Keep your shirt on," Mamma D shouted at him.

With Riel dead, then Alex would lose the profits from the sale of Riel's cigarettes. He kept that to himself and felt ashamed of thinking of his greed while Rani was in pain.

Vinny was walking about the kitchen, shooting at everything he saw with his clenched hand, a pointed finger sticking out like a pistol.

"They wouldn't find him until mealtime. I'll leave the gun in his hand, and they'll think he shot himself. What do you say?"

"Dog gone it, just settle down, Vinny. Let the police do their job. For land's sakes, and don't worry about me. My Lord, I'll be just fine and dandy," Mamma D said, holding him back by the arm.

"Fine and dandy, bullshit. How can you be fine and then dandy all at the same time, woman?" Vinny growled.

Alex gave Mamma D one of his barbiturates, which he always carried in his pocket. Vinny escorted her away into the living room. She went to sleep on the sofa, coughing even in her sleep.

Vinny and Alex left her and went outside for a smoke. "I phoned the hospital, but Rani was sedated and asleep; couldn't have visitors,"

Alex told Vinny while sitting on the back porch with a pile of Paulo's Playboys on the floor at his side.

Vinny took the cap off a Coca-Cola and drank from the bottle. Alex pulled out his Stromboli pipe and methodically filled it. He tapped the edges of the tobacco into the rim of the bowl and lit up.

They both smoked in silence.

Vinny opened the door and flicked his cigarette butt over the porch railing. He picked up one of Paulo's old Playboys.

"That Riel guy, doc. I heard the nurses talking about him when I was fixing the lights on his ward, some time ago," he said as he flipped through the pages of last year's magazine.

"Nice man in some ways, Vinny," Alex said, holding his nose. He added, "What are you using, Vinny? On your face?"

Vinny reached over and put his arm on Alex's shoulder. "Paulo's old after-shave. I'll give you a bottle, but they won't find Riel. He'll take off and live in the forest."

"He's a mountain man, Vinny; but no thanks, never use that stuff."

Vinny said something about the "Sunshine Girl" in the center fold and threw the edition down. "By the way. Heard you talkin' on the phone that night. To your mama."

Alex had his head down. He didn't look at Vinny. "You were sitting there, in your long johns?"

"Yep. Was in the kitchen. Lights out. Didn't see me, but I heard you talkin' for a long time."

Alex avoided talk about his mother and switched back to Riel. "I'll have to see Riel if he escapes, and they find him, before they cut his brain with the lobotomy. He won't remember his name after that."

"I'm sure he'll still be in the bushes down by the river, waiting for a freighter to take him east," Vinny said, pointing in the direction of the St. Lawrence.

Alex coughed on the harsh tobacco Vinny was smoking. He pointed to the massive Stanley padlock on the garage door. "Got gold in there, Vinny?"

Vinny grinned, said nothing, and left to get some exercise with a jog around the block.

A now-svelte Claudius, who had lost much weight following Vinny on his daily jogging routes, refused to budge. It was still too cold for Claudius. He was not farting as much, since master and dog were now eating less pasta.

Alex waited until Vinny had gone. Then he put on a jacket, took his fedora off the hook in the hallway, and went down the back steps and looked in the grimy window on the side of the garage.

He saw a gym with a full workout area. There was a leather punching bag hanging from the rafters. He peered in further. There was a stationary bicycle bolted to the cement floor, and a rowing machine in one corner.

As Alex wiped the glass, he saw the walls were covered with rusted army equipment. Blue helmets with NATO symbols in white, bayonets, tattered photos, and a few medals were pinned to the wall.

In the middle of the dirt floor were two barber's chairs. Complete with the footrest.

Claudius had jumped down from the porch and joined Alex for a leak outside.

"Look at that, Claudius. Two partially-dressed store mannequins, made of Styrofoam, are strapped into the chairs. Each Styrofoam head is full of holes, and dozens of empty pistol shells are still on the floor," he said to the mutt.

Claudius finished pissing against the wooden shed and came to sit near Alex.

Alex left the window and sat on the porch step. The sun coming through warmed Claudius as he curled up, in a ball, next to Alex.

302

Vinny trotted back and threw himself down on the cold grass outside and did twenty quick pushups. He looked up at Alex without panting, and then did ten more pushups, using only one arm at a time.

"Next week, doc. Next week, two of those punks who did my son in are going to get an anonymous gift from yours truly. A free shave and haircut, doc. Even a manicure."

He rolled over onto his back and did twenty quick sit ups with his arms behind his head. Alex laughed to see playful Claudius running around, in circles, barking at Vinny.

"At their favorite barber shop. Tip included," Vinny added as he wrestled Claudius to the ground.

"Very generous of you, Vinny," Alex said.

Alex smiled as he walked away. He knew that Vinny had some vile plan for revenge. He feared the worst, for what might happen to his new family, which now included Rani.

✳

CHAPTER 47

"Murder," She Cried

ALEX entered the doors to the Admin building the very next day. He was there to retrieve his American Journal of Psychiatry from his desk drawer.

Gabriella shouted out to him as he slowly mounted the steps. She almost ran into Alex and pulled him into the hallway. "Doctor Gage, I have searched everywhere. Nowhere is he to be found. Like, he doesn't answer his phone, Doctor. His cleaning lady said she hasn't seen him for days," she yelled, breathless.

Gabriella looked very distraught: agitated, unkempt, her hair disheveled, and exhausted. She looked like she hadn't slept for days.

"Doctor Cartier is unwell and on leave, Gabriella. Probably in the city somewhere," Alex explained, wanting to calm her down. He took her by the arm and escorted her back toward her office.

She broke away from his arm and whispered as nurses walked by to start their morning shift, "No, no, like, not the director. It's Aaron. It's Aaron. I know something bad has happened. Like, I can feel it in my bones, Doctor Gage."

"What are you talking about, Gabriella?"

"Three days ago. It was three, maybe four days ago. We were to meet and go out for dinner after work. Vittorio was here, lurking in the hallways."

"Sound like trouble."

"He came out after Aaron. They had a quarrel. Like, Vittorio was pulling me away from Aaron. He, Vittorio, punched Aaron in the face."

A nurse had stopped and asked if she could help Gabriella, since she was so upset. They were just outside her office.

Alex reassured the nurse that she would be okay with him.

"What happened? Come, sit down in your office and tell me what this is all about," Alex asked. He ushered her into the office and closed the door behind him.

Gabriella sat down in her chair behind her desk. "Aaron walked away. He was holding his head. Like, he seemed confused, Doctor. Vittorio punched me. Pushed me down on the floor. Then he followed Aaron out," she cried, speaking in rapid, staccato sentences.

"It's okay. Heard it before. Did you call security? Were you all right?"

"No. I was shaking. Bruised, like. He hurt my shoulder against the desk. When I fell, crying. He went after Aaron. I'm afraid. My God. What did he do, Doctor?"

"Aaron hasn't called you?"

Gabriella shuffled some accounting papers and ledgers on her messy desk. She tried to tidy the clutter and shook her head to think clearly.

She looked at Alex, pleading. "No. Not a word. He must have done something. I've looked everywhere. No one has seen him. Anywhere. Please help me find him."

Alex was thinking fast. "I haven't seen him either, come to think of it. He didn't attend ward rounds yesterday. He had a group meeting down in that cellar, where they used to do those hideous water torture treatments."

Suddenly the light bulb flashed for her. "Yes. The cellar."

"Maybe he collapsed there. Let's have a look. Come on."

Gabriella stood up, and for the first time, seemed hopeful. "Yes, like, he said that once to me. Can we go there? It is an awful, dark place, but I'll go with you."

Alex helped Gabriella from behind her desk. He buttoned his white hospital coat over his sport's jacket for extra warmth. He zipped up his parka and forced the fedora down on his forehead.

He helped her put on her heavy winter jacket. "Bring that flashlight, please," Alex suggested. He pointed to the emergency light attached to the wall, since the power often failed in the hospital.

Gabriella pulled the flashlight off the wall. They both walked outside into the frigid cold. Alex helped her around the corner to the entrance of the cellar; they entered the bowels of the building.

Alex pushed apart the large, steel doors with rusted hinges. "I can't understand why the Devil Aaron wanted to work down here, in this Hell-hole."

He helped Gabriella down a long flight of cement stairs into the yawning chasm. She was hesitant and scared, and held on tightly to Alex's arm.

Gabriella had trouble descending the stairs in her heels and shone the light ahead. "Told me, like, it was a peaceful place to work. Except for the mice and stray cats, which his group of patients hated, but fed."

When they entered the vast chamber, it was the same feral cats that welcomed the intruders. They jumped about at their ankles and onto their legs, seeking attention and scraps of food. The scrawny predators mewed and cried, wanting a hand out.

The cellar was cold, damp, musty, and devoid of light. The broken windows were shuttered tight to keep out the late winter gusts with snow.

Gabriella went to the near wall, where Aaron had an electric heater near his circle of chairs. She plugged it in. It rattled and whirled but offered a semblance of warmth.

"He's not here, Doctor Gage. It's an awful place. Let's go," she said with a shudder. She shooed away several cats, who milled about yowling, rubbed themselves against her legs, and nipped at her shoes.

Alex nodded in agreement, since his foot ached with the damp cold, but he continued to peer into the darkness of the room. It was the scurry of many rats, making a racket far off in one corner, that caught his attention.

A faint beam of light came in from a partially-opened shutter. It struck something silver hanging down from a water pipe.

"Over there, Gabriella. Over there in that corner. Let's just walk a bit and shine your flashlight there. Into that dark corner."

When she did just that, she screamed such a terrifying wail that all the cats and the mice scurried away with her ear-piercing shriek.

It was a horrendous sight that greeted them as they followed the beam of light into the darkness. It was her Aaron, hanging from his silver chain around his neck. It was strung up over a large water pipe, above his head.

"Oh, my God. Aaron." Gabriella swooned and fell onto the cement floor in a heap at Alex's feet.

Alex, aghast at the sight, went to her and cradled her head as she slowly revived. He helped her up. "Are you all right? Just stay here, Gabriella. Let me go closer and have a look."

She shook her head, and slowly got to her feet. "No. No, like, I want to see him, too."

Alex helped her walk the far distance toward the dark corner where the body was hanging. As they did this, Alex forced open a grimy shutter from a cracked window, to let some light shine on the gruesome scene.

Gabriella averted her eyes from the body, which was already starting to decompose. A few rats had nibbled away through Aaron's Italian leather shoes. They had devoured some of his toes and heels on his bare, exposed feet.

Alex slammed his hand at one large, aggressive rat inside Aaron's crotch. It had gnawed at Aaron's testicles, up his pant leg. As the rat dropped to the floor, he kicked it against the wall.

"Why, Aaron, why suicide? And to Gabriella, who was so good to you?" Alex asked, foolishly expecting an answer from the corpse.

Gabriella was somewhat composed at that point, and more alert as she looked over the horrific, tragic scene.

She pointed to a chair close by. "Look, Doctor Gage. Look, that chair is standing upright. See?"

"So?"

"So, Aaron couldn't have committed suicide by hanging himself. If he did, then he would have kicked the chair aside and toppled it over."

"My God, I think you're right. Also, his arm was paralyzed. He couldn't string himself up. Couldn't tie that chain around his neck and then push the chair over."

Gabriella put her hands to her mouth and gagged. "My God, the sadist pulled his pants partly down and hung his genitals out for the rats to feast on, Alex."

Alex pulled Gabriella away from the gross scene. He pulled the chair over, stood up, and loosened the chain from the pipe above Aaron's head.

He pulled the chain away, and the body fell to the ground in a thud. Aaron's false glass eye spilled out and rolled away.

Gabriella wanted to go to Aaron but was repelled by the odor of feces. His bowels had discharged their contents, and urine stained his legs.

She placed a kerchief over her nose and went to him. She cradled his head in her arms and wept softly, asking over and over, "Why, why, why?"

She looked to be in a daze as she did this. She turned Aaron's head slightly. "Doctor Gage," she shouted out, "He has a deep cut on the back of his head, a heavy blow. See?"

Alex went to her and looked down at Aaron's head, turning it slightly to expose the deep gash. He went to where the chair had been and picked up a large, metal pipe lying close by. It was used to transfer water from a hose into a water tub.

"It has blood on it, Gabriella. Clotted, but blood for sure."

"Murder," Gabriella cried out. "It's murder. He was murdered," she said over and over. She went to Alex, wanting to handle the pipe.

"No. Leave it. For prints. It will have mine. And maybe Vittorio's."

"Like, let me see for myself," she added, trembling again in despair at the obvious evidence of the murder scene.

Alex pulled her away. "No, don't. We must not touch anything anymore. We must let the police look at all this undisturbed. For evidence," he said again.

He ever-so-gently pushed Gabriella further away from the body, which was now gnarled and twisted and partially devoured by rats.

She pointed to the body. "See that. Vittorio. He said to me that he knew it was Aaron who killed his Celeste," she said as she pointed to the rats running about, ready to devour the corpse.

"Aaron said that it was Vittorio who collaborated with the Germans to send the Jews, and some of his family, to the concentration camps."

Gabriella put her hand up to her face to shield the awful sight from her eyes. She heaved, and Alex heard her gut gurgle. "Alex, I think I'm going to vomit my breakfast."

Alex turned her away just as she vomited all over the floor. He gave her his kerchief to wipe her chin of vomitus and helped move her away from the awful mess.

She painfully, agreed making her way with the flashlight, but muttered Vittorio's name several times as she walked. Alex watched her turn away into the darkness as silverfish, mice, and rats gobbled up her vomitus from the filthy floor.

As she walked away, Alex reached into Aaron's back pocket and retrieved the newspaper clipping that could potentially implicate him. He crumbled the clipping up and stuffed it into his white coat pocket.

Gabriella stopped for a moment and went to a passageway close by. It held heavy blankets and tarpaulins used to cover the unwilling victims after their baths.

She pulled them off the rails and hauled them over to cover Aaron's body.

"I don't want those filthy rats nipping away at him anymore," she said, tucking the edges into his sides and well over his head.

They left the body with vermin and predators scurrying about. Alex pulled the heater cable out of the socket as they sadly made their way out of the dungeon.

He locked the massive doors as they left.

Once out of the cellar and back in the warmth of the Admin building, Alex told Gabriella to get some tranquillizers from the hospital ward to calm herself down.

"Go home, Gabriella. Rest, and get some sleep after you tell the police what you know, and what we found. I'll do the same with the local hospital *gendarmes*. Maybe the *SQ* also. They'll be here soon. We'll meet again, but please stay away from Vittorio," he cautioned.

As Alex walked away, he reached into his pocket and pulled out the newspaper clipping. He tore it up into small, tiny bits and put them in his pocket to burn when he got home.

He gave a sigh of relief and walked out into the cool, crisp air.

✳

CHAPTER 48

Vinny's Sweet Revenge

IT was only a week later, on a Sunday, that Vinny was on the porch working at the crossword puzzle in the newspaper, *Le Devoir*. When Alex came down for breakfast, he marveled at Vinny's fortitude in developing a new physique; his paunch had totally disappeared. He was spitting sunflower seeds and exercising his mental acuities on the crossword.

One-time stout and flabby Claudius, curled up at his master's feet and snoring softly, was also no longer the over-weight, chunky hound.

Alex was also shocked to see Vinny wearing a leather jacket and heavy leather pants, like the type motorcycle gangs would wear. An electric heater was buzzing near his stockinged feet.

"Glad to see you're exercising your mind, Vinny. Good for you," Alex said as he pointed at the newspaper.

Vinny licked the tip of his pencil and pointed it at Alex. "Yeah, well, this is a tough one. What's the word for dimwitted? Six letters starting with 's'?"

"S?" Well, let's see, ah, how about trying 'stupid,'" Alex answered with a grin.

Vinny nodded and Claudius, lying close to the heater, wagged his tail in agreement, thumping it on the floor.

"That's it," Vinny muttered as he spat out the seeds. He bit into a McIntosh apple he was eating for breakfast. He dropped the apple core for Claudius to gobble up. He washed this sparse meal down with a large gulp of water from a glass on the floor.

"I've never seen you drink water before, Vinny. Well done."

"Shit, man, if you knew what those fish did in that water, you wouldn't either, big boy. You heard that the dictator is out in town somewhere, holed up? Sad to lose his pretty Katie," he answered in all seriousness.

"Yes. Back in Russia, but I fear she'll be sent to the Siberian gulags in the north once they pick her up."

"More likely for deserting Russia during the Stalin era. Shit. Now she'll be used and abused by those sadistic guards or other prisoners," Vinny said sadly.

"Maybe now she'll have that baby she wanted so much. But born in that Siberian wasteland."

"Yep. Won't need that doll her baba gave her to put between her nice, long legs anymore."

Alex nodded in agreement but heard Mamma D coughing upstairs.

"Sorry to hear about your good friend, Doctor Levy," Vinny said, looking up at Alex from his crossword.

"Yeah. Good friend, Vinny," he answered feebly.

Before much more was said about that, Mamma D's cough came rattling through onto the veranda. Alex was worried about her; he recalled poor Sister Denise and her bronchial malady with TB.

"Why all the leather, Vinny? Into weird, sadomasochistic stuff with your lady now?" Alex said as he put on his coat to go out.

"Ha, ha, ha, good joke, Mr. Freud." Vinny snorted. Vinny brushed Claudius' heavy coat, now shiny and healthy, as the dog got up with him. Both were going out for their daily run.

"Don't forget to buy the cough medicine for your wife," Alex said seriously, adding, "I'm very concerned about Mamma D's chronic cough."

Vinny muttered in agreement. He suddenly had a worried look on his face. He put his arm around Alex's shoulder. "You better see Riel before they fry his brains, doc."

"I guess so, now that they caught him, and he's locked up in the prison ward."

Vinny, dressed in his leather outfit, zipped up his black leather jacket and pulled on his heavy motorcycling boots.

"Where are you going, Vinny?" Alex asked.

"Just a quick bike ride for a haircut, my boy," was all he said.

Mamma D came out to the porch and said she had heard the men talking. "Golly gee whiskers, Vincent, do be careful riding around on that hog all by your lonesome."

Vinny patted Mamma D on the back, kissed his wife goodbye, and picked up his motorcycle helmet. Vinny then pulled on his heavy leather gloves and tapped Alex on the back.

He was dressed for bear, and there was no stopping him now as he ambled over to a Harley motorbike. It had been parked outside there by his neighbor friend.

"Good luck," was all Alex added.

After Vinny left, and Mamma D retired to bed again, Alex secluded himself and studied back in his room.

He could hear Mamma D rattling about in the kitchen again, and within the hour she brought him a small tray of ravioli, toasted cheese bread, lasagna, and a glass of homemade red vino, which he put aside.

It was in that very same late afternoon that Alex, needing a stretch after studying, did several sit ups, worked on his abs, and used the barbells to strengthen his shoulders.

He stopped his exercising routine when he heard Vinny talking to his neighbor friend outside his window. When Alex looked outside, he was surprised to see that Vinny was now dressed in a white sport jacket, black slacks, and sporty shoes.

Alex raised his window and shouted down, "Hey, Vinny, where's your leather outfit?"

Vinny stopped chatting and looked up. "What the Hell you talking about, doc? Never owned such stuff," he said, deadpan.

He turned and shook hands with his friend, who rode off with the Harley.

Alex went downstairs to meet Vinny, who was talking to Mamma D. "I was at mass with Father Champlain at the cathedral all morning, Mamma. The good Father gave us his blessing, and I lit a candle for Paulo," Vinny said as Mamma D gave him a hug.

Vinny winked at Alex as he reached for a cola in the fridge and brought out a Philip Morris cigarette. Mamma D quickly took the lighter off the windowsill and lit the cigarette for her husband.

The next day, a Monday, Alex got up early to study for the exams and get back to the hospital. He went downstairs for a break and found Mamma D in the kitchen, as usual, listening to her Italian Dean Martin tapes.

She was still watering Paulo's plants on the windowsill.

Alex grabbed a coffee and slathered Mamma D's homemade marmalade on the toast. He looked at the morning newspaper, which she had spread out in front of Alex. She smiled as she did so.

The headlines read, "*Two drug dealers shot, gangland style, in barber shop on Sunday.*"

Alex tapped his fingers at the paper and looked up at Mamma D. She averted her eyes from his and looked the other way. She continued whistling along to "Arrivederci Roma" with Dean.

Alex put his toast aside and read. "Look at this, Mamma D. The reporter said both gang members were having a shave and haircut in a barbershop. They were also having a manicure and a shampoo and sat next to each other in the chairs."

"That so? Golly gee, Doctor Gage, bless me if it ain't so."

Alex turned to the second page as he continued to read. The next page had photos of those two gang members, who had been shot in the head at the barber shop. Paulo's picture was also on that page.

"Look here. The barber's picture is on the second page, Mamma D."

Alex read out loud as he ate his toast. "*This motorcycle gang member came in through the back door. He then shot both men in the head at point-blank range and ran out the back door. Both men had just had their shampoo, and their heads were covered in a hot towel. The girl giving the manicure was hysterical, and had to be taken to hospital to be sedated. The barber shop was in chaos. The barber complained that his chairs and mirrors were covered in blood.*"

Alex continued to read out loud. "*The killer was gone by the time the police got there. Both men died instantly. One was Italian, the other Chinese. The police said he must have been a young hood; the motorcycle gear totally obscured his identity. He had parked his bike in the back alley and sped away before anybody could see him. The police are on the lookout for a well-built young gang member, probably from one of the Russian gangs in Montréal, they reported.*"

"Well, good luck with that," Alex said, and smiled at Vinny's plot and efficiency.

Mamma D didn't say anything as she rolled the pasta for the cannelloni but was smiling and now humming to "O Sole Mio."

Alex finished his breakfast and went out onto the front porch with his coffee. He found Vinny there, sitting in his rocker with svelte Claudius at his feet.

Vinny had his bare feet up, resting on an empty beer bottle box, unshaven. He had a fly swatter in one hand, ready for any little beasties that survived the cold spell, and a beer in the other. He chewed on sun flower seeds.

"How you doing, doc? Like a cool Labatt's?" he asked, sucking on a Sweet Caporal cigarette and picking his ears with a wooden match.

Claudius pulled himself from under Vinny's chair and ambled to the door, scratching to go out.

"Just fine, Vinny. No thanks. Too early in the morning for me. Were those two guys the ones that murdered Paulo?" he asked, opening the door to let Claudius out.

Vinny ignored the question. "I heard that you might be the next head honcho at that hospital, doc. The word is getting around about your good deeds."

"Thanks, Vinny."

"Our Looney Tunes chief is back in his office on some meds, I heard. Not playing with a full deck, he ain't. You gotta write and get those exams first, man."

"Will do, Vinny," he said as he sat next to Vinny.

"Our dictator sure was a sinner, from what I hears from that head nurse on Riel's sister's ward, my boy. Annette was in getting an oil and lube for her car. Talking like a motor-mouth and wanting to get at him. Some revenge, she said."

"Well, maybe he'll atone for his sins someday, Vinny. Oscar Wilde once said that every saint has a past and every sinner has a future, Vinny."

"Bullshit but keep away from that wop who might do the dirty on Gabriella. He may have a go at you too, since you both found Levy," Vinny said, very seriously. He pointed the wooden match at Alex, which he then used to light his cigarette and pick at his teeth.

Alex's gut rumbled at the potential threat. "What have you heard, Vinny?"

"Not much. That Vittorio guy must have flown the coop. Coppers can't find him."

"Yeah, I heard that they concluded Levy hung himself," Alex said.

"Bullshit. What about Vittorio's fingerprints on that pipe?"

"He swore that he was there some days earlier and used that pipe to kill some rats."

"Bullshit. What about Levy's bloodied skull and chair still standing?"

Alex thought about that. "Yeah, well, the *SQ* corporal had to agree with Vittorio. The rats devoured Levy's scalp. They figured that he was able to push that chair away enough so it didn't topple."

"Bullshit. But, there's a little bit of good in everything. Now we don't have to split that percentage to the poor passed and departed."

"I was glad you came to his funeral."

"The synagogue? Yeah, well, you said some nice things about him in your eulogy. It was a decent tribute to your friend."

※

CHAPTER 49

A Serious Predicament

"CAN we see *Breakfast at Tiffany's*, Alex? I'd love to see Audrey Hepburn," Monique asked as she snuggled up to him in his truck to keep warm. It was her day off that weekend. They spent the day shopping in town and just walking about, enjoying a warm spell early in the new year.

After the Saturday night movie, they sat at a local hamburger diner on the highway. "You have those lovely, flashing eyes, just like Hepburn," Alex told her as he looked at her dark eyes and lovingly touched her hand.

He munched on his fries, put some mustard on his hamburger, and waited for Monique to tell him what she was going to do with the notes she made about Beatrice.

She had told Alex about her notes earlier that night. It was about Cartier's examination and sexual abuse with the poor girl in his office. She gave her private notes to Alex to read at the drive-in.

"I just wanted your opinion as to the legality of my writings, Alex," she said. Alex had read her handwritten, but very precise, notes during the intermission and under the roof light in his truck.

What he had read worried Alex. "I have a moral and ethical medical duty to see Cartier and confront him with this information, my dear."

"*Mon chéri*, be careful. The director will defend himself now that he's back from sick leave. He will say that Beatrice is insane: not credible. He will call you to be a troublemaker, like Riel, if you go to him with what I told you," Monique cautioned as she gripped his hand at the restaurant.

"I have a duty to protect her and all other patients. I took an oath to do no harm," Alex replied worriedly, fidgeting with his fries.

"That man, he is wicked. Your fate and our future are in his hands. He could disqualify you, somehow, from taking your exams, and send you back south if you take my notes to him."

Alex smiled warmly at her when she talked about their future. "You're right, and my year could be in jeopardy," he said as he handed her back the envelope containing the incriminating evidence.

"I made copies of all my notes on our hospital Xerox machine. Just in case he got a hold of the originals and destroyed them."

Alex was very impressed with that and told her so.

Monique became quiet as she sipped on her vanilla milkshake and bit into her hamburger.

Alex stood, still shaken by the abuse, and muttered about needing to act.

Monique sat Alex down and pulled her chair close to his. "Calm yourself. The fastest road to Hell is by talking to the Devil," she whispered as she held his hands tightly.

Alex pushed the rest of his hamburger and fries aside. "That kind of behavior from a doctor makes me sick, Monique. Damn, it's abhorrent, immoral, and illegal," he whispered.

The foursome at the next table eyed him warily.

"Yes, and not nice either," she added in a joking manner.

Alex laughed. He loved this woman, who could calm him down with a sense of humor. "Riel will take his revenge on Cartier someday. The truth will out," Alex prophesized.

Monique told him to hush. She continued to stroke his hand gently to calm him further. She suggested quietly that they go back to his truck, so she could help him to relax even more so. She rubbed his thumb up and down with her fingers in a sensual manner.

Alex considered the erotic proposal but stayed on the subject. "I have a duty to go to the college with such information," Alex said, thanking her for the offer.

It was then that she got him to promise not to act impulsively. "Anger can lead to dire consequences for you, my dear Alex. Don't worry, I'll help you. Promise me that you will wait and not do anything until we talk about how to deal with this."

Alex hesitated as they both got up. He agreed and made his promise to her.

They left, both troubled. Monique was already forming a plan to help Alex, and to confront Cartier, on her own.

They drove back to her residence on the hospital grounds. She did what she had promised.

Alex, relieved and calmer, gave her a warm hug. "You know, Monique, your notes will be most effective. But I'll wait until my exams are over and I'm a qualified psychiatrist."

Alex watched her walk away from his truck. He knew that Cartier had some powerful friends in the medical community. But he was confident it would be her simple, handwritten notes that would bring him to justice.

✳

CHAPTER 50

Monique Meets Cartier

ONE morning, a few days into the early weeks of February, Alex sat in his office on the ward. He composed two letters, revising them both three times. They had to be just right. His future could be on the line.

Monique was busy charting her report on a new admission to her ward. She brought him a cup of tea from the ward kitchen when she was done.

Alex was pleased to see her and showed Monique the letters as he sipped his hot tea. "One is for the Québec College of Physicians, Monique."

"Is it about Cartier's abuse of Beatrice, my love?"

"Yes, and the other is about lobotomies, and the disastrous side effects of such permanent intrusions on the brain. It's barbaric. That letter is to the prime minister of Canada, and a copy to the Medical College also, Monique."

Monique went to Alex and put her arm around his shoulder. "Just put them in the top drawer in your desk, Alex. Wait until you pass the exams in a few weeks, and then he won't have a hold on you."

Alex wavered with the decision but knew that Monique was thinking clearly. "I guess so. Will do," he said, knowing she was right.

Monique gathered up the cups and gave Alex a tender kiss. He felt her watching him as he put the letters in a sealed envelope and into his desk. He locked the desk and put the key in his pocket.

❋

That very same week, Monique decided to confront Dr. Jacques Cartier. She called Gabriella to confirm that he was back in his office that day and was assured that he was, although for that morning only.

She decided to act for fear that her Alex might not contain himself as he had promised. She decided that this was the only way she could protect him.

She had a hot shower that morning, her day off, to quell her anxiety, only ate a light breakfast—so she wouldn't throw up—and prayed to the Holy Mary for added strength.

She walked slowly from her residence to the Admin building, protected by her umbrella from a heavy, cold rain that pelted down. She prayed that Cartier would still be there, since she may not be as bold the next time.

Once inside the building, she put her umbrella in the stand. She stood outside Cartier's office door and vacillated. She almost turned away.

Monique looked about as she knocked on the door. Then she opened his door and peered into the waiting room. There was no one else there in Cartier's inner office.

She was relieved; she feared to be publicly embarrassed and humiliated if he threw her out into the hallway.

She walked in and quietly asked the secretary, *Madame d'Albert*, the sign on her desk read, to see the director.

Cartier's secretary, with glasses falling off the tip of her nose, stopped typing and finally looked up. Monique saw the expression on the secretary's face: a young nurse in Cartier's office? "You should be talking to your nursing supervisor, not bothering the busy director of this hospital," she said brusquely.

D'Albert stood up, irritated, displeased, and looked about to dismiss the young nurse away. She asked Monique, who stood at attention when glared at by the officious woman, what she wanted.

Monique only said, "It is a highly personal matter, *Madame.*"

Madame d'Albert said she was too busy and added, "The director was not seeing anybody this day."

The young nurse just quietly stood there, determined.

The secretary turned away, gave a snooty snort, and then knocked on Cartier's door. Monique heard a gruff beckoning sound from behind the door.

The secretary feared Cartier's ire, as she knew that he had a volatile temper. He had fired his previous receptionist in a fit of rage over some inconsequential matter. But she persevered and opened the inner office door.

"A young nurse is waiting to see you, just before your lunch, Doctor. No appointment," she said sternly.

"She needs an appointment, *Madame* d'Albert," Cartier bellowed.

This howl caused Monique to gasp and her eyes to twitch, when she heard his fierce holler. It sent her legs to quivering as beads of sweat fell down the back of her neck.

"She didn't make an appointment. She's just sitting there now, Doctor. On the chair. Outside your office and she—" the secretary stopped, interrupted.

Monique stiffened as she heard Cartier cut her off with another muffled shout. He told his secretary that he was using his new Dictaphone machine to dictate a letter to the medical college, and again shouted indistinctly.

"Yes, Doctor. Well done. A patient's husband had reported that you were drunk and out of control one evening while you were making rounds. You must write to the medical association with an explanation," the secretary said quietly.

Cartier was thinking of a plausible answer. "I'll just say I had taken a cold remedy, and the medication and the fever made me unsteady on my feet."

"I am certain that would satisfy them," the secretary replied sweetly, sugar dripping from her lips. She clearly liked to appease her boss.

Madame d'Albert, his trusted secretary, returned to Monique, pointed a highly-polished, manicured finger at her, and ordered, "You will have to leave, right now, nurse."

Monique said nothing. She just sat down again, with hands folded on her lap. She decided to be patient, not smile as she always did, and be totally professional.

After an hour, Cartier shouted that he had finished the letter. He took the thin, plastic sheet from the roller on the Dictaphone, walked out, and gave it to *Madame* d'Albert for transcription.

He looked at the young nurse, who still sat there stiffly in her clean, white, starched uniform.

"She is still waiting. Waiting very patiently, sir. She is on her day off. That is what she told me," d'Albert said as she held the plastic Dictaphone sheet.

Cartier looked at Monique. He thought he might recognize her from the wards. The young nurse was sitting on the chair with her head down, holding her rosary beads with lips moving.

He would dispose of her quickly. She had some complaint about another nurse, he surmised.

"*Bonjour,*" Cartier said in French, addressing the young nurse.

Monique looked up when he spoke to her. She wore her white shoes highly polished and a nurse's cap from another hospital. This told

Cartier that she wasn't a graduate from his hospital, and she should be easy to deal with.

Monique waited, like she hoped to be taken into his office for more privacy.

He watched her lips moving as she softly recited a passage that the nuns often taught at times of stress.

"*Bonjour, Docteur Cartier,*" she said, looking up with her voice dutifully lowered. She stood up and curtsied slightly.

She was very nervous and looked straight ahead at his bow tie and buttoned, brown suit underneath his open, white hospital coat.

"How can I help you, my child?" Cartier asked with a paternal twinkle in his eye. He liked the fact that she seemed so deliciously innocent. She had a Madonna-like, virginal face, beautiful dark eyes, and a trim body. He swallowed hard to see that her uniform was amply filled above her waist.

He liked that. Maybe he could offer her something and receive something in return, he thought.

"May I come into your office?" she asked courteously.

Cartier hesitated. He again looked at his secretary, now sitting behind her desk. She was burdened with charts of patients being admitted. She was busy and ignored his look; she clearly resented any slight intrusion by this nurse.

Cartier waited. The older woman finally shrugged her shoulders, indicating that she knew nothing of the young girl's request. She rolled a white sheet of paper into her black Underwood typewriter and placed the headphones over her ears.

Cartier turned and opened his office door wider. He beckoned the young lady to enter. He cautiously asked, "How can I help you, Miss, ah, Miss…"

He looked at her small name tag, attached to her nurse's blouse above her left breast. "Miss Monique Joliette."

"*Oui. Merci,*" she answered respectfully, and then followed the director into his large office. Her eyes remained lowered as she waited. He liked the signs of respect and admiration that she showed.

Monique Joliette remained standing. She watched Cartier move into his protected position behind his desk.

"You may sit down, my child."

"*Merci.*"

Monique moved into the large, upholstered chair in front of Cartier's massive desk. She locked her heels together tightly and maintained a rigid back. She looked straight ahead, unblinking. She held a sheet of paper.

She sat there as Cartier pushed his chair forward into his desk and shuffled some papers. "As you can see, I'm quite busy, nurse. What is it?" he asked tersely, exasperated, and repeated again in French.

Monique quickly crossed herself and took a deep breath. She, a student nurse only in her twenties and her last, but still vulnerable, year at this institution, spoke to Dr. Cartier: the most powerful man at the hospital.

"It is I who will send a handwritten letter to your medical college and to the minister of health with a complaint, sir. With copies made." That was all she said.

She waited.

Cartier sat up, pushed the papers aside, and laughed nervously. He stared at her intently. She was so delightfully submissive, so purely innocent, and so deliciously virginal, that he felt an internal, visceral excitement. So much so, that his mind was elsewhere for a minute.

It was the word, 'complaint,' that stirred him from his fantasy while he stared at her breasts.

"A complaint? What the Devil about, my dear child?" he asked, with voice lowered but eyes raised from her breasts.

Monique waited. She took in a deep breath. "It is about *mademoiselle* Bonfleur, Doctor. With all due respect, she is my patient, and … and your patient, respectfully, sir."

Cartier pushed his chair back and looked at the ceiling. Confused, he tried to recall some patient, any patient, by the name of Bonfleur.

Cartier looked at Monique square in the eye, angry. "I have four thousand patients here or more. How in damnation would you think I knew every one of them?"

Monique didn't flinch, but she lowered her eyes in respect. "Beatrice. Beatrice Bonfleur."

"Who?" he shouted in anger. "Why don't you take this up with your nursing superior? A letter, did you say? To the college, eh? Are you mad, girl?"

"*Non,* my *docteur.* Her name, it is *mademoiselle* Beatrice Bonfleur," she replied in French, but emphasized the name again.

Dr. Cartier blanched and his shoulder muscles tightened. He gripped his desk. It was that name, Beatrice.

The name struck a chord.

He was about to stand and ask if this insolent girl knew whom she was talking to. Instead he controlled himself, shuffled his feet, and buttoned his white coat.

He thought that he should take another yellow capsule; he opened his desk drawer, looked at the bottle of prescriptions, but then closed the drawer.

Monique held onto her chair and the paper with her left hand, and gripped the rosary in her pocket with her sweaty right palm. To relieve the mounting tension in her chest, she shifted her eyes and looked around the room.

One wall was covered with black-and-white photos of men with beards. There was a photo of a nursing class graduation, but she couldn't read the years of either photo.

The other wall was covered with an oak bookcase from floor to ceiling. She couldn't imagine how anybody could read all those books.

She turned to look back at Cartier. "Shall I call my secretary to escort such impudence away, eh?" he asked Monique.

Before he could do anything more, the young girl stood up. With a tremulous hand, she placed the Xerox copy of the letter she had written on Cartier's desk, within his reach.

Cartier looked at her and then at the copy of the handwritten letter. His eyes glazed over as he picked up the sheet of paper, neatly written in her bold hand.

The paper shook in his grasp. She knew it was a grammatically correct letter; this one was directed to the Québec College of Physicians and Surgeons. The same college he had, apparently, just dictated a letter to. There was also a copy to the Minister of Health.

The doctor looked at the young nurse, but this time she avoided his eyes.

Monique felt the cold drops of sweat rolling down from her armpits and to her elbows. She pressed her arms into her side, fearing the salt would stain his carpet. She stared straight ahead.

Above the doctor's desk was a wall covered with six imposing diplomas. She squinted at them, but she couldn't read Latin. She wondered what '*Magna cum Laude*' meant.

She steeled herself and took the next step, speaking so softly that Cartier had to lean forward to hear her.

"I just wanted you to know, *monsieur docteur*. Beatrice confided in me, she did, sir. I have her notes after several meetings. That is, her history. The welts she had on her private person, she showed them to me. I have a witness, *docteur*."

Cartier coughed and spluttered. "A witness?"

"Time and again, sir. Each time, *mon docteur.* A witness. Annette, a nurse who was there …" she trailed off.

Cartier abruptly stopped her. "Annette? I, I don't know any Annette," Cartier shouted. He stood up and leaned forward, over his desk.

He glared down at Monique, but she didn't flinch. The cold sweat was now at her waist.

She looked down at her polished white shoes. "*Oui.* A letter from Annette, who was the witness. In writing. The nursing director dismissed her from work, as she was addicted to speed drugs. She said that, to me, she did."

"You mean that Fournier? A letter from her? Why? From that dyke?"

Monique knew what a 'dyke' was. She went on and explained further. "*Madame* Annette swore that you could have saved her position, but did not. She then swore on the bible as to her personal observations and that what she wrote was true."

Cartier looked like he was about to shout a response, but he contained himself. "Her personal observation?"

"Yes. Your late-night wickedness on that ward. Sir. Pardon me. Those were her words, not mine. Your late-night wickedness with Beatrice Bonfleur, the sister of monsieur Riel. Sir."

Cartier turned white. He looked at the copies on his desk. One held Monique's own notes with Beatrice's signature scrawled at the bottom. The other paper, more organized, thought out, and well-written, was the paper detailing Fournier's observations of his predilections for demented girls on her ward. It was signed at the bottom and witnessed by another nurse.

The papers trembled in Cartier's hand as he picked them up. She saw the gears turning in his head. He tried to laugh, and asked, "She swore on the bible?"

Monique held the papers in her sweaty hand. *"Oui,* sir. The college director asked me to do so when I phoned him. With profound respect, sir. Also witnessed with her signature that is, sir—ah, I mean, Director."

Monique felt that she had said all she wanted to say. She stared at the blue shag carpet for a second. She then stood up, turned, and walked to the door. She suddenly stopped, turned back halfway, and curtsied.

Monique saw Cartier frozen to the back of his red leather chair behind his desk. His eyes were lifeless. What was he thinking?

Monique left, and put her hand over her left eyelid to stop the tic. She hoped it wasn't visible to the secretary, who looked up at her as she left.

Once outside of Cartier's office in the waiting room, she took in a deep breath, gathered up the umbrella that she had left, and brushed the sweat from her forehead.

She then touched her small, nurse's medallion above her right breast and crossed herself again.

She recalled the words of her nursing mentor. "That precious piece of golden medal, that medallion, has been bestowed on you, nurse. Wear it proudly, and never bring shame to your nursing daughters and our holy father," her Mother Superior had told her.

It was just before she left the eastern nursing convent from where Monique had graduated. It was the only piece of authority that gave her credibility in Cartier's hospital.

Alex would be proud of her, she thought as she smiled and said *'bonjour'* to the secretary as she closed the door.

D'Albert didn't look up. She didn't reply and kept on typing.

CHAPTER 51

✳

Juanita, the Sacrificial Lamb

THE very next week, *Madame* d'Albert, Cartier's secretary, was on the phone with Alex. "Our hospital director, Doctor Jacques Cartier, has pneumonia, Doctor. He will be away on sick leave."

"Oh? I'm sorry to hear. Please tell him to see his own physician in town very soon."

"He said that since you are the most qualified here, you are therefore in charge for the short term."

She hung up, but stressed 'short term.' It was short. A command. Alex was not surprised.

Not only that, but Sister Denise, having been promoted to *Mère Supérieure* for the whole province, was moving to Montréal. Alex attended a going-away party for her in the chapel side room.

All the hospital nuns, many nurses, and staff were present. She, Mamma D, Justine, Rani, and other ladies from the town were also honored for their work.

The mayor of LaSalle praised their efforts in sending all the orphaned children back. The mayor gave Alex a sly wink, but avoided him throughout the ceremony. Christina's name wasn't mentioned.

It was a few days later. Six nursing students, seven fourth-year medical students, and three other doctors marched into the surgical room.

Juanita hadn't responded to the ECT or to the medications. Cartier had left specific orders for Dr. Walters to perform a prefrontal lobotomy on her. Alex tried, but was unable to postpone or cancel the procedure.

The Scot, Hamish MacDougall, was more cordial and pleasant to Alex since Aaron was no longer around. He would assist Walters.

In the middle of the room was Juanita, sedated and covered in a gray, but clean, gown. She had put on some weight with the higher dosage of chlorpromazine, and desperately gripped the arms of the large, metal chair that she had been forced into.

Her gray hair had been trimmed back from her temples, and her sunken eyes looked terrified. She looked at the crowd now surrounding her, but remained mute.

Two orderlies stood behind her. A nurse was at her side: it was Monique. Walters, on time at 9 AM sharp, walked in. As usual, he sucked on a long, fat, Cuban corona.

Alex winked at Monique. She gave an anxious smile in return. She nodded to Alex and turned her head toward the door. Alex got the message and went into the hallway.

Monique looked back to make sure they were alone. "You haven't said anything, have you, my love?"

She had already explained her meeting with Cartier soon after the confrontation. Alex just held her hand and thanked her again.

They both heard Walters starting his lecture while standing in front of Juanita. Monique followed Alex back into the room.

Alex came to Juanita's side as Walters' heavy body stomped over the wooden floor planks. He walked back and forth, huffing and puffing with his chest out, seeking adulation for what he was about to perform.

He ignored Juanita, the poor woman, now more anxious than ever. He pulled the metal tray on wheels close to his patient. He placed his smoldering cigar on the lip of the tray.

On the tray was a syringe, a small vial of sodium pentothal—the sedative—a wooden mallet, and a small milk bottle filled with alcohol. The icepick, his only surgical tool, was in the bottle.

Walters avoided the woman's eyes as he grasped her head in one hairy paw. "This here is Juanita. A crazy lady," Walters said with a grand gesture. He was on stage again.

Alex came to her side and leaned over. "Hello, Juanita. Don't be frightened. Everything will go well, and you'll soon be free of the demons plaguing you," he said kindly.

Juanita tried to shake her head free. She pursed her lips tightly, remaining mute.

Walters moved Alex away. He pushed down harder on Juanita's head. "Crazy, neurotic, psychotic, idiotic. She will be cured forever; will you not, woman?" the pompous doctor asked. It was more of a decree than a question.

He motioned to the group to come closer to the quivering victim. Alex, close by, recoiled from the garlic breath now filling the tight space. Hungarian sausage, he concluded, and expensive cigar smoke.

Walters looked at one orderly and demanded, "You will hold her head still. Those two orderlies there shall hold her arms: they must."

The surgeon then took the icepick out of the bottle. As he did so, his tremor caused the metal to vibrate against the glass. He flicked drops of the alcohol fluid on to the floor and readjusted his heavy glasses over his nose.

At that sight, Juanita gave a squeal and tried to stand up. She was forced back down by the two orderlies behind her.

"Now, now woman; this won't hurt. Sit quietly and don't squirm: else your eyes could be poked out," Walters said as he grasped the mallet in his right hand.

Alex came to Juanita's side, knelt down, and took her hand in his. "Would you like a washbasin and soap to sterilize your hands, Doctor?" Alex asked.

Walters stopped, icepick in his left hand, which now had a more obvious tremor, and mallet in the right. "No need, young man, no need. The nurse will clean the eyes with alcohol," Walters answered the impudent man.

With that, Monique dabbed Juanita's upper eyelids with the alcohol sponge and slowly injected the sedative into the upper lids.

Juanita blinked as the alcohol pierced the sockets.

In that split-second, Walters drove the razor-sharp icepick into the upper portion of her left eye socket, piercing the delicate bone. That thin layer of bone separated the top of the eye socket from the bottom of the brain's frontal lobe.

He then banged it up into the frontal lobe itself with the wooden hammer.

Students flinched. The audible crack of the thin bone above the eye socket reverberated around the room.

The icepick entered the bowels of her brain.

"You can see it slipped into the bottom of this woman's frontal lobes so easily," he lectured. "Then, with a deft flick of my wrist, the front of the brain will be severed from the rest of her cortex on one side."

Juanita swooned. Walters caught her head and held it tight. This simple procedure was then repeated on the right side.

After the swift tap with the wooden hammer, the icepick broke through the other orbital bone above her right eye.

Walters asked, "Did not hurt now, did it, woman?"

By then, poor Juanita had lost consciousness, and never answered. Orderlies held her head upright.

Monique took over. She held Juanita's head as she slowly regained consciousness. Surprisingly, indeed, it wouldn't hurt the poor soul; adrenaline flooded her body and obliterated the pain in her orbital skeletal structure. The inner brain matter is devoid of pain.

The sound of cracking bone was distressing to the spectators, but

Walters preached, "Piercing the thin bone structure might hurt, but the soft brain tissue is impervious to pain."

As Walters sermonized, Alex watched his fingers. He feared that, because of the tremble in his hands, he may have gone too far up into her cranium.

Juanita's eyeballs rolled up into her head as Alex held her hand. His hand went numb with Juanita's death-like grip.

One student nurse, pale as her legs gave way, slipped down to the floor. Her friend helped her up and ushered her out.

Thus, poor Juanita, confused and barely awake, gave a slight shudder, as students stared down at her. Tears streamed down her face. Her eyes were wide open, but vacant. The veins on her forehead were engorged from the rising blood pressure, and her heart thumped wildly through the neck of her gown.

She slumped forward.

Hamish stepped forward and told Monique to take her patient away. The two orderlies lifted the partially-inert body and placed her on a stretcher. Monique covered her with a blanket and rolled her out.

As Juanita was pushed past Alex, he was certain that he saw her have a mild convulsion under the blanket. Her eyes had rolled back, and her tongue hung limp on her lower lip.

The procedure was so quick that Walter's Cuban stogy didn't have time to go out. He picked up the soggy butt and stomped through the circle of students.

One very pale medical student followed the grand master out the room and asked, "Where did you get the idea for this procedure, Doctor?"

Walters sucked and puffed until the end of the corona was glowing red again. "Doctor António Moniz of Lisbon in 1935: he developed the technique of lobotomy, young man, he did. He observed that animals, and then people, became docile after any traumatic frontal lobe brain accidents."

The student and his friends scribbled notes furiously in small pads.

"Trephining, the burring of holes into the skull, was used by so-called physicians a thousand years ago. Primarily in Africa and Egypt, in order to let the demons out from those who were demented and irrational."

More notes were made as they followed the grand master out.

"Between 1939 and 1951, over twenty thousand prefrontal surgical lobotomies were performed in North America alone," he said proudly. He reached for a tablet hidden in his white coat pocket.

Walters then left to have a coffee. The others stood about, muttering about the procedure they had just witnessed.

Juanita was wheeled into the other room, and Alex saw the others awaiting the same fate in the adjoining waiting room. At the back of the row was Lafayette Riel, sedated heavily and snoring. Otherwise, the room was quiet as everyone waited for the next victim.

"Time for the doctor's coffee, first, and so we drink and rest," Walters said as he threw his cigar on the floor. He ground it into the walkway, swallowed his pill, and walked away.

Alex brushed the sweat from his brow. He was glad the demonstration was over; for now.

"We have to put a stop to this; but come on, Hamish, I'll buy you a coffee. Let's talk about it," Alex said, taking his arm.

"No, catch up to you. I must see our Juanita first."

"Good idea, Hamish."

Hamish smirked as he pointed to the Hungarian in the hallway. "You see, Alex, it was only the former USSR that banned this gruesome procedure. Josef Stalin, one of the world's most homicidal dictators, outlawed lobotomy in 1950 on moral grounds. Can you imagine?"

Alex shook his head. "If the murdering Stalin could do it, then we must," Alex said, determined.

Hamish went to Juanita's side while Alex gladly left the butcher's shop.

The group slowly disbanded. Students whispered amongst each other, waiting for the grand master's reappearance. The young nurse who collapsed had returned, but still looked pale and shaken.

Monique also went with Hamish. Alex walked to the ward to see a few patients.

It was soon after that Hamish walked past Alex in the hallway, turned, and put his arm around him. "I attended to her, but it was too late, my friend. She was convulsing soon after."

"How is she, Hamish?"

"Died, my friend."

Alex stopped dead in his tracks. "What? Juanita? You mean Juanita died?"

"Hemorrhage. He cut too deep; his hands were shaking," Hamish said with a whisper.

"That butcher's got Parkinson's. I saw his hands tremble when he used the pick. He missed taking his morning pills, for Christ's sake." Alex swore and slammed his fist into the palm of his hand.

Hamish walked away, looking very nervous. "Walters? He left so fast for Montréal in a swirl of dust, my friend. Cartier is not to be found. I heard that you are in charge."

Monique was by Alex's side.

"I am, and I will cancel all future lobotomies. Poor Juanita. She suffered so much," he said sadly to Monique.

"She is out of her misery now, my friend," Hamish replied as he left.

"I should have stopped all those procedures," Alex replied with guilt written on his face.

"It was ordered by Doctor Cartier before he left, Alex. You couldn't stop it," Monique offered, putting her arm around his shoulders.

"I'll cancel the rest. Riel will receive a reprieve," Alex said with a knowing smile.

Monique pressed his arm in comfort. "Well, well, how ironic; one sad death has saved many others, Alexander. Juanita was the lamb, sacrificed so that others are spared."

CHAPTER 52

The Esteemed College

MONIQUE was in Montréal for a week in late February and taking a few extra courses in hospital management. It was then that she and Alex were dutifully summoned to appear at the Québec College of Physicians and Surgeons in the city.

Each province in Canada had such a governing college, with a director, multiple medical departments, and various appointed groups. They governed the medical practice of each doctor in every province.

Monique knew that any physician who had a letter of complaint against them was then carefully examined before a board. If found guilty of a misdemeanor, then the misconduct was openly made public.

Such a transgression was sometimes of a sexual nature or of a financial wrongdoing. Or any act dealt medical or surgical harm to a patient.

After a careful examination of facts, that physician would be summarily fined and stricken temporarily, or permanently, from practicing.

Both Alex and Monique had been sent for by Dr. Etienne Champlain. He was the long-reigning director of the Québec College of Physicians and Surgeons.

They were both apprehensive as to what would transpire, as they knew that there had not been a complaint lodged against them.

"Maybe Cartier and Walters both filed a complaint against me as to the lobotomies," Alex worried.

Monique tried to reassure him. "I'm sure it's about that letter we sent, my dear," she whispered as they arrived promptly at 8:30 AM, and were immediately ushered into Champlain's inner office.

They sat nervously in front of his receptionist's desk, talking quietly about the letter that they had sent to the college and anxiously wondering if anything would be done about it.

Monique clasped her hands over her clean, sparkling, well-ironed uniform. Alex was fidgeting in a navy blazer, white shirt and tie, and brand-new slacks.

In the waiting room, behind her desk was a middle aged, attractive woman. She was on the phone. She had a warm, pleasant smile with graying hair neatly trimmed back in a bun. She wore a cotton, flowery dress and a small silver cross around her neck.

Champlain's receptionist finished her call. She looked up and kindly asked the pair to wait while she informed the director that they were there.

Monique was pleased to see the cross. She hoped that such a devout woman would be working with a similarly inclined, God-fearing employer, and he would make the right decision.

The receptionist got up and quietly rapped on the oak door. She respectfully waited.

Behind the door, Dr. Champlain sat behind his elaborate, Louis XIV desk in an opulent, brown leather chair.

He was well into his sixties, and was visibly irritated with this whole affair. As the esteemed director, he wore a dark blue suit, white shirt with cufflinks, and light blue bowtie to match.

A slight paunch desperately sought freedom from his snakeskin belt. It was from eating and drinking at too many medical and social gatherings that he was obliged to attend with his wife.

The man was asthmatic, with thinning gray hair and a red bulbous nose. He needed glasses to read.

As he put a small, white tablet in his mouth, he re-read the hand-written letter from Monique Joliette for the fifth time.

Exasperated, he took off his glasses and had a sip of water from the glass on his desk. He called to the woman to bring the visitors in.

She did, and Alex and Monique walked in. Monique went first, and Alex came close behind. Champlain, waving them into a chair, said nothing.

As Champlain peered over his reading glasses at Monique sitting in front of him, he swallowed hard and then emptied the glass. His first impression of the letter was that it was from another hysterical young woman from that asylum over there, somewhere beyond Montréal.

However, this young woman, Monique, didn't appear to be histri-onic: she sat there demurely, with her hands folded. He could see that she was well-composed, and organized both in her written statement and in her overall presentation.

"I've heard good things about you, Doctor Gage," was all he said, looking at Alex.

He could hear the sigh of relief from the young doctor, but he said nothing as he mopped his brow with the back of his hand.

Champlain looked at his secretary, who had come in and was sitting at the side of his desk in an oak chair. She stood up and refilled his water glass from a jug on the desk.

"Be sure of what you write. Word for word, *Madame* DelaPlace; word for word of this meeting," he said, tapping his desk with his pen.

"*Oui,*" the older woman respectfully replied. She opened her pad, looked squarely at Monique and Alex, and started writing in short-hand, the date, hour, place, and names of the four people in attendance.

Champlain pointed his pen at the two sitting across from him. He lifted several sheets of paper and directed them at Alex, but spoke to Monique.

"This Rose woman, daughter of the dead patient, must be overreacting to a deceased, demented mother in that institution of yours," he said to Monique, showing her the papers.

He waited for Monique's reply.

"I do not know that lady, *directeur.* Doctor Gage, he knows her; he met her. It is my letter, sir. I had an obligation to write it, as it was my duty to my profession, my patient, and the hospital. With all due respect, sir," Monique answered simply but firmly.

This time, Champlain directed his words at the young doctor sitting next to the nurse who had caused all this fuss with her letters.

"This six-page scrawl, from some woman called Rose, sounds like it does come from another lunatic, eh? She didn't sign her last name, or date the letter," Champlain said in English with a strong French inflection.

"Yes, sir. Rose, the daughter of Juanita, the lady who died by the lobotomy, is sane and realistic. Although she is still grieving, she is not well-schooled in writing letters," Alex replied in explanation.

"And you, young man, have direct knowledge of such vile deeds?"

Alex gripped Monique's hand. "No sir. I interviewed Rose, and this is what she said to me. Her mother was sexually violated by our director. She, Juanita, complained to her daughter of 'J.C.' coming into her. But, although she had religious delusions, it was not the Christ who was visiting her."

"Really?"

"Yes, sir, it was our director with the same initials. I am here to support my fiancée, only as to her letter to you, sir. Only her letter," Alex answered, not mentioning what Katarina had told him about Jacques Cartier.

"I heard that you are writing your examinations in psychiatry, young man."

"Yes sir."

"Ah, congratulations. I wish you well. *Bonne chance.*"

"*Merci.* I will need more than good luck, since my exams are near," Alex said with a grin.

Champlain had to act. He wasn't taking any chances now that he was about to retire. He needed a clean record and a good pension that wasn't to be compromised by some sexual deviant of a director.

He knew that this case would make the Montréal newspapers and affect his standing in the community, depending on his next decision.

He looked at his secretary. "I believe that I visited that asylum years ago," Champlain said.

The older woman shook her head in disagreement.

"*Non*, you have never visited *docteur* Cartier's hospital. I go once a week to see my ill sister there. It is not a pleasant place, but I tell you of it, sir, that this doctor sitting here has raised it into the present century and out of the medieval past."

"Really?"

"Yes. That young nurse, here, was very brave to do what she did, sir. Now, you must do the right thing," she replied in French, smiling at Monique.

"*Oui.* I can assure you both that we shall do the right thing," he replied in English.

Alex smiled. He knew some of the French by now. Monique gripped Alex's hand tighter. *Madame* DelaPlace recorded. A big, blue-bottomed fly bussed aloud at the window. Champlain took some water.

"*Merci*," they both said in unison.

Champlain smiled warmly. "This college will ask Doctor Cart-ier to step down with a full investigation. Your letter is paramount, well-written with other signatures, and I and my committee will act appropriately."

"*Merci*," they both said in unison again.

"I also have the copy written by the nurse Fournier," he added, again showing Monique that communication.

"*Merci*. The hospital will need a new director, sir," Monique offered bravely, looking at Alex.

"Yes, well, I propose that your fiancée here will be the interim director, my dear. I will send you an official letter in writing soon. I hear that he has already been fulfilling that duty often."

Champlain stood and thanked Alex and Monique. He kindly dismissed them, but again thanked Monique and reassured her and Alex that he would act appropriately. The meeting was over.

Alex got up and shook Champlain's hand. Monique did the same and expressed gratitude for his valuable time.

They both left.

The secretary closed the door and said, "That young man has made remarkable changes at the institution where my sister is, Etienne. I think that he should be the permanent director once he graduates."

"You may be right. I'll see to it. Remind me," he said. He walked about his room with a glass of water in hand.

Champlain looked at the wise old woman. The two of them had run the College for the past thirty years without trouble.

He crumpled up Rose's letter and threw it into his metal wastebasket in the corner of his office.

The secretary went to the basket and retrieved it. As she ironed it out and put it in the file, she added, "I will remind you, Etienne, but this time you must act, sir. There is a copy of it, this letter, and the nurse's astute letter, given to the Minister of Health."

"*Merde*. I forgot."

"No need to swear. Cow manure it will be in the newspapers in the morning, and you are not to be covered in it. I am sure of that, Etienne, if you disregard this complaint."

Etienne went to the window and opened it to let out the large, blue-bottomed fly, buzzing about in the Spring warmth and seeking escape.

"I'm over sixty, and retiring in three months; I don't want my image and this college tarnished in the newspapers," he said pointedly and then turned to look at DelaPlace.

DelaPlace knew what he was thinking. "We receive many letters of complaint from patients about their doctors. They are varied grumblings, and some refer to surgical errors, medication overdoses, and various mistreatments by the practitioners."

"Yes, *madame*, sometimes they were outright threats of mismanagement that caused further disability, or even death, in patients," he said sadly.

He handed her the notes he had made, together with Monique's letter and Rose's scrawl. On second thought, he took them from her.

He took her pad of transcriptions and set a paperweight over it. "*Madame*, I always wrote a very official letter, to any and all protesters. It always stated that we investigated the complaint, and after conferring with the committee, we found the doctor to be free of blame. But only some of the time."

"*Oui*, and nothing more was ever heard. That committee, sir, consisted of yourself and *moi*," she whispered quietly. She closed the window, shuddered from the cool draft that had blown in, and then returned to the desk.

Etienne looked at Monique's letter, unfolded it, and read it again and again.

"This letter, *madame* from this very bright young nurse who sat here, had no trouble writing in English, and is different from that of other letters that we have received."

"It is very revealing: very direct, very, very different, sir. Very different."

Champlain rapped his gnarled knuckles on his desk. "It implicates my ex-son-in-law, *madame*. It is an accusation of sexual abuse. She wrote that she had another witness, another nurse, and the patient endorsed her notes that very night. A certain Bonfleur had been violated sexually."

"The witness, is a head nurse from Bonfleur's ward. Her name is Annette Fournier; it was she who also wrote a letter of complaint to you, sir."

"Why the Devil did she?"

"That head nurse had been fired by the nursing director for being addicted to Dexedrine tablets. Such were stolen from the ward, but offered by her director, your son-in-law."

"Fournier?"

"Yes. She was angry at Cartier for not protecting her position," DelaPlace explained.

"We have heard rumors of such sexual depravity going on at that terrible place."

"*Oui*, but no one ever complained like this. With many letters and witnesses. Signed."

"Surely it was just endemic between some of those idiotic inmates and a few evil staff."

DelaPlace winced with the vision of her poor sister before her. "You must form a proper committee this time, Etienne. Take the pressure off yourself and me. Make this young, smart doctor the next director. A clean slate," the woman said firmly.

Champlain's eyes narrowed. "Yes, you are correct. That *fils de pute*, that son of a bitch, Cartier. He would get into trouble again one day. I knew such would transpire."

"I remember that you said he left your only daughter with three young children."

Champlain walked over, not puffing now that the white tablet was working, and spat into the basket.

"He took up with that Russian woman. You are correct. Now I'll form a real committee of local doctors, and turn the letters over to them. Let them deal with it, but with my correct recommendations," he said to his secretary.

"You did well to deal with Gabriella, to hire her for work in our accounting department, Etienne. She, too, was abused, and almost murdered by that man, Vittorio."

Etienne bristled in recalling that newspaper story. "That man abducted her from the hospital after the police sought him out for possible murder of that Italian. He used her for his vile purposes in his home," he recalled sadly.

"She did well to defend herself when he held his gun to her head as he raped her, Etienne. She was brave."

"*Oui*; she struggled when he whipped her with that pistol. That was when the gun went off, the detective said. In that struggle she was able to raise the gun up, and the shot from the gun blew his face off."

"And it was an accident, killing him in self-defense, the report stated."

"Good riddance."

"She also told us of the depravity happening at that hospital. Yes. Good riddance for Vittorio, and your son-in-law. She, Gabriella, is an excellent accountant now, working here for you and the college," *madame* DelaPlace said, crossing herself three times.

Champlain nodded in agreement. "That young man, Gage, has the will, youth, and a good woman by his side to clean up after that *chien* of a dog hound, Cartier."

"My sister told me that Vittorio, that other pig of a dog, grabbed my sister from behind in the laundry where she worked. That big Indian saved her from a rape; she told me that one day when I visited."

"That Sicilian was a predator," Champlain agreed.

DelaPlace gathered up her notes to leave. "Gabriella was fortunate to have your son, Henri represent her in court as her lawyer after Vittorio's attack."

"Yes. They will marry soon and his two children will have a wonderful mother again."

"Henri did well to recover after his wife's death from leukemia two years ago. Now he has Gabriella," DelaPlace said.

She walked away and closed the door behind her to type up her reports. She, too, would be retiring, soon.

Champlain knew she needed her pension to look after her ill sister, who lived with DelaPlace while on weekend leave.

Together, she and her sister cared for their senile, demented mother living in their basement room.

*

CHAPTER 53

The Attack on Monique

ALEX only saw Dr. Cartier once again after he returned from Montréal. Cartier put out a memo that he was on medical leave. He announced that he was awaiting another prominent position at a hospital, one that was more respected on the west coast of Canada.

The rumor mill was rife with late-night sightings of Cartier prowling about the hospital grounds. Cartier still had a standing order for Riel's lobotomy as soon as Walters returned.

However, Riel had avoided that by making an escape from his locked ward. Cartier had been furious to discover that an orderly had been bribed by Riel with a cartoon of cheap cigarettes. The orderly was on duty late at night, and Riel had not been seen again.

"Be careful, Monique. They say Cartier's manic again, and he could be out to get you for writing that letter. Call me when you get off work, and I'll come every night and walk you to your room," Alex said, nuzzling her cheek in the car. He drove her back to the nurses' residence after they had spent an evening out.

This time, he was pleased that she agreed to the use of his condoms; 'Shieks,' as they were called by embarrassed young men when they ordered a dozen at a drug store.

Alex always bought them in LaSalle, and kept them handy in his car glove compartment now that Monique had agreed to marry him.

When Alex returned home late that evening, he was happy to relax with Vinny. Vinny sat with a beer in hand, sucking on pumpkin seeds, picking his teeth with a match, and smoking his vile cigarettes on the porch.

"So, what transpired at the college, my boy?" Vinny asked, spitting tobacco bits and just missing Claudius nearby.

Alex was pleased to be able to confide in Vinny. He gave him all the details about his meeting with the college and Monique's letter.

Vinny pointed to Claudius, lying at his feet. "I know that the two of you are shit-scared with that dictator on the loose, doc. Take Claudius, here."

"Claudius? What for, Vinny?"

"He'll be a good protector for Monique. To keep and to use as an escort each evening. Cartier may be prowling about," he spat out, worried, but also angry.

"He came to see me once."

Vinny reared back, almost choking on his cigarette. "Fuck off. He did? Wanted our money, I bet?" he asked, worried.

"No. He was depressed," Alex replied, calmly.

"Get Walters to give him those treatments." Vinny guffawed and spat a large gob with seed shells into the beer cases in anger, just missing faithful Claudius.

"He was depressed, and told me he couldn't cope with all his losses."

"What the fuck about? He's fucking with you, man. Be careful," Vinny cautioned, standing up. He was so angry that engorged veins throbbed on his forehead.

Alex looked up at Vinny, who was glowering down at him. "It's okay, Vinny. Take it easy, man, or you'll have a stroke. He said he lost his position in France, but didn't explain. Lost his wife and children, then Katie. Lost his position here. Money. Job, future. He confessed all to me. He was suicidal."

Vinny wasn't going to let this go; he walked about with Claudius trailing on his heels. "Let him. Good riddance. So, did you tell the fucker to jump in that lake?"

Vinny opened the door to let Claudius out, fearful with his master so hostile.

"No. I put him on some Anafranil, a new anti-depressant. I had some samples. He threw them at me and stormed off."

Vinny closed the door after Claudius, calmed down, and put his arm around Alex. He patted him on the back and sat down. "You had to do the right thing, son."

"Thanks for that, Vinny. Appreciate it," Alex replied. He put his hand on Vinny's shoulder and said good night.

The very next night, the head nurse, a good friend of Monique's on the sick ward, ordered Monique to work overtime.

"I'm sorry, but you'll have to sit with this woman, Monique. She was kicked in the head by a horse while on leave. Had a chronic head injury, causing status epilepticus. Now she has recurring grand mal seizures, and the meds are not controlling her," the head nurse ordered, very concerned.

"It will be fine, Suzette; I have Claudius here to escort me after hours," Monique offered. She pointed to the hound, who was on his back with feet up, snoring under the hospital bed.

One hour after she was to leave at eight, Monique locked the outside ward doors. She left the building and made her way down the long path to the nurse's residence.

She felt reassured since her patient, also in the care of a young nurse in her second year, had finally responded to the anti-convulsant medications, and was slowly dropping off to sleep.

As she started her walk, she hooked her leather strap to the dog's collar. All the lights in the surrounding buildings were slowly shut down, and the grounds were empty of patients.

She felt safe enough, with only a few clouds in the sky and the light of the full moon. And good old Claudius was beside her, her protector that Vinny had so kindly offered.

Monique pulled the heavy, blue cape around her shoulders and fastened the clasps. She was walking quickly, since Alex would be picking her up quite soon.

Claudius, on the leather leash, was slobbering and craving his late dinner. He pulled Monique along to walk faster.

As she rounded the corner of the chronic women's building, she could see the three-story nurse's residence in the distance, just ahead of her.

"You see, Claudius. Some nurses are happily leaving as their boyfriends wait in their cars to take them out for the evening," she said to the dog, trying to hold him back.

She passed a thicket of rhododendrons, laden with purple flowers. They were just blooming in the early spring on one side of the path. A large, cedar hedge bordered the other side.

She quickened her pace as the moon slid behind a cloud.

Claudius stopped and growled at the rhododendron thicket with his fur standing on end. Monique pulled on his leash to keep him moving as she felt a cold breeze down her neck. She smiled; she was sure she saw Alex's truck coming up the drive, far in the distance near her residence.

Just as she approached the heavy bush on her right, a man covered in a black toque came through the thicket on her left.

Claudius pulled on the leather strap, wanting to charge at the intruder.

"It's all right, Claudius; it's a male patient, working late, and he must still be trimming the bushes." Monique cautioned the dog and slowed her pace to let the man pass.

Claudius strained at the leash, growling. Somewhere far in the distance an owl hooted, and several coyotes yapped playfully.

"*Bonsoir*, you are working far too late. You will lose your privileges if you're not back on your ward in time. The doors will be locked," she admonished the man, still talking in a kindly manner.

She didn't recognize the disheveled man. He had a grayish beard below the toque, now pulled down over his forehead and almost covering his nose. The man abruptly stood in front of her, kicked at the dog, and blocked her way.

She tried to pass around him, but he pushed her back. "*Qu'est-ce qui ne va pas?* Oh, sorry, I'll speak in English to you. What is it, are you injured or ill?" she asked.

She stared at the man, who wore a rumpled jacket, torn trousers, and shabby, black shoes.

He said nothing. Again, she tried to get by the man, ready to encourage him to get back to his ward. The stench from this stranger hit Claudius in the face and caused a barking fit in the dog.

It was then that the man lunged at her. She tried to dodge his attack, but his arms easily grabbed her throat.

"Ha, I have you now, *cochon*. You pig. You ended my career. You will pay dearly with your life. And then I will find that American swine of yours," the man said as he threw Monique to the ground.

Monique struggled for air, holding on to the leash. She was now on her back on the pathway. Her wind pipe was slowly being throttled, and she barely heard other vile, threatening words.

As her hands became weak, she let go of the leash. Her attacker pushed himself on her and pressed his knee into her chest. He held her on the ground as his spittle dropped on her face.

Claudius, now free of the tether, snapped at the man's trouser leg. He pulled on the rag with all his might, barking loudly.

The man turned and gave the dog such a wallop with his foot that it sent the dog yelping and howling into the bushes.

Monique could hear herself trying to plead with her assailant to let her go. But only garbled words came out. "Please let me go. I will take you to your ward. It is not too late, my good man. You can still be saved from further punishment," she wheezed, frightened for her life.

The man only tightened his grip on her throat further, and she felt herself fading into oblivion. She was sure she heard her father calling far away in the distance.

It was only the owl calling out and the coyotes barking as they heard the tussle and her cries.

Monique fought bravely and pulled at the toque. As the woolen piece fell away, she was certain that she knew her attacker.

Cartier was kneeling over her with his hands on her carotids as her face turned blue. She gave a slight shudder, not unlike the epileptic whom she had just nursed on the sick ward.

Cartier felt Claudius again nipping at his leg, yowling and barking. He kicked again, but it was the heavy thud of a gigantic colossus falling onto his back that made him loose his grip.

Cartier felt the powerful hands around his own neck. He was so shocked by the sudden and silent movement that he let go of Monique. He looked up, trying to defend himself.

Cartier couldn't see who it was holding his head in a vice-like grip with one arm from behind. He could feel the powerful biceps slowly crushing his neck, ever so tightly. It was like a massive boa constrictor squeezing the last breath out of him.

Cartier tried to focus in the darkness. All he could make out was a string. It was dangling from the neck of the person behind him. On the weathered string, he was sure it was a rabbit foot.

As he tried to free himself, slowly fading into the blackness, he felt the other hand on the side of his head. That was the last thing Cartier experienced.

The man behind him pushed Cartier's head forward, and his neck snapped. His upper spinal cord came free of the brain stem, causing immediate death.

Monique felt a body fall next to her as she shook her head to clear the darkness. Was there a struggle of men at her feet?

She thought so as she gulped fresh, moist air into her lungs. She felt the raspy tongue of Claudius licking at her face as she tried to stand.

Her knees were weak, and she collapsed again and fell over, injuring her shoulder on a rock near the bushes.

The searing pain helped her to focus, but all she could see was a man's leather, beaded trousers at her eye level. The figure silently moved away into the thicket of bushes, but she could still feel the warm, fur coat of Claudius against her face.

Monique raised her hand and tried to speak to the phantom. She wanted to thank this patient, if that's what he was, for saving her life. She held her throat and took in large gasps of air, still on her knees.

Again, she struggled on all fours and tried to stand. She saw the back of the man fade off into the darkness of the bushes. She valiantly again struggled to rise.

Monique desperately called out, knowing that Alex would be waiting, but she fainted again. She fell onto Claudius, who gave out a loud squeal and yelped in pain as Monique's body landed on his.

Moaning helplessly as Claudius whined in pain, Monique cried out for help in her mother tongue, but no one could hear her muffled pleas.

Monique, confused from the struggle and still breathless, wasn't sure how long she lay there. The pain in her shoulder stirred her awake. Her mouth was full of dirt, leaves, and bits of stone.

She spat out the debris and again tried to get up with Claudius barking loudly at her heels. As she got to her knees, she suddenly felt herself being lifted up into the air.

She had a vision of her father picking her up and throwing her into the air as he used to do as a little girl. He would catch her in his burly arms as she squealed and laughed in delight.

These arms were no different, and she allowed herself to be carried as her head slowly cleared. Nothing was said in those few seconds, until she heard car doors in the distance opening and slamming shut.

Women were shouting, and someone was blowing a whistle.

She heard a dog yelp somewhere far behind her. Was it Claudius?

She heard someone shouting. It wasn't her Alex. An older man, a father in a heavy, fur-lined winter coat visiting his daughter who was a nurse, rushed at Monique.

He pulled her away from the mountain man as he swore at the Indian, not knowing he was her savior. He helped her to stand.

Others were shouting. "It's the mountain man. Now we have him."

"Did he kill her?" someone asked.

A female nurse shouted, "He must have raped her."

"Get a gun. Call the police," another shouted.

Monique tried to speak, but all she could do was shake her head. She wanted to tell the nurse's father in the fur coat to help the man who rescued her.

She was helped up by two visitors who came to her side. She heard others in the dark, calling security.

She watched, blurry eyed, as several men scuffled with Riel, and finally wrestled him to the ground.

Her savior was forcefully taken away. Claudius was dragged into the building. Monique was placed onto a stretcher and carried into the residence.

CHAPTER 54

The Mountain Man's Story

AFTER the violent attack on Monique, Alex went to visit her three times daily on the medical ward. Her neck was bruised, her shoulder was in a sling, and she was on morphine for her hip pain.

The visiting orthopedic surgeon from Montréal assured them both that she would have a full recovery.

The exams were just around the corner for Alex, and he was studying furiously. In between his hectic days on the hospital wards, studying, and often visiting with Monique, Alex found the weekend daily papers were all about Cartier. A strong advocate for women's issues, Miss Abigail Norton, had a two-page article about the abuse of women by doctors.

Alex hung his jacket on the hall peg after work and walked into the kitchen. Vinny, sitting at the kitchen table, was scanning the papers.

"This fem broad's picture wearing pant suits is all over the papers, doc," Vinny sneered. He pointed at her photo with his fork as he sat eating lasagna and drinking vino.

"Yes, Vinny, but thank the good Lord, as Mamma D would say, that she said the right things about such abuse. By the way, Monique is recovering well after Claudius and Riel saved her life from that brutal assault and murderous attack by Cartier."

Vinny ranted on about them 'fems,' but agreed, "Yep, thanks be to God, Riel, and good old Claudius here."

Claudius looked up and wagged his tail with the acknowledgement. Alex looked at the newspaper, which was spattered with Vinny's tomato sauce.

"Yeah, well she's got a point, Vinny. Times are a changing," he echoed Mamma D's sage comments.

"She's got her fem knickers in a knot tighter than a bee's ass, that's all I'm sayin'."

Vinny read, smoked, chewed on his lasagna, and grumbled, "She's advocating for shelters for battered women. Had articles in all the papers on inequality of the sexes. This time, she's got her teeth into Cartier's poor, departed groin."

"Good for her, Vinny."

"She said doctors were practicing with their genitals instead of their stethoscopes." Vinny laughed at the picture he painted.

He enjoyed laughing at his new-found female victim as he read the papers to Mamma D. She came in and was now standing in the doorway, drinking a cup of steaming, herbal tea.

"Gee willikers, as the good doctor just said, Vinny: times are changing for the better, for gosh sakes. Keep your shirt on, God almighty," Mamma D wheezed, coughing up sputum into her napkin, which she always carried now.

Vinny had more to say. "Look here, Mamma, she listed all the women who had been abused by physicians in our *La Belle* Province. This broad even put in all the names of male physicians who have lost their licenses."

"Well, lordly lord, that is how it should be, by the good Lord," Mamma D shouted from the hallway as she left in a coughing fit.

"Yeah, but this lesbian legal beagle didn't list the women who screwed young girls. Or look here, even those dykes in high authority who had sexualized young, misfit girls. Like right in this place, here," he countered, thumping his finger on the table.

Alex poured himself a cup of the herbal tea and added quietly, but firmly, "There was a lengthy article about the College president and a woman lawyer. They discussed how the College was now dealing with such abuse."

"That fem lawyer said your College was too slow in persecuting doctors. She said she had many clients who were suing."

"Prosecuting, Vinny. Prosecuting."

Vinny shrugged and read out loud as Mamma D came back to the kitchen, "*The courts have paid out thousands of dollars to women who were abused. My client, Eileen Dodgson, has filed a civil suit against Dr. Cartier's estate for an undisclosed amount. He had sexual intercourse with her while she was a patient in the hospital. I will be representing my client. A certain unnamed nurse, and one Miss Fournier, are material witnesses.*"

Vinny continued. "Cartier has no estate. Katie emptied his bank account when she left him. She was mad as Hell with him, and turned his dollars into rubles."

Alex chuckled at Vinny's knowhow of what was going on at the hospital. "'Mad as Hell,' Vinny? An author two hundred years ago, William Congreve, wrote, 'Hell hath no fury like a woman scorned,' Vinny."

"Well, she was scorned, alright. Whatever that means."

Alex was ready to get back to his studies when Vinny was happy to change the subject. "Riel is in the maximum-security ward again after he saved your toots. I hear that the head slicer is in the next province, and is coming back here as quick as a bunny."

Alex nodded. "A troika of outside psychiatrists certified Riel to be dangerous. That's nonsense. But he did waste our director, and they said that was murder."

"Who called in those three shrinks?"

"The local *SQ* sergeant. He didn't know what to do with Riel. Some judge said he needed an opinion from a psychiatrist."

"Yeah, well, Cartier was about to waste your doll. He's a hero, not a killer. You better go and see Riel," Vinny replied. He pointed a finger, wet with Pesto sauce, at Alex in earnest. Claudius, at his feet, barked in agreement as he swilled up the plate put down by Vinny.

Alex agreed. "I wouldn't allow the lobotomy to be done here, so Riel will likely go to Montréal for the surgery. First, we need to know what transpired between Rani and Riel. I heard she will be living with you and Mamma D for the next three years, till she graduates."

Vinny stood and helped Mamma D to a chair, since she was weak from her coughing spasms. He put a heavy, woolen shawl about her wasted shoulders.

"It will be a pleasure to have her here. She told yours truly that she isn't wearing sexy outfits anymore. Said she learned her lesson," Vinny said, kindly.

Alex wasn't surprised that Vinny had a soft spot for Rani. "Good for her. By the way, the store is doing well, Vinny, and the government is now giving the patients who work a much better salary."

"You'll need that money you were handing out for your wedding now, and to help buy a house for your tootsie."

Alex nodded with a smile and left. He looked at Mamma D, and worried about her weight loss.

He still wanted to get the real facts about Rani from Riel, and what happened to her. But Alex had to call his mother one more time before he saw Riel.

He walked into the hallway and pulled the phone cord as far away as he could from Vinny's prying ears. It was getting dark, and Vinny had gone up to bed, escorting Mamma D gently up the stairs.

Alex waited until they were gone. There was a long delay before his mother answered. "Hello, mother. How are you?" Alex asked cautiously.

"Just fine, baby. Francine; it's Francine. How are you, baby?" she asked with a cautious giggle.

"Right, well, don't call me 'baby,' mother. Tell me some more about my father."

There was an abrupt silence as she laughed. "Like what?"

"Where was he born?"

Another nervous titter. "Oh, baby; that I don't know. Sorry: Alexander. I think, well yes, he was raised in a convent. By some nuns. Grey Nuns. In a place called Saint something, Saint Boniface. Some place in Canada."

"It's in Manitoba. Thanks, mother. Anything else you can tell me?"

"No, sweetie. Parents separated early. Raised by a grandmother, who gave him good luck charms to wear around his neck: rabbit's feet for good luck, he said to me. She died early. Ah, yes. He had a brother. Jean-Baptiste. Talked a lot about him." She again ended with a nervous, silly laugh.

Alex scribbled a few notes on a pad of paper. "Thanks, mother," Alex said, but had one more question. "Why did you marry him?"

"Ah-ha-ha, well he was wanted, by the Mounties. 'The Red Coats,' he called them. Said he was innocent, so I married him to give him citizenship. They couldn't get him after that, baby. Oh, sorry to call you that."

"That's the reason you married? To shelter him?"

Chortling again, she thought for a minute. "Well, only for a while. He vamoosed. Gone like the jackrabbit foot he hung around his neck. Okay, okay, I'll hang up soon," she shouted to someone in the room.

"How are your students doing with the cash I send you?"

There was that titter again, as usual. "Ah, baby, that's so nice. I make them a nice, warm breakfast and then some lunch before recess. Thanks for the money orders. And Garth is starting up Al-Anon meetings and another AA group in the next town."

Alex wanted to calm her down from that nervous laugh or to extend his compliments with what they were doing in that town, but the phone went dead.

✳

CHAPTER 55

The Truth from Lafayette

A few days later it was overcast and raining heavily, but warm for a change. It was just before his exams that Alex went to see Riel.

Alex called the ward ahead to say that he was coming to see him before his lobotomy in Montréal. He walked down the hill toward the river, and had to use the two keys to open the reinforced door on the security ward.

As Alex walked in, he found female nurses attending to the patients. That was part of his plan. An occupational staff worker was having a group meeting with those who were capable of such in a quiet corner.

Alex was pleased to see that the ward had been newly painted, with new beds, and that the staff were wearing proper new uniforms. The men wore short, white coats again, proper shirts, and black trousers on his direction.

In the back of the room, Alex saw that Lafayette Riel was strumming on a guitar. Alex pointed at Riel and raised his hands in a questioning manner at a nurse.

The male nurse, now dressed in a clean, white jacket with a nametag, explained. "Riel has permission to entertain us. Some female know-it-all said Lafayette can use his music therapeutically," he said derisively.

"That know-it-all is a highly respected occupational nurse on this ward, Marcel," Alex replied, looking at his nametag.

"Nice to have them here, doc," Marcel said sarcastically and walked away. Alex knew that women on that ward were still not welcome, and he heard sexist and racist comments from some of the male guards.

But Alex knew that a woman's presence could tame the wild beast that was inside any man. Especially those on this ward. All it took was a smile, a soft voice, the lack of a threatening stance, and possibly a gentle touch to quiet a patient down.

He made sure that female nurses and the female OT worked there most days, including other female group therapists. And they were told not to accept any abuse, silent or otherwise.

Alex made his way through the ward, which now had the new beds, good mattresses, and clean bedding that he had requested. He came up to Riel, but moved around to the other side of his table for safety's sake.

Riel looked up and smiled. "Okay, man, I don't want any more of that chlorpromazine shot in my ass. Don't worry; I'm not blaming you for them there. Ordered by those who signed the papers."

"Right on, Lafayette."

"What did you want to see me about?"

Alex hesitated, looking about as other inmates tried to listen in on the conversation. "Well, I need to know what happened with Rani. I know you saved Monique. Thank you for that," he said quietly.

Riel tossed back the long braids over his shoulder. "Being a savior won't save me, man. Three doctors wrote that I was crazy, you know, in their report, because I killed that man. I could talk all you want for a cigarette," he said with a wink at Alex.

"It's a deal."

Riel pointed to the office. "Let's see if Mr. Riel and the doctor here could have that private room over there," Riel said to the brawny nurse standing to one side.

Alex gave a sign in agreement. The nurse nodded and escorted Riel, with Alex following, to the office at the other end of the ward. They went into one of the consulting offices, and all three sat down.

Alex was hesitant to be in the room alone with Riel. Riel was very much at ease.

Riel looked at the nurse. "This man, I want to talk to him alone," he said as he lit a cigarette that the nurse had given him.

Alex shuffled his bad foot under the desk and looked at the weightlifter. "It's okay. I'll be all right," he said, somewhat hopeful.

"There is a button on the desk, Doctor. Punch it in an emergency."

Alex looked at the button, handing another cigarette to Riel. "I wouldn't reach it in time if I had to."

"I know that," Riel said with a grin as he saw Alex's concern. He enjoyed the tension, palpable in the small office.

The nurse left and closed the door. Alex looked at the closed door, wondering how long it would take to reach it.

Riel saw the worried look but puffed on his cigarette, sat back, took his moccasins off, and put his bare feet up on another chair in front of him.

There was a long silence.

Alex waited.

"Look, Yankee man, worry none about the button. Riel is glad you came. You want the truth? Okay. You had guts to come see me. *Merci*," Riel said in guttural French.

"So, what happened?"

"With that pretty nurse of yours? She is the kind, gentle soul. Kindly to my dim sister, Beatrice. I couldn't leave her there in the bushes with her little dog barking."

"No, not Monique, but thanks for helping her. You could have taken off, but you didn't. Just like at the lake. *Merci*, again. I owe you one."

Riel's shrugged that off. His eyes focused on the river, looking through the clean windows with bright, new curtains drawn back.

"Yeah, Yank, her pleading for help. Knocked out. That hound whining. It did it. I couldn't leave that nice girl, or that dog." he sighed.

"Some say you snapped Cartier's neck."

Riel shrugged his shoulders again. "Some say."

"Some say Cartier fell. Drunk and cracked his neck."

"Some say," Riel said, over his shoulder as he got up and walked the room.

Alex waited through a long silence.

"No, I was asking about Doctor Rani. What happened with her?"

Riel talked as he paced the room in his bare feet. "Lafayette, he freaked out, man. Those fucking cops said I raped her, over and over. And that lawyer, she only wanted her legal aid fees and to get another Indian by the balls," he spat out.

Riel stubbed his butt in an ashtray. He wanted another cigarette. "I don't smoke those things you provide us," Alex said meekly.

Riel came back to the desk. Alex stood up and stepped back as the hulking mass leaned over him. Riel reached over and slammed his fist on the button.

Alex reared back. The office door flung open. Three male nurses rushed in. One held a syringe.

Riel sat down, straddling a chair. The nurses surrounded him.

He just looked up, grinned, and told them to bring him some more cigarettes and a glass of juice.

"My mouth, she is dry from those pills you make me eat," he said, ordering the nurses away.

They looked at Alex, who nodded. The brawny head nurse scolded Riel for pulling that trick.

Riel laughed heartily.

"Just leave a few here, and some matches. He won't burn the place down, not with me here," Alex suggested as the trio walked out.

Riel lit his fresh cigarette and inhaled deeply.

Riel watched the smoke rings rise in the air and bounce off the ceiling. "Look, white man, that woman was the best thing that ever happened to Lafayette. She was kind to him. She, she is the one who reminded him of his grandmother," he said with head bowed.

Did Alex see tears in those dark eyes, he wondered? "Your grandmother? Where's your grandmother, Mr. Riel?" Alex asked, staring at him.

The question was ignored. "She, that kind woman doctor, she was younger. But same dark color as us. And kind like us. Religious, like my grandmother, and those kind nuns I had."

Alex seized the moment. "Nuns, Lafayette? Where?"

Riel sucked on the last puff before he burned his fingers on the hand-rolled cigarette. "Yeah. After my grandmother died. They, all those white men, they sent me west. That's far away, Mister Doctor. Somewhere west."

"How long were you there?"

"Till I was kicked out for fucking with one of the young nuns who had just came there. She was a horny, good-looking kid. Liked to screw, even in her black garb." he grinned.

Alex ignored that. "Nuns?"

"Yeah, nuns. But only one horny, young one."

Alex plunged in. "Were you always here? I mean, in Canada? Québec?"

Riel picked up the glass. He spat out a spray of juice. "Lafayette hates this grapefruit piss," he swore as he poured the juice into a wastebasket.

Alex remained seated.

Riel picked up another cigarette and pulled out loose strands of tobacco from the thin roll. "Long time ago, I lost faith in God, any god. To me there was no God never, whatever."

"How come?"

"My mother, she left me in the bushes as a little baby."

Alex pulled out a scrap of paper and read the notes he had made when talking with his mother. "Who was your mother?"

No answer. "This doctor, she called herself 'Rani' to me, she kept telling me to have faith and to pray. This Rani, she was a believer, just like my grandmother. I think; whatever."

"What was she to you, Lafayette?"

"She's a religious, spiritual woman, dark like my people, the real people of this world."

Alex repeated the question. "Were you always in this country?"

"Naw, like mister, I was like the wind. Free like the deer. They tell me you're a Yankee, a real Yankee, like some I knew."

"You had a brother. Jean-Baptiste. Killed by the Red Coats in a shootout. In La Verendrye, I think," Alex said, reading from his notepad.

Riel shrugged. "Never heard of any brother. All my kin are brothers to mister, here."

Alex waited. Nothing happened. Riel used the butt of the last cigarette to light a fresh one.

"So, what happened with Rani, Lafayette?"

Riel had his head down, troubled. "It was the drink that troubled this here man. He had head accidents, and in a rage like a bull in heat after that. He rolled three cars, and the red coats were kicking him in the head. Kicks to this man's head," he said quietly, as though he was talking far off and about someone else.

Riel stood up, walked about, and struck the door hard with his fist. Three nurses ran in again.

Alex told them to give him another cigarette. "It's okay. Nicotine has a calming effect on schizophrenics and brain-damaged patients," he offered.

Riel stopped. He strummed his fingers on the desk as blood slowly oozed from his knuckles.

"I, Lafayette, I played my guitar for her. She told me in her clinic office that it would be the last time that afternoon; late afternoon it was. I was mad. I was furious, and in my rage, like that bull, I swore at her and then …" he trailed off. He stopped in midsentence.

The room was quiet. Riel's cigarette dangled from his lips. Ash fell on his bare toes.

Alex leaned forward. "So, what happened, Lafayette?"

Riel looked up with a glazed looked. "She got up to give me a bible that was on a table in the corner. Said to me that Riel must have faith. Fucking high heels, she wore." He swore again under his breath.

"So, what? She always wore very high heels, Lafayette. So?"

"So? So, she walked with the bible, but tripped on the frayed carpet. One heel broke off. She fell. Poor girl. Fell flat on her face. Poor girl," he repeated sadly.

"Really. Then what?"

"Hit her head on that table. Table with the bible.

"She was unconscious?"

"Sorta knocked out. I went to her to help her up. Picked up her heel and kneeled to help her up. Like with your woman. In the bushes."

He stopped again. Riel flicked the live cigarette against the wall. Live ashes spewed all over the floor. Alex walked over and stomped on the glowing flecks.

Alex was getting impatient. "So? What happened then, Lafayette?"

"The door flung open when she cried out. From the blow to her noggin."

"They said you had sex with her."

Riel jumped up and put his face square in front of Alex. "Fuck no. She was not right to do that. A fucking nurse came in when she was on the floor. I didn't touch her none. That doctor later said that I tried to rape her."

Alex had read Riel's past history. "You had temporal lobe seizures from the head injuries. You could easily have blacked out, be in a daze with any stress."

Riel nodded and went on, talking with his head in his hands. "Lafayette, he didn't touch her, I swear on my grandmother's grave."

Alex nodded. "I understand. Go on, Lafayette."

Alex waited as tears welled up in Lafayette's eyes. He became more tearful as he talked. He squeezed one nostril and blew his nose on the floor.

"No more to say. How is she? Nice lady. Kindly to all others. Lay on the highway to stop buses. Young children should not be here. She stopped that."

"Yes. She and others. She'll be all right, Lafayette. She's gone to stay with her parents in Toronto. They moved there to open another restaurant."

"This kind of work, at her hospital, is too hard on her. Too many bad types there. For her kind."

"She phoned me. Said she was sorry you got into trouble. She said she should have listened to me about being careful running about in her high heels."

Riel looked up at Alex, pleased to hear that. "That is better for her kind. To listen to a wiser person," he said kindly and pointed his cigarette at Alex.

Riel sat for a long time, smoking, spitting tobacco strands on the floor, and blowing his nose into his sleeve.

The two men just sat there together, not looking at each other.

Minutes went by. It was quiet. Peaceful.

"I believe you, Lafayette," Alex said.

Riel stood up. He looked dumbfounded, like a little boy. "You believe me? Well, nice to meet you, Yankee man. Like a good son to me, you is. I had one little boy, once. Couldn't deal with a baby cripple with a bad foot. Many, many, moons ago."

Alex gulped hard. He wanted to ask where and when that was, but all he could say was, "Likewise, Lafayette. Nice to meet you, again."

Riel's voice softened. He looked at Alex and put out his hand. "Yeah. Nice to meet you, Doctor. Those three fuckers, those all white men, they believed wrong. Once he has the operation, this man will know nothing: nothing, nothing more."

"Yes. I guess so," Alex said, downcast.

"Is that kindly nurse better? The one that was choked?"

"Yeah, she's just fine now, thanks, Lafayette. O'Rielly, her supervisor, gave her a week off."

Alex stood and walked to the front of the desk and took Riel's bloody hand in his. He forced a smile. "Look here, Lafayette: have faith, man. You never know what's around the corner."

Lafayette rolled his eyes to Heaven, turned, and stretched. His massive chest strained at the buttons on his deer skin vest. He stood there, looking at Alex for the longest time.

Alex felt awkward. He said nothing. Embarrassed to ask more.

Lafayette finished his last cigarette and ground the butt into the ashtray. His knuckles, bruised from hitting the wall, continued to bleed. He sucked the blood off.

He spat on the floor, opened the door, and walked out.

Alex sat on the edge of the desk and turned his hand over. The palm of his right hand had Riel's blood on it.

He looked at the red globs and sat in silence, thinking about what he had just heard.

✳

CHAPTER 56

Flora's Illness and the Finals

IT was the second Sunday morning in mid-March, and just before Alex's exams. He went onto the front porch to study his textbooks and make notes again.

Vinny walked out, quietly closing the door behind him. "I don't want to wake Flora; she's still resting," he whispered, concern written all over his face.

Alex had never seen him so serious. He was dressed in a dark blue suit that didn't fit him very well, after many years on the hanger. He had a black tie, poorly tied in a Windsor knot, and a rumpled white shirt with a button missing. His garb just covered his hang-dog look.

The smell of wax from his polished, black shoes caused a sneezing fit for Claudius. He crawled away into the corner.

"What's going on, Vinny? Where are you off to? Where's the funeral?" Alex asked, and immediately regretted those words. "Oh, sorry."

"Yeah, well, I thought I'd go to church this morning," he said. He clutched the large, very old, family bible under his arm.

He sat down beside Alex. Silence. Did he want to talk?

After a long, uncomfortable minute, Alex made the first move. "How's your wife?"

A longer silence. Claudius wanted out.

Finally, Vinny said what Alex already knew. "Flora isn't well. Coughing in the night. You heard her?"

"I did. Is she raising blood in that cough?" asked Alex. He had never heard Vinny refer to his wife by her first name before, ever.

Vinny nodded. "The doctor said more tests. They found something in some lung of hers. Shit, she never puffed a fag in her life." He swore.

Vinny got up and stood there, thinking of what else he should say. There was nothing else to say.

Claudius followed Vinny to the door. He looked sad and more forlorn than his master.

Vinny stopped. He took his package of Sweet Caporal cigarettes out of his pocket and threw them on the ground. He stomped on the package.

Alex said nothing. He looked at Vinny with sad, moist eyes.

Vinny just had to change the subject. He was about to break down. "That hot-shot surgeon with the icepick is in Montréal, doc."

Thank God, Alex thought. *He is still lecturing. That's good.* "Riel's operation date is set for a week from now. Just after I get back from writing my finals, Vinny."

"I'll pray for Riel, and you, at the cathedral," Vinny said as he turned and blinked at the bright sun rising in the east.

"He and I will need all the help we can get. Thanks Vinny."

"I had to fix the lights on his ward yesterday. Told me that we'd get the last shipment of fags from his supplier on the reserve soon."

"Do you have enough to pay for the delivery?"

Vinny smiled. "Nah, he just laughed. Said this one is free, since he won't need money anymore."

"Kind of him, Vinny. Kind, but sad. Listen, you make doubly sure he gets the money. Make sure he hides it real good in his pants. Give him big bills. Get it? Give him a few one hundred-dollar bills. Tell him to secret them in his shorts. Will you?"

Vinny was taken aback by the request. It was more of a command, coming from the doctor. "Yeah? Well, okay. Will do. Will do. Gave me a good luck charm off his neck, also. To help Flora, he said," Vinny replied, not asking about the big bills. He let Claudius out.

"He has a strong faith in those amulets."

"Yeah. I'll give it to Flora to wear. Big bills?"

"Yes. Big bills. Easy to stuff in his leather pants, or into his shorts. You tell him, and you do it, Vinny. You hear?"

Vinny clearly wanted to ask more, but he didn't. "What kind of stuff do they ask you on your final exams, doc?" Vinny asked, pointing to the book on Alex's knee.

More talk? Alex was surprised by Vinny's genuine curiosity. "The exams consist of two written sessions, three hours each, and a two-hour oral exam, Vinny."

"You're full of it, man. Eight hours?" Vinny asked, counting it out on his fingers.

"Yep; during the oral exam, a patient has to be examined by me, and then I present the findings to the examiners. They are always two respected, older psychiatrists from other provinces."

Vinny whistled. Claudius came back in and perked up at the whistle. "What the dickens can you write for six hours?"

"Well, Vinny, the first written exam is on the basics, which includes psychology, biochemistry, neurophysiology, neuroanatomy, pharmaceutics, and sociology."

"Lots of 'neuro' and 'ologies' stuff."

Alex continued as Vinny bent down to clean the muck off the dog's feet. "The last written exam, lasting three hours in the same day is after lunch, and it consists of practical knowledge of patients. Diagnoses, procedures, medical, and psychiatric treatment applications."

"You know all that stuff? Learned it here? In this coo-coo place?" Vinny asked, leaning against the doorjamb. He looked at the trampled package of smokes in the corner. Alex wondered if he yearned for a drag.

"You betcha, Vinny. You have to know the medical diseases that could produce emotional and psychiatric problems."

Alex feared Vinny had had enough. He got up to prepare for his trip to Montréal for the exams.

Vinny looked at his watch. "Like what, man? Like what medical stuff?"

"Well, that includes thyroid, diabetes, eating disorders, neurological conditions, tumors, hormonal dysfunction, early Alzheimer's, and other organic brain disorders like trauma, multiple sclerosis, ALS, and pancreatic cancer that could present with depression. All the illicit drugs cause psychiatric problems."

Vinny became thoughtful for a moment. "You got that right, soon to be head-honcho man. Drugs. Like what happened to our Paulo. Poor guy," he said sadly.

"Yeah, sorry about that, Vinny. But it took four years of University, five years of medical school, and four years of psychiatric residency. I'm almost there."

"So, what's with the oral stuff? No funny stuff there is there?" he asked, screwing up his face and trying to be funny.

Alex smiled. "No, Vinny, but the oral examination could be problematic because of possible personality differences between the examiners and me. I'm a foreigner, you know. One or the other may not like us guys: Americans. Rebels."

"Just brown nose a lot, kiss ass, and you'll be okay, doc. Just kiss ass," was Vinny's best advice that day. He waved his hand and left.

Alex packed a small case and said goodbye to Mamma D in her room. He kissed her on her cheek. She looked withered, had lost weight, and was pale. He wished her well, reminding her to take her medications.

She gave him a feeble hug with wasted arms and went back to bed. She whispered, "The special surgeon told me they will take out part of my lung soon. Said I'll be well. Do you think so, Alex?"

Alex took her hand and held it tight. "Monique told me about that pulmonary specialist. She thought you had a good prognosis, that is, a future, since there is no spread, Mamma D," Alex replied with a genuine smile.

Alex drove to Montréal after seeing Monique, who said she would pray for him and for Mamma D. She gave him her small, gold cross to wear under his shirt.

When he got to Montréal, he studied in his hotel room all that day.

The written exams were finished the next day; Alex took them with thirty other hopefuls from across the country at the College auditorium, where he had met the director with Monique some time ago.

Alex had one hour to physically examine his patient and then take a complete psychiatric history on the man. He was an elderly, depressed gentleman farmer from up north. He had early Alzheimer's and was blind in one eye after a car accident.

Alex examined him and found he had a large liver from drinking too much, his memory was faulty, and he had just attempted suicide. He had walked into the side of a bus. Four times in that hour of examination, the man asked to relieve himself. Once, he didn't make it to the toilet.

After calling in a nurse to help his patient with his soaking-wet pants, Alex made notes and went into the examiner's room.

When Alex walked into the room, he found one professor who was no more than five feet tall, with a wispy beard, glasses, and a balding pate. He seemed to be kindly, and greeted Alex with a smile and a nod. The other was chunky and quite obese, still munching on a hot chicken sandwich. He sported a red beard and a healthy head of red hair, but seemed cold, distant, and indifferent.

After an hour of grilling on all manner of subjects psychiatric, it was the dour, overweight, red-faced doctor from Glasgow who did the talking. Dr. Scotty Argyle looked over his bulky reading glasses at Alex and finally asked a lengthy, disjointed question.

"So, Doctor Alexander Gage, tell me: if your fifty-year-old, chronically depressed patient, about whom you've just read in that additional copy of his history I gave you, doesn't respond to those anti-depressants that you so quickly prescribed, what else would you do for him?"

Quickly? Alex thought. After all, the man was suicidal, and he needed the meds; but he kept focused. "Well sir, I would consider changing the medication. Slowly. I would add thyroid medication to give him some metabolic energy, and some of the newer anti-depressants that can be mixed together. Sir."

There was no response from Argyle.

Alex felt warm. The room was devoid of a window, and the temperature was rising.

"If all that fails, what would you do next?"

"Well sir, I would admit the gentleman to hospital for further observation and protection. If he was very much younger, sir, and was a chronic depressive with recurrent mood swings, then he might benefit from lithium. It's very popular in the British Isles, sir," Alex replied with a forced smile, trying to suck up, as Vinny had suggested.

No smile in return.

"Lithium? You would prescribe lithium? A heavy metal? And if that failed, young man?"

Alex looked at the other examiner, who continued with his crossword puzzle and made no eye contact.

"Well sir, then a course of ECT."

The Scot's lips quivered into a painful twinge. Was it the wrong answer, or was it his dyspepsia—or perhaps a need to pass wind? Was the chicken sour?

It was gas.

Once Argyle burped and felt relieved, without excusing himself, he growled, "The man is still a raving suicide: uncontrollable, aggressive, and on a rampage on your ward. What do you do then, Doctor?"

Alex would have liked to have said that he would have referred the man to Argyle here, but Vinny's words rang out in his head again, "*kiss ass, Alex, kiss ass.*"

Alex screwed up his courage. "Well sir, I know that in the Scandinavian countries, and throughout the British Isles, they would recommend a prefrontal lobotomy, sir. That would certainly be in order for this gentleman to quiet him down."

The crossword man put down the weekend puzzle, looked up, and smiled. Did he find an answer to a puzzle, or was he pleased with the answer?

Alex broke into a sweat. Argyle, the other examiner, returned to his notes and wrote frantically. He never looked up.

The room got hotter. The shirt that Alex was wearing was soaking wet; the gold cross was stuck to his chest. The silence was deafening.

Alex recognized the white, hand-carved clay pipe on Argyle's chunky thigh, and pointed to it. "Is that a meerschaum, sir? Very elegant pipe. Does it give a cool smoke, Doctor Argyle?"

Ha, good one, Alex thought. Brown nose. Kiss ass. Vinny's advice.

Argyle put his pen down, and for the first time looked Alex in the eye. "Bought it in Istanbul, at a medical meeting. It does provide a refreshing smoke, come to think of it: nice and cool, young man," Argyle said, almost cracking his face with the hint of a smile.

"I'll have to buy one, sir; a real beautiful pipe. When I can afford it."

"You'll be able to, young man. You're excused."

Alex got up, expecting something more. There was nothing. He left the room recalling the words, "*You'll be able to, young man.*"

Vinny would be proud of me, Alex thought as he made it to the toilet just on time.

Once he calmed down, he called Monique and told her about the exams. She was sympathetic and reassuring. "I'm sure you passed. I got a favorable sign from the Madonna when I prayed to her at the cathedral," she replied.

The Madonna is swathed in marble and doesn't respond, Alex thought, but he kept that to himself.

Waiting was nerve-wracking. It would take a week after Alex got back to the DaCosta's to get the results. Evening meetings with Monique helped to relieve his stress and anxiety.

In the late afternoon, after work a few days later, Vinny asked if he had received the results. "Not yet, Vinny. Other consultants from across the country mark the exams. It was all very anonymous, Vinny." Alex explained.

Vinny was sitting on his veranda, with the bible on his lap. "They phone you, do they?" he asked, scratching Claudius, who seemed to be fretting.

"No, Vinny. The college sends the results by special mail. If the envelope is thick, then you get a huge, three-page re-application form to re-apply for next year. A thin envelope means one piece of paper, a simply-typed note that you passed and some kind of congrats."

"Thin, is good, doc. Thin is good," Vinny said. He tightened his belt another notch on his belly, which was getting wasted after Flora had stopped cooking. He was bringing home salads, ham and rye bread for himself from the grocer's, vitamins and soup for Flora, and dry dog food for Claudius. Rani was there often, cooking curried dishes. Claudius didn't take to curry.

"Good luck, son," Vinny said sincerely, and then had some news for Alex. "Clarice is gone, doc."

Alex wasn't surprised that the Ice Queen had moved. He heard on the wards that she had a sister in Halifax who had offered to look after her.

"Gone to Halifax, Vinny? Good for her."

Claudius got up and chased after a wasp that had made its way through the holes in the screens and was annoyingly buzzing about. Vinny ignored the beast.

"Naw, gone through the thin ice at the lake, she did, doc."

"What? Didn't they save her?" Alex asked. "What was she doing down there?"

"Yeah, poor lady said she didn't want to be a burden to her sister. Moved her motorized wheel chair to that small hill above the lake, let go of the brake, and rolled down through the thinning ice."

"My God. Those brakes must have given in, Vinny. No one there to save the poor woman?"

Vinny watched Claudius swatting at the wasp with his paws as it skimmed the floor. He missed.

"Poor woman, indeed. I serviced her motorized chair that week; the brakes were good. The Ice Queen went through the ice and is still at the bottom. Poor woman, indeed," he added again.

"Poor Clarice and Juanita. One committed suicide, and the other was murdered," was all Alex could say.

Vinny got up and opened the door to shoo the wasp out. "Yeah. Well, they will drag her out when the ice melts in the spring," he said sadly.

"Give her a proper funeral, Vinny. We'll get *Mère* Denise to do it."

Vinny thought for a second, but had another piece of info for Alex. "Yeah. Well, she had Cartier's final biblical message, clipped to the back of her wheel chair in bold letters. Saw it when I did her brakes."

Alex was curious. "What did he write, Vinny?"

Vinny thought for a minute. "'And know that I am with you; yes, to the end of time. J.C.'"

✳

CHAPTER 57

Saving Lafayette

ALEX had one more important duty to perform.

Several days after his visit with Riel, Alex drove Monique to her residence one late afternoon. There was a light snowfall, which would be the last, according to the weatherman.

As he dropped her off, he told Monique that he would make the visit to see Riel that very night.

Monique didn't ask any further questions. She knew what his plans were, and they had both decided that she would be involved. She gave him a long hug and a short, wet, passionate kiss.

"I'll make the arrangements for the meds and I'll be on the ward tonight, my love," she whispered in his ear, left, and closed the car door.

Later that evening, Alex made partial ward rounds to see one of his patients, who had just given birth.

"Both mother and baby are doing just fine," Lydia, the nurse on duty, was pleased to report.

Alex fretted all that evening and waited for the right time. Finally, after making notes on some of his patients who were ready for discharge, he phoned Lafayette's prison ward and asked for the orderly in charge.

"Doctor Gage here. I'm making ward rounds tonight. I'm just checking that you've got that big Indian ready. He's slated for surgery in Montréal in the morning. Doctor Walters wants his own special surgical nurse here at the hospital ward to have him ready."

Marcel, the head orderly on the prison ward, was almost gloating. "Yes, Doctor. He's well sedated. We've got that Mohawk, mad-killer Indian shackled to his bed," the sadist said with confidence.

Alex let the slur pass. "Well done, my good man. Well done. I'm assisting the surgeon in the morning, and Riel is first on the list."

"You're the lucky one, Doctor. Wish I could be there to see it."

"I'll see if I can arrange it, my good fellow. We want him in surgery here overnight so that he's well prepared, sedated, and no trouble once he's in the Montréal hospital. Surgeon's orders," he lied, doing his best to be authoritative.

Marcel hesitated. "Isn't that highly unusual, Doctor?" Marcel asked with a questioning tone.

Alex sensed the hesitation. "Extra special case, Marcel. Highest priority. We don't want any trouble with him, now do we, when he's moved from your ward to surgery and then by ambulance to Montréal? We have to be doubly careful. Doctor Walter's very special orders."

There was a slight pause. "Okay-dokey, doc. Pretty special for you?" the man asked, laughing. Alex heard another orderly chuckle in the background.

Alex answered with a forced laugh. "You got that right, man. A knockout punch he'll get. I'll escort him to the hospital ward tonight, together with a special nurse from surgery. I'll be on your ward at nine sharp tonight, to take him to the surgical unit."

"He'll need a shot, Doctor."

"I'll give him a double dose of Amytal, up where the sun doesn't shine," Alex said, using a tone only a sadist like Marcel would understand.

"Ha. Up where the sun don't shine! If you say so, Doctor. Wish I could do it."

Alex added a little drama to the scene. "The surgeon, Doctor Walters, is doing me a favor. I'll use the icepick through the left eye socket, and Walters will do the right eye. I can hardly wait."

"Wow. Wish I could be there. The dueling duo. Like the matadors in Spain brandishing icepicks: *olé, ole*," the sadist shouted to his buddy in the office, imitating the Toro bull ring cry.

For good measure Alex added, "Strap him to a wheelchair, with ropes around his legs, before I get there at nine. I don't want any trouble from that Mohawk. My nurse from the surgical unit will be there to assist me, and I'll give him the intramuscular shot when I get there, just for good measure."

"Yes, sir," Marcel shouted, almost apoplectic.

Alex asked for good measure, "Oh, one last thing. Is the front of his head shaved?"

"Done this morning, Doctor. We didn't touch his braids around the back."

Alex closed the phone with, "Thank you. Well done, my good man. Well done."

Alex left his office and walked into the late Juanita's ward that evening at eight. Monique had made sure that the nurse's station would be empty, and that all the nurses would be busy getting beds ready, handing out meds, and dimming the lights.

All the patients were in the day room watching the 1942 movie *Casablanca* with Humphrey Bogart and Sam, the piano man, singing, "*It's still the same old story, a fight for love and glory, a case of do or die ...*"

As he listened, he thought that this was indeed for love and glory and a case of do or die as he looked about. All the nurses were busy. Once in the nurse's station, Alex made sure no one saw him.

He reached down into the waste basket and pulled out an empty vial of sodium amytal where Monique had placed it under a paper napkin.

Monique had secretly arranged the next two requirements. Alex opened the medicine cupboard and put a syringe into his pocket. Then he took a bottle of saline solution from the shelf and went to his office.

"Well done, Monique," he mumbled to himself.

Alex closed his office door. He laid the syringe, the empty sedative vial, and the full saline solution bottle on his desk.

Next, Alex took the syringe, pushed the needle into the bottle, and filled the syringe with saline water. He picked up the empty vial with the rubber stopper, and filled it full of the salt water solution from his syringe.

He wrapped the empty syringe in his kerchief and put the 'amytal' vial full of liquid saline in his pocket.

Alex waited. At fifteen minutes to nine, he stopped writing progress notes. It was a dark night with low, heavy clouds, a cool fog, and a light drizzle coming down. The light snow covering the grounds had cleared away.

As he made his way to the prison ward, he noted that the gardens were empty of staff and the wards were in lockdown.

Alex unlocked the heavy metal door to Riel's ward down near the river and walked in.

Marcel, the burly oaf, met him with a wide grin and flexing his muscles. "Riel is held at the Queen's pleasure, Doctor. According to the certificates. Not my queen, though," the orderly said, derisively.

"Yes, Marcel. Canada still uses the British rule of law. You Canadians are still considered to be the Queen's subjects," Alex reminded the lout as he looked around the ward.

"Well, Riel committed a crime, and the psychiatrists from Montréal said he was mentally ill, Doctor. We have the committal papers."

"Well done, my good fellow. What did you give him, Marcel?" he asked, still buttering him up.

"Those sedatives such as paraldehyde, chloral hydrate, chlorpromazine, and the barbiturates don't even touch him, Doctor."

Alex looked at all the patients in the room snoring loudly. "Looks like they worked on all the other patients," Alex said. He spied Monique, who was busy checking Riel's blood pressure and temperature.

Marcel nodded wisely. "Many of these violent men don't respond to massive doses of sedation. The surgical nurse has arrived," he answered and pointed to Monique.

Marcel looked out to the windows. "You ordered spot lights to surround the buildings, but the wiring is still incomplete," he said, concerned.

Alex knew that, since Vinny had agreed to Alex's suggestion of not connecting the cables for that night. He needed the darkness. That was one of Vinny's jobs in this caper. The other was stuffing large bills in Riel's underwear.

"I'll be all right. Is he well-strapped in as ordered, Marcel?"

"Well-strapped in indeed, as ordered, Doctor."

Alex scanned the room again. Snores and soft farts reverberated off the walls and the air stank of foul smells that emanated from every possible human orifice.

One male orderly, half asleep on a chair, quickly got up for the doctor as Alex walked by. Alex was in good shape, but was half the size in height and weight of this burly guard.

The big gorilla arched his shoulders in combat. "You want to arm wrestle, let's do it," the ape said jokingly.

"Ah, no thanks. You're in much better shape."

The hunk, called 'Tarzan' by his mates, pointed to the corner. "There's your man."

Alex's eyes slowly accustomed to the darkness. He focused on Riel strapped in the wheelchair. Marcel was next to Alex and Tarzan, the gorilla, followed behind.

"Your nurse has finished checking him over, and his hands are tied to the arms of the chair. His feet are wrapped together with rope, and a heavy, leather strap is around his waist. As you ordered," the gorilla said. He pointed to the corner of the room.

"Well done. Well done," Alex said patting the ape on the back.

The ape flexed his shoulders and puffed out his chest. "He's ready for you, Doctor."

"I'm taking Riel personally to surgery. Let's go see him." They walked to the corner.

Alex found Riel, lashed to the wheelchair, with his head down on his chest and Monique busy writing in his chart. She looked up and only said something in French as a greeting.

Riel heard the footsteps of one man dragging a leg. He knew that shuffle. The other heavy boot with steel toes approaching him from the side belonged to the sadistic guard, Marcel. He could also smell Tarzan, the ape. The scent of Monique's body lotion was still in the air beside him.

Alex slowly approached Riel. He lifted his chin.

Riel remained perfectly still, as his brothers had taught him when they were hunting in the bush.

"I gave him a shot of paraldehyde earlier, Doctor. He needed a double dose," Tarzan said. He pulled Riel's head back roughly by his long braids.

Alex cautiously went to the back of the chair. He put his hand on Lafayette's right shoulder and squeezed the muscle.

The Indian was careful not to wince.

Alex nodded. "He could be better sedated. I've got the double shot just to make sure," he said as he pulled the vial out of his pocket.

Alex opened a kerchief holding a syringe and a vial of amytal.

"Hold his arm tight. I don't want a broken needle in his shoulder if he bolts," Alex ordered.

The caretaker laughed at his immobile quarry and viciously tightened the strap around Riel's chest. "No response from the Indian," Marcel gloated.

"Oh, sorry. I forgot the sterile swabs, my good man. Can you get some for me from your office? Don't want any infection in his shoulder now, do we?" Alex said with a forced laugh.

"Have to be careful, Doctor." Marcel and Tarzan laughed in unison, and both took off for the office.

Alex bent over Riel and whispered, "Say nothing and do nothing. This won't affect you at all; it's just water, Lafayette."

The weight lifter came back with a swab dripping in alcohol. "Thank you," Alex said, taking the sponge.

Alex thrust the needle into the vial and withdrew the fluid. "This shot of extra-strength amytal should knock him out for a few hours while we take him to the surgical ward for the night," Alex said to Monique.

He cleaned the deltoid and thrust the needle into Riel's shoulder muscle. Riel's arm gave a slight quiver, an automatic muscular contraction. Alex pocketed the vial and gave the syringe to the orderly.

"Need a good man to go with you, Doctor?" the weight lifter asked hopefully.

Alex had grasped the handles of the wheelchair and turned it toward the door. He pointed at two male nurses grappling with one patient who was thrashing about violently. The psychotic was in a frenzy and had his arm around a nurse's neck.

"Naw, I'll manage just fine. This kind nurse will help me, and they need your help over there. Prepare a syringe of one hundred mgms of paraldehyde for me, just in case."

The orderly followed Alex, Monique, and their wheelchair-bound patient to the office, unlocked the door, and prepared a syringe.

Alex wrapped it in white gauze and handed it to Monique. She put her blue nurse's cape around her body, a blanket over Riel, a woolen toque on his head and mitts on his hands.

Marcel locked the office door and patted Alex on the back. "You got the last laugh now, doc."

"Yeah, the last laugh."

Alex smiled and waved goodbye to both men. He pushed the chair down the hall as Monique dutifully followed. Alex zipped up his parka and pulled the fedora hard onto his head, turned, and made sure the door locked behind him.

The three were alone, and walked out into the night.

Once outside, Riel took in a deep lungful of the cool night air and carefully opened one eye. His chest heaved as the leather strap strained to hold him in the chair.

It was a very dark evening; a light fog continued to roll up from the river below. The clouds had parted and the drizzle stopped. A half-moon lit the pathway ahead of Riel's wheelchair. A family of raccoons skirted across their pathway.

As Alex slowly pushed his chair away from the building, Riel saw the river scows and tugs in the darkness far below. Monique gently pat him on the shoulder.

The tugs were tied to the wharfs along the St. Lawrence River, holding the freighters at bay and waiting for the tide to turn. Monique had checked the tide tables earlier, informed Alex and both were satisfied with the timing.

The grounds were empty. All the buildings were quiet. It was dark. The nursing staff were shutting the lights down as the patients were bedded for the night.

"All is right, my love," Monique whispered as a pair of coyotes were heard scurrying after their prey in the bushes.

Riel heard that, but said nothing. Alex leaned down over Riel.

"Be quiet and don't struggle, Lafayette," Alex said, as he unexpect-edly pushed the wheelchair off the sidewalk and into a small thicket of bushes.

Monique loosened the straps from behind Riel's chest.

Riel grunted and shifted his chest and back muscles. He snorted, breathing heavily through his nose.

"Just be quiet, Lafayette. I know you're awake. Don't yell and don't struggle. I'll get these off you," Alex whispered in his ear.

He released the straps first from his arms and legs, and Monique freed those around his waist.

Riel raised his shoulders. He massaged his arms to get the blood flowing. Alex grasped the big man by the arm and he and Monique eased him out of the chair.

"That shot I gave you was only water. We'll have to work fast. You're going to have to hit me pretty hard, Lafayette."

"Hit this man? You?" Riel asked, throwing his mitts into the bushes.

"Yes, so it will look good and very real before you take off."

Riel looked at Alex sideways as he rubbed his eyes. He raised his hands behind his head and stretched.

Alex reached into his pocket. He handed Riel a large wad of bills, whispering, "Here's another four hundred dollars: payment for that last shipment of cigarettes."

Riel put his hand down to his crotch. "I have more. From Vinny," he said quietly. He took the extra bills and stuffed them in his pockets.

"Good for Vinny. Look, there's a ship at the docks below waiting to leave. It might stop at Halifax, or at New Brunswick, or in the eastern States."

Riel looked beyond Alex and into the hills. "Riel likes the forest, man."

Monique shook her head. "Be on the ship below. Don't go into the woods, or they will send the dogs, and the Red Coats, after you and bring you back. Do not."

"Riel will do as the kindly nurse say to me."

"Good. I'll tell them you went into the forest. Go to the river, instead. They won't think of that," she said firmly and gave Riel a small hug.

Riel straightened his back and shook his head to clear it. He looked at Alex. "Lafayette, he can hit you, man, but this he'll be sorry to do it. And sorry to not see this kind nurse anymore."

Alex cautioned Riel before the blow came. "Hit me on the side of my head. I need my teeth," Alex said with a smile, offering his left side.

Riel put out his hands with palms up. Alex took his hands in his. They both looked at each other for a minute.

Monique waited and watched the two men embrace. "I'm leaving, and I'll wait for you in the surgical sick ward, Alex. Don't hit him too hard, please, Mister Riel."

Riel nodded in agreement as he watched her leave. "I feel like that big white guy. You know: who had his head shaved off, by that woman in the Bible," Riel said in a hushed tone, rubbing the now-bald frontal areas of his head.

Alex smiled and took off his fedora. "You mean Samson? Well, you've still got your braids, and they didn't shave all your hair. Take care of yourself, man, and stay out of trouble. I don't want to see you here, ever again."

"Yeah, that's the man. Samson. Don't worry. Lafayette here, he will be gone forever," said the Indian, as he sent his fist flying at Alex's head.

Alex hit the ground with a thud.

Riel bent over, lifted Alex's head in his rough paws, and whispered something in his ear.

Alex was dazed. He tried to sit up, but continued to lie there as he saw the back of the big man start his run down the slope.

Riel quietly loped down the grounds and to the river, hunched over and quiet as a deer. He faded in the distance, out of sight for a moment.

Alex slowly got to his feet. He looked around again. He was alone. He rubbed his aching head. At the bottom of the hill, Riel turned and waved.

Riel disappeared into the cool, rising mist from the mighty St. Lawrence, as the fog horns wailed. The partial moon slowly sank in the south.

Alex sat down on a large bolder for a few minutes. He massaged his head, and then rolled about to get his white coat dirty and his parka mussed with leaves. He scuffed his arms with rose branches to draw blood and then put on his fedora.

As he waited in the bushes, he gouged his forehead with a rock where Riel had stuck him to cause a deep cut. As the blood flowed down his face, he limped back to the surgical ward close by. He left the wheelchair on its side, but pulled it onto the path.

At the entrance to the hospital building, he rang a large bell used for emergency purposes. He waited a minute and started shouting and kicking at the door.

When the door opened, he recognized O'Rielly, who was in charge for the night, making rounds. Monique was there, aghast and looking terrified.

Monique looked at Alex, bleeding from his forehead. She gasped and shouted for help from the orderlies.

"My God, Doctor. Doctor Gage, is that you? What happened to you?" O'Rielly asked. She reached for Alex as blood filled his eye socket.

Alex was on one knee, holding onto a rail beside the door. Alex rasped, and put on his best act. "Riel was vomiting from the sedative. Aspirated, and started choking. I loosened his straps. That was a big mistake," Alex said, dramatically.

He struggled to catch his breath as he held his head in one hand, wailing and crying. He put on his best theatrical performance yet.

"Who, Doctor Gage? Who did this to you?" O'Rielly asked, pulling Alex into the building with Monique's help.

Alex became even more dramatic. "He jumped me and knocked me down once Monique here left us," he mumbled, and he feigned collapse again.

As Alex fell to the floor, he recalled Shakespeare's words, *"All the world's a stage."* He felt like he was one of the major actors, full of sound and fury, signifying nothing much.

He grabbed at his throat, grimaced, wailed, and hysterically fell down again in a heap.

"Who, Doctor? Who was it?" O'Rielly shouted again, trying to help him up. An orderly, now on the scene, tried to lift the injured doctor off the floor.

Alex shook his head, rolled his eyes into his forehead, and showed the nurse the blood on his sleeve.

"It was the big Indian. Riel. I was bringing him here to await his lobotomy in Montréal tomorrow." He gasped melodramatically.

"My God. You poor man. How ghastly," they all said in unison.

Alex was lifted by both arms into a wheelchair, brought by another nurse. The surgical nurse dabbed at his forehead with cotton gauze.

"Don't you worry, Doctor; we'll get him," said the beefy orderly.

Alex was wheeled into the hospital ward by Monique and one of the other nurses.

An assistant nurse brought a bottle of iodine. "Bandages, nurse, for after you clean the doctor's head wound," Monique ordered.

Alex listened as the orderly phoned the hospital police. He shouted at Alex, "Corporal LeFleur wants to know which way he went, Doctor."

Alex shook his head and blinked a few times, enjoying being on stage again. "I saw Riel running up into the hills, into the forest and away from the river. He must be looking for his Indian brothers, his mates," he wailed, ending 'act three.'

"The forest, Corporal. Use the dogs. Get the dogs," the orderly shouted, jumping up and down in a frenzy.

Alex winced as the nurse slapped iodine on his cut. "He went into the bushes, and is now heading for the north highway," Alex yelled.

"He has gone to his relatives in Montréal, I'm sure," the orderly shouted back into the phone. He slammed the receiver down.

Alex pointed to the hills. "He took off behind the hospital, into the forest. Tell the corporal."

"They're getting a group together. We'll get him for you, sir," the orderly said. He put on a heavy coat in glee to join the posse. He was so excited that he was literally dancing up and down, frothing at the mouth.

"Good man. Get him for me, but he knows the bush well. So be careful."

"I'm going to help the police. We'll drag him back by the neck," the silly fellow said as he ran out to join the party, who were already gathering outside.

"He'll be hard to find in those bushes up the hill. Take a flashlight," shouted Alex. He pointed in that direction again.

"*Bonne chance*," O'Rielly yelled as she placed a bandage over the cuts on Alex's arm. Monique brought Alex a cup of tea and covered him in a blanket as he brushed the dirt off his hat.

"*Oui*. Good luck," Alex shouted, since the orderly had left the door open.

Alex felt better after the tea, and later, the hot soup. O'Rielly and the other nurses fawned all over him. Monique told him and all the other staff how brave he was.

Alex smiled, enjoying the admiring glances from the staff, and winked at Monique.

He composed himself, blew her a kiss, and left around midnight. He drove home in his truck, which had been left outside by Monique that night. He unwrapped a stick of Juicy Fruit gum, lit his pipe, and drove down the highway.

The radio was playing Gerry and the Pacemakers' new hit song, "You'll Never Walk Alone."

"I'll have to tell Monique about this tune. So appropriate," he said, laughing at the British group.

Alex traveled the highway, which ran parallel to the raging St. Lawrence. The tide was coming in. He pulled over, turned the motor off, and heard the engines of the freighters struggling against the rising waters as the Atlantic washed in.

The tugs and freighters inched their way forward, searching for the massive gulf and the open waters of the Atlantic.

Riel would be on board with one of them. They were always happy to have the extra help of a strong back.

"Good luck, my old man," Alex said as he sucked on his pipe. He fired up the engine and threw the white bandage circling his forehead, placed there by Monique, on the floor.

When he got home, he was glad to see the house in darkness. Flora was coughing softly, and Vinny was snoring.

Alex phoned the hospital police.

"Hello, Doctor. Heard you got a bad wallop. We searched the hills, eh. No trace of Riel yet. He's in the bushes, but we'll get him for you, eh? We got the hounds on his trail, eh," the *SQ* officer at his desk said with a vengeance.

"I'm sure he can't be far away. I hope you blocked the highway to Montréal, officer," Alex offered, in great seriousness.

"We've got the area covered, eh."

Alex replied with a wide grin on his face, "Good work. Well done, eh."

✳

CHAPTER 58

A Final, But Fatal, Request

ALEX knew that the *Sûreté du Québec* police force would never find Riel, and they never did. They had the dogs out and combed the forest, stopped all cars on the highway to check their trunks, and tried to bribe the local Métis for information.

Riel's friends were only too happy to assist the *SQ* for some *wampum*, as they jokingly called the Canadian dollar. "Yes, we saw him go that way, officer. West. Go west."

The police went that way.

"*Oui*, I saw him running this way," Riel's good friend, Gerard, said, pointing south.

The local police went that way, south.

"He stopped here for a bowl of soup, and then went north to be with his brothers," the café owner said.

The *SQ* headed north with the dogs.

But Riel was never seen again. He was on the river, heading east.

Alex reluctantly agreed to visit Casa Loma one more time before leaving town with Monique. They were going to get married in Montréal. Her mother, Christina, was very intense and strident in her request to see him, almost demanding, which was unlike Christina.

He sensed that she was anxious, but she didn't explain the reason for her demand on the telephone. He wasn't interested in any sexual dalliance with her, or any need for the sadomasochistic teasing, now that he was engaged to her daughter.

When he arrived at Casa Loma on that Sunday afternoon, he found the entrance hallway crowded with politicians from Ottawa and Montréal.

He carried his briefcase full of blotters soaked with LSD for Christina, and felt safe enough when he saw the police chief and the mayor.

The weekend crowd were all happily paying their dues to two young, sultry girls at the entrance. The girls welcomed them and stood at the door provocatively, but only worked by way of accepting cash for Christina.

Alex found Christina busy escorting Jasmine, her new obsession, out of the kitchen where she worked. He hesitated briefly in the large, opulent living room, and told Christina that he was in a hurry to get home. He was not interested in a three-way, nor in passing any time with pretty Jasmine.

Christina understood, nodded, and pointed upstairs to her bedroom. Before he went up the stairs, Alex stopped to speak briefly with Theodore, and thanked him again for saving his life with that rifle shot at Bruno.

Both men watched Jasmine stop for a few minutes in the ornate room. She refilled the long-playing Motorola record player with several LPs.

She pushed the button to start the music, and Alex was pleased to hear Édith Piaf, the renowned French chanteuse, with her signature song "Non, Je ne Regrette Rien."

He recalled the words, so meaningful to him now: *"No, I regret nothing, I don't care about the past; Today, it begins with you."* Such nostalgic words and poignant thoughts made him think of his beautiful Monique.

As Alex listened to Piaf, Christina waved to him again, blew him a kiss, and told him to come up the grand staircase with her and Jasmine. He followed them up to their boudoir, but at the top of the landing, Alex turned and pointed down at the hairy colossus of a man in the large room below.

He was walking about only in his shorts, with his pockets bulging full of candies, chocolates, and lollipops.

"Never saw him here before. Who the Hell is that, Christina?" Alex asked.

Christina winked and nodded in that direction. "Stanislaus, Alexander. Bruno was his cousin. Stanislaus also works the river in those barges, but they all call him Santa Claus. He hands out lollipops and candies to young children, especially young boys."

Alex recoiled in disgust. "Christina, he's trouble for you, and shouldn't be here. Vinny knows him, and told me about that greasy pervert. He likes young boys and seduces young, teenaged girls. He entices them with money and sweets. Get rid of him." He scowled.

Christina laughed and chided Alex, "He pays double for my girls. There are no children here, my sweet. Maybe you can treat this pedophile and cure him. He would pay you well, Alexander."

"Hell no, Christina. Homosexual pedophiles are born homosexual and can't be cured, so to speak. It's in their genes," Alex said, looking at Jasmine next to him on the staircase.

She nodded in agreement.

Christina had more information. "He paid me a deposit for information on a transfer of a riverside land property. He and a bunch of his Russian partners want to develop the land for a large housing project. I have all of that cash for you in a suitcase, under my bed, my dear boy."

Alex was not willing to accept money from such a transaction. "No thanks, Christina. It might implicate me in a bribe, and in some wrongdoing in the future. It's unwise, and way too risky for me. I don't need a scandal."

Christina shrugged her shoulders and said nothing as Alex followed the two women into the bedroom. Christina closed the door and locked it. Jasmine stripped down naked and slid into their bed, waiting for Christina to follow.

Alex watched the beautiful, mulatto girl reach over to her bedside table and pick up a small perfume bottle. She then sprayed herself and the room with a magnificent scent of a floral, spicy odor that was most enticing.

Christina interrupted Alex's vision of Jasmine and pulled him away. She went to her desk and pulled out two paper documents.

So … this is the reason for her phone call.

"Alexander, I need you to fill in this disability form for Jasmine. She needs long-term medical assistance from the government."

"What are you talking about? She makes good money here," Alex said, angry to be called for such an unprofessional request.

"Not enough. The money is to help her out, since I don't want her working like the other girls here," Christina said as she pulled him over to her desk.

She pushed the forms at Alex. She sat him down and gave him a pen.

Alex pushed the pen away. "You want me to do what?" Alex asked, horrified. "I can't believe what you're asking of me, woman. You've never asked me to do anything improper, or illegal, before. Well, only to be around for that one abortion."

Christina put the pen down near him and moved around Alex. She gently put her hand on his shoulder and sensuously massaged it, cooing into his ear. "She's disabled, and has severe periodic migraines. You can write that she is cognitively disturbed, needs meds for her post-traumatic stress and long-term treatment."

"To Hell, Christina. Post trauma? From what trauma?"

"Yes, and she is permanently disabled from employment and can't work. It's commonly done, Alexander, my dear."

"For Christ's sake, Christina. I can't do that. I've never even examined Jasmine, seen her with migraines, or taken a history, woman. You know that."

"Yes, I know that. Jasmine is beautiful, isn't she?" Christina said, pointing to the bed

Alex ignored that seductive suggestion. "It's illegal, and I could be disbarred by the medical college. I'm going to be the next director at the hospital as Monique must have told you, Christina."

Alex pushed the papers away and was ready to walk out. He was furious, but Christina had an ace up her sleeve and showed it.

"Business is slow, Alexander. The politicos are anxious because of all those women of yours who protested and marched on parliament. They lay down on the highways with that Rani. The children are back in the community and causing trouble for them. It's bad for my business."

"Too damn bad. It will pick up."

"Jasmine needs some money to send to her family. I can't support her forever. Of course, you can. I can tell the college about our secret business here with the acid." She hesitated. "And that you helped me with that abortion months ago."

"Christina! That's blackmail. How could you, after our great relationship. We cared for each other, woman. We were good for each other. Think of your daughter, Monique," he shouted, enraged, standing and ready to leave.

Christina held him back, moved her hands down his chest, and slid her hand down on his crotch. She began to manipulate his genitals as Jasmine threw the covers off her body.

"Jasmine and I will help you one last time. She will use the cat-o'-nine-tails. It will be the best sex you've ever had, Alexander. Now, just write," she said, getting him hard as he looked at Jasmine and she kissed him softly on the lips.

Alex was between a rock and a hard place, but he had to acquiesce. He knew she would do anything to get her own way, the sly bitch.

He sat down and quickly filled out the form and signed it. Christina smiled, kissed him on the forehead, took the forms, folded them, and put them in her bra next to her left breast.

"Come to bed, Alexander. Jasmine will play with you willingly while I watch, and then you can have me also, whip or not."

"Bugger off, Christina. I wouldn't do that to Monique. You know that," Alex said angrily, with his voice raised. He pushed her away and started for the door.

He didn't get to the door before it came crashing down, and wooden splinters struck his leg. Alex staggered back from the blast and Christina, in shock, fell to her knees when he backed into her.

It was Stanislaus. He was almost stark-naked, hairy, sweating, and in a drunken rage: just like his cousin, Bruno. He only wore small, tight, jockey shorts and heavy, leather gumboots from his stinking barges.

Stanislaus had smashed the door down with his massive shoulders and a kick from his work boots. He was mad, drunk, on acid, and out of control. He had a German Luger in his right hand, which shook wildly. Red in the face and furious, he aimed it right at Christina.

Alex had moved just behind Christina and tried to hold her up from her fall. He stepped aside as Stanislaus moved forward, wildly brandishing his pistol and babbling incoherently. He was psychotic and completely out of his mind.

With this chaos, Jasmine sat up in bed, covered herself in the sheet, screamed, and kept on shouting in French. Christina fell back again as the pistol aimed right at her, but Alex caught her just in time.

Christina pushed Alex further back, but she staggered and fell. Jasmine kept swearing in French at Stanislaus as she leaped out of bed, wrapped her chenille night dress around her body, and went to Christina's aid.

She helped Christina up. Alex was stunned with the sudden change of events. He moved away from the two women, and went behind the desk for protection.

Stanislaus was livid, in a sweat, and fuming. He took several lurching steps forward, toward the two women. "Bitch, you cheated me out of that property on the riverbank," he shouted at Christina. He came at her pointing his Luger with his finger on the trigger.

Christina staggered up, and came face to face with Stanislaus, now unafraid, defiant, and spitting fire.

"Listen, you big ape: get the fuck out of my room. You'll pay for that door, and you didn't pay me enough for that property transaction. You said you wanted that piece of land, but I told you there was a time limit on it, you motherfucking ape. You were too late because you were fucking with those kids on the riverbank."

Stanislaus seemed momentarily confused by Christina's aggressive stance. He began massaging a bulging erection in his shorts, seeking an immediate escape from the tight, cotton underwear.

This sensual excitement was the result of his acid trip and booze, the overpowering floral scent in the room, and beautiful Jasmine. All the while, the sensuous rendition of Piaf's melody drifted up from downstairs.

He tried to pull himself together and became rational for an instant. "I was moving beef down into Maine, the States," Stanislaus shouted. "I told you to wait, bitch. I'd be back," he added, spewing forth venom with spittle dripping down his chin. He was now face-to-face with Christina.

Christina wiped his saliva off her face. "I'm not going to wait for three months for your stinking scow, full of cow shit, to return. Alex, go to my desk, in that drawer. Give this Russian prick the thousand dollars that he paid as a deposit," she said, pushing his Luger away from her.

Alex, uncertain what to do, turned away and opened the drawer. He looked in and pushed her leather outfit and the whip aside. The drawer was full of large bills. A small hand gun sat on top of the money.

Alex looked at the small gun. He knew that it was always loaded. Just then, he heard the gunshot.

With Christina's aggressive push at Stanislaus' Luger, he had felt more threatened by her, and so, with his twitchy finger on the trigger, the gun went off twice.

Jasmine gave out an ear-piercing scream. When he looked up from the open drawer, he saw Christina slump to the ground, with two bullet holes in her chest.

Stanislaus was standing over Christina, stunned and uncertain what to do next. Jasmine rushed at him with fists flailing at his bare chest, shouting, "You killed her. Killed her. Christina. No, no."

Stanislaus, bewildered by Jasmine's attack, raised his Luger again and pointed it at Jasmine. It was at that moment that Alex, acting on reflex, quickly took the small pistol from the drawer and pulled the trigger.

In quick succession, he pumped two bullets into Stanislaus.

Stanislaus was stunned; wide-eyed, he stumbled back from the two shots, one of which hit him in the fleshy part of his left thigh. The other bullet missed and hit the wall.

Alex was waiting for Stanislaus to drop. Just as he staggered back from the minor flesh wound, Theodore rushed into the room with his pistol drawn.

"Heard the commotion, Christina. We know that Stanislaus was trouble. Came to help," he shouted. His gun pointed at Stanislaus. Theodore, the sharp shooter who had saved Alex from certain death, was almost on top of Stanislaus.

"Watch out, Theodore, he'll shoot Jasmine," Alex yelled out, moving back behind the desk.

Jasmine paid no attention to the men. She continued to cradle Christina in her arms on the floor. She was crying, and asking Christina to open her eyes. Alex knew that wasn't going to happen.

Stanislaus turned to look up at Theodore. Theodore hesitated for a moment as he looked at Christina with blood oozing from her chest. It was in that moment that Stanislaus made his move.

He easily picked Jasmine off Christina's body. He wrapped his free arm around her waist and carried her, limping, to the side of the bed.

Theodore was ready, and aimed his pistol at Stanislaus, but stopped abruptly.

Stanislaus put his Luger against Jasmine's head, shouting, "Back off, or I'll kill this whore too, and then that doctor."

Jasmine was surprisingly calm. Theodore lowered his pistol. "Easy, big fella. Take it easy. Throw your gun down, and you can go back to your country. I'll see to it. Give you safe passage on that barge of yours," Theodore said calmly.

Alex knew that Stanislaus wouldn't buy that line. He was stupid, but not that stupid.

"Russia? Fuck, no. Not Russia. They'll send me to Siberia. The gulags." He swore and tightened his grip on Jasmine. He tried to pull her toward the door.

Alex saw that some of the girls who were in the hallway were screaming. Several men came to the open door and tried to pull the girls away when they looked in. Stanislaus was waving his Luger in that direction.

Alex put his gun down on the desk. "Stanislaus, give me the gun. Just give me the gun. No Russia. I'll help you, just give me that Luger," he said taking a few steps toward him.

Agitated, Stanislaus thought of his options. "Help me? Fuck you," he said as Alex came closer and reached out to free Jasmine.

Alex was thinking fast. "Look, I'll admit you to my hospital. You'll be cared for after I sign papers saying that you were insane from drink and drugs. You'll live and be cared for by me. You have no choice," Alex offered as he took his arm away from Jasmine.

Stanislaus wavered. "Your hospital? You promise?" he shouted.

"I promise, Stanislaus," Alex added again, since he was in front of the killer with his Luger now pointing at Alex's chest. "Just give me that gun."

Jasmine freed herself as Alex again reached out and pushed her away. Stanislaus still pointed the gun at Alex, thinking to shoot.

Alex came closer.

Stanislaus lowered his Luger and hesitated.

Theodore moved in closer and was thinking to shoot, but feared that Stanislaus would shoot first. Alex looked at Theodore and waved him off.

Jasmine went to Christina.

Everyone at the door stopped shouting. Alex offered his hand to Stanislaus. "Just give me the gun, Stanislaus. You'll be okay," he said calmly.

Stanislaus wavered. He was thinking of his options. He gave Alex the Luger.

Jasmine fell on top of Christina and tried to wake her. She sobbed and prayed to the Holy Mary that she was still alive.

Alex threw the Luger on the ground and went to Christina. She was not breathing, and her carotids showed no sign of a pulse. The bullets had gone through her sternum and into her heart.

"Sorry, Jasmine; Christina is dead. Sorry," he said sadly. He cradled Jasmine in his arms and pulled her to the bed.

Theodore had gone to Stanislaus, and with help from his friends who had entered the room, they escorted him out the door. "Have no fear, Stanislaus; they will take you to the hospital, and I'll see you there," Alex assured him.

Theodore went to Alex and picked up the small gun he had used off the floor. He wiped it clean of Alex's prints and put it in his pocket. "No, you don't need to be involved, Doctor. You cured many of my friends with those new medicines at your hospital. I'm grateful to you. You'd better get out of here fast," he said to Alex.

"Thanks again, Theodore."

"The fucking bastard was caught robbing Christina, and in defending herself, he shot her. I came to her defense, and it was I who shot him in the leg. That's what my friend, the chief will hear about what happened here, and nothing else. We'll get him to your hospital. Brave thing you did here. It could have been a disaster for everyone here tonight. More people could have been shot."

Alex wiped the sweat off his brow, nodded in gratitude, and went to Jasmine. Jasmine covered Christina's body in a blanket from the bed. She was calm, cool, and collected, thinking fast and in charge.

The crowd outside had scattered, and Stanislaus was safely escorted away.

Jasmine put her arms around Alex and embraced him with a warm hug. Alex calmed down, still shaking, but with that affection and comfort he relaxed.

She then showed Alex the disability forms that she retrieved from Christina's blouse. She tore them up and stuffed them into her bathrobe pocket.

"There's a large suitcase full of money under the bed. Maybe two hundred thousand dollars, which we made this week. Take it and buy Monique and yourself a nice house. Christina would have liked that," Jasmine whispered in Alex's ear. She watched Theodore go to the phone to call in his police buddies in town.

Alex cupped his hand and replied in Jasmine's ear. "Jasmine, you'll need that money for yourself."

"No. Christina made out a will, and left Casa Loma to me and to her daughter, Monique. I'm going to sell Casa Loma and give Monique half. This house is finished without her," she said, tears in her eyes.

Alex only waited a few seconds. He left Jasmine and bent down to retrieve the suitcase from under the bed. Theodore finished his phone call.

Alex said goodbye to Theodore. Theodore waved to Alex as he walked out to meet his chief, who was downstairs with one of the girls.

Alex turned back to Jasmine. "What are you going to do now, Jasmine?"

Jasmine took off the housecoat and dressed. She was very composed and calmly explained, "I'll open up a half-way house in the poor district of Montréal. A safe place for lost girls, hookers, and destitute women, where they can rest, have a meal, see a doctor and a social worker. A safe house. Maybe build some low-cost housing for women."

Alex was amazed with her forward thinking and self-sacrificing attitude. She had it all figured out. "Good for you, Jasmine. Congratulations. That's an excellent plan, and if I can be of help, then let me know."

"I'll call you for sure. We'll need some doctors and a good psychiatrist, occasionally." Jasmine kissed Alex on the cheek and pushed him out the door. "Now get out of here. As Theodore said, you've never been here. I know the chief is downstairs with one of the girls, and sure to come up soon," she added.

Alex left, in despair. He slowly walked down the elegant stairway with his suitcase. He passed the chief of police, who was pulling up his pants and buttoning his shirt, taking two steps at a time up the stairs.

They both nodded to each other as Theodore, meeting his chief up the stairs, winked at Alex and said, "*Adieu, docteur.*"

Theodore was holding a folded, canvas stretcher that was always available in the side room for any emergency. He would use it to transport Christina's body to the morgue.

Alex turned to look up and see Jasmine at the doorway. She waved goodbye, still sobbing quietly into her kerchief.

✳

CHAPTER 59

Some Good News at Last

THE funeral in the Montréal cathedral for Christina was magnificent, if funerals can be described that way. Jasmine had a large choir singing Christina's favorites: "Amazing Grace" and "Nearer My God to Thee."

The pews were full of all the girls who had ever worked at the Casa Loma, many politicians, policemen, and those who worked in government institutions. Hundreds of women who had paraded in front of the parliament buildings in Ottawa to change the abortion laws also attended. Christina had been very generous in assisting many charitable organizations to help the unfortunate women.

It was a solemn affair, but after the long service Jasmine had a sumptuous banquet in Christina's honor for everyone who attended.

After the feast, Monique and Alex walked about, meeting and talking with all those attending. Jasmine told Alex, Vinny, and Mamma D, "A wealthy businessman has already given me an empty building where I can open our women's safe house in that tough neighborhood."

"Good for you, Jasmine. We will be glad to help out. Just call," Vinny said, giving her a hug as he and Mamma D left.

Jasmine had decided to call the new halfway house 'Christina's Casa.'

"A great honor to a great lady and my wonderful mother. We will all miss her," Monique added.

A week later, after the sad affair, Alex limped down the stairs for a late breakfast. He still had a bandage around his right knee after the injury from Stanislaus' attack. He also had a small, tight, elastic bandage around his left foot following day surgery to correct his clubfoot.

"Mamma D is making a wonderful recovery after her lobectomy for that benign pulmonary tumor," Alex said to Vinny, who was sitting on the porch spitting out sunflower seeds and chewing on sticks of gum. He was desperately trying to quit smoking.

Vinny stopped chewing and spitting for a minute. "I see that one of Christina's last requests was for you to see that orthopedic surgeon who often visited Casa Loma. The staples and pins in your left foot let you walk pretty good," Vinny observed, pointing at Alex's leg.

"Christina was always looking out for others, Vinny."

"She had a grand funeral compared to the dictator's."

"Yes. There was hardly anybody there for Cartier. No relatives or close friends, Vinny."

"You made a nice eulogy for him. Said a lot of nice things about him. Hard to do, that speech."

"It was much easier to get that judge to agree that Stanislaus was insane and have him admitted to the hospital, Vinny." Alex got up to leave. "By the way, he's a master mechanic. He worked in Russia and on those cattle barges for years."

"I need a good mechanic in my shop. Let me know when you're ready to give him a day pass."

"Will do, Vinny. Will do."

Alex left Vinny and Claudius and found Flora in the kitchen for the first time in weeks. Her clothes still hung on her bony shoulders, but she looked much better. Her cheeks had some color, and she had a better appetite. Today, she heartily spooned up chicken soup at the table that she had made for Vinny.

Flora looked up and gave Alex a smile. "Golly gee, Doctor Gage. There was a courier who brought you a letter at nine this morning," she said as she ladled more soup into her own bowl.

"Was it thick or thin, Mamma D? A thick one or a thin one?"

"Oh, gosh almighty, don't know. My lordy, lord, it looked official, maybe thick, or maybe it was thin. My Goodness gracious, I even had to sign for it." She pointed to the other room.

Alex almost ran into the adjoining dining room, which was brighter and more cheery again. It was no longer the dark, sad place with dust gathering and the carpets dirty.

He found a fabulously slim envelope on the recently-polished table.

He ran into the veranda and put it up to the bright sun shining through the windows. He smiled. He could almost see through it. There was nothing inside but one thin, single, lonely page.

"It is a skinny one, doc. Skinny. Slim and lean. Congrats." Vinny chortled as he shouted from his chair where he was doing the crossword.

Alex pulled up a patio chair and sat next to Vinny, who was slouched over, attempting last week's crossword puzzle with Claudius nearby.

"Skinny is good, unlike my examiner, the chubby Scottish doctor."

"Yeah, congrats my boy. But I heard you got another gift, from the kiddies."

"Kiddies? Ah, yes. Some of the few older orphan girls who were just about to leave, Vinny. They had a small going-away party. For those still waiting to be adopted out, Vinny."

"You did well, kid, to get all those children outta' here."

That was one of Alex's proudest achievement, and his finest hour yet. The others were saving Riel, finding the love of his life, taking this hospital out of the medieval age, assisting his mother, stopping

Stanislaus from killing him and others, and helping Jasmine set up Christina's Casa.

Alex stretched out in the chair and folded his hands behind his back. Proudly, he explained to Vinny the other story that the girls had told him.

"Some of the girls saw *Mère Supérieure* fall: she was all in white under her black robes, with sheer, gossamer robes flowing in the wind. The girls working underneath pulling out weeds saw her flying through the air, Vinny. Some of the older nuns said it was like a holy vision, prophetic like, to release the children."

Vinny had already heard that story from other mechanics. He was impatient. "Yeah, yeah; so what gift did they give you. They gave you a present."

Alex took his time. It was his story to tell. "Well, when she hit the pavement below, she lost her medallion cross. She used it to pray with. The girls found it in the bushes they were trimming and they kept it."

"So, so what?"

Alex was on stage again. He raised his hands heavenward. "So, they said it was Heaven-sent, Vinny. Heaven sent. They kept it, and prayed to it in their rooms in the basement. Prayed to *Mère* and to Saint Denise and to the doctors. For salvation, deliverance to be rescued, and for their freedom, Vinny."

"Oh, no kidding. I didn't know that. So, did they give you a cake?" Vinny asked again, impatiently. They both heard Flora singing with Dean Martin on her Italian tapes in her bedroom upstairs.

"No, Vinny. They gave me the cross. The cross from *Mère Supérieure*. The same one given to her by Sister Denise; she was given it as a young girl in that French convent. They said they didn't need it anymore."

"Very impressive, kid."

"Most of them, almost all, have been adopted to nice families in this province or further away. They said that their prayers have been answered, and they wanted me to have it."

Vinny sat up and put his crossword down. "Really? So, show me. Let's see it, buddy."

Alex shrugged his shoulders, "Can't do, Vinny. Can't do."

"Why the dickens not. Go get it, man,"

"Can't, Vinny. I gave it to your wife, to Flora."

There was a long silence as Alex waited.

"That was nice of you; thanks, son. She wore it to the hospital during her operation," Vinny said with a spasm in his throat, choking up.

Alex only nodded and brushed his hair over the bruise on his forehead. The slash from the rock he had used was almost healed. He took off his slipper on his surgically-corrected foot and pulled on a sock. Alex was pleased that he could now wear a proper shoe, even though it was quite loose, so it could cover the thin bandage.

Alex got up and walked about the porch without hardly the usual shuffle.

Vinny looked at Claudius. There was an audible rumble from a gut, but it came from Alex and not from Claudius, who was eating Mamma D's cooking again. "Stomach upset, doc?" he asked Alex.

Alex tightened his abdominals. "No, Vinny. Just a bit of an upset. I'm going to get married, Vinny."

He felt that he could confide in Vinny; he had some other news for him. "Monique missed her period. We weren't careful, just that one time," Alex said.

"Shoulda pulled out, my boy. Like my old man told me to do. Shoulda pulled out."

"Yeah, Vinny. Shoulda. Coulda. Didn't. But she's happy to be pregnant. That's why the quick wedding. In Montréal. Lots of her family and friends coming: Jasmine, and all the friends from Casa Loma."

"Well, I'll be. Gonna have a baby you two, are you. A new life. Shit, life is just a sexually transmitted, lifetime disorder, my boy."

"For some, I guess it is, Vinny."

"You got some? Family, I mean?"

"No. Not here. Just me."

"I'll come. Stand in with you. What do ya say, my boy?"

Alex reached over and slapped Vinny on the knee. "Really? That would be great. You'll be my best man, Vinny. My best man."

"Got a name for the little bugger, doc?"

"Monique said we'd call her Flora, if it was a girl."

Vinny looked up from his crossword puzzle. "Might be a boy, doc. Take after you, smart and sassy."

"If so, then we'll call him Vincent."

Vinny only smiled and said nothing except, "I'll have to buy a new suit, with a tie and tails for your wedding." He gave a throaty laugh. "Good luck," he added as he waited for the newspaper boy. The boy was late, and Alex knew that by now he would need the answers to last week's crossword puzzle, still sitting in his lap.

It was then that the young lad bicycled past and threw the Montréal Evening Post over the fence.

Vinny swore at the boy as it struck the screen door, waking Claudius out of his reverie. Alex got up, patted the dog, and walked out. "I'll bring in the paper for you, Vinny."

He unfolded the paper and scanned the news. There was nothing there on a Mohawk Indian escaping from the institution.

Vinny emptied the beer bottle and sucked on his match stick. "You and me, us, are lucky to have two good women at our side." Vinny said.

"Yeah, you bet, Vinny."

"Those ladies, yours and mine, but all women have the capacity to love twenty-four-seven, but men, us guys can only do it once or twice a week, son."

"Ha, quite right, Vinny. I'll try harder."

Vinny pointed to the case of beer beside him. "Have one for the road, to celebrate your new position."

"No thanks, Vinny. I won't be the new director until the minister of health gives his approval for it in the next few days."

Vinny pulled out a beer from his case. "Are you on the wagon, doc?" he asked, offering the bottle to Alex.

Alex pushed it away. "No thanks, Vinny. You know I don't drink. Vinny, those two adages, 'one for the road' and 'on the wagon,' came from hundreds of years ago."

"No shit?"

"Yep. When convicts were sent to the Tower of London for execution hundreds of years ago, or even further to Tyburn prison, they were transported by a horse-driven cart. The cart, full of prisoners, always stopped at a pub. The English were very civilized."

"Stopped to have a piss?"

"No. The pub owner came out and, in a caring manner, asked each if they would like a pint of ale for the last time."

"No shit? Good of him."

Alex passed the newspaper to Vinny. "Those who were to be hanged in the nearby Tower, said, 'Yes, one for the road,' and the men who went to prison, knowing they would be fed and watered, said, 'No thanks, I'm on the wagon'."

"Well, I'll be damned. Good story, doc." Vinny laughed and spat his match stick out.

"Any word from Rani yet?"

Vinny had some news for Alex. "Fuck, yes. Rani phoned from her parent's home in Toronto. She said you'll be one of the best, since you already turned that place around. She's in the kitchen as we speak, man."

Alex was surprised with that. "Didn't see her come down. You're pulling my leg, Vinny. Here? Now?"

"To help me and to nurse Flora till she's fully recovered."

"Wow. She's a good cook, but you will have less lasagna and cannelloni, Vinny. Now it will be lots of samosas and curried chicken," Alex replied with a chuckle.

Vinny snickered and pointed to the newspaper. "Anything about that big Indian's escape?" he asked, looking at Alex's fading bruise on his forehead.

Alex buried his head in the newspaper. "Nothing yet. Heard anything, Vinny?"

"That pea-souper, Detective Treudeau. Good friend of mine. We're old buddies from the army. Said Riel knocked you down and took off in the woods."

"Yeah, Vinny. Tough guy. Knocked me down and took off in the woods."

"That pea-souper shoulda' checked the river. I would have told Riel to hop the freighters, don't you think?"

Alex coolly shrugged his shoulders, trying to look stupid, which was hard for him to do. "Really? Good idea, I guess, Vinny."

That was all Alex was going to say about that. He saw the perceptive look on Vinny's face, and he knew that Vinny was in on saving Riel.

Vinny moved his chair closer and slapped a creeping spider on the floor with his fly swatter.

Alex got up to pat Claudius for the last time.

Alex was thinking about the next few days. Monique and he would drive to Montréal to get married, and then buy a house nearby in the village, close to the DaCosta's; they were now his family. He wasn't going to live on the hospital grounds.

He had opened four different bank accounts and deposited the money that Jasmine gave him in the suitcase in various amounts in each bank. He didn't want to rouse suspicions as to the quantity of funds. He would use the funds to buy furniture for their house and give some to his mother.

Alex continued to read in the newspaper that America was in turmoil, with the Vietnam war still raging. Students were rioting, Hollywood stars were marching in the streets, draft dodgers were appealing their convictions in the courts, and politicians were debating the escalation of the war in the senate.

At the hospital the previous day, before he left on holidays and left Hamish in charge, O'Rielly gave Alex a small going-away tea party. Everyone signed a card to congratulate him in his new position as the hospital director.

After that, Alex had gathered up his books and files from his office on the ward and moved them into Cartier's former office in the Admin building.

At the end of the day, Alex had his truck lubed and oiled by Vinny, the tires checked, and then had it washed. The inside had been scrubbed for the journey to Montréal with Monique.

While he was still chatting with Vinny that afternoon, Alex heard Mamma D come downstairs just as Monique walked in. Monique wore her new, light-blue suit and jacket. It looked great over her svelte, trim body and over a pretty, white blouse. She wore new, high-heeled shoes and looked very happy and beautiful.

Mamma D gave Monique a long hug and led her into the kitchen. "My lordy lord, you look gorgeous; I want a picture of all of us. At your last supper with us, Alex," Mamma D said, setting up the camera on the kitchen counter for an automatic photo.

Alex looked at Rani, who was currently cooking up a storm. "Smells great, Rani. I love curry," Alex said, coming over to the pot on the stove. He put his arm around Rani. "Great to see you again, Rani."

Alex looked at Mamma D. Her lasagna was front and center, together with Rani's chicken curry.

There was a loaf of freshly-made bread and a bottle of red wine on the table. It was bought at the store, and not Vinny's home-made hooch.

Alex sat with Monique in the center, with the others on each side. He said, "I feel like one of the twelve disciples at the table of the last supper with Jesus, who said, 'If you want to get in on the picture you better be on this side of the table.'"

Everyone laughed and clinked their glasses.

Vinny was wearing a large, silver cross on a chain around his neck. They ate samosas, chicken curry, and the best lasagna Mamma D had ever made. They finished the bottle of red wine as Rani helped clear the table.

Claudius was under the table, slobbering on a plate of leftovers. Monique, Alex, Rani, Vinny, and Mamma D reminisced and laughed about the past year. Monique talked about her excitement in seeing some of her relatives soon at the wedding.

Rani had some news. "I saw him."

Silence. It was Vinny who piped up. "Him? Him, you saw? Saw him? Who's him?"

Rani and Monique cleared the table. Vinny finished the last dregs of vino. "Lafayette Gagnon," Rani answered Vinny.

"Gagnon?" Alex asked, surprised.

Vinny could see that Alex was surprised by the name.

"Yep. He told me that he changed it back to his other name. No more Riel, he said. So that the police couldn't touch him."

Rani waited for Mamma D to wipe the juice off Vinny's chin. "I met him at the new Christina Casa in Montréal. Brought in a wad of cash for Jasmine from the reserve straddling the border with America. Cigarette sales, he said."

"No shit," was all Vinny could say. He was about to repeat that, but was admonished for swearing by Mamma D. "You're pulling my leg, girl."

"No, Vinny. And I apologized to him for what happened back then when I interviewed him. Sincerely apologized, I did."

"Good for you, Rani. Shit. We lost that cigarette trade now that he's helping Jasmine." This time, it was Vinny who apologized to Mamma D as she swatted him with her napkin.

"He told me that he was pleased that Alex had his foot corrected. He told me that he was looking forward to seeing him soon," Rani added as an afterthought.

"Where does he live, now?" Alex asked, still very surprised by the name change.

"He lives out in the reserve. Changed his name, cut his hair, has a beard. Came back after the *SQ* gave up on him. They told him that they concluded that Cartier died after falling on that rock," she said.

"Amazing man," Vinny said proudly.

"He's helping to finance Jasmine. To care for the poor, wayward aboriginal girls hooking on the streets. Gets them cleaned up, off the drugs, the booze. Finds them low-cost housing, also."

Alex couldn't believe what he was hearing. "Good for Riel. Ah, I mean, Lafayette Gagnon," he said, looking at Monique, who knew his history with his father.

"It's okay, Doctor Gage. We still do well with Vinny's store," Mamma D piped in.

After the grand dinner and Rani's news, Vinny helped his wife up to her room for a rest as Monique, Rani, and Alex washed the dishes, talked about Cartier, LaGlace, Juanita, and the former Riel and what might have been.

Once they were finished, Monique helped clean up the kitchen. Alex finished his glass of vino, and they both walked out.

Mamma D came down the steps for some fresh air. She had on her new dress that Vinny had bought for her at the Hudson's Bay store in town.

Alex hugged Mamma D. He smiled to see her so pretty in her new dress and told her so. Vinny and Alex at first shook hands, and then

Vinny put his arms around Alex and gave him a big bear hug.

Vinny's eyes watered. He quickly turned away from the others, dabbed at his eyes, and watched Alex walk to the truck, where Monique was patiently waiting. Rani joined Vinny and Mamma D outside.

Alex sat in, closed the truck door, and started the engine. Monique reached over and held his hand, feeling the pain. They had waited for a few minutes when they heard Vinny shout, "Hey, you two, hold up a sec."

When Vinny came out to the truck, he asked Alex to turn down the window.

Vinny took the rabbit's foot that Riel had given him for good luck when he had handed Riel the wad of bills, before Alex sent him free. He hung it onto the rear-view mirror.

All he did was wink and give a toothy grin with, "Good luck, Yank."

Alex and Monique drove off, waving at Vinny. Mamma D threw kisses. Claudius was at her feet, licking at her open toes in her sandals. She was leaning against the maple tree and supported by Rani, who was also waving goodbye.

Alex looked back through the rear-view mirror as he slowly drove away. He saw that Mamma D was wearing the cross around her neck that Alex had given her from Sister Denise and *Mère Supérieure*.

THE END.

✳

History of Psychiatric Institutions

THE first written knowledge of such intuitions came from the Islamic Arab states, as explained by travelers to that area. Cairo had such a hospital in the 9th century for the care of the insane and employed compassion, support, and music therapy as treatment.

In medieval Europe, the insane were housed in some monasteries or in village and city towers, called "fools' towers." The hospital in Paris, Hôtel-Dieu, had a few cells only for lunatics. The Teutonic Knights also had hospitals with small attached madhouses.

Spain had many institutions and in London, England, The Priory of Saint Mary of Bethlehem was built in 1247, which later became known as the famous Bedlam.

In 1285, a treatise by Sheppard, *Development of Mental Health Law and Practice*, described a case of a "frantic and mad" individual due to "the instigation of the devil."

Throughout England and Europe, the parish authorities assisted families both financially and with nursing care for their mentally disabled. Such a parish might further help by housing a family member in a private madhouse or boarded out with other caring families. Some charitable institutions were available, mostly supported by religious groups, such as Bedlam.

In the early 18th century, many cities throughout England had private institutions. Unfortunately, there are recordings of some institutions selling or renting out their patients in the form of slavery. Such individuals worked in various workhouses, mills, and mines as serfs. In the early 19th century, the College of Physicians in England put a stop to that practice.

Privately run asylums developed in the 1600's, and in 1632 the Bethlem Royal Hospital in London recorded that in the lower levels there was "a parlor, a kitchen, larders, and several rooms where distracted people were held." Those who were violent were chained, but all others could roam about, even out to the public areas.

When King George III had a remission of his mental disorder in 1789, such disorders were seen to be treatable and curative. Moral and compassionate treatments prevailed with the French physician, Philippe Pinel, in 1792 at the Bicêtre Hospital near Paris. Pinel, and then others, freed patients of chains and dark dungeons were abandoned. It was agreed that such illness was the result of social and psychological stress or hereditary and physiological damage. Attendants and other nursing personnel were taught to be compassionate, supportive, and humane. Patients were encouraged to work in the hospitals, and on discharge were assisted within the public workplace.

In England particularly, larger institutions developed smaller, cottage-like homes to house those who required less supervision. Such cottages held 50 – 70 patients, and it produced a family-style environment, with patients encouraged to perform chores to allow a sense of contribution. They were rewarded at Christmas, Easter, or other holiday incentives with special meals or even with a small glass of sherry or a small tankard of ale.

The author and his wife, a nurse, had the opportunity to work in such humane and very modern cottage hospitals at the Runwell

Hospital in Wickford, east of London, England, and at St. Ebba's Hospital in Epsom, Surrey, in the early 1960's. They were light-years ahead in housing patients; a sharp contrast to the huge, red brick, four-story monstrosities that held 4000 – 5000 patients in the provinces of Canada and throughout the United States.

In the USA, the first psychiatric institution opened in 1768: The Eastern State Hospital in Virginia. Later, in the early 19th century, many such hospitals opened throughout the States.

In Canada, every province had immense, 3 to 4-story, red brick, very ornate hospitals, fronted by Corinthian columns to each building with grand staircases in some. However, a few levels had bars on the windows and padded cells. Each was a community within itself, and in the 1960's, they became more civilized, with beauty parlors, cafeterias, movie houses, some game rooms, private showers on each ward, and overnight sleeping rooms for families from afar who came to visit with their relatives.

The author worked at the Weyburn Mental Hospital in Saskatchewan in the summer of 1951, the Brandon hospital in Manitoba in 1956, and Essondale, later called Riverview, in British Columbia in 1958 and again in 1961 and 1964. I was impressed with the caring, supportive, considerate, and compassionate attitude of all nursing, medical, and personnel ancillary care workers.

In the 70's and early 80's, there was an international movement to decentralize such large institutions and move patients into their communities. Thus group homes were established. Patients were encouraged to be treated at home, with therapists visiting close by. Out-patient units were attached to every medical facility in the area.

However, there has been an outcry by the public that many such patients were seen to be on the streets, addicted to drugs and alcohol and sleeping in storefronts or in alleys. The prisons now house many such mentally ill individuals. Housing for the poor, the destitute, the indigent, and the mentally ill is obviously wholly inadequate.

"The Mad House" Glossary

<u>Asylum</u> – A safe haven: a sanctuary and a refuge. It was used to house the mentally ill in order to protect the public rather than a place for treatment.

<u>Bedlam</u> – The Priory of Saint Mary of Bethlehem was the first hospital in England, as a religious sanctuary, with areas for the mentally ill. It was built in 1247, and was later known as the famous Bedlam.

<u>Electroconvulsive Therapy</u> – The electrical production of a modified convulsion. Epileptic seizures, febrile, or traumatic convulsions were known to be curative for centuries.

<u>Equinovarus</u> – A clubfoot present at birth. Now surgically corrected with pins, screws, and staples.

<u>Filles du Roi</u> – Daughters of the king. King Louis XIV sent more than 700 young women to colonize Canada due to a scarcity of women. He feared that the British were doing better, and would take over the country.

<u>Galloping Consumption</u> – An early medical term describing Tuberculosis. The tubercle bacteria rapidly consumed the whole body.

<u>Gonorrhea</u> – The gonococcus bacteria spread by any form of sexual contact, causing severe pain, discharge in the pelvic area, and beyond. Called "the clap" after the "*clappier*" brothel area in Paris in the last century.

<u>General Paresis of the Insane</u> – Also known as GPI after syphilitic infection. Invades the whole body and the spinal cord, causing paralysis and for the brain to produce insanity.

<u>Hysterectomy</u> – Greek "womb" is *"Hyster,"* thus, "Hysteria," or "Hysterical," an emotional disorder usually consigned to women. It was thought that the womb roamed about, creating havoc. Thus, the only cure was a hysterectomy.

<u>Insulin Coma Therapy</u> – The production of a convulsion via injection of insulin to produce a diabetic coma and a seizure. Last used in the early 1960's.

<u>Korsakoff's Psychosis</u> – A chronic, debilitating insanity due to alcoholism destroying the brain.

<u>LSD</u> – A hallucinogen, lysergic acid diethylamide. Albert Hofmann produced lysergic acid in 1938 from a fungus.

<u>Lithium</u> – A metal found to have a beneficial therapeutic effect for bipolar disorder.

<u>Manic-Depressive Disorder</u> – Now called bipolar. A prolonged disturbance of emotional lows and depression, alternating with highs or hyperactivity.

<u>The Mad House</u> – In 1812 the Spanish painter, Francisco Goya, painted a stark, bleak canvas of a ward in a local hospital called *The Mad House*. Now in a Madrid gallery.

<u>Ménage à Trois</u> – 'A household of three,' or sexual activity with three participants. Several historical figures are known to be involved in such.

<u>Prefrontal lobotomy</u> – The frontal lobes of the brain are cut to produce tranquility in the mentally ill. Antonio Moniz in 1935 received the Nobel Prize for his work on the brain and the practice of lobotomies.

<u>Psychiatrist</u> – A medical doctor who studies another four years to specialize in mental health.

<u>Pyromania</u> – The thought of planning and setting of fires for an emotional, or often sexual, gratification. Arson is fire-setting for a financial, insurance, or homicidal reason.

<u>Padded cell</u> – A small room with all walls heavily padded to prevent disturbed patients from harming themselves.

<u>Psychoanalysis</u> – Coined by Sigmund Freud in 1910. A "talking" therapy to explore early trauma and dreams.

<u>Schizophrenia</u> – Coined by Eugen Bleuler. "Schizo": a splitting. "Phrenia": the mind. The mind is split from the emotions.

<u>Sterilization</u> – Removal of the ovaries, the fallopian tubes, or the womb. In males, the vas deferens tubes are cut from the testicles. Often performed on the intellectually deficient in the past.

<u>Syphilis</u> – The spirochete bacteria invades the body similarly to gonorrhea, but is more lethal, producing GPI.

<u>Sadomasochism</u> – The production of a sadistic, painful sexual activity elicited by some, along with the reception of such masochistic action acceptable by others. Coined by the Marquis of Sade and then later by Leopold von Sacher-Masoch.

<u>Straightjackets</u> – A heavy, cotton jacket worn backward for hostile, aggressive patients. The arms were then tied around to the back to prevent movement.

About the Author

DR. LAWRENCE E. MATRICK received his degree in Medicine from the Manitoba Medical College, and then worked at the Provincial Mental Hospital as a resident in psychiatry. He continued his studies in London, England and received his British degrees in Psychiatry, and later his Fellowship in the Royal College of Physicians, Canada. As an Assistant Professor in Psychiatry at U.B.C., he also had a full-time private practice in Vancouver for almost 50 years. Qualified by the courts, he often attended as an expert witness, dealing with those involved in motor vehicle accidents.

www.ingramcontent.com/pod-product-compliance
Lightning Source LLC
Chambersburg PA
CBHW051554100726
47898CB00001B/86